Prologue

Ever since the 1906 hurricane, Frederick Davenport knew storms had the power to change lives. It was no surprise when he huddled with his family in their downstairs hallway on July 5, 1916, a hurricane would alter his life once again. Five-and-a-half-year-old Bethany sat on Frederick's lap, and little Louisa hugged his arm. Phoebe held Doff beside her stepmother, watching as Melissa rocked six-month-old Frederick Junior. Feverish and inconsolable, the youngest Davenport whimpered though Melissa did all she could to comfort him as the wind and rain continued to beat upon their home.

Needing to give his son relief, Frederick kissed Bethany's forehead and Louisa's auburn locks before setting them together and facing Melissa.

"If you'd allow me to bring him to the hospital—"

"It's too dangerous."

"Then give him to me a few minutes. You need a respite, Beloved."

Frederick took his namesake to his heart, fretful to feel the lack of energy in his son's body. Stepping toward the study, he looked back at Melissa. "I'll stay away from the windows."

He carried Junior toward the bookshelves. Since Alabama outlawed liquor the year before, Frederick kept hidden stockpiles of his and Melissa's favorite drinks so they could still share a glass of wine on special occasions, or he could indulge in a shot of something harder when the mood struck. Their make-shift wine cellar was elsewhere, but the tonics were scattered about the study in false books. Taking the leather-bound case labeled *Paradise Lost*, Frederick set it on his desk and removed the bottle of brandy.

He loosened the blanket around his only son and looked upon his weakened form. Not since Bethany was overcome with an evil spirit four years before had he seen one of his children as bad off as Frederick Lionel Davenport, Jr. Wispy russet hair damp with fever and brown eyes glassy, the once sturdy baby continued to fuss.

"You need relief, my prince."

Frederick pressed his lips to his son's cheek and removed his handkerchief. Opening the brandy with one hand, he dipped a corner of the cloth into the amber liquid and brought it to Junior's mouth for him to suck. Then Frederick took a swig from the bottle, briefly closing his eyes.

Once more, he dipped a clean corner of the handkerchief into the bottle before taking another swallow and returning it to its hiding spot. He paced the room, swaying Junior as he gnawed the liquored cloth.

Wind lashed the house—the walls of his enchanted childhood with the Easton family. He thought of his ex-mother-in-law. After losing her husband, Mrs. Easton sold her house and traveled between her children's homes. Frederick hoped she wasn't in Grand Bay with Susan that month, but he believed she was with Emma in Monroeville.

When Junior fell asleep, Frederick shoved the handkerchief into his pocket and fixed the blanket around his son before returning to the hall.

BARREN DEVOTION

The Possession Chronicles #7

By

Carrie Dalby

Book formatted and published by Olive Kent Publishing

Mobile, Alabama

First print/digital edition ©2021

www.carriedalby.com

For Stephanie Thompson, who loaned me the Mystics of Dardenne society,

featured in her book Want, *by Stephanie Lawton,*

and

David Gandy for inspiring the face of Claudio

Melissa stood. "You got him asleep."

In his attempt to seek comfort, Frederick tasted her with a deep kiss. Melissa pulled back and leaned over her son's mouth to inhale. Eyes narrowed, she looked to Frederick with scorn. "Freddy, how—"

"It was just a dab for medicinal reasons. He's exhausted, and needs rest. I had to do something since you won't let me go for help."

"We need to stay together." Melissa put a hand out to Phoebe, whose blue-green eyes were luminous in the dim hall.

She clutched her stepmother's hand in return. "Do you think Momma, Poppy, Asher, and Miss Naomi are safe?"

"They have big porches to protect their windows and the lovely hallway downstairs to gather in," she answered.

Phoebe turned and wrapped her arms about her father's waist. "May we go there?"

Frederick smoothed her blonde hair. "It's too late for that, Princess."

"What about Kade and his family on the island? Are they safe?"

"God will watch over the Campbells." Frederick smiled for his brave girl. "Why don't we get more comfortable?"

He shoved the parlor sofa across the floor and into the hallway, Melissa's favorite armchair diagonally across from it for her and Junior. Frederick took three-year-old Louisa in his arms, and Bethany and Phoebe claimed either side of him as they waited out the storm.

***

The next afternoon, still blustery and wet, found Frederick and Melissa at the roofless hospital with their son. They'd dropped the girls with Lucy and Alexander and driven the debris-cluttered roads to get the help Junior needed. The infant was declared to have pneumonia, and the hospital had neither the space nor supplies to care for him.

"Make him as comfortable as you can," a nurse told them as she ushered Melissa out.

"What do you think we've been doing since the hurricane?" Frederick yelled as he grabbed the doorframe, blocking the exit to keep Melissa and Junior in the exam room. "We came for help as soon as we could leave our neighborhood!"

"I'm sorry, Mr. Davenport, but there's nothing we can do for him."

"Freddy," Melissa whispered as she touched his taunt arm, "let's find Darla."

The telephone lines were unserviceable, so they drove to the Adams's home. Horatio ran about the yard in a rain slicker as his parents collected the largest felled branches. Darla came to the vehicle when they pulled alongside the pile of tree limbs.

"We were going to—is Junior still sick?" Darla's hand went to the infant's forehead.

Melissa choked back a sob. "It's pneumonia, but the hospital turned us away."

"The nurse had the nerve to tell us to try to make him comfortable as if we'd not been doing that for days!" Frederick hit the steering wheel.

Henry rushed over at the shout, and Darla grabbed his hand. "I need to go with them. Come in a little while to check on us."

Soon Frederick, Melissa, and Darla were huddled around the baby in the Davenports' parlor. Darla showed them how to hold Junior to open his airway when breathing became difficult.

"It's a blessing convulsions haven't set in," Darla said, "but I know Frederick is experienced in keeping fevers down."

"How can we save him?" He couldn't keep the pleading tone out of his voice.

Darla's lower lip trembled. "At this stage, it's as the nurse told you."

Fists clenched, there was nothing left for him to do but punch.

"Freddy, please!" Melissa cried as his knuckles broke through the partially closed pocket door.

He stomped across the hall into the study and went for the brandy.

Sometime later, Melissa set a sandwich on his desk and cracked open a window. The wind still howled off and on, but the rain had slacked. On her way out, he reached a hand to her. She intertwined their fingers and fell against his solid chest.

"Don't shut me out. I need you more than ever."

"Is there any change?"

"He's sleeping, but his breathing is shallow. Henry has gone to pick up the girls."

"I can't deal with the girls."

"Darla is going to see to them, and we'll bring Junior to our room. And don't tell me you can't come with me. I need you, Freddy."

Through tear-blurred vision, he gazed at her in defeat. "I can't."

"You've done noble things for your previous wives, and now it's time for you to do something for me. You needn't say anything, just stay with me. Stay with me until the end, Freddy. That's all I ask."

He nodded.

"Keep in here until they come if you'd like. I love you." She closed the door.

After a few more swigs of brandy, Frederick laid his head on the desk and wept. His Christmas Eve son had been ripped from his hands, and there was nothing he could do about it.

She came in a cloud of lavender, lifting his head as her green eyes drove the shrapnel of his shattered heart into his soul.

"Goosy." He collapsed against her shoulder. "I'd rather it be me."

Lucy shushed him with the stroke of her fingertips along his back. "It may not feel like it, but you'll get through. I know what it's like to lose a precious one, though you had Junior much longer than I carried Camellia Alexandra. The ache stays with you, but Melissa needs you—Louisa, Bethany, and Phoebe too. And I need you, Frederick Lionel Davenport, my first husband and forever my knight."

She kissed his cheek, but he cupped her face in his large hands and pressed his lips to hers. It felt like home—her warm mouth and cool hands trailing his neck—and he pressed for more. Then her hands were pushing his chest as she leaned away.

A curving smile rather than a frown graced her pretty face. "Brandied tongue and kissing another man's wife. Don't tell me you're turning into Alex."

Frederick buried his face in her veil of blonde hair and tugged her against him, remembering the evening he almost took her in that very room though she was married to Alexander. "I'm sorry, Goosy."

"Don't be. You're half-drunk and fully hurting. Besides, you were always a fine kisser." She left a peck on his cheek. "But how will I explain brandy on my breath to Alex?"

"I hear mint covers a myriad of infractions."

Her laugh momentarily lightened his mood.

"I love you, Freddy. I had no one when I went through my loss. Keep Melissa close." Lucy replaced the brandy in its hiding spot. "Be there for her and the girls. And let me know if there's ever anything I can do."

Frederick kissed her forehead. "Thank you."

He brought Lucy to the entry hall, and she followed Henry and Horatio to their automobile. Stopping in the parlor to hug and kiss each of his daughters, Frederick gave Darla a nod of thanks before retreating upstairs. Melissa lay atop their bed, curled around the still form of Junior. He watched several seconds before seeing the pathetic rise of the baby's chest beneath his white gown. Frederick took the spot across from his wife—their dying son between them.

She trailed a hand down his arm. "Thank you."

He lifted her hand to his lips, kissing her knuckles. "Remember, I'm not perfect."

They lay in silence until the gray sunset turned black when Frederick Lionel Davenport, Jr. took his final breath. Frederick held Melissa in his arms for several minutes. Then he kissed his son goodbye and ran out the door.

One

In the predawn quiet of Saturday,

Melissa held her breath as she leaned against Freddy's back. Friday had marked nine months since Junior left the world. She'd spent the day alone, save for Louisa, as typical. Phoebe and Bethany were staying Easter weekend with their mother—taking Holy Friday Mass at the cathedral and their Saturday morning equestrian fun with Alexander—and Freddy hadn't come home until Louisa was in bed for the night.

Melissa brought her arm around Freddy's waist and placed her forehead against his shoulder, exhaling in relief when he reflexively shifted into her. Too often, he turned away from her touch, but this time he lifted her hand and kissed it. Knowing that he knew she was there, she tucked her knees behind his and snuggled closer, trying to ignore the flutter of want that began in her chest and crept lower.

Dawn glowed through the curtains as Freddy turned to her fully. For the first time since the hurricane, his hands went to her hips. Rather than the kneading caress of years past, he explored the sharp angles beneath her cotton gown. After birthing two babies, her body had rounded into *pleasing curves*, as Freddy called them. But over the months of heartache and loneliness, she'd whittled to less of herself while Freddy continued to increase his bulk at the gym six days a week.

"Melissa, what's happened?" His hands roamed to her waist, and he fingered her ribs. "Where's my soft wife?"

"She walks away the lonely hours and can't bring herself to sit at the supper table without her husband."

"But you have Louisa, plus the girls when they're here."

"Are you going to tell me you were completely fulfilled after your divorce because you had your daughters?" Hurt more than bitterness carried her words.

"What have I done?"

His arms felt foreign about her, and Melissa's pain manifested as tears.

"Beloved, forgive me."

Clumsily, his lips went to hers. Beside empty kisses on the cheek as he came or went from home and brushing her hair before bed, Melissa had been untouched since last July. After a minute of indulging, Freddy slipped from the bed and locked their door that had been left open through the passionless nights. Melissa marveled over his physique while he disrobed as he returned to the bed.

"If you wish to turn me away, I'll understand," he whispered. "I warned you I'm not perfect, but I've been a poor excuse for a husband these months."

Part of her wanted to punish him for his neglect by turning from him, but her long-buried desires spurred her to respond to his attempt to heal her wounds. Fingers trailing down his pectoral muscles, Melissa raised her chin to accept another kiss. His attentions were slow and tender while they rediscovered each other.

Afterward, Freddy pulled her on top of him. "Promise me there will be no more hunger strikes."

Wanting to trap him into the truth, she asked a baited question. "Am I too thin? Is that why you haven't touched me?"

"Beloved, I've not seen you these months. I've been trying to beat the pain the only way I know. I've had no interest in anything but surviving another day. I've been to work and the gym, turning to no one for comfort except that terrible day. Seeing Lucy when she stopped by brought all my previous pains to the surface and—"

"She told me. She told me after the funeral and apologized. You two shouldn't be allowed in the study unchaperoned."

His laughter gurgled as though afraid to let loose. "It was my fault that day, but I'm glad she told you."

"Don't hide from me, Freddy. We have nothing without each other. The girls will grow up and leave, and we'll be empty if there's no love between us."

"I never stopped loving you. Forgive my neglect, but please be patient as the ache still stings. I don't deserve your devotion." Freddy's hands were about her body, feeling like a stranger's touch.

Sharing the ultimate a second time proved urgent. Melissa marveled over his increased mass, but it could have been her frail size in comparison to his strength that made her feel like he could break her with one false move. He had, after all, already broken her heart.

Lying quietly in his arms when they were both spent, she heard Louisa in the hallway before her knock.

"Mommy, Pancake Time!"

"Have you—"

"Yes," she breathed out the pain with the word. Each Saturday after their son died, Freddy had slipped from the house before the girls were up, not returning until noon. Rather than disappointing his daughters, Melissa donned an apron and mixed pancake batter while the girls accompanied her with a less exuberant rhythm section. "Every Saturday, even when Phoebe and Bethany are with Lucy. Some traditions need to be carried on despite heartache."

His kiss rivaled the passion he'd shown when they were caught in the rain during one of their first dates. Then he stood, pulling on his pajama bottoms and reaching for the door while Melissa tugged the blankets to her neck.

"Daddy! Are you home sick?"

"No, Littlest Princess." He took Louisa in his arms, hugging her as he kissed her cheek. "I'm here for Pancake Time. Do you think I remember how to cook?"

"The king never forgets! Mommy said you'd join us again. Phoebe and Beth will be jealous they missed it."

"Tell your sisters I'll see them next Saturday." He turned to Melissa. "I owe you much, Beloved."

***

Hoping Freddy would return from the gym sooner than normal, Melissa and Louisa took a walk around the neighborhood. They went by the Spunners' house, but Hattie, lying in from her newest arrival, wasn't taking visitors, and Sean was out with their son, which was a bit of a relief for Melissa. She had avoided Hattie's weekly science club gatherings since Junior passed away. The few times she'd gone that winter and spring, she'd sat numbly with her empty arms, not participating in the discussions with the other ladies and young women.

On their way back up Catherine Street, Mrs. Conner stopped them.

"Have you heard the news, Mrs. Davenport?" she asked as she turned from her azalea bushes.

Melissa paused, releasing Louisa to skip ahead, her striped dress flapping about her knees. "No, what is it?"

"Yesterday, President Wilson declared America is going to war. All that talk about drafts will go into effect in the months ahead. It's a blessing our husbands are too old for that, isn't it?"

"Yes." But a pang of worry over their younger friends like Henry, Chuck, and the other regulars at the gym struck Melissa.

Louisa stopped at the next corner. "Come on, Mommy!"

"Enjoy your day, Mrs. Conner. Your garden is prettier than ever this spring."

When they reached home, Louisa brought paper and crayons to the front porch, and Melissa settled in the swing with her journal. She stared at the blank page half an hour before being secure enough to put pen to paper.

He loves me still. As strangers, we reconvened at dawn, he seeking forgiveness and I wanting nothing more than my husband's arms about me. He didn't realize what I'd suffered alongside him until he felt the emotional scars that altered me during nine months of loneliness. From here, we'll cleave together, especially as war reaches our friends.

At eleven-thirty, Freddy still hadn't returned. Melissa went inside to prepare lunch while Louisa swung in the backyard. She was about to call Louisa when the sound of Freddy's automobile came through the open windows. Watching him toss their daughter into the air and hug her warmed Melissa's soul. While he hadn't blocked his daughters as he had her, he hadn't been as present for them. Knowing Louisa missed the attentions of her father concerned Melissa. But Freddy, the devoted father she'd married, appeared to be back after his period of mourning.

He piggybacked Louisa inside, allowing her to slip to the kitchen floor before urging her to wash. Then he embraced Melissa, kissing her fully.

"Welcome back, Handsome. I've missed you."

As though sensing she spoke of more than the morning, he gave her a shy smile before dipping her back for a deeper kiss.

Toward the end of the meal, Melissa remarked about the news she'd heard from their neighbor.

"The dispatch was all the men talked about." Freddy took a drink of his iced tea and looked to their daughter. "Naptime when you're done, Princess."

"Daddy tuck me in?" Her brown eyes were warm, completely trusting.

"So long as I'm home, Louisa Constance."

Freddy hurried Louisa to bed and rejoined Melissa in the kitchen as she finished the dishes. "I'm glad you ate well at breakfast and dinner. Will Miss Sharon be here to fix supper tonight?"

"I gave her the weekend off since the girls are gone, though she's helping Naomi tomorrow."

"Would you like to go to the diner instead of cooking?"

"There's chicken that needs to be used, but if you want to take us for dessert—"

His lips were on hers as he lifted Melissa off the ground and carried her to their room. He tossed papers from his pocket onto the dresser before hastily removing his bottom layers and joining Melissa on the bed.

After their coupling, Melissa stood to straighten her clothing. The breeze through the windows rustled the papers Freddy had thrown on the dresser. Her heart splintered when she read the bold words across the top.

Volunteer Enlistment

"Freddy." His name came out like a thousand nails sealing her coffin.

Seeing where she looked, he quickly hugged her. "I had to do something. They might not take me as I'm beyond the standard age. They'll be in touch for a physical and—"

"Of course they'll take you! You're in perfect health. How could you do something like this without discussing it with me after what we finally shared this morning? And you came home and made love again like nothing changed." Her voice trembled.

"Chuck, Thomas, and a handful of others were enlisting. We were the first ones at the armed service office. Henry is waiting for the draft. On Monday, I'm making him a full partner and changing the company's name to 'Davenport and Adams Allied Accountants.' But if Henry is drafted, Mr. Peabody can step in as manager. If anything happens to either of us, you and Darla will have a share—"

Her hand struck his cheek with a sickening *thwack*.

"All these boys are going off to war. Knowing how it feels to lose a son, I have to try to protect others from that pain."

"And what of *my* pain?" She clutched his arms as hot tears rolled down her cheeks. "What are the girls and I left to do but worry? Who will protect and console us when you leave?"

"There's Alex, Lucy, Darla, Claud—"

"A hell of a lot of good that's done me these past nine months!"

"You're strong and have lived without me that long. I'm sure you can handle another nine months or a year on your own."

In her agony, she raised her hand to lash out once more, but he caught her wrist. She trembled to feel her weakness beneath his grip. Seeking to shield herself from more pain, she laid a wall between them with her words.

"How dare you throw your life away when you have so much to live for! Don't touch me after what you've done today, and the emotional neglect you've put me through." She yanked her arm free and glared. "In case you forgot, I lost my son that day too! You've been a selfish bastard all this time, and then you toss me a nugget of what we once had only to shove it down my throat as a parting gift."

"Beloved—"

"You have no right to call me that! Not one thing you've done shows that you've cherished and loved me since Junior died. I'm tired of being ignored, of being in the same room and afraid to touch you lest I be spurned once again. One day of intimacy doesn't heal a gaping hole."

Melissa ignored his pained countenance and pleading words, locking herself in the bathroom to scrub his scent from her skin.

When she emerged in her bathrobe, Freddy was gone. She pulled on a simple blue dress, tugging the sash as tightly as it would go to accentuate the narrowness of her waist. After braiding her long hair, she went to check on her slumbering daughter.

Alarm at seeing Louisa's empty bed sent Melissa rushing downstairs. She found Louisa with Freddy on the front room floor, making a fort out of the furniture and blankets.

"Mommy, come help."

"Not now, sweetie. I need to prepare supper."

"Daddy said we were going for ice cream!"

"You're more than welcome to go with Daddy, but I need to stay home."

"Go on and get your shoes, Louisa. We can finish the fort later." He nudged her from under the blanket.

Freddy caught Melissa around her waist, nuzzling against her neck. "Forgive me."

She tensed. "I can't."

"Melissa, I—"

"I need time, something you'll give me plenty of when you leave—possibly for good."

"I'll return. Just as your kiss made me victorious at the tournaments, send me off with your love, and I'll come home."

She shook her head. "War isn't a boxing match among friends."

"Have faith in me."

Melissa turned for the kitchen. "I'm sorry, but it's all gone."

Two

Naomi Joyner situated the basket of
rolls on the Mellings' dining room table in preparation for Easter
dinner. The floral china gleamed amid the polished silverware and
crystal place settings as someone entered behind her.

"Don't worry, Miss Lucy. Sharon and I have things under
control. Everything will be perfect."

"She's too busy getting Asher to keep his bowtie on to fuss
about the table." Alexander grabbed a roll from the basket and
winked. "Besides that, she trusts you impeccably."

Naomi took in Alexander Melling's half-unbuttoned shirt and
shoeless feet. "Company will be here in ten minutes, Mr. Alex. If
you're not going to show them respect, you ought to show some to
your Savior by dressing proper on His glorious day."

"You may be right, Miss Naomi." He kissed her cheek and
shoved the roll between his lips so he could fasten his shirt.

Lucy entered and studied her husband tackling his buttons.
Approaching him, she took a bite off the roll hanging from his
mouth, a hand on her lavender hat to keep it from falling.

"Really, you two!" Naomi feigned shock. "What would your
mother think of that display, Miss Lucy?"

"She'd probably prefer us sharing than draining her bread basket."

Alexander removed the roll. "And we'd never want to disappoint Mrs. Easton."

He popped it back in and leaned to his wife, offering more.

Naomi laughed. "I hope y'all got everything out of your systems during Asher's nap. I swear y'all made Sharon blush with that racquet. Did you even bother to shut the door?"

"With the girls here," Lucy said, "of course we did, though they were happily playing in the yard."

"Miss Bethany wanted to run up and tell you about a caterpillar she found, but I stopped her."

"Thank you." Lucy's rosy glow was becoming against her purple gown.

"Let's find my tie," Alexander said, "and make sure Asher knows if I have to wear one, he better keep his on or else."

"Or else what?" Lucy challenged.

"Or else that room makeover isn't going to happen, and he's stuck with yellow ducklings on his wall until he goes to college."

"You wouldn't be so cruel." Lucy kissed him.

He tugged at her with a thrusting motion. "Oh, I would unless you soften me with your touch."

She teased him back with a slower kiss. "What you seek appears to be what makes you harder."

"But because you love me, you'll make sure it's only temporary."

"I need to get some air after all that," Naomi said as she went for the hallway.

"Your time will come, Miss Naomi," Alexander called after her.

Naomi had given up longing for a beau when she passed her thirtieth birthday two Februarys ago. She'd convinced herself her station with the Mellings—complete with the snug apartment over the garage she'd moved into after their son's birth—was as fulfilling as anything she could expect out of life with her blind eye.

The doorbell chimed, and she offered a smile upon answering it. "Welcome, Mr. Frederick and Miss Louisa."

"How do you do, Miss Naomi?" The girl curtsied.

"Well as anything. Your sisters are in the yard."

Louisa scampered toward the back, nearly running over Alexander.

"Louisa, slow down!" Frederick called as he closed the door.

"Sorry, Mr. Alex. Thank you for having us." She paused long enough to hug Alexander's knees before continuing.

"She's growing up right quick, Mr. Frederick," Naomi remarked.

His smile seemed pained. "That she is."

Alexander joined Frederick. "I want a kiss from Melissa. Where is she?"

"She didn't feel up to coming today."

Lucy joined the group and took his hand. "Freddy, is she feeling unwell because there's news?"

His cheeks went red. "Nothing like that."

Disappointment clearly on Lucy's face, she hugged him. "I'll continue to hope for you."

"Don't, Goosy. And please don't say anything of the sort to Melissa. We aren't trying because there's no way to replace who we lost."

Naomi wiped a knuckle under her eye and moved around the corner to avoid seeing the heartache on Frederick's face. He and

Melissa hadn't been the same since they lost their son the summer before. Still, she'd never heard Lucy mention Melissa's weight loss or the fact that Frederick stayed late at the gym, having Phoebe and Bethany take supper with them every weekday evening.

"Naomi," Lucy called out, "don't let me forget to send a plate home with Freddy for Melissa."

Naomi stepped forward. "We'll send her a feast, Miss Lucy."

"Go get comfortable, Freddy. Alex and I need to see to Asher a moment."

Frederick wandered into the front room as the Mellings went upstairs. Naomi—about to turn back to the kitchen—returned to answer the next door chime.

"Happy Easter, Naomi." Darla, lovely as ever in a yellow dress that showcased her womanly figure, embraced her.

"Thank you, Miss Darla. It's always good to see you, Mr. Henry, and strapping Horatio."

"Where's Asher?" the blue-eyed rascal demanded.

Naomi ruffled his wavy hair. "He's in his room, putting up a fight about his Easter clothes."

Henry gave his greeting and mounted the stairs behind his son.

Darla turned to the living room, a frown setting in. "Frederick Davenport, in all my years of knowing you, I never would have expected such selfishness as you displayed yesterday morning!"

Naomi caught her breath and held her position in the hall. Frederick came to his feet, a look of despair etched across his face as Darla approached him with a wagging finger.

"After all Melissa's been through, you had to march off and enlist when you're beyond draft age and have three lovely daughters who need you at home. Not to mention your wife, who you gave no thought to when you rushed to sign your name! No amount of patriotism is worth tossing that trust aside."

"I know." He hung his head.

"Where is she? I need to give her a sympathy hug. I about strangled Henry when I heard he stood by while you, Chuck, and the rest of the guys tried to show off by being the first to join the army."

"Melissa refused to accompany me today."

Darla huffed and crossed her arms. "You've made a muddle of things."

"I realize that."

"What's this?" Lucy asked as she entered the room.

Darla turned, scorn on her face. "Frederick enlisted in the army yesterday without a word to Melissa or anyone else except the fools at the gym."

"Frederick Lionel Davenport, a man your age has no business running off to war!" Lucy crossed the room, pulled her hat from her head, and thrashed Frederick with it. Flowers rained around them from the force, but he did nothing to shield himself.

Darla smirked and plopped onto the loveseat as Alexander rushed in.

"My queen, set down your sword." His arms went about Lucy's, pinning them to her side. She dropped her hat and proceeded to kick at Frederick—which did little damage with her bare feet.

"I'll not have my daughters left half-orphans for you to go play knights with real soldiers!"

"What?" Alexander released Lucy.

"He enlisted without discussing it with Melissa."

Alexander slapped Frederick across the face.

"Alex!" Lucy yelped. "We didn't invite Freddy here to abuse him!"

He turned to his wife. "Then what were you doing when I walked in?"

"That's completely different!"

"Why, because you berated him like that exactly five Easters ago at your parents' house?"

"I have every right to express my concern when my daughters are involved." Lucy kissed the red splotch on Frederick's cheek. "Freddy, you know I don't wish you harm. I'm sorry my husband is such an insufferable, chivalrous cad that he thinks he can slap you because you did something that wounds Melissa."

"I've made a mess of things, but I have to go if my enlistment is accepted."

"Perhaps Alex could challenge you to a duel and sever a finger or two."

"You'd enjoy that too much, Goosy."

"Daddy!" Phoebe led the charge of the Davenport girls. "It's not fair you did Pancake Time without us!"

Frederick embraced his daughters, oldest to youngest. "I've already promised Louisa I'll be back for it again next weekend. No more skipping, so long as I'm in town."

"Are you going to be traveling with Sissa again?"

"I never know what might happen, but I promise to be the pancake maker as long as I'm home, Phoebe."

Before retreating for the kitchen, Naomi took in the sight of Frederick's daughters—blonde, brunette, and redhead—and smiled over their perfection. But three children, no matter how glowing, didn't replace the loss of another.

Three

"We're back, Sissa," Bethany's soft voice said.

Melissa slid a bookmark into the atlas and smiled at her stepdaughter. "I'm glad of it."

Bethany left, and Phoebe bound into the study.

"Sissa, you missed it all!" Unabashed, the nine-year-old climbed onto the desk, shoving the massive tome toward the typewriter so she could be the center of attention. If she kept up like that, there would be no living with her in another few years. "Kade brought the Gilbert Erector Set he got for Christmas he's been telling me about and built the tower as quick as anything on the patio after dinner. Then he helped me place Rummy on top like Rapunzel, and silly Horatio climbed up it to get my rabbit. Miss Darla started shrieking, but Kade built it so well, it didn't fall apart. It's made with steel like the big skyscrapers in New York City. I wish you could have seen it. It was taller than me!"

"It sounds spectacular." Melissa could feel Freddy watching from the doorway but refused to turn. "And how were Kade and his family?"

"Kade's terrific. Tabitha and Beth were off together playing dress-up with their dolls. Mr. Douglas talked a long time with Daddy and Mr. Henry about President Wilson and other boring things. And

Miss Maggie and Miss Darla talked about babies and islanders like they always do." Phoebe sighed like a tired old woman. "Louisa played yard games with Asher, Simon, and Horatio. She scuffed her new shoes and ripped a hole in her sash."

"I'll be sure to look over Louisa's clothes tomorrow. And what of your mother and Poppy?"

Phoebe's eyes shone with pride. "She wore the prettiest lavender outfit, but the hat she wore to Mass was all busted to pieces come dinner. Poppy said it was a casualty from a Melling Militia battle but wouldn't disclose who she fought or the winner. At least he made Asher pick up the flowers instead of me. He was in trouble for not keeping on his bowtie."

A laugh blurted out before she could stop it. Melissa reflexively looked to her husband to share a smile. Just as his mouth turned up, she looked away. "You tell stories as well your mother, Phoebe. Now it feels like I was there."

She jumped into Melissa's lap and hugged her. "Everyone missed you, and Miss Naomi sent a plate of food. Daddy put it in the icebox."

"Thank you."

Phoebe ran for her room.

Freddy stayed in the doorway several seconds before approaching. "Louisa fell asleep on the way home. I carried her to bed."

Melissa folded her hands on her desk, glancing at her loose emerald and diamond ring before meeting his eye. "I'm glad the girls had fun. Sounds like everyone enjoyed themselves."

"Not me. There's no joy without you, Melissa." His finger trailed her jaw to keep her chin up. "That battle in which Lucy's fine Easter bonnet lost all its flowers was against me. Darla scolded me and then told Lucy what I'd done. She unleashed her fury with words while she pummeled me with the over-budded hat."

Melissa bit the inside of her cheek to keep from smiling.

"Alex stopped her, but when he heard what I'd done, he slapped me. I think I have a bruise forming on my cheek, and it serves me right. I've been numb these months, and when I woke to your touch yesterday, the world came alive. The next thing I knew, there was talk of war and fear over facing death once more took hold. I acted impulsively to protect others in harm's way, but now I see that in doing so, I've lost your trust. I'll work the rest of my life to repair that, Beloved."

His soft touch and pleading voice loosened the knot in her throat. When he pulled her into his arms, his kiss tasted like tears. She weakened further as he caressed her back.

"Please allow me back into our bed tonight, Melissa. I don't want Phoebe or Bethany asking why I'm in the guest room. I'll not touch you if you prefer, but if our days are limited, I'd like them to be happy ones for my daughters, and you, if at all possible."

"How long would you have?" she whispered.

"The recruitment office said I should get an appointment for a physical and interview within two weeks. If I'm accepted, there would be a few months of training before anything happens."

Melissa sniffed and rested her head on his chest.

"If I could do it over, I'd come home rather than enlisting, but my signature is on the paper. If duty calls, I can't back out, but know that I love you and will do everything in my power to return to you and the girls."

She nodded and clung tighter to her fallen champion.

"Phoebe told you about the food Naomi sent, but I also have a message to go with it. Naomi pulled me aside and told me she's been worried about you, and if Sharon wasn't doing a good enough job over here, she'd be willing to deliver you a supper plate every day until you fill out properly." Freddy's hands gripped her boney hips. "As for Naomi, she's going to question me about how much you ate when she sees me tomorrow. I have to give her an honest report, so please eat something. I even wrangled a piece of carrot cake from Lucy to be sure you got dessert."

"And was another hat victim to that battle?"

He responded to her teasing by crushing her to him in an embrace. "I owe you everything. Your smile is the reason I'm alive."

***

After one night apart, Melissa and Freddy shared their bed, but it wasn't until Friday turned to Saturday the following week that she reached for him, curling against his side.

"I knew they'd want you," she remarked on the result of his appointment with the recruiting office and health inspection.

Freddy's arms encircled her. "These last few days, I hoped they'd think me too old, but my age helped in their decision to put me in as an officer."

"Leadership experience, education, fitness. You're golden to them."

"But forever tarnished in your eyes."

Her hand went under his shirt, feeling the warm skin across his abdominal muscles. "It hurts worse than you withdrawing from me during your mourning. Next time, drag me to the boxing ring. I'm sure I'd heal quicker from a physical beating than from this."

"What can I do for you right now?"

Melissa thought of small boxes of chocolates he'd brought to her when he returned home each day that week, his eagerness to help with the girls in the mornings and evenings, and having his eye contact and smiles once more—the best of all. Knowing it was temporary, she tried to enjoy his attentions without the bitterness of his impending departure, but it proved difficult. The advice Alex gave her during her first year of marriage came to mind. *But for now, take it whenever and wherever you can get it.*

Her hand under Freddy's shirt trailed toward his waistband, where she slipped the tips of her fingers beneath. "Help me feel like the most adored woman in the world. Make love to me like you did on our wedding day."

"It would be an honor."

After locking their door, Freddy opened the drapes to the clear night, the half-moon shining in a rectangle of silver that touched the bedpost. Freddy left his shirt on the bench before scooping Melissa into his arms. He set her on the chair so he could smooth the bedsheets and then cradled her in his massive arms, his lips upon hers.

Once on the bed, he unbuttoned her cotton gown enough to tug it to the side, exposing one of her shoulders, which he kissed. "Are you ready to explore each other as we set out on this grand adventure of life together?"

She smiled her appreciation for him remembering the words he had uttered. She replied in kind. "It feels like I've waited my whole life for this moment."

He knelt beside her on the bed. Soft kisses that urged her to lay back began at her lips and worked their way down her throat. A tender touch trailed up her leg, slowly raising her nightgown until he kissed the inside of each knee.

"You've blessed my life, Beloved. We'll be one, forever."

Under his sinuous attention, Melissa warmed and awakened, dropping all sense of loss in the glorious hour they shared. They slept in each other's arms until Phoebe's shouts roused them.

"We want pancakes! We want pancakes!" Banging on the door accompanied the chant, soon joined by a second pair of hands and lungs, and then a third.

Melissa snuggled into his solid form. "They've missed you."

"That sound is music to my ears." He tugged on his pajamas and did a two-step with the flare of one of Alex's sultry gyrations to the chanting.

Laughing, Melissa reached for her robe. "I better be the only one you share those moves with."

Freddy took her hands in his and started Turkey Trotting. After a few seconds, it melted into a tango of sorts with more hip rotations and roaming hands. In the hallway, the clamor increased. He danced Melissa to the door and kissed her long and deep before opening it.

"Daddy!" The girls flung themselves at him.

Freddy allowed them to pull him to the ground in a jumble of flowered nightgowns and giggles. They bounced on and hugged him until Phoebe started them back to chanting.

"We want pancakes! We want pancakes! We want pancakes!"

"Phoebe, arrange the ingredients. Beth, pull out the mixing bowl and pans. Louisa, gather the noisemakers." Freddy looked at each girl as he gave instructions and then smiled at them all. "On the count of three, Knights of Kingdom Davenport! One. Two. Three!"

They ran for the stairs in a mass of glee. Melissa dressed in a simple skirt and blouse and twisted her hair into a bun before joining the family in the kitchen. She accepted Louisa's offered pot and wooden spoon, adding her clanging to the din the girls made while Freddy whisked the eggs.

When Louisa and Junior were both born, Pancake Time was more subdued the first few months of their lives. Junior had just reached the point he could sit in Melissa's lap and bang a pot when he took ill. So while Freddy hid at the gym all those months, Pancake Time became more restrained as the girls' heavy hearts missed both their brother and father. But that second Saturday in April, all their bottled exuberance was set free in the Davenports' kitchen.

When Alex arrived at nine-thirty to pick up Lucy's girls, he stayed on the porch rather than enter the chaos. Laughing, Melissa joined him.

"While it's terrific to see Freddy back to his old self, the rowdiness I can do without."

"They'll be a few minutes. We lost track of time, and the girls just ran up to change."

Alex fingered a tendril of hair that slipped loose. "Are you well, Melissa?"

She smiled, but it wasn't her natural one. "The ache comes and goes. They're making him an officer—have you heard?"

Alex shook his head and angled his stubbly chin toward her. "He'll be great, you know."

"Yes, but it doesn't make it easier for me. He'll be training for a few months and then shipped overseas this summer. He's going to tell the girls tomorrow. He wants them to enjoy today."

"I don't envy him that conversation."

Louisa came to the door, still in her nightgown, complete with syrup stains.

She stood beside her mother. "Hello, Poppy. I mean, Mr. Alex."

He squatted to hug her. "You can call me Poppy if you want to."

Her dark eyebrows rose in surprise. "You'll be my Poppy? Phoebe says you can't."

"Your biggest sister doesn't like to share, but you're special to me, Louisa Constance." He kissed her cheek. "You might have a different mother than your sisters, but I'm as close a friend with your parents as I am anyone else in this world."

"Does that mean you can teach me to ride a horse when I turn five?"

He laughed. "We've got more than a year to figure that out, but I'd love to, Louisa. I'll talk it over with your parents soon enough."

Alex straightened and took Melissa's chin in his hand and dropped his voice as he stepped forward. "I'm here for you and the girls. I'll be Poppy to all while Freddy's gone. And for you"—he winked—"I could fulfill other needs. Don't be shy."

"Now I know why Maggie punches you."

Freddy came outside, giving Alex a narrow stare. "What's this?"

Alex flashed a grin. "Just offering my services for when you're engaged elsewhere." He jumped off the porch to distance himself from Freddy.

"Poppy!" Phoebe ran to Alex.

He twirled her around until her hat flew off her brassy locks, and she squealed in delight.

Freddy sighed, taking Louisa into his arms. Bethany joined her family on the porch, dressed as the other two riders but with her hat strapped under her chin. She only joined Alex and Phoebe on Saturdays when they kept to the ring at the riding club. Wednesdays, Alex took Phoebe on the trails and more advanced jumping courses.

"Goodbye, Sissa," Bethany said. "Thank you for Pancake Time, Daddy."

"You're welcome, Little Princess." Freddy kissed her head.

Bethany patted Louisa's arm and ran to join the others.

"He'll spoil them rotten when I'm not around to keep things in check," Freddy remarked. "He's level-headed enough with Asher, but it's all fun and frills with those two."

"Mr. Alex said I can call him Poppy, and he wants to teach me to ride when I turn five." Louisa hugged Freddy around the neck. "But I'm glad you're my daddy."

"And I'm blessed to have you as my littlest princess." Freddy looked from Louisa to Melissa and back. "What shall we do with Phoebe and Beth gone for a few hours?"

"Go visit Miss Lucy and Asher!" Louisa exclaimed.

"I'll take you one day next week," Melissa told her. "Why don't we drive to the bay and go for a walk?"

Freddy leaned around his youngest daughter to kiss Melissa. "That sounds perfect."

Four

On Monday, Naomi kept an ear out for the doorbell while Lucy and Asher were in the yard. The plans for Asher's bedroom update were in full swing, and the final contractor was expected that morning to see the project and offer a bid.

As she finished dusting the living room, the doorbell rang. Tucking the used cloth into her apron pocket, Naomi wiped her hands on the underside of the covering and straightened her striped blouse before opening the door. She stared a moment at the man before her. Though wearing denim overalls and a simple work shirt, his posture held the same dignity as Frederick. He was dark, broad-shouldered, and his deep-set eyes were piercing in their intelligence.

He removed the cap from his head, showcasing short, curly black hair with the tiniest hint of gray above his ears, and gave her a nod that felt like a bow in its distinction. "Mr. Paul Rollins here to see the Mellings about the possibility of redecorating a room."

"Yes, sir, please come in." She stepped back with her left side to him as he took in the grandeur of the vestibule from marble floor to gleaming decorative trim with quiet appreciation. "You may have a seat in the front room. I need to collect Miss Lucy from the yard."

"If it's not too much trouble, may I accompany you?" A thin mustache highlighted his upper lip, and she found herself staring.

Turning fully to him, she narrowed her good eye at him. Unfortunately, the gesture accentuated her blind eye, and Naomi tried to recover from what she wished to hide.

"The house is a Rogers's design, isn't it?"

"Yes, sir. Mr. Alex's parents had it built a decade ago."

"I'd like to see more of this work of art if you don't think the Mellings would mind."

Naomi smiled. "Those two are as welcoming as anything."

"Mr. Melling was pleasant to work for when I remodeled his office building five years back. He called me himself to set up today's appointment and took a few minutes to catch up on how I'd been. He was saddened to hear that my wife passed two years ago. A sympathy card showed up at my home the next day."

"I've never known a man more prone to kindness," Naomi said as they went through the kitchen. "I'm sure Miss Lucy will show you more when she brings you in."

Lucy stood on the edge of the covered patio, her white tea gown bright against the lawn as she watched Asher kicking a ball.

"Miss Lucy, Mr. Rollins is here about the room."

She approached them with a smile. "Thank you for coming."

"It's my pleasure, Mrs. Melling."

"Call me Lucy, please."

"Miss Naomi didn't want to overstep the boundaries, but any part of the home you'd be willing to let me see, I'd be more than pleased. I enjoy Mr. Rogers's designs and have worked on a few of his projects over the years."

Naomi found herself drawn to his smile above his strong, square jaw.

Lucy glanced between the two and turned fully to her. "Show Mr. Rollins the main floor before seeing to the second. I'll meet you in Asher's room as soon as I can get him inside."

Nodding, Naomi brought the carpenter through the kitchen, pausing for him to look over the cabinetry and trim before leading him through the den, dining, and morning rooms. He appeared to savor the details that most visitors overlooked. When they stepped into the front room, he behaved as if he were in a sacred place.

"The use of natural light and the veranda out front are perfect." He gazed at the unused grand piano in the far corner. "And the furniture is well placed."

As they ascended the staircase, he caressed the banister. Naomi tried not to look at his large hands—they were impeccably clean. She wondered how they would feel upon her and immediately heated. *I've been subjected to too much around here to keep scandalous thoughts out of my head!*

Mr. Rollins followed her to the guest wing and explored the rooms while she waited in the hallway. "That's always been my favorite, but I've never understood why," she said as he went to the yellow room.

After being inside a minute, he came to the doorway. "You have a fine eye, Miss Naomi. Come see."

While he pointed out the window placements in conjunction with the fireplace, Alexander's cheerful voice called from the stairwell.

"Naomi! Have you made it up here?"

She stepped into the corridor as Alexander reached the top of the stairs.

"We're touring the last guest room. Miss Lucy insisted Mr. Rollins see the house first."

"Excellent!" Alexander left a quick kiss on her cheek—embarrassment from his touch reaching her for the first time—

before he went for their visitor. "Mr. Rollins, it's good of you to come."

Alexander embraced the man with a quick handshake and one-armed hug like an equal.

"Call me Paul as you used to, Mr. Melling." Mr. Rollin's smile was bigger than ever.

"And call me Alex." With an arm angled up around the man's broad shoulders, Alexander looked to Naomi with a huge grin. "Paul here ripped apart the upper floor of Melling and Associates—tearing out the vileness of my father and Rupert Lyons so I wouldn't have their rot hanging over me."

"That was good of him."

"Poppy!" Asher ran past Naomi, flinging himself at his father.

Alexander took him in his arms and introduced him to Mr. Rollins. Lucy arrived, and Alexander ushered them over, setting Asher on the ground and drawing Lucy to his side with a slinking arm about her hip.

"Paul, meet my queen, my everything, my Lucy."

She blushed prettily under the attention, and Alexander nipped a kiss at her neck.

"Hello again, Miss Lucy." Mr. Rollins looked to Alexander. "You have a charming family and a lovely home. I hate to think I need to redo Mr. Roger's handiwork, but where's the room in question?"

"It's already been tampered with, so you'll be restoring it." Alexander walked with an arm about Lucy and Mr. Rollins on the other side down the wide corridor. "My wife wanted ducklings on the wall for our boy. That was fine for his younger years, but he's nearing school-age. I'd like a room that will last him until he reaches university so we aren't remodeling every few years."

"I understand."

"That's our girls' room there." Alexander pointed to the Davenports' open room a few feet away and then motioned to the one he stopped by. "In Asher's room, we want a deeper hue on the walls—a blue or green. The pastel blue stripes are already beneath his discerning taste. We were thinking a library-style shelving unit on one wall with room for a desk for his studies while allowing plenty of space for a full-size bed and armchair."

"And my toy box!" Asher declared before throwing open the lid and tossing his animals and blocks out until he found his hobby horse buried on the bottom. He circled the adults, swinging his arm with an invisible lasso and shouting, "Giddy-up!"

Alexander laughed then looked to the contractor. "What do you think of the space, Paul?"

"I think this interior wall would be perfect for a built-in unit. I could copy the molding from the rest of the house to trim it out. I could stain the wood to give the room a masculine air, like the downstairs den."

Alexander's arm returned to Lucy's middle. "What do you say?"

"It sounds lovely."

"Allow me to take measurements, draw up a plan, and bring it by the end of the week for you to look over."

"Perfect." Alexander gave one of his dashing smiles.

Asher galloped for the stairs on his stick horse. Naomi hurried behind him, leaving the Mellings to see Mr. Rollins out. She slowed when he took to traveling the length of the downstairs hall and kept an ear out for him as she removed ingredients from the icebox and pantry for their midday dinner. A few minutes later, Lucy asked Asher to slow down, promising him outside time after eating.

"Send him in if you'd like," Naomi called. "I've got crayons and paper on the table."

Eager to create—whether mischief or art—Asher clamored to the square table in the corner and set to work. Lucy smiled at him from the doorway, but when her husband's groping hands encircled her waist, her face took on a less motherly appearance.

"Go, you two." Naomi waved a dish towel at them.

Alexander scooped Lucy off her feet. A moment later, the click of the door to his den echoed down the hall.

***

On Thursday evening, Frederick took Melissa out, so all three Davenport girls were over for supper. Phoebe and Bethany stayed with their mother after school most days, but Louisa was a bright addition with her mother's smile and father's eyes. Alexander showed her extra attention, sitting her beside him at the table—Lucy on his other and Asher and his half-sisters across from them.

"Poppy," Louisa said over her bowl of ice cream during dessert, "will you show me how to hold a horse strap?"

Phoebe huffed. "It's called the reins, and you're not old enough to learn."

"I can learn before I go to the stables."

"You're just a baby." Phoebe sneered before shoving another spoonful of ice cream into her mouth.

Naomi collected a few dishes off the table and paused near the door.

"I'm almost four." Louisa held her head with the dignity of her mother. "Poppy said he'll teach me."

Phoebe shoved her chair back from the table and stood. "He's not your Poppy!"

"Phoebe Camellia Davenport." Lucy often used that tone when rebuking her ex-husband.

"Poppy belongs to me! When Daddy leaves, she'll have no one but Sissa!" Phoebe ran from the room as Louisa burst into tears.

Naomi set the dishes on the credenza as Alexander pulled the sobbing child into his lap.

"Louisa, my darling, you know that's not true. I love you. When your father is out of town, I'll be here for you. I told you I'm your Poppy." He kissed her auburn hair and hugged her.

Then Bethany and Asher were beside Louisa, patting her back.

"I'll share Poppy," Bethany whispered.

"Yeah," Asher added, "don't cry. I'd trade you for Phoebe any day."

Naomi choked on a laugh as Lucy's mouth quirked at the edge.

"Here, Louisa, let Bethany sit with you while I go talk to Phoebe." Alexander stood, but Lucy grabbed his hand.

"Let Freddy deal with her," she whispered.

"He'll need to address the issues too, but I'm going to let that stubborn knight know she can't talk to her sister like that in my house. I'll not let anger and bitterness rule within these walls."

Fear darkened Lucy's face.

"I've got these three," Naomi told her, and Lucy rushed after Alexander.

Asher and the two youngest girls helped Naomi clear the table and wash dishes. They joined Alexander and Lucy in the front room when they were done. Alexander took Louisa onto his lap, and the others gathered on the floor before Lucy with one of her fairy tale collections.

"Good night, all." Naomi waved from the doorway. "I'll lock up on my way out."

"Paul Rollins comes first thing tomorrow morning with his designs for Asher's room. If you want to make an early appearance, I'm sure it would be appreciated." Alexander caught her eye and winked.

"You tease, Mr. Alex." Naomi tried to sound irritable, but she couldn't hide her smile before she turned for the kitchen.

She let herself out the gate that opened onto the driveway and took the last few steps to the garage. Passing Alexander's automobile, she climbed the stairs to her apartment. What was first Eliza Melling's art studio and later Mrs. Melling's chauffer's apartment was now hers. As a reminder of the cheeky young lady who first graced the space, Naomi kept one of her works over the sitting area—an oil painting of the front of the mansion.

Memories of the Mellings' passion coupled with Alexander's teasing about Paul Rollins equaled a difficult time falling asleep. For consolation, Naomi collected her copy of *Winter of My Heart* and curled in bed to read until her eyes were too heavy to stay open.

Five

The final Pancake Time before Freddy left for training proved tense for Melissa. Two nights before, Phoebe had an outburst at Alex's house while she and Freddy were on a supper date. That morning, Phoebe still snubbed her half-sister while Louisa idolized her every move.

"Daddy, make her stop copying me!"

"Louisa is eating her pancakes, the same as everyone."

Phoebe folded her arms and glared at her father. "Everyone knows she's your favorite because you love Sissa more than Momma."

Melissa held her breath.

"You're all my daughters, no matter who your mother is. I love you the same, Princess."

"But I asked you to stay, and you're leaving Monday. You care more about being a soldier than you do being my father!"

"I gave my word I'd go to protect our country and help keep you safe. I can't back out after promising something. That's how it is in Kingdom Davenport."

"Then I'm joining Melling Militia!"

Freddy gave her a look of utter heartbreak but kept the pain out of his voice. "Momma will enjoy the extra time with you and Bethany."

"I love living there and might not wish to return. I have to share *you* with Louisa, but not Poppy and Momma."

"They're her family too, Phoebe."

"She's nothing to them! I don't want her at my house ever again!"

Freddy pushed back his chair so hard it fell against the wall as he jumped to his feet. "Go wash your hands and face and get yourself to bed, young lady!"

"I have to dress for Pop—"

"You aren't riding today." Freddy's Saturday stubble stood out on his face through the splotches of red anger. "I'll not stand for my daughter talking about family members like that!"

"But Daddy!" she whined as tears fell.

"Go right now, Phoebe Camellia, or I'll—"

Phoebe shrieked and ran from the room.

Both Bethany and Louisa were in tears. Melissa forced a smile and kissed each girl. "It's a difficult time, but we'll make it through."

Freddy stood where he'd jumped from his seat, fists white, arms trembling.

Melissa waited almost a minute before he looked to her. "If you need to go to the gym—"

"No." He shook the tension from his arms. "I'm not leaving the family this weekend."

He gathered Bethany to him. Her thick brown hair was the same shade as his, except for the hint of gray that began showing at his temples the past year. "You know I love all of you, don't you, Beth?"

"Yes, Daddy." She snuggled into his neck. "You love all the princesses in Kingdom Davenport. When Phoebe's sad, she pretends to be mad so people don't think she's a crybaby."

"There's nothing wrong with tears. Even Daddy cries sometimes." He hugged her tighter and kissed her forehead and cheeks before gazing into her eyes that mirrored his own. "Don't let anything Phoebe says hurt you. It's her anger, and you don't need to take it upon yourself. Now get dressed for riding. Poppy will be here soon."

"I can go?" Her brown eyes brightened.

"It's only Phoebe that needs to understand how her words affect others."

She left a smooch on his cheek before rushing from the room.

Freddy turned to Louisa. She sprang into his hug, arms and legs wrapping around him like the monkeys that climbed upon Melissa when she was in India.

"I know you love us, Daddy. You've been sad about Junior, that's all."

"You're right, Littlest Princess. I miss Junior every day, just as I'll miss all of you when I'm gone."

The tears in Freddy's eyes stirred Melissa's emotions to the surface. He set Louisa down, and she gathered her dishes, bringing them to the sink. Melissa took the moment to get a hug of her own.

"Have I failed as a father?" Freddy whispered.

"No. And don't think it's entirely your fault. After all, Phoebe's her mother's daughter."

He laughed. "Thank you for putting up with me and reminding me what's important."

The kiss began innocently, but his lips turned hungry, and he reached around her with a kneading touch as he tugged her against him. She felt the flush of want creep down her neck and went for his buttons. Booted feet scampered down the stairs ending their private moment.

"Thank you for opening to me, once again." His breath flickered across her face as he gazed at her with desire. "Making love to you while parked in the Melling's driveway Thursday night was an adventure."

It was the most scandalous thing they'd ever done—from having an illegal bottle of wine in their automobile to partially disrobing within a stone's throw of the main road. Melissa blushed at the mention, though her body happily responded to the images in her mind and the sensations they evoked.

"You were amazing."

Freddy caressed her warm cheek. "But now it's time for me to be a father to a hurting child."

Melissa left a kiss on his lips as she reached behind him to untie the apron strings. He went upstairs, and she joined Bethany pacing the front hall.

"You look ready," Melissa remarked over the riding clothes Alex had the girls outfitted with each season.

"My hair feels loose. Phoebe usually helps, but she's pouting."

"I'm happy to help you, Beth." Melissa settled on the stairs, and her stepdaughter sat a few steps below her. After removing the riding hat, she untied the blue ribbon holding the brunette waves at the nape of Bethany's neck.

"What if Poppy doesn't want to take me?"

"Of course he'll want you to go riding. Why do you think he wouldn't?" Melissa raked her fingers through the girl's hair.

"He's only taken me with Phoebe. I don't know if he likes to spend time with me."

"Sweet Beth," Melissa crooned as she wrapped her arms about her stepdaughter. "You were too young to remember, and I'm not sure what's been said to you in recent years, but your Poppy loves you so much he risked his life to get you to safety when you were in danger."

"The Melling Militia Rescue Phoebe talks about? I thought it was another play story."

"No, Beth. You were being held captive, and Poppy ran through the night to find you. When the bad guy heard him freeing you, he shot at him with a gun. Poppy has a scar on his leg and one in his arm because he loves you so much."

Bethany turned to Melissa, a hand on her knee. "Poppy has lots of scars."

"He has a big heart, and every scar he has is from helping someone he loves."

"Which one is for Momma?"

"In part, the ones on his hands and arms."

"Those are his biggest." Her earnest face was thoughtful. "He must love Momma most of all."

Melissa finished securing Bethany's ponytail as Alex pulled into the driveway. Through the screen door, they watched him cross the yard. His familiar swagger in his riding breeches brought a smile to Melissa's lips.

"Poppy's handsome, isn't he?" Bethany's soft voice said.

"Very much."

"Momma watches Poppy whenever he's in the room. Her eyes twinkle like she's imaging all the fun they have together."

A laugh tumbled out before she could catch it. "I'm sure she has plenty of joyful memories."

Alex stepped inside and looked at the two conspiring on the stairs. "And what's this, my darlings?"

Bethany hugged him, and he leaned down to kiss her forehead. "We're talking about you."

"And should I be pleased Sissa finds me amusing?" He looked to Melissa with a grin.

"She thinks you're handsome," Bethany whispered as though it were a secret.

Alex pursed his mirthful lips. "And are the knights ready to go with their *handsome* Poppy?"

"I'm ready." Bethany clasped her hands behind her back and looked up at him.

"And you're pretty as an iris, Bethany."

Melissa leaned close to speak into Alex's ear. "Phoebe's not allowed to come today. She exploded at Louisa and Freddy during breakfast."

Alex shifted closer. "Should I go talk to her?"

Melissa shook her head then dropped her voice even more. "Beth's worried about you not wanting to bring her without Phoebe."

A dangerous spark burned in his crisp blue eyes as he turned his mouth to her ear. "Then I'll reassure Bethany rather than ask why Freddy returned alone Thursday night smelling of wine and sex when he collected the girls." His lips brushed her ear before he stepped away and fell to a knee before the girl.

"So it's just you and me today, Knight Bethany?"

She nodded, swaying in her boots.

"Then it will be an extra special adventure. I've wanted to try you on the trails. Do you think you're ready?"

Her smile said it all. "Yes, Poppy."

"Excellent! I'll meet you at the automobile."

Bethany dashed out the door. Alex laughed and moved to follow, but Melissa took his arm.

"To answer your unasked question, I stayed outside when he got the girls because I couldn't walk straight and my clothes were severely rumpled. Freddy had to carry me to bed after he got the girls inside."

"And did he have another go after that?"

"Wouldn't you like to know?"

"And yourself? Were you too wasted to remember?"

Melissa laughed. "I remember, but it was nothing compared to the backseat."

"You naughty woman, but it makes me love you more." He kissed her cheek. "I'll watch the girls tonight if you wish."

"Freddy wants us to have as much time together as possible, but thank you." She nudged him out the door. "Focus on Bethany."

Once Alex left, Melissa went in search of Louisa. She played with a doll in her room—the old guest space Melissa stayed in when she first came to work with Lucy. Junior had shared the room his last month of life, his crib still in the corner piled with his clothing and supplies Melissa hadn't been ready to face. She silently vowed to tackle those things when Freddy was gone. Returning to the hall, she peeked in the room across the hall. Freddy snuggled with Phoebe on her bed. Both their eyes were closed, but she doubted they slept.

***

As though her body didn't wish to miss a moment with her husband, Melissa couldn't sleep Sunday night knowing she'd be lying in bed alone for weeks. Her head rested on Freddy's chest, and he kept an arm about her in the darkness. At two in the morning, Melissa trailed a hand down his abdomen.

"I'll ache for your touch every day, Beloved." He held her to him and fingered her braided hair. "When I think of the months I've neglected you this past year, I grow sick. I've missed so much with you—with the girls. I'd give my life to get that time back."

"Don't say that, Freddy. Not with what we're facing." Melissa kissed him long and deep.

The familiar touches built slowly as their garments were removed. They surged together in quiet passion. Afterward, he nestled into her bosom.

"Tell me what you need, and I'll fulfill all your desires."

"Don't hold back, and don't stop, but allow me to lead sometimes." She kissed his neck. "Maybe we'll wear ourselves out and be able to sleep."

An underlining level of desperation drove Melissa, making up for what they'd missed after losing their son. She clung to Freddy in hopes of filling her reservoir against the coming drought as they savored their final hours together.

When the alarm clock rang, Melissa found herself wide awake rather than sluggish from only two hours of sleep. She washed and dressed. Then biscuits, bacon, and eggs were prepared. When the kitchen door swung open, she caught her breath. Freddy stood outfitted in his khaki uniform and boots. She fell into his arms, holding back tears while she fingered each button and symbol, marveling how the cut of it gave him even more distinction.

"Captain Davenport, the keeper of my heart."

"Melissa, my beloved."

Louisa arrived next, and after a hug from both her parents, she settled at the table. Bethany and Phoebe entered together, wearing their matching school dresses for St. Mary's Catholic School.

"Daddy," Phoebe shrieked, "you look like you could take on Melling Militia!"

Bethany kissed his cheek. "I'm proud of you, Daddy."

After breakfast, Freddy donned his campaign hat, and Melissa gathered the girls on the front porch for photographs. Louisa stood in front of her father with Phoebe and Bethany on either side. Then Melissa took a candid one of them all piled around him on the swing.

"I'll take one of you and Sissa, Daddy!" Phoebe captured them standing respectfully together and another while they kissed.

Alex's automobile drove up, and Lucy streaked across the yard in a pink dress, followed more slowly by Alex and Asher.

Melissa stepped to the side and watched Lucy tremble a moment. Then her arms were about Freddy's neck, and she went to her tiptoes to leave kisses on his cheeks. A moment later, she buried her face against his chest and shook from tears.

"Sorry for the display, Captain Davenport," Alex said, "but at least she's doing it here rather than at the station. I refuse to bring her there."

Lucy turned, wet face shining in the morning sun. "Alexander Randolph Melling, you're insufferable!"

Freddy laughed, hugged Lucy once more, and kissed her quickly on the lips. "I'm just going for training, Goosy, but take care of our girls."

"And we'll watch out for Melissa and Louisa." Alex put an arm around Melissa's waist and pulled her to his side. "I think I'll claim a kiss from your wife as you have from mine."

Freddy playfully tossed Alex aside before taking Melissa into his arms. "I only kissed her lips because I didn't wish to taste her tears," he whispered.

Then Freddy stepped back, smiling. "Thank you for coming, Lucy, Alex, and Asher." He paused to hug the boy—something Melissa knew pained him. Even though he looked nothing like Junior, Asher reminded him of his own son no longer with them. "I'm walking the girls to school, and then Melissa and Louisa are bringing me to the train station."

Alex took a photo of all five Davenports before offering a brotherly hug. "The noble Frederick Davenport, I'm sure you'll do Mobile proud. And I bet you'll be at least a Major by the end of the year."

Freddy laughed. "I might not even survive the officer's training."

"I'm certain you'll beat all the records," Lucy said with a melancholy face. "I'll miss you."

The Mellings stayed to wave Freddy and the girls off, and then Lucy reached for Melissa. "If you ever need us, please telephone. And come over anytime. Daytime for Louisa to play with Asher or suppers to see the girls—you're always welcome."

"Yes, darling Sissa." Alex placed his hands on her as though ready to tango. "And if you should need more than friendly companionship, look no further."

Lucy backhanded his arm, causing him to laugh as he released Melissa.

"I don't think I could handle you, Alex." Melissa smiled. "Your intensity and prowess appear too great for me."

"After your drunken display in the backseat of Freddy's automobile in my driveway—"

"Melissa Stone Davenport, if you can get Frederick to go at it in an automobile, you could surely handle Alexander." Lucy took Alex in an erotic hold, kissing him like she had no business doing with the youngest children on the porch. "But you won't have the opportunity."

"I'll try to overcome my heartbreak," Melissa said.

"Come for supper tonight," Lucy begged.

"Not today, but thank you."

"But you—"

Alex stopped Lucy with a kiss. "She wants to be alone with her thoughts for today, and then she'll have the girls tomorrow." He turned to Melissa. "How about Friday, Melissa? You should be ready for stimulating adult conversation by then."

"Friday evening sounds perfect, Alex."

"And every Friday," Lucy added, "but come over during the day too. Asher's room is getting remodeled, and Louisa would be a welcome distraction."

"Then why don't you come here?" Melissa offered. "I could manage a luncheon Wednesday."

It was agreed upon, and the Mellings left.

While Freddy was at training, Melissa would only have her stepdaughters overnights on Tuesdays and every other weekend, after their Saturday morning rides, going from a full house to a nearly empty one. Regular company and supper dates would be welcomed.

When Freddy returned from walking the girls to school, he collected his haversack, and they loaded into the automobile for the cross-town drive—Melissa at the wheel. The train station bustled with men in uniforms and women crying. Freddy kept Louisa on his shoulders so she wouldn't get stepped on in the commotion. Many of the newly joined officers were being sent to Ohio for training. Then they would return to work with their local units before heading to Europe for further training and placement. Chuck Brady and Thomas Charles were there, both with their wives and Thomas also with his son. Rachel didn't look herself with the tear-streaked face and puffy eyes. Chuck tried to console her with kisses, but she continued to weep.

Freddy leaned close to Melissa. "Don't hang around here. See to yourself and Louisa as soon as I'm gone."

"Don't worry, Melissa," Chuck said. "We measly first lieutenants will take care of Captain Davenport."

Melissa hugged Chuck and then Thomas. The train whistle blew a warning for the passengers needing to board. With Louisa still on his shoulders, Freddy took Melissa in a tight embrace.

"I love you." His fingertips traced her jaw. "I'll remember you always and write every day, though I might not be able to mail a letter as often."

"Weekly is fine, Handsome."

"Same for you, Beloved." He left a kiss on her lips and stepped back so he could bring his daughter into his arms. "I love you, Louisa. I'll see you after your birthday, but that means you'll get another cake when I come home because I don't want to miss one of Miss Sharon's special treats."

"Love you, Daddy! Mommy and I will be brave."

"I know you will, Littlest Princess." He handed her his handkerchief. "Keep this safe for me. I'll see you when you're four."

Freddy clasped hands with Melissa and kissed her once more. Then the men were boarding and waving from windows, the iron beast pulling them away. Melissa took Louisa's hand and started for the automobile.

"A moment of your time, Mrs. Davenport!" a voice called.

She stepped to the side, and a man in a gray suit and fedora offered his hand. "Thank you for stopping. It saves me the time of making a telephone call. I'm Benjamin Paterson, an editor with The Daily Register."

Melissa switched her hand holding Louisa's to shake his offered one. "Pleased to meet you, Mr. Paterson."

"I hate to bother you on this emotional day, but we at the Register are more than eager to offer you a weekly column detailing life for a family with a husband involved in the war effort. It would be an honor to have a distinguished writer from our community on staff during the trying months ahead."

"I hardly know what to say."

"I don't expect an answer now," Mr. Paterson said with a grin. "We'll send over a contract and details, and you may telephone the office at your leisure with your response."

"That sounds fine, Mr. Paterson. Thank you for thinking of me."

"We've considered no one else, Mrs. Davenport. With your experience writing for *Noble Travels* and your two essay collections, there's only one voice we want for our readers."

Six

When Naomi opened her apartment door
Tuesday morning, the sound of sawing filled her ears. Paul Rollins
had the garage space arranged as a woodshop so he could build the
bookcase and desk unit for Asher's bedroom onsite. Smiling to
herself, Naomi straightened her white blouse and navy skirt before
descending the stairs.

Paul lifted his cap. "Good morning, Miss Naomi."

"Morning, Mr. Rollins."

"I'll be here for weeks, and the Mellings are so relaxed, please
call me Paul as they do." His intense gaze seemed hopeful as he
watched for her response.

She couldn't stop the grin as she tilted her blind side away.
"All right, Paul. And you needn't call me 'Miss' either."

"As you wish, Naomi." He nodded and returned to cutting a
piece of chestnut.

A quick glance behind her proved Paul watched her go. She
smiled to show she appreciated the attention. Mind wandering,
Naomi heated at the thought of Alexander's blatant words. *I think
Paul will enjoy working at the foot of your stairs.* She could image all too
well the type of things a man like Alexander would say to another

man in private and hoped he held her in high enough regard not to embarrass her.

Like most days when Naomi let herself in at nine o'clock, she found Lucy and Asher in the morning room. Lucy appeared pensive, sipping her coffee at her desk as she stared out the window.

"Morning, Miss Lucy." Naomi looked to Asher pushing a shiny fire engine before the unlit hearth. "Morning, Phoenix Asher."

"Hello, Miss Naomi! I'm going to get my ship." The boy ran over to give her a hug.

She kissed his pale hair before he ran down the hall and then laid a hand on Lucy's shoulder. "Everything good?"

"I wonder how she did last night." Lucy fingered the telephone on the edge of her desk. "I keep thinking of calling Melissa, but Alex told me she needs space, to wait until I visit tomorrow."

"That's probably for the best. You don't feel like being conversational when you're sad, do you?" Naomi thought of the way Lucy had cried after supper while Alex held her.

Lucy shook her head, dark blonde waves falling over the shoulder of her red dress. "But I ache for them. They love each other so much. After losing Junior, I could tell their relationship suffered. But why Frederick had to sign his life away without discussing it with anyone, I'll never understand."

"Worry over your daughters and make sure those sugars don't go without."

Lucy's mouth curved into a smile. "Alex is going to spoil them. He's talked about bringing the girls to the stables a second afternoon each week when his schedule allows. He telephoned when he got to the office to tell me about walking them into school when he brought them this morning. He said Phoebe was over the moon and held his arm like a princess going to court, and even Bethany giggled and kissed his cheek. What the sisters at St. Mary's must think of them with their father in uniform bringing them one day and their debonair stepfather the next, I do wonder. Especially with Claudio stopping in to dote on them as well."

"With Mr. Alex and Father De Fiore looking after the sugars, they'll be well seen to. Not to mention the love they get from you and Melissa."

"She does love them." Lucy sighed. "I often wonder what I'd do if Alex had a baby with someone else—if I'd love the child without qualms as it seems both Alex and Melissa do for Phoebe and Bethany. I've decided I'd be resentful and jealous. Melissa's a better woman, and I worry Alex will pick up on that. He might try to comfort her in her aloneness and—"

"Hush now, Lucy. Asher will be back any minute, and he doesn't need to hear you talk that way about his father. Nor do you need to be saying such things. We all know your husband's a flirt, but he's completely devoted to you. What's wrong?"

Lucy wrapped her arms around herself, rocking slightly. "I ache to my bones with melancholy. I haven't felt right for weeks, but Freddy leaving made it worse."

Naomi took a hand and squeezed it. "Anything I can do for you?"

"Beside Freddy, you're my dearest friend. You've been through it all with me. Please find joy for yourself. I want to see you shiningly happy, know you're taken care of when I'm no longer here."

Not since Lucy's pregnancy with Bethany had Naomi seen her so despondent. A cold trickle of fear crept down her spine as she embraced her friend. "Don't talk like that, Lucy."

Asher returned, and Lucy looked to her son with a bittersweet smile. "I hope he adapts well to his sisters being here more often," she whispered.

"Your boy will take it all in stride because, like his father, he'll be pleased there are more females to dote on him."

Only when Lucy's laughter reached her eyes did Naomi feel secure enough to leave her so she could dust the bedrooms.

***

Naomi anxiously awaited Alexander's return that afternoon. Once the casserole was in the oven, she rushed out the backdoor. Forgetting Paul worked in the garage, Naomi ran to the driveway before thinking about the scarf tied about her head and the soiled apron at her waist.

"Afternoon, Naomi. I'll be out of your way in a few minutes."

"Don't mind me, Mr.—Paul." She bashfully looked at her brown shoes when the roar of an automobile came up the driveway.

Alexander parked beside Paul's truck and walked around his automobile.

Not wasting time, Naomi got right to the point. "I need to speak with you before you see Lucy."

It must have been her downcast expression that made Alexander's smile falter. "Excuse us, Paul." Alexander took her elbow and led her through the gate, straight to the camellia maze. He set Naomi on the bench and sunk beside her. "What is it?"

"Lucy's not herself. I haven't seen her this gloomy since she was pregnant with Bethany and mooning over you."

Alexander rubbed a hand over his face and hair. "Must be Freddy leaving."

"It's been coming on longer than that."

"Since Junior died." Alexander rested his elbows on his knees. "It was like losing her baby all over again. She relives her pain with everyone else's."

"She needs you, but she might need someone else to help her this time."

Alexander nodded. "I invited Claudio to come for supper Friday along with Melissa and Louisa. I think we all could use a bit of brightness, and Claudio brings that. But for tonight, I'll do what I can for Lucy."

"Does that mean I need to bathe Phoenix Asher after supper and put him to bed?"

"Is there something he could help you with right now as well?" He winked.

"I'll see what I can do, you rascal."

"I'll give you a three-minute head start." Alexander nudged her toward the path.

Naomi checked the chicken and rice casserole before looking for Lucy. She and Asher were in the front room, she curled against the arm of the sofa, and he looking through a book about horses by her feet.

"Would it be all right if Phoenix Asher helped me with the green beans?"

"Of course, Naomi."

Asher stood on the footstool at the kitchen sink when Alexander came inside.

"How's the best boy in the whole world?"

"Poppy!" He ran to his father.

Naomi smiled, knowing the name the man once found horrifying was second skin to him. After a hug and kiss between father and son, he greeted Naomi.

"Front room," she whispered. "She's already lying down, but make sure the drapes are shut at least."

Alexander laughed. "There would be no complaints with my queen and me on display."

She snapped a dishtowel at his backside, which only made him giddier. A minute later, her curiosity took hold, and she inched open the swinging door.

"Are you lonely without the girls this evening?" Alexander's voice floated down the hall.

She couldn't hear a reply, but a moment later, Lucy's laughter rang out. Then Alexander carried her to his den. Soon after, Naomi brought a tray of dishes to the dining room. A few steps from the den, Lucy cried out on the other side of the door.

"My angel!"

Naomi bit her lip and quickly set the table. She returned to the kitchen, trying to ignore Lucy's impassioned cries.

At supper, Lucy's green eyes sparkled once more, but by morning she was melancholy. She put on a brave face when she and Asher left to walk to the Davenports' house at ten o'clock. Naomi, not having immediate work to complete until supper preparations, locked the mansion and went for her apartment.

Paul smiled. "Off duty for a bit?"

"Yes, but I'm going to the market in a while."

"If you wait for my lunch break, I'd be happy to drive you so you don't have to manage your load on the streetcar."

As she tried to decide if he showed kindness because he was that sort of man or if he was interested, the nervousness in Paul's eyes betrayed him.

"I appreciate it and accept. Thank you." Naomi paused, a hand on the railing of her stairs. "What time should I be ready?"

Paul looked at his watch. "Noon."

She nodded and started up the stairs.

"Naomi, I'd be pleased to take you to a luncheon counter while we're out if you'd like to accompany me."

The smile that found her lips felt as dazzling as one of Lucy's. "I'd enjoy that, Paul."

Once she closed the door behind her, Naomi spun around her sitting area. *A man finally looks at me as though he likes what he sees, and I plan to enjoy it!*

Not wanting to appear too eager, she kept her same clothes on but did her hair so the frizz around her face laid smooth, the back in a tidy bun beneath her cloth headband. She dispelled nervous energy by wiping counters and dusting her little bookshelf.

Unable to wait any longer, she descended the stairs five minutes before twelve. The smell of freshly cut wood greeted her, followed by a charming grin from Paul.

He removed his cap. "I'm ready, are you?"

Afraid to speak, she nodded. With a touch almost as soft as Alexander's, he took her elbow and led her to his truck. On the bench, she scooted away from the door-less opening. When Paul took his seat opposite, she worried she looked too forward by sitting in the middle.

"I've never ridden so high without a door." She gave a nervous smile as she met his gaze.

"I won't let you get hurt."

They stopped to eat at one of the nicer luncheon counters with a colored window at the back. Paul seemed to know almost everyone, and she was given equal esteem. They ate their pulled-pork sandwiches at a picnic table on the side of the restaurant.

Not long after, Alexander strolled down the sidewalk, chin high as his eyes took in everything—including Naomi. He strutted through the invisible line separating the whites from the blacks, looking all too pleased as he removed his gray hat.

"This is a beautiful sight!" He slapped Paul on the back as he shook his hand, and then he kissed Naomi's temple. "I love to see my favorite people getting along, like when Frederick Davenport and Melissa Stone got together. It makes a happier life for all involved."

"Paul only offered to bring me to the market. We just stopped here for a quick bite to eat." Naomi was sure if her complexion had been fairer, it would be as ruddy as Darla's often turned under Alexander's attentions.

"Of course, Miss Naomi." Alexander winked at her, then gave Paul one of his mischievous smiles. "Remember, she's like a sister to my Lucy. I'll see you this afternoon."

Paul watched Alexander down the street and turned to Naomi, who studied her plate. "Men like that mean well, but they don't understand how their attentions have the possibility of being uncomfortable. Tell me about yourself, Naomi. How did you come to work for Alexander Melling?"

She relaxed as she told of her days as a child at the Eastons' house—how she and her cousin would meet Sharon's mother there after school. Her aunt was the cook, and she and Sharon were raised learning to keep house, but the rambunctious Easton clan was always eager for more playmates.

"Lucy is less than a year older than me, and when she wasn't running wild with her brothers and Frederick, she was often alone reading. She always shared books and welcomed my company. By the time she was out in society, I was officially working part-time at the house. When she married Frederick, the Davenports' hired me full-time. They divorced four years later, and I went with Lucy to the Eastons' old house—the pretty Queen Anne off Catherine Street, if you know it."

"I do."

"Frederick bought it from her when the Mellings moved into Alexander's parents' home. That's where her daughters have lived most of the time, but they're with the Mellings now that Frederick joined the army."

"The divorce was because of Alex when he came back to town?"

Naomi nodded. "They were young lovers, but he needed to mature before they could settle together. Lucy married Frederick when she thought Alexander dead, but she never got over him."

"And how do you manage to look so young and vibrant amid all the drama surrounding your employers?"

Naomi laughed. "It's been difficult to see the heartache, but I'm not one for getting swept up in other people's affairs. I keep my life simple and quiet."

"And how has that served you?"

"I've been happy enough."

Paul's square jaw seemed to tighten. "How would you feel if I told you I'd like to get to know you and see you socially?"

"I'd say it's well past time for me to step out a bit, but first, I'd like to hear about you."

He grinned. "After working with an uncle at handyman jobs a few years, I married my sweetheart at sixteen. Willa and I had two girls, Jessa and Mattie, that are still on this earth—married with families of their own—and two boys that didn't make it past the age of five. When my uncle grew too ill to continue working ten years back, I took over his workload and started gaining a name for myself. Willa took sick two and a half years ago, and after hanging on to see our fourth grandchild born, she slipped away."

"I'm sorry."

"There's been more good than bad, but any sorrow seems overwhelming at the time." He briefly touched her hand that rested on the table between them. "I think I've got a decade on you, Naomi, but I assure you I'm healthy and spry."

She laughed and reached for her sweet tea. "I'm not worried about anything like that, Paul, but I'll keep an eye on how well you carry my purchases at the market."

Seven

Father Claudio De Fiore hesitated on the veranda of the Mellings' home. He patted the letter in his pocket, feeling the weight of it in his soul before pressing the bell. The massive door opened, and the light of heaven filled his vision, complete with angels.

"Claudio." Lucy hugged him, and they kissed each other's cheeks.

Phoebe tugged his arm, bringing him over the threshold. "How come you didn't see me at school this week? I wanted to show you how well I know my multiplications."

"You are very smart, *Principessa*. I shall come to you next week, I promise." He kissed her and allowed Phoebe to bring him into the sitting room, lush in gold and cream tones. There Bethany came for a hug. "And are you doing well at school?"

"Yes, Uncle Claudio. I got everything correct on my spelling test."

"*Eccellente*, Bethany. Your parents must be proud."

She smiled and nodded. "Momma wrote Daddy a letter all about our week when we got home from school today. Poppy is going to take us to the post office tomorrow to mail it."

Alexander galloped into the room, Asher on his back.

"Uncle Claudio!" the boy reached for him as Alexander trotted past.

Claudio snatched him from his father, gathering him in his arms. The perfect blend of Alexander and Lucy—fair hair, blue eyes, coupled with his father's self-assurance and Lucy's tender heart. "Have you been good this week, Asher?"

"I'm getting a new room. A man named Paul is building me a special desk and shelves, and the green paint is going on the walls soon!"

"Very good." Claudio turned to Alexander to ask to speak to him in private, but his friend put an arm around him first.

"Lucy, excuse us a few minutes, but there's something I want to discuss with Claudio before Melissa arrives."

"Of course." She kissed her husband when he leaned close.

Asher took hold of Alexander's arm. "May I come to?"

"Not this time, Phoenix Asher."

Claudio followed his friend to the den and hoped what Alexander wished to discuss would leave time to address the note he carried.

"I need your help, Claudio," he said as soon as the door shut.

"Melissa is unwell?"

"I threw that out so Lucy wouldn't suspect we're talking about her."

Claudio raised his eyebrows and took out his cigarette case, offering it to Alexander. He pulled one free and went to open the French doors to the patio, motioning Claudio to follow him. They stood in the double-entry, cool evening air wafting over them as their vapor dissipated into the twilight.

"Lucy's sad, and I can only refocus her for short periods. Before, her afterglow would last until the next time. Now she's as depressed as she was before I gave her attention."

Claudio laughed. "Are you worried you are losing your touch?"

"I'm worried I'm doing her more harm than good!" Alexander gripped Claudio's arm. "She's told Naomi some disturbing things this week. I fear she's slipping away, and I don't know what to do to hold her here."

"*Amico*, it is Lucy. She feels deeply and is upset because Frederick left. She will improve as the days pass, and he is well. He will return next month, no?"

"But then he'll leave again, and I don't know what it will do to her once he's on the battlefield. Please help her have peace."

He took a deep drag and held his friend's gaze. "I will do what I can for her."

"Bring her in here after supper and bless her, I beg you."

A quick knock sounded at the door, followed by its immediate opening. Melissa rushed in wearing a straight blue evening sheath that showcased how slim she'd become, her thin arms bare.

"A smoke, gentlemen, before the girls come for us."

As Claudio opened his case, Alexander doubled back to the door, locking it. Not until she brought the cigarette to her lips and exhaled did she lean in for kisses.

"Thank you, Claudio. Good evening, Alex."

Alexander snuffed his cigarette in the ashtray and took her into his arms. "And how are you holding up?"

"It feels like a dream—one I hope I'll wake from soon." Her hand trembled as she took another drag. "Days are long, nights longer. I started to go through Junior's things and—"

"Don't push yourself." He tightened his embrace, hand caressing her back. Claudio heated as he watched them, wishing he offered the comfort. Alexander kissed her cheek and gave her a handkerchief for the tears brimming in the corner of her eyes. "You shouldn't be alone when you sort through Junior's things."

"It sits there in the corner of Louisa's room, and we see it every day." A fist went to her heart. "I'll keep him always in here, but the constant reminder needs to go. I have enough pain seeing Freddy's empty pillow and...I just can't."

"There's nothing as calming as a priest when dealing with heavy memories and loss. And Claudio probably knows how best to pass along the things you don't wish to keep."

Her brown eyes, drowning in sorrow, turned to him. "Would you come to me, Claudio?"

"*Sí.*" Claudio opened his arms to her. Melissa tucked against his chest, a wave of citrus scent enveloping him. He kissed the top of her head and tried to ignore the press of her body against his. "I will come tomorrow."

"Poppy!" Phoebe shouted through the door. "Supper's ready!"

"We'll be right there!"

Melissa stepped away, puffing on her cigarette. "I don't know what I'd do without all of you. I'm not used to feeling isolated. Abandoned, really."

"Leave it to Frederick Davenport that the one time he makes a rash decision is when it has the biggest impact." Alexander offered his arm. "May I escort you to supper?"

She smiled. "Only if you promise not to sit next to me."

"There's my feisty redhead." Alexander nipped her cheek with yet another kiss before reaching for a mint.

Claudio ground his cigarette forcefully into the ashtray and stalked from the den, knowing his letter would have to wait for another time. He found himself at the table with Bethany to his left and Louisa to his right, Melissa on the far side of her daughter. They caught each other's gaze over Louisa's head and smiled. Across from them sat Asher, Lucy, Alexander, and Phoebe.

When not humoring the children, the priest watched Lucy as much as possible. She appeared subdued but not nearly as sad as Melissa. Alexander brought a spark to his wife's eye with every well-placed touch and kiss, but he knew it was a knife to lonely Melissa. While they waited for dessert, Alexander whispered in Lucy's ear—as well as tasted her neck. Claudio caught his eye and frowned, slightly angling his head toward the other guest.

Alexander immediately straightened, and Naomi entered with a pecan pie. "Would you cut it, Claudio?" he asked.

"Of course." He joined Naomi at the end of the table and set about slicing the pie without getting his fingers sticky. "Bethany, you shall be the server."

When she brought Melissa her plate, they hugged. The way Melissa stared into her eyes—as though she were looking for Frederick's face—caused Claudio's stomach to sour.

"I've missed you this week, Beth."

"I miss you too, Sissa."

"I do have a bit of news," Melissa addressed everyone. "I've accepted a weekly column with the newspaper to discuss home life while the husband is away called 'From the Heart of the Home.'"

"That's wonderful!" Lucy exclaimed.

She'd given up her magazine column when pregnant with Junior, and Claudio knew she missed working. "I am glad to hear it, Melissa."

"I haven't had a column of my own in two years."

As though wishing to change the topic, Alexander sprang from the table. "Dancing commences in five minutes. Please join me in the morning room when you're finished."

Phoebe giggled. "Poppy's such fun! I love it here."

Melissa looked to their hostess as she stood. "Thank you for having us, Lucy, but I better get home."

Claudio rose to his feet, a hand going to her shoulder. "I would like for you to stay."

She shook her head. "I'm not in a danc—"

The sounds of "The Turkey Trot" started down the hall, and Melissa paled. Alexander danced into the room, heading straight for her. His moves were practiced and precise. Lucy laughed, and the children clapped. He took Melissa around her waist and tugged her toward the hall without missing a beat.

"I had to beg Darla to teach me, which was no easy task, mind you. Henry had to stand in on all my lessons, but I didn't want you to grow rusty with Freddy not around."

"Alex, I haven't danced since before—"

"It's high time you got back to it, Melissa. Stop shuffling your feet and set yourself free!" Alexander increased his efforts and pulled her toward the phonograph.

Claudio followed, the children not far behind. By the time Melissa was in the center of the morning room, her face had lost its seriousness, and she made the efforts to remember the dance she had last enjoyed before her son died. The four children piled on the sofa, giggling. Lucy stopped beside Claudio in the doorway.

"He isn't one for dancing like that," Lucy whispered, "but he looks to be enjoying it. He wants to make sure Melissa doesn't hide away while Freddy's gone. I hope he behaves himself."

Claudio's hand went to her cheek. "Is that what worries you, Lucy?"

"I feel myself slipping from this world, and if Alex and Melissa were to fall into transgression, it would be the end for all of us."

With an arm about her, Claudio led Lucy into the den, sitting together on the blue chaise.

"Alexander loves you. He loves and cares for Melissa in a different way. His esteem for Frederick and his family—your family, as I know you claim them—is what has him seeking to please her." Claudio wrapped her in a brotherly hug. "Alexander is devoted to you. You will not lose him."

"He will lose *me* because my grasp in this world is slipping."

Cold settled in his chest, but he managed to raise his hand to do the sign of the cross over her, praying in Italian. She wept silently, and Claudio felt the veil draw thin between heaven and earth. There was truth in what Lucy said, but he did not understand. His prayer quickened as though he raced to save her. The chill slowly left his body, and warmth spread across her pale face.

"You feel it?"

She nodded.

"Hold to the light of the Holy Spirit, Lucy. Cling to joy when it is within your reach. Alexander only wishes to please you, to see happiness in your eyes. Give him all that you can when you are able."

"I belong to him, body and soul. I give him my everything."

Alexander waltzed in, bowing before her. "Melissa is changing the music, and I'd like to claim the next dance."

She raised her left hand, which he kissed before resting it on his shoulder. He captured her right one and placed his other hand on a voluptuous hip, which brought a wanting smile to Lucy's previously downturned mouth.

"For now, we dance for all to see, but tonight our bodies will sway to the music of our hearts." Alexander's lips went to the base of her neck.

Part of Claudio wanted to be angry with his friend for only seeking joy for his wife through sexual gratification, but then he realized that was how they communicated. To Alexander, intimacy— even when he had paid for it—was always emotional. The lightness of Tchaikovsky drifted through the air. Alexander deftly guided Lucy through the hall in a modified waltz before flourishing her in the middle of the morning room. Claudio offered his hand to Melissa, who stood by the phonograph.

"I was not expecting to dance tonight," he told her as he held her close, "but it is a pleasant surprise. It does brighten the mood."

"I can't believe Alex went to the trouble of learning to Turkey Trot. You both are wonderful to me."

"What time shall I come over?" he asked.

"If you'd like to take lunch with us, arrive at noon. Otherwise, around one, when Louisa is down for her nap."

"I should enjoy lunch with the Davenport ladies, thank you." Claudio adjusted his hand at her waist. "I would like to know you are eating properly. I will care for you, Melissa. You shall not be allowed to waste away."

Eight

For the first time since Freddy left, Melissa rose with a purpose other than caring for Louisa or the girls. She dressed in a functional green skirt and ecru blouse and then brushed through her hair—which had become a tangled mess that week without Freddy's attention. Even when withdrawn, he took a few minutes before bed to brush her hair, and she'd braid it for the night to save it from tangles. Clutching her unruly copper mass, she decided to do something about it after breakfast.

Determined to keep Freddy's tradition going, Melissa whipped up a small batch of pancake batter. Louisa stared, unmoving while holding a pot for a drum.

"What is it, Sweetie?"

"I don't feel like making noise, Mommy."

Melissa set down the mixing bowl and held her. "You don't have to, Louisa. The important thing is that we're together. That's what Pancake Time is about—family—not the noise."

She sniffled. "I miss Daddy and my sisters."

"So do I."

"I miss Junior too."

Melissa kissed her daughter. "Though the house is empty, our hearts can be full."

"Why do Phoebe and Beth get to have a brother and Poppy and each other while Daddy is gone? Why do we have to be alone? Did I do something bad?"

"No, Louisa Constance Davenport, you've been a wonderful helper and a good girl. Phoebe and Beth share your Daddy, but their mother is Miss Lucy. When Daddy is gone a long time, it's good for them to be with their mother. And since Lucy is married to Poppy, they have him as a stepfather. And Miss Lucy and Poppy had a baby together, so the girls have Asher as well."

"Why can't we live there too?"

"We can visit, but we need to take care of things here. Phoebe trusts you to care for her cat while she's with her mother, and Daddy expects us to keep the house ready for him to come home. I think we'll do a great job, how about you?"

"Yes, Mommy."

"Good. After we eat, we're going to town for a little while, and then Father Claudio is coming to have lunch with us."

Louisa smiled. "Is Father Claudio a daddy or poppy to anyone?"

"No, but he's like an uncle to all of you."

"Asher and my sisters call him Uncle Claudio. I want to call him something special too."

After they ate and cleaned the kitchen, Melissa drove downtown to a beauty shop for a modern style. Melissa felt freedom in the movement of her natural waves that looked more like curls without the weight of two feet of hair pulling them straight. It softened the angles on her now gaunt face, and she felt beautiful for the first time in months.

They stopped in Bienville Square to feed the squirrels, and Melissa accepted many kind words for her husband's bravery. Then they went to the bakery and delicatessen, where she selected Italian meats and cheeses for their luncheon with Claudio.

Once they unloaded the groceries, Melissa pulled the gramophone into the dining room and propped the kitchen door open to allow the strains of Paganini to fill the space. Melissa rolled her sleeves to her elbows and set about creating a platter displaying the bread, salami, pastrami, mozzarella, provolone, apple slices, and olives in a decorative pinwheel while Louisa settled at the breakfast porch with her art supplies.

Just as Melissa pulled a bottle of *Brunello di Montalcino* from the hidden wine closet in the wall of the downstairs bathroom, a knock sounded at the front door. Tucking the wine behind her back, she peered around the corner.

Claudio stood on the other side of the screen, a finger under his priest's collar.

"Welcome, Claudio."

His kisses left warm spots on each cheek as she returned the greeting. He touched her new style. "Your hair is most agreeable. *Molto bella*, though you were beautiful before."

"Thank you. I needed to do something to spruce myself up. Do you feel like indulging today?"

"What do you have in mind?"

She pulled the wine from behind her back and presented it to him.

His dark features took on a new light, and he reverently turned the bottle in his hands. "*Brunello di Montalcino*! The grapes are grown near my family's home. It has been so long! *Sí*, let us indulge. If we are caught, I shall beg forgiveness."

"I thought we'd eat in the kitchen as I'll need to grill the sandwiches."

Claudio pulled her to a stop outside the dining room, his masculine scent invigorating her senses. "Paganini played as only Valentino can. Do you wish me to miss my homeland? Ah!" He sniffed the air and went to the kitchen. Upon seeing the platter, he set the wine bottle beside it and tossed a stuffed olive into his mouth, grinning. "You spoil me, *Eroina*!"

He pulled her to him and left a kiss on her lips.

Reflexively, her hand touched the spot of contact. "What does *Eroina* mean?"

"A lady hero. You have rescued many people in your life. You may count me and my hunger for Italy among them."

Melissa relished the fact she could still bring joy to a man. "It's not much, but pile on what you want, and I'll grill the sandwiches."

"It is perfect."

Louisa came in the open door from the screened porch, carrying her drawing. "Father Claudio, look!"

So used to humoring other people's children, the priest immediately took a seat and brought Louisa onto his lap. She presented him with a drawing of black, red, and other colors. "It is you and me," she explained. "Will you be my father while Daddy's gone? It's already part of your name."

Claudio coughed and sputtered on the last olive he'd put in his mouth. Then he turned to Louisa, and Melissa warmed to him more.

"I am honored you asked me, Louisa, but while you may call me 'Father Claudio,' it does not make it so. I love you and your mother, but it would not be fair to your real father for you to pretend that of me."

"Then may I call you 'Uncle Claudio' as Asher and my sisters do?"

"*Sí*, I feel at home here as I do at Asher's house, especially with your mother having prepared this thoughtful meal." He kissed Louisa's cheek. "Have you ever eaten a hot Italian sandwich?"

When Louisa shook her head, he continued. "You must fill the bread in the right order for it to taste the best. Shall I teach you to stack your food appropriately?"

She hugged him. "Yes, please, Uncle Claudio."

He took plates from Melissa. "Allow me to prepare the best sandwich of your life while you grill Louisa's. I love working in the kitchen, but the rectory cook frowns upon the priests taking over."

His voice stirred base desires within Melissa so that she felt his touch of friendship as more—and she wasn't sure she should feel the relief it gave her. Melissa laughed off the feeling and went to the stove to prepare the pan with olive oil. Happiness filled her soul until the sight of Freddy's favorite glass in the cupboard sent her heart crashing. Quickly removing two stemmed wine goblets, she closed the door to the ache.

With Louisa's sandwich ready, Melissa sliced it into four equal pieces and handed Claudio the plate. He helped Louisa add fruit to her dish and poured her a glass of milk while Melissa spread olive oil on the outer sides of the bread for her and Claudio. By the time theirs were ready, Louisa's sandwich was cool enough for her to eat.

"Forgive me, but I must pray in Italian over this feast."

Rather than closing her eyes, Melissa studied how Claudio's eyelashes cast shadows on his chiseled face as his head bowed in prayer. The line of his Romanesque nose gave him a harsh edge, but his deep, lyrical voice softened his aura. The remembrance of his spontaneous kiss haunted her, and she blushed when he looked up.

"Did you over-heat by the stove, *Eroina?*"

"I think I did."

"Allow me to pour the refreshment." As Claudio opened the bottle of wine, the music in the other room ended. "Do you have more of Valentino's recordings?"

"Yes, several." Melissa stood to change the scores. Claudio rose from his seat across from her. "No formalities, Claudio."

With a new recording set, they ate with little conversation. When Melissa finished her second glass of wine, she remembered the last time she'd drank—in the backseat of the automobile with Freddy. Rather than crying in front of her guest, Melissa hurried upstairs with Louisa. Since she needed access to the child's room, Melissa tucked her into the master bed, marveling over how tiny her daughter looked in the bed big enough for two adults.

"Rest well, Sweetie."

"Will Uncle Claudio still be here when I get up?"

"I'm not sure how long it will take to put things away."

Back in the kitchen, Claudio filled their glasses once more. "Sacramental wine is not enough to fortify man. This has been most refreshing, from drink to food to music to companionship. Let us finish the bottle so you may gather bravery to face the memories."

"Bravery or numbness, I'll take either." She accepted her glass and led the way to the front room.

Claudio settled on the sofa, a respectable distance from her. "Your mood has darkened since we started eating. Have you been apprehensive?"

"Remembering." Melissa took a sip. "What about you? You've seemed a bit distracted since supper yesterday."

He raised his eyes to hers. "You noticed?"

"You're dear to me."

"To know you recognized my trouble cheers me." Claudio lifted her hand to his lips.

"But what is it?" She squeezed his hand as he held hers.

"It is Magdalene. Douglas joined the Navy, and she is anxious, as I well know you understand."

"Does Darla know? Alex?"

"She told me she wrote Darla, but she wanted me to tell Alexander. He was worried over Lucy last night, and I did not get a chance to tell him. I will try again tomorrow."

Melissa sighed. "Worried or happy, Alex acts the same."

"*Sí*, Alexander's approach is similar for all instances." Claudio jumped to his feet and copied Alex's gyrating moves.

Laughing, Melissa stood too quickly and grew light-headed. Claudio took hold of her and set her glass on the coffee table.

"Do not tell me I made you swoon." His brown eyes were mischievous, and he began to caress her bare forearm.

"And what if you did? Would moving like that cause you to rush to the confessional?"

He tucked a loose strand of her shortened hair behind her ear, never looking away. "I fear I shall have many reasons to go to the confessional by the time the afternoon is over."

Melissa felt the heat in his gaze. Though a priest, she knew he wasn't perfect, so she stepped away and drained the rest of her wine to save him from himself. "We should start on Junior's things, but first, I need to dispose of the evidence of our illegal activities."

She felt his eyes upon her as he followed her to the kitchen, where she rinsed the empty glasses. They were soon in Louisa's room. The stacks weren't as daunting with Claudio beside her. To keep were the layette pieces that Louisa and Junior had worn, plus a few special items, like the blankets, hats, and booties Mrs. Easton crocheted for him. Diapers, other clothing, and blankets that weren't as sentimental were gathered to be dispersed to those in need.

The crib that all four Davenport children had slept in needed to be disassembled to fit through the attic door. Claudio unbuttoned his cassock, his broad shoulders narrowing to where his shirt tucked into his black pants. Learning he was well-shaped beneath the sack-like coat startled Melissa, for she had never seen him without it. Sitting on the floor beside the crib with the tools she'd fetched from the carriage building, Claudio went to work without glancing at her. The memory of how he supported her when she grew faint at

Freddy's tournament years ago came to her. Claudio had stood strong and silent, a gentle hand at her elbow within the heat of the crowded room. And before that, he encouraged her to share her heart. Friendship and devotion were what he offered—then and now.

"You are like Magdalene, marveling over me when I removed my cassock before her so we could walk in the bay at Seacliff Cottage. She saw me as a man rather than a deacon for the first time and never looked at me the same again." He set the first bolts into a cookie tin, acting as a collector for the small parts of the crib. "I am older now, but tell me, *Eroina*, will you see me as a man rather than a priest?"

"I've always seen you as a man, Claudio. A handsome Italian who happens to work for a church." When he turned from his spot on the floor to look up, she sank into the chair a few feet away. "Do you forget I was unattached when we first met? That you reminded me of my stay in Tuscany."

"*Sí*, and I told you one day you would be a part of this family." He returned his focus to dismantling. "I hope you will continue to rely on me should you need help."

"I will, Claudio. Thank you."

He finished taking apart the side rails, and Melissa led the way to the attic door. When the crib and crates were stored, they carried the items to donate downstairs, where they would be collected by someone from the parish the next day. As soon as Claudio set his load in the foyer, he slipped his arms into his cassock.

"Forgive me, *Eroina*," he said as he buttoned his vestment, "if I have unwillingly placed you in an uncomfortable situation."

"You did nothing wrong." She stepped closer, wishing she could help him button it to show she wasn't afraid of their closeness. "We're good friends, and you've brought me much comfort. Louisa will be sad she missed saying goodbye, but come see her another day."

They stepped onto the porch.

"I would come to see her—and you." His smile was soft, inviting.

She planted lingering kisses on both cheeks. "Thank you, Claudio."

Nine

On the second week with the Davenport girls in the house, Naomi came as a surprise to cook the Monday morning meal. Lucy thought the relief of not preparing breakfast divine, asking Naomi to come each school morning the girls were there. The flurry of activity proved draining compared to the leisurely mornings Naomi was accustomed to.

Tuesday morning, Alexander looked to Naomi with his impish grin as she loaded a tray with dirty dishes from the dining room. He rounded the table, kissing her cheek. "You're getting a raise. Five more a week, or do the girls merit ten?"

"Ten!" Asher shouted. "My sisters are priceless!"

Alexander laughed, catching his son in a hug. "As is their mother, Phoenix Asher. Always treasure the ladies in your life." He kissed his blond head and let him loose. "Tell your sisters five minutes!"

Naomi smiled as she continued clearing the dining room table. "You aim to raise a charmer."

"That's all I know." He trailed a teasing hand over her shoulder as he went for the door. "And I mean it, Naomi. You're getting a raise. Check with Sharon, too. I doubt Melissa has her more than a day or two a week. If she wants more work and you need a hand, bring her in. She can fill in as needed if you get too busy taking outings with Paul."

"Hush now, Mr. Alex."

"Has he brought you dancing yet?"

"We've only had lunch last week and a moving picture show Saturday." She took the tray toward the door.

"Don't make it too difficult for the man." He followed her into the hall and went for Lucy, who waited near the staircase. Alexander's hands were about her red gown when Naomi pushed through the kitchen door with her load.

Bethany scampered in while Naomi washed dishes. "Goodbye, Miss Naomi. I'll see you tomorrow after school."

She wiped her hands on a towel and opened her arms to the girl. "You tell Miss Melissa I said you've been a good helper. And be sure you give her lots of love, your little sister too. I bet they're lonely over there without y'all."

"Phoebe spends all her time cuddling Doff, but I'll hug them."

Coming over to cook breakfast made Naomi miss seeing Paul arrive, but he'd made great progress on the furniture, and she hoped to spend some idle time that afternoon watching him work.

Once Asher settled for his nap, Lucy followed Naomi into Alexander's den. Lucy plopped onto the chaise with a sigh while Naomi started dusting the bookshelves.

Hoping to get Lucy's mind off what worried her, Naomi started talking. "Alexander told me he was going to give me a raise, but be sure to tell him I don't expect one."

"Nonsense," Lucy said as she straightened. "We talked about it last night while we—"

Naomi looked at her incredulously. "I don't want people engaged in such speaking about me."

"He's excited for you and hopes Paul romances you good because you deserve pampering." Her smile caused Naomi's face to heat. "And before things got too intense, he said you're working the hardest with the girls being here. We want you to know we appreciate you."

"I know y'all do, and it's a joy to be in a house with those sugars once again. But if you really respect me, please don't discuss my business while he's seducing you."

"You can be sure it was nothing of the sort. I was leading things."

She wanted to say *for shame, Lucy,* but gave a secret smile instead. "You're as incorrigible as he is."

Lucy hopped to her feet with renewed energy. "I have to fulfill everything I can while I'm here."

"I wish you wouldn't talk like that."

"Not saying it doesn't change the fact that I won't be here forever." Lucy opened one of the drawers and removed the package of mints to refill the bowl on Alexander's desk.

"You're young, and your mother is seventy. You've got decades to carry on with your husband. Are you ready to start work on a new novel?"

Lucy frowned, her pale face darkening as she fingered the empty ashtray on the desk. "I'm afraid my story well is dry. My time from now on will be spent penning letters to my favorite Army Captain and poems to my first and last love affair."

"Have you heard from Frederick?"

"No, but I'm sure he'll send anything he has time for to Melissa first. Freddy's been hurting, and now he's away from home. I want to make sure he knows he's still loved." She sighed as though the weight of the world were upon her shoulders. "I'm going to try resting. If you happen to hear Asher about before you leave, please send him to my room."

Lucy went for the hall as Asher ran in.

"Momma, I can't sleep."

Lucy scooped him into her arms. "Let's try napping on Poppy's chaise."

Naomi gathered two pillows out of the morning room and brought them to mother and son. Lucy settled the velvet throw across their legs. "I love you, Phoenix Asher Melling."

"I love you too, Momma." He touched her cheek with his little hand. "You're priceless."

Lucy's radiant smile warmed the whole room. "And you are your father's son."

***

Lucy and Asher both slept when Naomi finished dusting. She was about to pull the drapes across the French doors to the patio when Alexander stepped through the back gate.

Meeting him in the yard, she offered a smile. "Your loves are sleeping on the chaise." To answer the unspoken question in his raised brow, she continued. "Asher is snuggled to his mother, so don't get any ideas about climbing upon her."

"Indeed, I might have to join them. A nap before our early supper reservation sounds tempting. I'm sure my queen won't complain about being surrounded by her angels."

"Devils masquerading as angels. You've never wasted naptime with sleep, have you?"

"Probably not." He loosened his tie and grinned. "You're off for today?"

"I'll need to figure out what to do with myself."

"Don't worry about that. I let Paul know you weren't working this evening. I'm sure he'll have thought of something before you reach the garage."

Naomi yanked off her apron and snapped it at Alexander, who only laughed. "You keep your nose out of my business."

"Love *is* my business." He sauntered to his den and pulled the drapes shut behind him.

Naomi hung her apron in the kitchen. Noise from the hall pulled her curiosity. She nudged the door open an inch. Alexander had Lucy in an impassioned hold, and their lips were all over each other, inhibiting their vision as they stumbled toward the front hall.

"Alex, I can't wait." Lucy's hand went for his belt while the other tugged his head to her neckline. After a gasp of pleasure, she arched back. "Take me on the stairs!"

Naomi caught her breath and eased the door closed. *Mrs. Easton claims Alexander's spoiled Lucy, but she doesn't know how thoroughly Lucy has ruined him by indulging his appetites.*

When Naomi exited the yard, she met Paul coming toward the gate.

"Afternoon, Naomi."

"Where are you going?" The question came out sharper than she intended.

Paul lifted the cap off his head, knocking the pencil stub out from behind his ear. He bent to pick it up, brushing her hand as he straightened. "I wanted to double-check a few measurements in the room before building the sideboards for the shelving unit."

Hoping to soften her previous tone, she smiled. "How 'bout a coffee break instead? I'll go up and start the water."

His eyes brightened. "Are you inviting me over?"

"Yes, or we can take the coffee out here."

"But I can't go to the house to take measurements?"

"Not now." Naomi stepped toward the garage, looking over her shoulder at him. "Do you accept?"

"I'll be up in a minute." He grinned.

With the kettle on her little stove, she rethought her situation. *Maybe I shouldn't have stopped him. He has permission to come and go in the house while he's working, and he's bound to interrupt the Mellings at some point. But the thought of Paul finding them sprawled on the stairs ... I'd rather compromise my standing than subject him to the Mellings' lovemaking. Once you witness that, there's no going back.*

Both the little windows in her front room were open, and she propped the door ajar with her iron to allow a better cross-breeze. Naomi set the circular table with cups, saucers, and dessert plates. By the time she brought the cookies and coffee over, Paul knocked on the door.

"Come in," she said from her position by the table.

Naomi was pleased he appeared as nervous stepping into her home as she did in having him there. Paul took in the space with a slow, casual glance. Secondhand settee and rocking chair—compliments of Lucy—plus the bookcase, Eliza's artwork, and tiny dining table.

"It's right pleasant. You've done a fine job making the space into a cozy home."

"Thank you." She motioned to the table. "Ready to join me?"

"I'd like to wash up, please."

She motioned to the miniature kitchen, which made the room like a capital L. When he returned, he pulled her chair out, leaving a gentle touch on her shoulder before sitting.

As she poured the coffee, he cleared his throat. "What's going on in the house that has me needing to stay away?"

Naomi barely controlled the pot, righting it before it spilled on the lace tablecloth. She set it on the trivet and met his handsome face.

"The Mellings are an amorous couple and take advantage when the children are occupied. Asher was napping when Alexander returned. I don't think I need to say more."

"There's nothing wrong with a married couple enjoying their time. I could have come and gone without—"

"They don't always keep it in the bedroom," she blurted and then covered her mouth.

Paul laughed straight from the belly. "Should have known with a smooth talker like him."

Naomi looked at her folded hands in her lap.

"But that's nothing for you to worry over."

Still, she kept her eyes averted.

"Naomi." His hand reached across the little table and lifted her chin. "You're sweeter than honey. May I kiss you?"

She held her breath as she stared at his earnest face, slowly nodding.

Paul could have leaned across the table, but he stepped to her side, taking her hand to help her stand. Never had Naomi felt so small than when his broad shoulders towered over her. Her head reached his chest, barrel-shaped and massive. Hand still holding hers, he locked their fingers together as he lowered his mouth. Having waited so long to feel a man's lips on hers, Naomi expected it not to be as exciting as she imagined.

It was more!

His full lips were softer than anything she thought possible. She felt her insides melt and gather in a hot rush in her pelvis, creating the urge to press her body against Paul's. *That explains the gyrating motions so often displayed at the Mellings' house. I've been an ignorant fool all these years!*

Before Naomi could understand everything happening to her, Paul stepped back. His smile was all she wanted to see in life, but she took her seat as he returned to his. He lifted his cup to sip the steaming drink.

"If the next thing you tell me is that I make good coffee, I'll be disappointed."

Sputtering, Paul set down the cup.

Naomi heated under his scrutiny. "I'm sorry for being foolish."

"You're nothing of the sort. It just surprised me." He took her hand across the table, his dark brown skin enveloping her fawn complexion, complements of her mixed heritage. "Naomi, was that your first kiss?"

Nodding, she finally met his brown eyes.

"You told me you'd never had a beau, but I didn't realize.... Are you worried if you did well?"

"It's silly of me."

"You're fine, Naomi, but the bigger question is if I've let you down, having waited for this milestone."

"I wanted nothing more than for it to continue."

"If you'd like, we can try again later."

Naomi smiled at him. "I'd like that."

"I'm glad." Paul took another sip. "And you do make great coffee."

Ten

Melissa sat on her bed after breakfast on Wednesday, staring at the sampler of chocolate delivered to her two days before. She took a bite of a pecan turtle, savoring it as she reread the note in Freddy's precise handwriting.

Beloved,

It has only been a week, but I imagine it has been long and hard for both of us. I am sure I have dreamt of you each night and miss having your scent on the bunk I sleep in alone. If you have not received a letter from me by now, I apologize. I can only assume it is on its way. I look forward to any news from home. Nothing is trivial. Tell me everything you have time for. And please be sure to eat three meals a day, with chocolate indulgences in between.

Love and Devotion,

Freddy

She sniffed—proud tears didn't fall for the first time when rereading the words. Knowing Freddy had planned ahead by writing the note and arranging the delivery filled her with love. Phoebe and Bethany had stayed overnight, but Phoebe's constant chatter about

Alex and Lucy did little to cheer Melissa. Her first newspaper article was due Friday, and she still debated how personal she should make it. Yesterday, she thought mentioning the delivery of chocolates lovely, but today it felt like it would be gloating over the men without the means to secure that luxury or the women whose husbands weren't as romantic to dream up such a thing.

Louisa ran in as she placed the box on top of the dresser. "Mommy, is it time?"

Melissa checked the clock and nodded. "Would you like to wait on the porch?"

"Yes!" She bounced like Phoebe, her auburn locks springing about. "I'll get my ball!"

They were on the porch swing when Lucy arrived hand-in-hand with Asher, his navy sailor suit bold beside her neutral skirt and blouse. A straw hat covered her hair with a pink band and a few tasteful roses, but Asher's pale hair shone in the sunlight. When Louisa grabbed her ball and ran into the yard, he broke away from his mother.

Lucy smiled at the children kicking the ball and continued to the porch. "Melissa, your hair! Frederick will have an absolute fit when he sees it, but it is becoming on you. It brings out your natural curls. Now I know where Louisa gets hers."

Melissa settled beside Lucy on the swing and squeezed her hand, knowing she would understand her feelings. "I couldn't face it anymore. Freddy always brushed it at night, and I didn't have the heart to keep at it myself."

"He brushed mine as well. I found that one of his sweetest attributes. With Alex, I have to do most of the work. He'll start brushing but kiss my neck and roam from there." Lucy sighed. "I miss Frederick terribly, but I know it's nothing compared to you. Your pain must be unfathomable."

"I've grown used to pain these months, but I'm all Louisa has to rely on, so I plod along."

"A sense of purpose is good, something I often lack."

Melissa noted Lucy's downcast face and took her hand once more. "Lucy, your purpose is just as clear as mine, if not threefold as you have the girls and Asher. Not to mention Alex."

Green eyes brimming with tears stared back, misery on display. "The girls have you and Freddy. Asher has his father. Even Alexander would have no trouble replacing me."

"Whatever are you talking about?"

Lucy shook her head and turned to watch the children in the front yard. "Nothing."

They swung in silence for several minutes, Melissa smoothing her hair behind her ears and trying not to stare at Lucy. "Shall I prepare sandwiches now?"

"I'm not hungry."

Melissa bit back the words threatening to spill out. *What right do you have to come here needing to be coddled when it's my husband preparing for war? You should be comforting me!* "I know the feeling, but we must eat. Freddy had chocolates sent. Would you like one?"

Lucy straightened. "No, but thank you. What type of cake would you like Friday? We'll celebrate your birthday at supper."

"I don't expect anything."

"Nonsense, we must have a bit of fun if we can. Darla and her family will be there. Alex will insist on dancing. He enjoyed Turkey Trotting with you." Lucy sighed. "It's the Campbell's regular weekend to come, but I doubt they're making it this time. Have you heard about Douglas?"

"Claudio told me. I sent a letter to Maggie offering my support and for her to visit."

"It might be better if she doesn't come." Lucy rushed into the house.

"Louisa! Asher!" Melissa called as she stood. "Why don't you play inside?"

The children ran upstairs. Melissa found Lucy standing in the middle of the parlor, arms wrapped about herself as tears rolled down her face.

"Do you know how many hours I spent in this room with Frederick? Hundreds! Hundreds of chaste, companionable hours of devoted friendship. As children, we played, as teenagers, we danced, and as a ruined young woman, he kept me company, reading together and talking. But I didn't acknowledge his respectable courtship until I thought he was my last option."

Disgust masquerading as anger tightened Melissa's muscles to immobility and Lucy's lavender scent began to choke her.

"I welcomed him only when I thought Alexander dead. I allowed him to love me completely while my heart left only a corner for him. I let him treat me as his everything though Alexander was all I ever wanted. Tossing Frederick and our wedding vows aside the moment Alex returned was the easiest thing I've ever done." Lucy's face hardened. "I mistreated him all those years, but still, he was willing to love me. Me, the whore who disgraced her family by loving Alexander Melling! I'd do it again, every day, because I need Alex like I've needed no one else. But just as I've trampled Frederick's heart, my husband has the power to wound me."

Not wanting to hear more, Melissa reached for the trembling woman. "Lucy—"

"Don't touch me! I deserve my pain! Alexander would be more than happy with you or Magdalene. If your husbands don't return, he will take one or both of you. Concubines, lovers, or even a new wife. I'll be left to suffer as I did to dear Freddy. Opal should have killed me that day. It would have saved everyone a lot of trouble."

Lucy crumpled to the floor, and Melissa went for the telephone.

"Melling and Associates," the secretary answered.

"It's Melissa Davenport. I need to speak with Alex right away. It's about his wife."

"I'm sorry, Mrs. Davenport, but Mr. Melling is in court this morning. He—"

"Give him word to come to my house as soon as possible." She broke the connection and immediately asked the operator for her most used number without thinking.

"Davenport and Adams Allied Accountants."

Sharp pain in her chest rendered her speechless.

"May I help you?" Ms. Neves tried again.

She took a deep breath. "It's Melissa. Is Henry there?"

"Hello, Mrs. Davenport. I believe Mr. Adams is free. One moment."

Henry's jovial voice came over the line. "Good day, Melissa."

"Sorry to bother you, Henry. I asked for the number before—"

"It's quite all right. I'm happy to help."

"It's Lucy. She's unstable and collapsed in the parlor. I don't know what to do with her, and I'm not sure when Alex will come because he's in court."

"Shall I send Darla? I'll go home to give her the automobile and bring Horatio back to the office with me."

"Would you, Henry? I'd appreciate it."

"It's no problem. Darla has dealt with Lucy's breakdowns many times."

Fortunately, the children played upstairs without incident until Darla arrived a quarter of an hour later. Melissa met her at the front door.

"She's crying on the parlor floor."

Darla peered around the corner and sighed. "She hasn't been this bad off for years. What did she do?"

"It's more what she said and how dead her eyes looked." Melissa recounted Lucy's crazed claims about her feelings for Freddy and Alex's lust-filled life.

"That might be true with how she treated Frederick, but Alex is devoted to her."

"And she can be sure I'd never run to Alex as a lover."

Darla laughed bitterly. "I wouldn't put it past Maggie. Only if Douglas was gone from this earth, mind you. I've seen how she looks at him and might be jealous if I were in Lucy's shoes. The way Opal fawned over Henry at the boxing tournament was bad enough."

Melissa's hands went clammy as she remembered seeing Opal Easton five years before. The lack of empathy in Lucy's eyes today rivaled Opal's penetrating stare.

Darla placed a hand on her shoulder. "Go see to the children, and I'll deal with Lucy."

"Where's Momma?" Asher asked as Melissa led him and Louisa to the kitchen.

"She's in the parlor with Miss Darla. You'll see her after lunch."

Louisa's brown eyes looked up at her mother. "I thought we were all eating together."

"That was the plan, but Miss Lucy isn't feeling good right now."

"Momma's sad a lot. When Poppy's gone, she lies on the sofa or writes to Louisa's daddy."

Melissa's stomach tightened. Once the children were eating their sandwiches, Melissa stole to the parlor. Lucy still cried, but she lay on the sofa, Darla in an armchair beside her.

"Could you bring some cinnamon?" Darla whispered. "Unless you have lavender."

Melissa managed a smile. "Freddy wouldn't stand for it."

Darla checked the laugh that looked ready to spill out. When Melissa returned with a teabag full of cinnamon, Darla held it under Lucy's nose.

"Deep breaths, Lucy. It's time to calm down."

The sound of an automobile careened to a stop out front. Melissa rushed for the door, meeting Alex at the foot of the steps.

"The secretary sent a clerk to wait for me." His blue eyes were frenzied, and he gripped Melissa's arms with strength she didn't realize he possessed. "What's going on? Where are Lucy and Asher?"

"Asher's having lunch with Louisa and Darla's in the parlor attempting to calm Lucy."

"Bless you for knowing who to call." He hugged her, a hand going to her shoulder and his mouth toward her ear. "Your haircut is attractive. I bet while you're going at it, the length would allow it to bounce as well as a pair of—"

"That's in no way why I cut it, and you best not speak like that to me in front of your wife!" Melissa pulled back. "That's exactly the type of thing she went to pieces over."

Like a boy scolded, the light left his eyes, and he stepped away. "What did she say?"

"She confessed about her cruel treatment of Freddy in her younger years. Then she raved about all the pain she caused him would be heaped upon her because you'd take me and Maggie as lovers if our husbands fail to return."

"But I'd nev—"

"She's hanging by a thread."

He took Melissa's elbow and marched up the porch steps. "I'll see to Asher first."

"Poppy!" Louisa dashed from her seat when they entered the kitchen.

Alex scooped her to his arms, kissing her cheek. "How's my girl?"

"Asher and I played ball and with Doff. I take good care of Doff for Phoebe."

His genuine smile helped Melissa forgive his earlier infractions. "I'm sure you do, Louisa." Turning to his son, he ruffled his pale hair. "Are you having a good day?"

"Yes, Poppy. I like coming to visit the Davenports."

"They're a marvelous family."

"Why can't Sissa and Louisa live with us like Phoebe and Bethany?"

Alex met Melissa's gaze before turning to Asher. "They'd be welcome, but I think Doff needs them here. Besides, Freddy will be back in a few weeks."

"Will we have a supper party when he returns so Momma can see him?"

"Of course, and it will be the biggest party we've ever had."

Eleven

A little after twelve, Naomi sat at the bottom of the stairs to her apartment, waiting for Paul to finish sanding the top of the desk. Seeing Alexander's automobile pull to a stop near the veranda set her insides squirming.

"Naomi!"

She ran down the driveway, stopping short when she saw Darla supporting Lucy in the backseat.

"She had one of her episodes," Alexander said. "I need to get her in bed, but could you fix—"

"Tea, right away." She dashed for the front door and unlocked it with the key from her pocket. She paused to watch Alexander carry a paler than usual Lucy to the house.

Only when she caught her breath in the kitchen as the water heated did she remember her date with Paul. Going out the back, she waited to speak while he wiped down the freshly sanded desktop with a damp rag.

"I can hear you, Honey." Paul glanced at her but kept cleaning. "Is there some kind of trouble with the Mellings?"

"It's Lucy. She has these spells every so often. I'm afraid I'll need to stay nearby."

"Could I bring food here?"

"That'd be nice. Hopefully, things will settle down soon."

He walked with her to the gate, where he rinsed his hands at the spigot. When he leaned in for a kiss, Naomi couldn't help but brighten.

"I'll be back soon." Paul squeezed her hand.

"Wait for me in the kitchen if I'm not there."

She fixed a tray for two, complete with cookies and a few finger sandwiches, and carried it upstairs. Lucy wore her silk slip, covered to her waist with the bedspread. She appeared to be sleeping, but Lucy was an excellent pretender. Darla offered Naomi a smile on her way out, and Alexander took the tray, setting it on the side table.

"Thanks, Naomi. I hope we didn't interrupt your plans."

She looked away from his blue eyes. "Nothing that can't be changed. Paul's gone to get some food for us."

He grinned. "I'll stay with Lucy while you eat, but it's my day to take the girls riding. Melissa said she'd keep Asher until afterward. So if you could watch Lucy until I return with the children, I'd appreciate it."

"And what about supper preparations?"

"Just open cans of soup after I return, but you'll have over an hour for your dinner break. That should be plenty of time to eat and partake of other things." He winked.

"I told you to keep your nose out of my business."

"Alexander Randolph Melling," Lucy's said with her eyes still closed, "you've struck a nerve with Naomi."

With the lightness of a cat, he sprung upon the bed. He straddled her hips and leaned over to get at her throat. Trailing kisses to her mouth, Lucy arched seductively beneath him.

"Please wait until I leave the room and Lucy has something to eat."

Lucy giggled and tugged Alexander's necktie. "Then you better feed me, Alexander, because I'm ravenous for you."

"Your wish is my command, my queen." He jumped off the bed as nimbly as he'd alighted and went for the tray.

Voices came from the kitchen as Naomi approached the door. Prepared to defend her turf, she pushed through the swinging door. Darla and Paul halted their conversation and turned to her.

"Naomi, make sure you let Alex know if Lucy says anything odd when you're with her," Darla said. "She went off at Melissa today. It shook her up, and you know how stalwart she is."

"Lucy's already a minx with Alexander."

Darla rolled her eyes. "Then I got out of there just in time. Call me if you need anything. Otherwise, I'll see you Friday evening." She hugged Naomi and turned to Paul, offering her hand. "It was lovely to meet you, Mr. Rollins."

Darla left, and Paul motioned to the sack of food on the table. "Shall we?"

Not wanting to be under the same roof as the Mellings, she suggested eating on the patio. She poured two glasses of sweet tea from the icebox and led Paul out the door.

When they were halfway done with the shrimp po' boys, the door opened on the screened porch above them. Lucy's laughter carried through the air, followed by the squeal of chains supporting one of the bed swings. It was too early in the year for Naomi to have seen to the sleeping porch, and each motion of the couple sent the unoiled metal squeaking, but it didn't drown the sounds Lucy made.

Naomi gathered dishes and jerked her head toward the kitchen so Paul would follow her. As soon as their things were on the table and the door closed, they looked at each other and laughed off their embarrassment.

Paul grinned, a twinkle in his eye. "You were right about them not keeping things in the bedroom."

"You may be sure I'll oil all the chains as soon as possible."

***

The following Wednesday, everything ran smoothly at the Mellings' house. Asher had a pallet on the floor of the girls' bedroom because his room—now painted hunter green—was under construction with the installation of his shelving. Lucy left with him for their visit to Melissa's, so Naomi perched on the corner of Asher's new desk and watched Paul's backside while he moved the pieces around. Two workers were expected to help attach the shelves to the wall, but for now, she enjoyed their privacy.

Turning abruptly, Paul caught her studying him and grinned. "Like what you see?"

She tried to downplay her racing heart. "You're wonderfully formed."

He laughed. "For an old man."

Her countenance grew serious. "For any aged man."

Paul crossed the room, knees brushing hers from his closeness. She stood and set her hands on his shoulders, exploring his lines as she trailed her touch over his broad chest. He closed his eyes, the hint of a pleased smile on his face. Marveling that she could bring him such enjoyment, she grew heady. Her arms went under his, hands migrating across his back as she stretched on her toes to reach his lips.

Feeling secure in her power as a woman, their embrace heated as the intensity of the kiss grew. Paul's tongue tasted her mouth as his hands caressed her hips. A soft moan escaped, and her body tingled beneath the attentions. Naomi hoped she did right with returning the deep kisses. When Paul firmly grasped her backside and lifted her against his pelvis, she was assured of the potency of her technique. Having learned a thing or two in her time with the Mellings, Naomi wrapped her legs about his waist. Her A-line skirt afforded the move, and she switched her concentration to the rhythm of Paul's movements. A primitive thrumming resonated between them. The need to give more of herself to him fueled her desire.

Paul braced himself on the desktop, leaning back enough to balance Naomi on his lap while he opened the buttons at her neck. His lips on her throat caused a current of electricity to travel her body, and her legs clung tighter around his waist in anticipation. She arched back, which pressed their sensitive areas together.

"Naomi, you're sweeter than honey."

Feeling like a beautiful flower under his stroking movements, she warmed as though lying in the sun. The drumming in her core continued to build. Her breath came in gasps. His warm mouth continued to tease along her throat and lips. She vaguely realized the grinding motion her hips were making against Paul increased, but she couldn't still her body. It was part of the cadence of the moment.

Then his big hands were gripping her waist, massaging upward across her rib cage as they glided over her blouse. Urgency swelled until it funneled between her thighs. Bewilderment stung her over-taxed senses with the throbbing there.

A panting cry rang out.

So often she'd heard that sound through a closed door, it took her a moment to realize it came from her. Naomi sobered immediately.

The doorbell chimed far away in the vast house. She looked at Paul in bewilderment.

"Honey, you're fired up, but I think you got what you need for now." He kissed her on the mouth. "I don't want to let you go, but that'd be my boys here to help."

As soon as she stood, the strangeness of her body's sensations doubled. Wanting nothing more than to cling to him and relive the deliciousness of the contact, she began to get an inkling of what she'd done.

She ran for the stairs and locked herself in the downstairs bathroom. Splashing water on her face, Naomi calmed her breathing.

We're both adults and enjoyed a few weeks of courtship. Naturally, physical attentions were bound to increase. He's been nothing but respectful. It was me that started touching and—now I know why Lucy wants to climb upon Alexander with the slightest provocation! She bit the towel to keep from crying out. *I behaved like a bedeviled Melling, complete with a rendezvous in someone else's bedroom! Did I defile little Asher's new desk? Alexander might be proud, but Lucy....*

Naomi wanted to keep the secret, but there were so many questions—things she couldn't ask Sharon or any other member of her family without complete embarrassment. Yes, Lucy would be the one to hear of her actions.

Not wanting to show her upset, Naomi waited an hour to bring a tray of iced tea to Asher's room. The framing of the bookcase was in place, as well as the top shelves. The young workers whipped off their hats.

"Don't fuss over me, gentlemen. I thought you might be thirsty, but if not, I can leave the tray in the hallway to keep the dust out of it."

"We'll take it now, Naomi. Thank you." Paul relieved her of the tray and nodded introductions. "This here's Bert, my Mattie's husband."

"You're even prettier than Paul hinted at, Miss Naomi." Bert shook her hand and grinned. "Mattie will be sore I met ya first."

"And this rascal," Paul elbowed the man in a yellow shirt as he spoke, "is my cousin's lad, Grover."

"You're much too young for this old man, Miss Naomi. How about I take you out Friday night and show ya a good time?"

She laughed and shook his hand. "I'm older than I look and quite happy at the moment, thank you."

Paul caught her eye and grinned as though he knew all too well how satisfied she was.

A few minutes later, Naomi returned to the kitchen with the empty glasses as Lucy and Asher came in the back door.

"Welcome home," Naomi said. "It's a bit noisy up there today with the installation. Asher should try to nap down here."

"I wanna see my room!"

Lucy rested a hand on his head. "Take a good nap, and then we'll go up. Do you want to sleep in Poppy's den or the morning room?"

"On the big sofa, Momma."

"Take off your shoes and wash up in the bathroom down here." Lucy kissed his forehead and watched him scamper off. Then she sighed like the weight of the world crushed her.

Naomi finished with the glasses and dried her hands on her apron. "Did the visit go all right?"

Lucy nodded. "It's difficult to talk to Melissa after reading her stirring words in the newspaper each week. All her gushing about Freddy will have the whole female population of the city swooning over him once more."

"Did they ever stop?" Naomi teased.

"Probably not, but the stories no longer reached me after he married Melissa. Have you ever noticed how Louisa has Freddy's eyes? From her dark brows to the warm brown color, she's just as much Freddy as Bethany."

"Bethany has the Easton chin, and there's just enough of Melissa in Louisa for those two to look related but be different, like Phoebe and Asher."

"Asher's his father all over again. The angel will strike down the hearts of all the girls like a militant Cupid."

Naomi's laughter brought a smile to Lucy's face, and she took courage from the momentary spark in her eyes. "If you have time after Asher's down, could I speak with you?"

Lucy patted her arm. "Of course. Make coffee if you'd like. I wouldn't mind a few cookies if you have them. I'll be in the den."

Twenty minutes later, Naomi set the coffee tray on Alexander's desk and took the armchair across from Lucy, who tucked away a piece of paper she'd been writing on.

Lucy chewed a bite of shortbread before speaking. "What did you want to talk about?"

She felt like a child going to the headmaster with the massive desk between them. Stirring her coffee nervously, Naomi glanced up at her friend. "I was hoping you could help me understand a few things. Paul and I—"

"How are things going?" Lucy took another bite.

"Wonderful. He's been respectful and kind. I never thought the attentions of a man could be so fulfilling."

Lucy angled closer, dropping her voice. "Is he a good kisser?"

"I think so, but I've nothing to compare him with." Naomi sipped from her cup.

"I've only Alex and Freddy. They're both delightful, though different. Alex has many techniques, depending on the mood and situation. Having him is like a bouquet of lovers."

"While I've seen and heard quite a bit in my time with you, there are a few things I'm not certain about. I hoped you'd be able to—"

Lucy's eyebrows scrunched together. "Paul's not pressuring you into anything, is he?"

"Not at all."

Dalby

"Good. He's a nice man, but he knows what he's missing and might want to move your relationship along quicker than best."

"What's best, Lucy? You were with Alex all of a month before you were engaged, and then you gave yourself to him."

"That's not the norm, nor was it a wise thing to do with all the havoc it caused. It's my cross to bear, now and forever, but I wouldn't trade it for anything." Her cup rattled against the mahogany desk before settling. "Once you feel the rush of a pinnacle with the man you love, there's no going back."

"But what if…what if you have that experience without the full contact? Is that possible?"

Lucy's laughter was as mystical as the wind chimes from the Orient Edmund gifted the family last month. "It is." Her eyes widened. "Did you—"

"Yes." She looked toward the partially opened door before turning back. "Promise not to tell a soul, especially your husband."

"I promise!" Lucy pulled her desk chair around Naomi and sat beside her, holding her hands. "What happened?"

Naomi described her touching turning to full kissing, how her body moved of its own accord, pleasuring in the contact on areas previously neglected. "I was embarrassed, but Paul took it all in stride. Then the helpers were here, and we haven't been able to talk."

"He probably down-played it because he knew you were unsure. I bet when you're alone, he'll take you in his arms and talk it over with you real lovingly. He seems that kind of man. There's plenty of time for you, Naomi. Enjoy the courtship."

Twelve

Each Monday, Melissa's column was printed in the paper, and a box of chocolates with a note from Freddy was delivered—besides one or two letters that arrived by post on different days of the week. On her birthday, another box of chocolates, an enormous amount of fresh gladiolas, and a striking gold and emerald pendant necklace were delivered. She wore the necklace to the supper party the next evening and felt Freddy's absence weighing on her heart as she danced with Alex, Henry, and Claudio.

Her new pattern of life was simple. She and Louisa visited Lucy and Asher on Wednesdays, supper parties with the Mellings on Fridays, and church service at Trinity the Sundays when Phoebe and Bethany were home. Once or twice a week, Melissa would stop by the Spunners' house while out on a walk because she knew Hattie would come looking for her if she didn't. Louisa would play with Brandon while the ladies talked on the veranda—Hattie nurturing her newest arrival, which pained Melissa to see. Claudio came by sporadically, sometimes after supper when Louisa slumbered. Those visits included a glass or two of alcohol, cigarettes, and lengthy conversations.

On the evening of May thirtieth, a quiet knock on the front door roused Melissa from the book she read in the parlor. The press of Claudio's lips on her cheeks was the balm she needed after the last twenty-four hours. She kissed him in return with an accompanying hug.

"I believe you know how much I need you on Wednesdays."

"I want nothing more than to ease your burdens, *Eroina*." The light in his eyes burned startlingly pure. "Do not think I come only because I am thirsty for your amazing collection of illegal beverages."

Laughing, she kissed his cheek again. "I'd never assume that. I had hoped you'd come tonight and stopped at the delicatessen for cheese after I left the Mellings'. How about we indulge with a bottle of wine?"

"If that is your wish, I gladly accept. Allow me to help you."

The nearness of Claudio's cologne-scented body in the kitchen tugged at her loneliness. She'd spent too many hours in that room with Freddy to be unmoved by the presence of another attractive man.

"If you could finish this, I'll get the wine."

She left without waiting for his reply and collected a bottle of *Brunello di Montalcino* like they shared in April. Claudio leaned against the counter, arms crossed when she returned.

"What is wrong today, *Eroina?*"

Her gazed traveled the length of him, settling on his lips and eyes—the only soft things amid his features. She could not speak of her pathetic need to feel a man's arms about her or the hunger for a hug and kiss to feel fortified in a life of barrenness, so she complained.

"Lucy is worse than ever. She trudges around as though she's the only one experiencing heartache." Allowing the anger to conquer her pain, she raved on. "She has the nerve to expect me to cater to her because she feels inferior to me. Between her brooding and Alex's lavish attentions, the girls are utterly spoiled. Yesterday all Phoebe could talk about was how Alex sings to them every night. She didn't think she'd be able to sleep without *Dear Poppy* crooning, but

Doff's purring would have to do on the lonely nights she's forced to come here."

A hint of a smile teased at the corner of Claudio's mouth. "But Bethany is not like that."

"Of course not. She's Freddy's girl, through and through. Phoebe's too much like her mother and amplified in the worst possible ways. I love them both, but some days, biting my tongue and holding back the tears is the best I can do."

His arms went about her, tucking her to his chest as Freddy used to do. "I shall remind the girls on Friday what is expected while their father is gone. Hopefully, the weekend with them will not be too painful."

"Thank you, Claudio."

They settled in the parlor with the wine and cheese. Claudio went to the corner behind Melissa to put on one of Valentino's recordings, the volume soft since Louisa slumbered upstairs. When he came back, his cassock and collar were gone, and the top buttons on his shirt opened.

"I am here as a friend to ease your burdens." Claudio settled beside her. "I know you need physical comfort, *Eroina*. Allow me to hold you."

She drained the remainder of her wine and collapsed against his shoulder. His arms went about her, his head gently resting on hers as he whispered in Italian. Warmth spread across her skin, but one nagging thought kept her from complete relaxation.

How did I grow from an independent woman to a weak damsel who requires a man's touch to be fulfilled?

As the fervor of the Vivaldi score reached a crescendo, she made the mistake of looking at Claudio.

A finger trailed her cheek, and his eyes were intense. "You are not alone, *Eroina*."

Stimulated by the tender moment, Melissa leaned toward his face. Her eyes closed for the kiss, but she didn't deceive herself that

Freddy held her. Instead, her mind transported her to the Tuscan vineyard of her past. The flavor of the kiss, the looks of the man, and the music were all the same. As the kissing continued, Melissa slid a hand around his neck, relishing the heat within his open collar. The other hand played through his hair before traveling to his back. Claudio's effort increased, lips going to her jaw as he grasped her waist. Her body responded as it had always done under similar circumstances, welcoming more as she pressed closer.

Minutes later, Melissa pulled away. Smiling, she met his gaze. "Thank you."

His deep lines and dimples brought giddiness to her soul, and his laughter sent her soaring. She took the wine bottle rather than her glass off the table and swigged before cozying beside Claudio once more.

"For you, *Eroina*, I would do anything."

Melissa's core heated with the knowledge she had the devotion of that striking man.

***

On Sunday, June seventeenth, Melissa stood on the train platform in the midday heat, one hand firmly gripping Louisa and the other holding her green parasol above them for shade. Bethany and Phoebe stood beside her, clutching a shared umbrella of their own.

A hand touched her raised one, followed by a peck on her cheek. "Allow me."

"Poppy!" All three girls clamored for him, but Louisa jumped at Alex first.

He heaved her up, setting Louisa on his shoulders so she'd be able to see over the crowd when the train arrived.

"Is Lucy here?" Melissa whispered so the older girls wouldn't hear.

"She's been in bed since yesterday. I put Asher down for a nap after Mass before coming."

"I'm glad you're here," she remarked.

"I didn't fancy you standing alone, especially if the train is late."

She squeezed his arm. The sounds of the approaching train—a wistful noise from her previous lifestyle—roused Melissa. Rachel Brady pushed past the other wives, wanting to be the first to see her husband.

Alex poked Melissa's side. "Go on, and I'll keep the girls. You need to get yourself a good kiss before they're climbing on Freddy. You've waited nearly two months for a little action."

Melissa's face heated, but the temperature could be blamed rather than her indulgences—kissing and being held several times in the past few weeks by a priest.

Chuck Brady jumped off the train, embracing his wife. Melissa felt like a fish swimming upstream with the flow of exiting soldiers filing past her. Then Freddy stepped out—his haversack on his back and a drawstring sack over one shoulder. His eyes went to the rear of the crowd where the emerald parasol shaded Louisa, who waved his handkerchief from Alex's shoulders. He smiled and focused his eyes to the front of the throng.

Mere seconds separated the time he spotted Melissa to when he lifted her in his arms. She ran her hands over his uniform, falling deeper into his embrace.

"Beloved, why are you crying? I'm not upset. You look gorgeous." He raised her shortened locks to his nose. "I'll miss the length, but you smell the same. I've missed you."

Her arms went over the top of his pack to reach around his neck. "I've missed you too, Handsome."

"Daddy!" Bethany's voice cried louder than Phoebe's.

Melissa stepped to the side and watched as he greeted his oldest daughters with hugs and kisses. Then, he straightened and turned to Alex.

"It was quite the disappointment to spy the parasol and find you beneath it rather than Melissa." Freddy lifted Louisa from Alex's shoulders, and she wrapped her limbs about his girth as best she could. "I love you, Louisa. Will you bring me home?"

"Yes, Daddy. Miss Sharon is cooking my birthday supper today."

"Your second one?"

"The first for our house. I had a supper party at Poppy's, but Mommy gave me the tricycle already. At Poppy's, we had strawberry cake, and I got a pretty dress and book from Poppy and Miss Lucy. Asher gave me a toad."

Freddy's laughter caused a lump in Melissa's throat. *I've missed his smile, that laugh. I'll cherish every moment he's home.*

As though feeling her watching him, he turned fully to her, shifting Louisa to his side so he could kiss Melissa before turning back to Alex. Freddy clasped his arm. "Thanks for watching out for my girls."

"It's been a pleasure."

Freddy's eyes narrowed in teasing suspicion. "Just don't let me catch you under Melissa's parasol again."

Alex's bawdy laugh turned heads in the crowded station. "If only! I'll see you later, Davenports. Wednesday afternoon for the girls, and Friday evening at the latest for everyone else. We'll be celebrating Lucy's birthday." He kissed each girl and then left a lingering one on Melissa's cheek just to goad Freddy.

Melissa drove home, and Freddy sat in the back with his daughters, hearing about Bethany riding the trails, Phoebe's new scarf, and Louisa's playdates with Asher. His conversations with the girls continued into the afternoon, with them piled around him on the sofa. Melissa watched from an armchair, planning how best to share their private time.

After supper and chocolate cake, Freddy dug into his large bag and removed three stuffed animals. He gave Phoebe a bear, Bethany a tiger, and Louisa, a rabbit.

"Now I have a bunny like Rummy!"

Phoebe huffed, but Freddy kissed her cheek. "Could you start the bath for your sisters?"

"Yes, Daddy." Phoebe tucked the brown bear under her arm and stalked upstairs.

"Now, you two run along and ready for bed."

"I'm glad you're home," Bethany said. "Thank you for the tiger."

He kissed her and Louisa. When they were gone, he opened his sack further.

"Now for your presents, Beloved. I stocked up while in states still selling." He began unrolling uniform pieces, exposing wine, brandy, and various other bottles. "If you see to the girls, I'll put these away."

Melissa hugged him. "Don't take too long. I have something for you in our room."

His hands roamed her backside as he gave her a stirring kiss. "Nothing like motivation to get a man to work faster."

Melissa readied a bath for her husband. While it filled, she changed into a sleeveless nightgown and put on the emerald necklace Freddy sent her for her birthday the previous month. Over that, she tied on her bathrobe so what lay beneath would be a surprise. She brushed through her hair and shut the water off before going to the hallway.

The girls, eager to be with their father, were already in their nightgowns and brushing their teeth. Freddy dropped his bag in the bedroom.

"There's a hot bath ready for you," she whispered.

"Bless you." He kissed her cheek.

When the girls completed their brushing, the family gathered in Phoebe and Bethany's room for prayers, a purring Doff rubbing against Freddy's legs.

"But we haven't heard about your training yet," Phoebe said as her father kissed her.

"I'll tell you everything you want to know tomorrow." He went to Bethany snuggling with her tiger. "I'll see you in the morning, Little Princess."

Freddy took Louisa's hand and walked her across the hall. His eyes lingered in the corner where the crib once stood, now housing a rocking chair from the guest room.

"I'll see you tomorrow, Louisa." Freddy kissed her and went for his bath.

"Thank you for all your help these weeks, Sweetie." Melissa hugged her. "We'll enjoy Daddy while he's here."

"He looks happy. I think he missed us."

"I know he did. I love you. Sleep well."

Melissa closed the master bedroom and turned down the bed. She tucked Freddy's haversack against the far wall and knocked on the bathroom door.

"Do you need anything?" she called.

"You."

Freddy lounged in the deep water of the clawfoot tub. His eyes went to her as she removed her robe.

"The necklace looks beautiful on you."

"You spoiled me across the miles."

"You deserve it." He leaned back. "I couldn't help but notice how many bottles were gone when I put things away. I hope you haven't been drowning your sorrows."

She met his drowsy gaze. "It wasn't all me."

"Don't tell me Alex is back to drinking. Or have Henry and Darla been over much?"

She fingered the pendant. "I've shared with Claudio."

Freddy pulled the bath plug, staring at her as the water *whooshed* down the drain.

"He's been a good friend to me these weeks. He helped me sort through Junior's things."

"I noticed it was all gone."

"Gone from sight but not forgotten." Melissa handed Freddy a towel as he stood. "Claudio comforts me after the difficult days."

Freddy wrapped the towel about his waist and stepped out of the tub. "I suppose it's better for you to be drinking with a priest than with a cad like Alex."

Melissa nodded, lost in her thoughts as she looked upon Freddy's bare chest and remembered Claudio's last visit. She'd longed to touch more of him, but he continued to keep things simple. *"Frederick will be home soon," he'd said. "You can wait a few more days."*

Freddy's hand went to her shoulder. "I know you're strong, but I hope it hasn't been too difficult."

She embraced her husband, his hot, damp skin clinging to her gown. "I've missed you, but I'll do better this time, for all our sakes."

"You're wonderful." He carried her to their bed and knelt over her. Gently, he felt her body beneath the thin covering, hungry eyes studying the curves he explored. "You feel and look healthier than when I left. I'm glad about that. I don't want you wasting away."

"And you're stronger than ever." Melissa's hands roamed his body. "I've missed the feel and sight of you. The sound of your voice and laugh."

"Every night, I've dreamt of you. I wanted nothing more than to feel your skin and taste your kisses." He flipped their positions so she was on top, her necklace hanging near his chest. Leaning forward, he kissed it. "That's just a small token of my love for you. Now I wish to express it physically."

"I'm yours, Freddy."

Thirteen

Friday afternoon, Lucy rushed into the kitchen, where Naomi mixed a bowl of remoulade sauce. "I need fresh flowers for the dining table! Why didn't I think of fresh flowers?"

"Telephone Alex and ask him to pick some up on his way home."

"He's taking Phoebe riding and better return in time to shower before supper, but I need flowers! Do you think I could get someone to deliver for me?"

Naomi kept stirring. "I've never known you to be particular about a table setting."

"Mother always fussed over it. I never understood until today. Maybe I'm growing up."

"Wouldn't that be something?"

Lucy huffed and stomped out while Naomi continued with supper preparations, trying not to worry about Lucy's manic episode. It was too late to retract the invitation to Paul to come over for supper. Lucy had voiced the idea earlier in the week so Naomi could enjoy his company while the Mellings celebrated. As Lucy had been melancholy lately, Naomi extended the invitation to please her, though she didn't like the idea of entertaining while she waited on the family.

Fifteen minutes later, Lucy returned. "The telephone operator helped me find a florist that could deliver next hour. I'll get a check ready in case you need to accept the delivery."

A short while later, the telephone rang. On the fourth bell, Naomi reached for it. "Mellings' residence."

"Naomi, I hope my sister and her scandalous husband aren't driving you crazy."

She laughed. "How are you, Mr. Edmund?"

"Very well. Would you pass on a message to Lucy for me?"

"Of course."

"Inform her Mary Margaret respectfully declined the invitation."

"She expected as much," Naomi said.

"But tell her I'm bringing Mother and Oscar. Maxwell and Lottie are coming, but they're going to leave after supper and bring home my two charges for me. I plan to stay late and live it up as long as they'll have me."

"It'll be right nice to see more of the family. I'm sure Lucy will be pleased."

Lucy shrieked when Naomi delivered the message. "Mother and Lottie! The table better be laid perfectly!"

"I'm capable of setting a proper table, Lucy."

"It's just all too much. And Oscar! At least he will keep Phoebe happy. Should I do place cards?"

"You're liable to frighten everyone if you get too formal. Just arrange the flowers and wear your prettiest dress. It's your party, after all."

"But it's a homecoming for Freddy. This might be his only time at our house before he leaves again."

At five-thirty, Asher ran through the kitchen in his navy suit, minus a tie. He dove under the table in the corner, peeking out at Naomi with a finger to his smiling face. The imp couldn't look more like his father if he tried. The next moment, Alexander came in the backdoor, fresh from the stables—looking and smelling the part.

"Phoenix Asher Melling!" Lucy's voice carried down the hall.

The boy bumped a chair leg, and his father saw his hiding spot.

"What has your mother calling out for you like that, Ash?"

He pointed to his unadorned neck, and Alexander nodded knowingly.

Lucy burst in. "Phoenix Asher, you better not be hiding behind Miss Naomi!"

Alexander caught Lucy around her the waist of her red dress that looked more like an undergarment than a proper gown—the newest French fashion, Mademoiselle Bisset promised. "What has you upset, my queen?"

"Unhand me!" She slapped at his arms. "You're covered with dust!"

"Only if you tell me what's wrong."

"Asher won't put on his tie, but who can blame him with a scoundrel like you as a father?"

Alexander made a stabbing motion to his heart and fell to the tiles as though dead, causing Asher to giggle.

"I knew you were in here!" Lucy lunged for the table, but her husband caught her ankle and pulled her on top of him.

"Alexander Randolph Melling, if you ruin my dress, I'll never forgive you!" Her fists went at him.

He caught them and bucked his hips, so she shifted toward his middle as her dress crept up her thighs. Alexander released her hands and went at her hairpins, pulling apart the chignon. "Your hair's not down."

Lucy gave a wordless scream and collapsed on his chest.

He looked at Naomi. "What did I do?"

"In case you forgot," she said, "there's a supper party tonight for our lady with a birthday Sunday. The guests happen to include Mrs. James Easton and Mrs. Maxwell Easton. I believe Lucy is going for respectability tonight rather than the typical comforts you enjoy when hosting."

Alexander groaned. "I'm sorry, my queen. Let me help you up, and I'll see to your hair."

She sniffed. "And what do you know about woman's hair other than how to pull it apart with wanton passion?"

"Lucy, my queen, forgive me." He lifted her chin and kissed her all over her pale face. "Allow me to begin by making sure Asher knows how important it is to be properly dressed at supper."

He sat up, bringing Lucy with him, and turned to the table. "Asher, you need to wear a tie tonight as a sign of respect for your grandmother coming."

"Yes, Poppy." He crawled out from under the chairs and ran for the door.

"And as for you," Alex said as he pulled Lucy to her feet, "you still look lovely and not a mite over thirty-two. The dress didn't wrinkle, but I'd be happy to brush it off for you."

His flicking movements turned to groping touches, but Lucy stiffened. "Not now, Alex. I need to reset my hair, and you need to shower and change."

"But you forgive me?" His hands settled on her hips.

Lucy smiled. "Yes, Angel."

"Then help me remove my clothes while I tell you about all I have in store for you on your special weekend."

Lucy giggled as he pulled her toward the stairs. Naomi shook her head and turned to the crab cakes.

A knock on the kitchen door startled her.

"You're a bit early."

Paul greeted her with a kiss. "I thought it best to get a parking spot by the garage. It'll be a good excuse to stick around until the driveway is clear, but I do know my way around a kitchen and am happy to help."

"I might take you up on it. Usually, I have Sharon with me on party nights."

They chatted while Naomi worked. The doorbell chimed, and Asher thundered for the front.

Mrs. Easton's boisterous voice carried down the hall. "I want a word with Naomi, Lucy. I'll be back in a moment."

Naomi hastily wiped her hands clean and turned for the door as it swung inward.

"Naomi, dear child, it will be a blessing to have your cooking. Your aunt taught you so well, and I've missed—" Mrs. Easton's gaze went to Paul sitting at the table, and he stood. "Naomi, there's a man in your kitchen!"

"I'm aware, Mrs. Easton."

"Does Lucy know?"

"She's the one who told me to invite him. This is Paul Rollins. He—"

"Asher's room! I've heard so much about it. I'm going to have one of the men bring me up. It might be best to go before supper as I tire early these days. There isn't much rest to be had at Eddie's house. His children run as wild as he did. I looked forward to a quieter evening, but Eddie insisted on bringing Oscar. He's the worst of the lot. I'll be glad when my time comes to stay here once more. I do miss your cooking." She smiled and turned back to Paul. "It is good to meet you, Mr. Rollins. I hope you treat our girl right. She's an absolute gem."

"That she is, Mrs. Easton."

When she left, Paul laughed. "I don't believe she took a breath between all that. Miss Phoebe surely gets her social skills from her grandmother."

A few minutes and many door chimes later, the Davenport girls were heard in the hall. The next time the kitchen door opened, Frederick entered. Dressed in a tuxedo, he looked nothing like an Army officer.

Naomi turned off the burners and rushed to him. "Mr. Frederick!"

"Hello, Naomi." He took her in a hug and kissed her cheek. "I didn't want to embarrass you by greeting you in the dining room, though I see this could be just as awkward since you have a guest with you."

She laughed. "I'm glad you came. This here is Paul Rollins. Paul this is—"

"The heavyweight champion of Mobile." Paul shook his hand. "The Army is lucky to have you, Captain Davenport."

"And you're blessed to have caught this fine lady." Frederick looked to Naomi. "Tell me right quick, how did the girls do? And Lucy?"

"Mr. Alex's spoiled them all, but Phoebe and Lucy are the worst for it. Phoebe doesn't like going home anymore, and Lucy's been all over the place with her moods."

"I was afraid of that, but thank you for telling me. I'll see you later, Naomi."

Paul let out a whistle when they were alone. "And I thought Alex teased when he said you were like family. There aren't many help who would be greeted so warmly by guests."

"Mrs. Easton and Mr. Frederick have both known me since I was a knobby-kneed girl."

Alexander found them next—locked in an impassioned kiss. "I was going to ask if you will be ready in five minutes, but it looks like you might need a half hour to finish off."

Naomi straightened her apron. "Get your guests to the table, Mr. Alex. "I can serve in five."

Fourteen

When he followed the group to the dining room, Claudio realized he should have declined the supper invitation. Seeing Frederick's hand on Melissa's back as he brought her down the hall sent an ache through his soul. He did not expect the jealousy, but seeing them together after the tender hours he had shared with her gnawed his heart.

Claudio paused in the doorway. Alexander led his mother-in-law to the head of the table, Bethany and Asher flanking her. Maxwell and Lottie took the opposite end. Lucy motioned Claudio to the empty seat beside Darla—across from Frederick and Melissa.

"Before you sit, please lead us in prayer," Alexander said.

He managed a rote prayer in Italian, followed by one asking for the safety of men at war that only Alexander might understand. Claudio focused on the Davenports as Naomi brought several platters in. He distractedly filled his plate as the service pieces came around. The first time Melissa's brown eyes met his, she immediately turned to her husband without so much as a smile. Claudio's countenance hardened.

Darla laid her hand on his sleeve. "Have you heard from Maggie since Douglas left?"

"Just once, though I write her weekly."

"I'm worried about her," she whispered. "She's afraid to come while Douglas is gone because she can't afford the hotel and doesn't want to stay here. Not that I blame her. She and Alex have no business under the same roof without her husband."

Claudio laughed. "*Sí, Posseduta* can get herself in as much trouble as Alexander can."

Alexander, three seats away, cocked his head toward them. "Did I hear you mention Magdalene?"

"Yes," Darla said. "Has anyone heard from her this month?"

"About two weeks ago," Melissa said. "I invited her to bring the children and stay with me in July. I hope she accepts."

"I'll encourage her to come as well." Darla grabbed Claudio's arm. "You write and tell her we miss her and the children."

"Shall I write her?" Alexander asked.

"No," Darla and Lucy said at the same time.

Only Alexander laughed. When he noticed Lucy's grim face, he kissed her. "You're all I need, my queen, but Magdalene is dear to me."

Across from Claudio, Melissa frowned at the Mellings. It pained him to see her unhappy. As though Frederick felt the same way, he planted a kiss on her neck. A flush of pleasure bloomed on her cheeks, and Claudio balled his napkin in his lap.

The remainder of the meal consisted of tedious talk and a few exchanges with Darla. After the carrot cake was eaten, Maxwell collected his wife, mother, and nephew while the others said their goodbyes. Phoebe made a fuss about losing her cousin but settled into her role as eldest child at the party with ease.

"Phoebe," Edmund called to her, "why don't you bring the children upstairs for a few minutes. The ladies may wait in the morning room as there is something I need to share with the men."

Lucy's green eyes narrowed. "Edmund—"

He patted her hand. "Be a good hostess and keep Darla and Melissa happy until we join you."

The children ran for the hall, but Frederick took Melissa around her waist. Pressing their bodies together, he went at her lips, and she responded in a way familiar to Claudio.

"Come on, Davenport." Edmund took him by the shoulder. "It's a few minutes, not a world tour. She doesn't need any more fodder for her articles. Once more, the whole damn female population of Mobile is swooning over you."

Claudio, Frederick, Edmund, Henry, and Alexander gathered in the den.

"What's in the box you brought earlier?" Alexander asked.

"A bit of Dardenne mischief to celebrate Freddy's homecoming and soon departure. I had to smuggle it with one of our shipments, but I thought tonight was a worthy time to partake of it." Edmund smiled and lifted the lid, removing two bottles of brandy.

Frederick looked amused. "I appreciate it, but you didn't need to, Eddie."

"Nonsense. You were never a Mystics of Dardenne member, but you suffered through that final masquerade with us, and this felt a fitting tribute to your bravery putting up with my sister and Alex back then, as well as your courageousness in joining the army."

Alexander laughed. "You should have told me, Eddie. I could have provided glasses."

"We don't need glasses." Edmund opened the bottles and shoved one at Frederick. Lifting the one he held, he shouted, "To the hero!"

"To the hero!" the men echoed as Edmund and Frederick drank.

The bottles went to Henry and Claudio next.

"To victory!" Henry cheered and partook generously.

Claudio lifted the bottle. "To Frederick's safe return." He swallowed a shot.

Alexander found himself with a bottle in each hand. He lifted them in a toast. "To Freddy, the best ex-husband for my wife!"

He bent forward and placed both bottles into his mouth and then leaned back, guzzling from them in unison.

"Save something for the rest!" Edmund grabbed the bottles—spilling some of the contents on Alexander's suit in the process—and sent them around again. "To drunken encounters with loose women!"

"To our wives!" Henry cheered.

"To Douglas and the Navy," Frederick offered.

Claudio took only a sip each time. Frederick and Edmund held their drink well, but Henry and Alexander grew tipsy as the minutes passed.

"To Lucy," Alexander slurred. "The sexiest woman I ever bedded. Just thinking about her gets me hot. I need her cold hands on—"

Edmund yanked the bottle from him. "If you say something crass about my sister, you'll get a black eye."

Alexander peeled off his tuxedo jacket and tugged at his bowtie. "You mean you don't want to hear how she—"

Frederick had him by the throat. "Nor do I. I'm sure Claudio and Henry can do without the details as well."

"I don't know," Henry said with a smile. "Darla thinks Alex is awful, but I've personally never heard anything too shocking from him."

"Our young friend needs to be educated!" Alexander unbuttoned his shirt. "If I cannot speak of my wife, allow me to speak of Magdalene, the woman for whom I clawed the demon from myself. Sensual, sweet Magdalene Jones. And her husband isn't here to stop me!"

"But I am, *amico*. You do yourself a great disservice in boasting of your encounters. Lucy will be displeased to see you like this."

"Once a Dardenne, always a Dardenne." Edmund slung back the remainder of a bottle and clapped Alexander so hard he almost fell over. He and Henry laughed, and then Alexander joined in.

Frederick came to Claudio's side. "You didn't drink much."

Claudio met his gaze. They were nearly the same height, though Freddy's muscular build made him appear larger. "I am not in the mood tonight."

"Is that because you often drank with Melissa while I was gone?"

Claudio forced his face to remain calm. "Ever since I helped get Alexander drunk the time Lucy was pregnant with Asher, I do not enjoy the thought of him indulging."

Frederick nodded. "But what of your time with Melissa while I was gone?"

Claudio would not lie, but he would not offer all the information either. "She shared with me, mostly wine from Tuscany, which reminded me of home. She is compassionate, and I believe it helped her through her pain to lift another."

"Did she confide in you?" Frederick whispered.

"*Sí*, of many things." *I should have drunk more of the brandy when I had the chance.*

"How difficult was it for her to go through Junior's things? Did she speak of her pain?"

"She was brave. Her heart is open, but she was neglected for a long time. I did not like seeing her lose her luster for life this past year, but it displeased me more to know she suffered without your support."

Frederick's knuckles whitened, and his jaw tensed. "Are there no secrets between you?"

"That I cannot say. She bore much to me, but I do not know what she omitted. I am comfortable saying that if you ever neglect her again, I will strike you down."

"And I'd deserve it."

Alexander's bawdy laughter turned their attention to the other side of the den. Their host clutched his bare chest while he made thrusting motions.

"Thank you for your friendship with Melissa, but I can't stay in here anymore."

"It is my pleasure." *And heartache.*

When Frederick opened the door to the hall, he came face-to-face with Lucy. Hearing Alexander's drunken laughter, she pushed around her ex-husband and saw the lewdness on full display.

"Edmund Albert Easton, how could you? I know it was you because everyone else has come and gone dozens of times without bringing"—she picked up a discarded bottle from a side table—"brandy! You wretch!"

She threw the empty bottle at her brother's head, but he caught it and snickered.

Alexander sauntered toward her with a suggestive gait. "I've been naughty. You know what I need, my queen."

Frederick stalked toward the morning room, Henry following.

"My lovely Lucy." Alexander nestled against her, hands roaming her thin gown. "Heal me."

She remained unmoving, unsmiling.

Edmund laughed. "Don't blame me, Lucy. You're the one who married him. It's been great, but I'll go now. Maybe I'll meet you inside a confessional sometime, Father De Fiore."

Once Edmund was gone, Claudio pried Alexander off his wife. "You have guests, and you must begin the dancing."

As the words were spoken, the sounds of The Turkey Trot started down the hall.

"They don't need us. Lucy will set me to rights." Alexander reached for her, but Claudio stepped between them.

"Lucy, do you wish to be left in here with your husband?"

She shook her head.

"My queen!" Anguish poured from Alexander's soul. "Forgive me!"

Claudio grabbed mints from the bowl on the desk and shoved them at Alexander. "Join us when you can behave."

The priest offered Lucy his arm and escorted her to the morning room.

Fifteen

Melissa was halfway through The Turkey Trot with Freddy when she felt Claudio's eyes on her. Unnerved at the way he stared at her all evening, she did her best not to look his way. She focused on her husband or stole glances at Henry and Darla dancing.

Phoebe, Bethany, Louisa, Asher, and Horatio ran in as The Bunny Hug began.

"I want to dance! Where's Poppy?" Phoebe demanded.

"He is indisposed at the moment," Claudio said from his seat beside Lucy.

Freddy squeezed Melissa's hand. "Allow me to see to Phoebe."

Once father and daughter were dancing, Melissa slipped out of the room to find Alex. He sat on the edge of the chaise in his den, elbows on his knees and hands over his face.

"What's wrong, Alex?" She sat beside him, trying to discern the details of his forlorn face in the shadows from the hall light.

"Eddie brought brandy to toast Frederick, and I drank too much. Lucy's livid, and I don't blame her. I'm a rowdy fool and then an angry drunk afterward. She probably won't let me touch her all night—a sorry way for us to start her birthday weekend."

She patted his leg, resting her hand above his knee. "Then we'll try our best to sober you. How about I fix some coffee?"

"You're a dear." He kissed her cheek just as Lucy came to the doorway.

"I heard that!" She flipped the light switch. "You can't keep away from her even when her husband is in town. Are you going to blame this on the brandy?"

"My queen, it's—"

"Does Frederick know you meet my husband in dark rooms?"

Melissa stood. "I came to see if I could help."

Lucy's laughter bordered on hysterics. "I know exactly what *help* he seeks. If you think I'll stand by while you two make a mockery of my marriage—"

Freddy encircled her from behind. "Goosy, let's not frighten the children."

"Don't you want them to know what type of harpy you're married to?"

"I rested my hand on his knee and offered to make coffee." Melissa's voice sharpened. "He kissed my cheek in thanks, nothing more."

Lucy gave a snort of disgust. "And is that what bringing Magdalene to town will do—*help him*? Gather Alexander's harem before him while their husbands are overseas."

Freddy turned her to face him. "Goosy, you're being ridiculous."

"Don't you wish! She's after my husband and a priest!"

"Goos—"

"Haven't you seen the way Claudio is looking at her tonight and how she's refusing to meet his gaze? If that doesn't prove she—"

Freddy shook Lucy by the shoulders. "I'll not have you discuss my wife in this manner!"

"No one loves me!" Lucy broke free and ran for the stairs.

Melissa folded her arms. "I don't care if it is her birthday—I'll not sit by and let her twist my pain into something that gives her attention!"

She stormed out the French doors and across the yard. Too angry for tears, Melissa trod around the grass near the gate. A minute later, Alexander crossed the lawn with two lit cigarettes in his mouth. He passed one to her.

"Naomi's making coffee. Freddy told me the night air would do me good. He thinks we should let Lucy stew for a bit, but I don't like leaving her alone when she's like this." He took a long drag and exhaled. "I'm sorry for what she said about you."

"Why? It's true."

He perked to full alertness. "You're trying to get in my pants?"

She laughed despite her torment. "She was wrong where you're concerned."

Alex stared, eyes slowly widening. "Dear God, *Claudio?*"

She nodded and turned away to hide her trembling lips.

"I'll slap him with my glove or … or something! Freddy will—"

Melissa grabbed his arm. "He mustn't find out. I can't send him off to Europe thinking I don't love him because I do, desperately! I care for Claudio, but all he did was offer comfort."

Alex guffawed. "I bet he did, that Italian lover. I ought to march him down to Bishop—"

"Please don't. It was as much my fault as his. Things didn't go too far, and it was with good intentions. I don't see how God would judge us too harshly. And Freddy mustn't find out until he returns. Promise me, Alex."

They stared at one another, puffing on their cigarettes while Melissa willed him to understand.

Naomi crossed the shadowy yard to hand Alex coffee. "Need anything else?"

"No, thank you."

"Are the children all right?" Melissa asked.

"Those sugars are fine, dancing like there's no tomorrow with Darla and Henry."

"Thank you." Melissa looked up at the sliver of the moon and filled her lungs with smoke.

Naomi returned to the house, and Alex stood silently beside her, drinking his coffee. Several minutes later, he held out his empty cup to collect her spent cigarette.

"I promise not to say anything to Frederick or Lucy. I'm going to her now. She's getting worse in her moods, and I must try to help. And just so you know, you can't hide everything from Freddy. He's been watching us from the den this whole time."

Her smile was bitter. "It's just as well. He can see I'm not perfect little by little."

"No one's perfect, Melissa. Don't be too hard on yourself." Alex kissed her on the cheek and went through the kitchen door.

As soon as Alex went inside, Freddy came onto the patio. Melissa ran to his open arms.

"I'm sorry for my anger. I shouldn't let her get to me the way she does."

He cupped her face with his hands. "Have I failed you so completely you seek relief with cigarettes?"

"I indulged long before I met you. I would smoke in the magazine office to blend in with the men and have only infrequently partaken since moving here."

"With Alex?"

"And Claudio. I'm sorry if it disgusts you."

He enfolded her in his massive arms and rested his head against hers. "Don't do it in front of the girls or allow it to take over your delicious scent."

"Can we go home now?" she whispered.

"Not until I get another dance with my gorgeous wife." His lips went to her throat, his hands teasing across her back.

"I love you, Freddy."

"And I love you."

When they entered the den, Freddy pointed to the bowl of mints, and Melissa claimed one. The morning room showcased the lively party with moving bodies and fast music. Darla broke away from Henry when the dance was over and came to Melissa.

"Is everything all right?"

Melissa nodded. "Thank you for keeping an eye on the children."

"We're having fun, aren't we, Louisa?" Darla took the girl's hand when she came over.

"I danced with Mr. Henry, Horatio, *and* Asher." Her auburn head turned to Freddy. "May I dance with you, Daddy?"

"It would be my honor, Littlest Princess."

Henry started a quick-moving Strauss waltz, and Louisa took Freddy's hand. Blue-eyed Horatio curled in the corner of the sofa, half asleep. Bethany and Asher joined him, leaning against each other for support in their weariness.

"Darla, would you honor me with this dance?" Claudio bowed before her.

"I'm afraid I need to sit this one out. I'm running tired these days and expect to have official news to share soon."

"I'm pleased to hear it, Darla." Melissa then turned to Claudio and offered a smile.

"You would dance with me tonight, *Eroina*?"

She nodded and accepted his arm. Once they were moving about the room, she spoke. "I'm sorry for ignoring you, Claudio. I wasn't sure how to channel my feelings."

"I understand."

"Even with what he's done, I love my husband," she whispered.

"I know you do, *Eroina*." His brown eyes were too kind. "He thanked me for being here for you. If he only knew—"

"He can't know, Claudio. I'll tell him one day, but not until he returns." Her whisper was vehement. "I did tell Alex."

Claudio frowned.

"Lucy guessed as much based on my behavior toward you this evening. I needed to tell someone who would understand."

The score ended, and Freddy came to claim her. "One more dance. Then I'm bringing my girls home and making love to you."

His words and strong embrace created a rush of longing. Heedless of the others in the room, Melissa kissed him with fervor, savoring his brandied tongue.

Freddy led her into Alex's den, locking the doors and shutting the drapes. Without speaking, he removed his jacket. She hiked her dress, and he lifted her against him. Her legs about his waist created a smile on his handsome face.

He paused. "You don't mind us in here?"

"No." Her breath already came in gasps, and she felt her body readying for the event. "It's been too long since you've held me like this. I want you, Freddy."

Bold and completely driven by emotions, Melissa dropped all sense of propriety. She brought forth sounds from Freddy she'd never before heard. Afterward, they righted their clothes, and—not caring about the telltale flushing across her neck—she opened the hall door.

Lucy stood red-faced with green eyes glaring. "How dare you defile our chaise!"

"We never touched it or any other piece of furniture. We didn't even lie on your carpet." Melissa shouldered past her, going toward the front while Freddy gathered the girls.

Alex stood at the intersection of the hallways. "I just pulled her out of her mood before we came downstairs. She heard Frederick enjoying his release, and I lost her again."

"I'm sorry about that, Alex. She seems concerned about your precious chaise. Be sure to reiterate we soiled no surfaces with our actions."

He gave a guttural growl. "Just go, Melissa."

She let herself out the massive front door and waited on the veranda for her family. Guilt tried to creep in. *I've done nothing more than what Lucy herself has done over the years—seeking comfort from a close friend and allowing my husband to take me in an unoccupied room during a party. Alex is overreacting, the same as Lucy.*

The door opened, and Freddy herded the girls out.

"Can't we stay with Poppy?" Phoebe whined.

Freddy took her hand. "You'll see him when he picks you up for riding in the morning."

"Why is Momma upset at her party?" Concern etched Bethany's face.

"She's worried about many things, Beth, but she'll get over it soon enough."

Louisa fell asleep on the drive home, and Freddy carried her to bed while Melissa oversaw the other girls' preparations.

Locked in their bedroom for the night, Freddy wrapped his arms around Melissa. "Maybe I should be ashamed for what we did, but I'm not."

She kissed him. "We're married and have a scant amount of time together for an undisclosed period. The only thing I'll be upset about is if you fail to do that with me again."

Sixteen

Naomi waited until the yelling subsided before turning to the hall.

Paul took her hand. "It sounds like you'll have your hands full. I better go."

"You don't need to, but I understand. Should we see if the driveway is clear?"

"I'm sure it is, Honey. Supper was great." His strong arms went about her waist, and she leaned against his chest. "You aren't going to back out of Sunday dinner at Mattie's house, are you?"

"Nothing will stop that. The Mellings know they have to do without me until supper that day."

The sensation of his lips on hers never ceased to thrill. Knowing she had a colorful night ahead with the Mellings, she leaned in for more when Paul moved to step away.

"I better go, or you'll be stuck with me indefinitely."

She narrowed her eye at him. "That wouldn't be so bad, would it?"

Hands low on her hips, Paul grinned. "It would be terrific."

With a final kiss, he was out the back door. Sighing, Naomi went to the hall.

"—to progress when he leaves!" Alexander's voice sounded menacing as she approached the den. "She's beautiful, smart, and sensual, but it's no excuse!"

"She is a friend and was in need." *Father De Fiore!*

"You cannot allow it! What will Frederick think when he finds out? And he will—she's said as much. He lost his first wife to death, I stole his second from him, and you're courting an affair with his third!"

Naomi covered her mouth to muffle the gasp.

"I will not deny her comfort when I know she is in need."

"Then, for God's sake, stay away from her! How many times have you forced me to my knees? Now it's time for me to do likewise. You know this can't end well. You've seen where behavior like this leads from your time with Eliza."

"This is nothing like what happened with Eliza!" The priest raved further in Italian.

Naomi took a few steps back and then went hurriedly for the morning room.

"Naomi," Alexander called out, "a moment, please. There's been some trouble tonight, and Lucy is out of sorts. Would you mind keeping an eye on her and Asher when I take the girls riding tomorrow?"

"No problem, Mr. Alex. I'm just checking for wayward dishes before washing what's left. Then I'll be going home if you don't need anything."

Alexander ran a scarred hand through his dark blond hair. "I don't think so, but would you check with Lucy before you go?"

"Of course, Mr. Alex."

"She's upstairs." He put a hand on her shoulder. "Thank you, Naomi. Supper was fabulous."

Naomi hastened up the stairs, eager to get away from Alexander and the priest.

Lucy sat in the armchair in Asher's room, the pathway of light from the hall revealing her bare feet on the plush carpet. Naomi went in, and seeing the boy asleep in bed, took Lucy by the hands and hauled her upright.

She allowed Naomi to lead her to the master bedroom. "Are you wishing for a shower or bath tonight?"

"A bath, please." Her eyes were almost as red as her dress, her nose puffy. "Where's Alex?"

"Downstairs with the last guest." Naomi started the taps, adding a dash of lavender to the tub.

"Claudio?" When Naomi nodded, Lucy slumped against the wall. "They might think me daft, but I'm not blind. I know what I saw, and I don't appreciate it being used to turn Freddy against me."

Naomi stayed silent as she tidied the bathroom counter.

"I'm wearing thin, and the complications with everyone aren't helping. But maybe they'll miss me when I'm gone."

"Lucy!" Alexander rushed to embrace her. "Why must you speak like that?"

"My flame is suffocating."

He scooped her into his arms and carried her toward the bed. "Then I must breathe some of my fire into you, my queen."

"Her bath is ready, Mr. Alex."

He turned to her, still cradling his wife in his arms. "I'll take things from here, Naomi."

As she closed the bedroom door, Alexander's voice reached out like tentacles. "Off with that gown, my queen. Submerge yourself in the bath, and then I'll immerse myself in you until your heart is aflame once more."

***

Sunday with Paul's family was a joy. Mattie and Bert were welcoming, and doting on their two children brought happiness to strained Naomi. Then a week and a half of quiet followed. The Davenport girls stayed at home with their father while he finished training with the local infantry. Only Alexander saw them as he brought them to and from the riding club. Naomi spent several hours with Paul, pleased to escape Lucy's moodiness.

After a subdued Fourth of July, Naomi readied to go to Alexander's office with the Mellings' at seven in the morning on the fifth so they could watch the army march through town on their way to the mobilization camp in Montgomery. In the middle of packing a picnic lunch to bring with them, the doorbell rang. Naomi beat Alexander to it by a few feet.

"You look dashing in that uniform, Mr. Frederick."

He removed his hat. "Thank you, Naomi." Seeing Alexander behind her, Frederick addressed him. "I wanted to give Lucy one more chance to allow me to say goodbye. Once I'm with the regiment for the parade, I can't leave."

Alexander offered a hand and clapped the other around his shoulders. "She's still in bed, a captive audience, you might say. I know she'll regret not speaking to you. We'll be watching the parade from my office window. Be sure to wave."

Frederick followed Alexander upstairs, and Naomi went back to the kitchen. With the basket packed, she began scrambling eggs for breakfast.

Lucy's raving carried down the hall. "That was entirely rude, Alexander Randolph Melling!"

"I'm sure Freddy wasn't too shocked." Alexander strode through the kitchen door. "He has seen you naked, my queen."

Lucy stomped into the room behind him, wearing only a tiny slip of a gown. "So you have no qualms with men seeing me as am I when you lie with me? Am I to be on display for all your friends in the future?"

He looked her over with an appreciative eye. "I wouldn't trust anyone but honorable Frederick, though I saw a glint of longing in his eyes when you rushed to him at the top of the stairs. I'm sure the sight of you will give Captain Davenport plenty to think of when he's sitting in the trenches."

Lucy charged at him so hard he hit the wall, knocking his head.

His arms went about her though he looked slightly dazed. "I love it when the passion burns through you. And it got me excited to see you in his arms—to know you had strong, dependable Frederick Davenport and chose wayward me. Kiss me, my queen. Kiss me like you kissed him, and I won't be mad you took liberties with old Freddy."

"You absolute scoundrel!" Lucy's arms flew at him in a rage.

Fearing Alexander blinded from her anger by his teasing nature, Naomi pinned Lucy's arms to her side—the same way Mrs. Easton had to handle Opal during her fits.

Alexander looked incredulous. "What—"

"Dampen a washcloth with cold water, quickly!" Naomi commanded as Lucy struggled.

When Alexander returned from the sink, Naomi gave Lucy to him. She gathered Lucy's hair to the side and placed the cool cloth on the back of her neck. Lucy struggled to break free, but her husband held firm as Naomi pressed the cloth to her.

"You need to calm down, Miss Lucy. We're here to help."

"Let me go!"

"My queen, I went too far. You know I love you and never wish to upset you." He kissed her face multiple times. "Frederick is your sacred one, your golden calf. I'll tread carefully."

"He's been nothing but good to me! I'll always love him!" Lucy collapsed against Alexander. No tears, no wailing, but it was more disturbing than her typical demonstrations.

He nodded to Naomi, and she stepped away.

"Allow me to bring you back to bed so you may rest a few minutes more." Gathering Lucy in his arms, he carried her upstairs.

Naomi returned to breakfast preparations, stewing over Lucy's erratic behavior as she ground coffee beans.

Alexander joined her a few minutes later. "Asher's with her. I told them I'd bring breakfast in bed." He slumped into a chair at the corner table. "What are we going to do if she doesn't come out of this rut she's in?"

"You're going to keep loving her, Mr. Alex. And we won't leave her alone."

"I don't want you tied here when you have Paul." Alexander rubbed his stubbly chin. "I'll need to bring on another worker, but Lucy will get suspicious."

"There's no way she can keep up with the girls and Asher this summer." Naomi turned off the burner and transferred the eggs to a platter with the toast.

"I'll speak to Melissa. Magdalene arrives tomorrow, and I hear she's bringing the Walkers' oldest daughter with her. Maybe we could work something out between all of us in regards to Lucy not being left alone."

"I didn't think Melissa would come back after the fiasco at the last party."

Alexander shrugged and took the tray off the counter. "I'll figure something out. Thanks, Naomi. We'll leave at the top of the hour."

By the time they loaded into Alexander's automobile, Lucy appeared emotionally collected though somber. Naomi rode in the backseat with Asher, the lunch basket between them.

Lucy rarely made an appearance in her husband's office. The secretaries awkwardly remarked on her stylish hat, the clerks were keen to show Asher the massive file room, and the other lawyers complimented Alexander on his family. Alexander escorted Lucy up the stairs a few minutes later, Naomi following. He brought her to one of the windows overlooking the square and stood behind her, arms wrapped about her middle. When Asher bound up, Naomi caught him in the hall to give his parents a bit of privacy.

"It's difficult to think back on the dozen years since that day I spied you dancing in the fountain." Alexander's voice was soft, but it carried to the hall. "So much agony, but now we've been together longer than we've been apart. It was all worth it."

"Demons, death, disfigurement, divorce—"

Alexander stopped her list with a kiss and pressed his forehead to hers. "This, what we have, is worth it. You, our son, and your daughters are everything to me. Promise me you'll fight to keep what we have alive. Promise me you'll love me to the end and allow me to love you in return. That's all I ask—to be free to love you no matter what."

"I promise, my angel." Lucy kissed him with desperation.

Naomi squeezed Asher's hand and led him to the secretary's desk at the top of the stairs. There she pointed out the telephone switchboard.

Several minutes later, a red-lipped and cocky Alexander sauntered down the hall. He offered his hand to Asher. "How about we go buy colas for everyone?"

"Yes, Poppy!" He looked like a replica of Phoebe as he bounced.

"Go kiss Momma goodbye."

When Alexander and Asher were gone, Naomi settled in a chair beside Lucy in front of an electric fan. She opened windows to watch the boisterous well-wishers fill Bienville Square and the surrounding streets.

Seventeen

Melissa tried not to be upset about arriving downtown later than she wanted, but managing three girls on the crowded streetcar was a worse idea than finding a parking spot would have been. They caught one of the last rides before the roads closed. With over a thousand local soldiers leaving, a multitude lined the streets on the parade route. A swarm of spectators was all she could see on the sidewalks when they exited near Bienville Square. Melissa led the girls toward the park in hopes of finding a bit of shade, though they were all outfitted with wide-brimmed hats.

"Let's try for the far side," Melissa called over her shoulder to Phoebe and Bethany, who held hands directly behind her and Louisa.

"By Poppy's office!" Phoebe declared. "And look, there's Momma!"

Lucy, a beacon of royal blue in Alex's second-floor window, sat regally with Naomi beside her. The women waved to the girls—equally eye-catching in matching white dresses.

"May we go see Momma?" Bethany asked.

"We haven't seen her since her party," Phoebe whined.

"Just for a few minutes. Mind the crowd."

She watched them cross St. Francis Street. A minute later, the girls were in the window hugging Lucy and waving.

"Melissa!" Alex, carrying a crate of cola bottles with Asher on his shoulders, came toward them. "Could you take the box a moment while I set Ash down?"

She assisted him, and when he took the crate back, he kissed her cheek. "Where are Lucy's girls?"

"They wanted to say hello, but they'll need to come back soon." Melissa pointed up at the window while Louisa hugged his legs.

"I'll escort them. Are you excited to see your father in the parade, Louisa?"

"Yes, Poppy, but it would be nicer if he stayed."

"You're a wise girl." He turned to his son. "Stay close, Asher."

"Come play with me soon!" Asher said to Louisa in parting.

Melissa forced herself to make conversation with the neighboring people. Then Ethelwynne Graves was beside her, one of the young ladies from Hattie Spunner's science club. She had graduated high school the month before.

"I appreciate your thoughts in the newspaper each week," Ethelwynne said, brown eyes sincere. "I know it must be difficult to write most of the time."

Melissa nodded. "And it will grow more so as soon as he's crossing the Atlantic."

"May God bless Mr. Davenport."

Studying Ethelwynne's face, she saw the stress. "And your beau, Winnie. Are you still with Nathan Paterson?"

She smiled and nodded. "He joined right after graduation and is training in New Jersey for the signal corps."

"And will Benjamin Paterson try to leverage that to get the inside scoop for The Daily Register?" Melissa asked because the editor who hired her was the young man's uncle.

Ethelwynne shook her head. "Benjamin is always trying to work an angle, but you'll continue to speak for all of us left behind."

"Do you have an understanding?" Melissa asked.

"We're to be married after his training is over, during his window of leave." She raised her left hand to showcase a simple diamond ring. "You know my mother. She wouldn't allow us to have a wedding directly after graduation though several of our classmates married the next day for that very reason. She said if Nathan and I could make it through the separation during his training, she would finally sanction it."

"I wish you both the best, Winnie."

"Thank you. I hope to see you at club meetings in the future. We could all use the support these days."

A minute after Ethelwynne moved on, Alex returned. He took Melissa's elbow and ruffled Louisa's curls. His grin was infectious despite her heavy heart.

"Lucy and the girls are begging to stay together. Could we keep them with us until after their riding time Saturday?"

"Maggie arrives tomorrow, and I know Phoebe was looking forward to seeing Kade."

"It's only one more day, and it would mean so much to Lucy."

"Anything for Lucy," she said with a bitter tone.

Alex's smile faltered. "I need to speak with you and Magdalene about that. Would it be all right if I stop in around two tomorrow?"

"They aren't expected to arrive until noon and—"

"That will be plenty of time for Magdalene to get settled. I won't stay long, and I don't wish Lucy or the girls to know about the visit if it can be helped."

"I'll see if we can clear out the other children as well."

"Thank you, darling Sissa." He kissed her cheek and dashed back to the office.

"Poppy forgot to say goodbye to me."

"He has a lot of things on his mind, Louisa. You'll see him soon, though."

The parade arrived with great fanfare. Melissa held her daughter on her hip so she could better see the soldiers marching past, a steady stream of khaki uniforms under the July sun. Freddy—Captain Davenport—on the front row of his regiment was a commanding figure. Melissa yearned to touch him again. Just one more taste of what they shared in the early morning hours, and she would be able to carry on until he returned. Swallowing the lump of feelings rising in her throat, she protected Louisa from her emotions with a set smile.

When the last of the parade moved beyond Royal Street on the way to the docks, Melissa was grateful not to have the other two girls in tow. Hugging Louisa to her chest, she hastened south to catch a less crowded trolley on Government Street.

As soon as they were home, she fed Louisa a sandwich and put her down for a nap. Melissa collapsed on her bed and wept.

At supper, Melissa drank coffee as her attention jerked to every sound in the empty house.

Louisa picked at her food. "When will Phoebe and Beth come home?"

"Saturday at lunchtime." *The anniversary of Junior's death.* "But Miss Maggie, Kade, Tabitha, Simon, and Clara Jane will be here tomorrow. Eat up so you can get to bed. The sooner you sleep, the sooner they'll be here."

"Are you going to eat, Mommy?"

Melissa sighed and took another sip of coffee. "Maybe later."

"Daddy told me I need to make sure you eat."

"Don't worry about me, Sweetie. You have enough to take care of. Be sure Doff has water in his bowl before you go upstairs."

Louisa readied for bed and hugged the stuffed rabbit from Freddy. Melissa read a Beatrix Potter book while Doff settled at the girl's feet.

"I think Phoebe is upset Doff likes me now," she whispered.

"That's what happens when people are gone—those who love them look to someone else for care." She clicked off the light.

"Who will you go to for love?"

Melissa caught her breath. "You give me lots of love, Louisa."

"But not like Daddy can. I love you, Mommy."

"And I love you."

Melissa turned on the hall and parlor lights before stopping in the study. Looking over the books on the shelf, she couldn't decide if she wanted something to read or drink.

A faint knocking sounded from the front door.

The one I turn to for care.

Without a word, she opened the door for Claudio. He led her to the sofa and allowed her to cry on his shoulder.

***

On Friday, Joe and Claire Walker—along with their four children—accompanied the Campbells to the Davenports' house. Melissa had Miss Sharon on hand for the arrival and presented a casual luncheon spread. When Melissa told Joe and Claire that Alex wanted a private word with her and Maggie, they agreed to take all the children downtown for ice cream.

With Miss Sharon preparing supper in the kitchen, Melissa helped Maggie unpack upstairs. Tabitha would share Louisa's bed, and a single bed had been arranged in the corner for sixteen-year-old Clara Jane Walker, who came to help with the children. Maggie had the two-bed guest room for her and her boys. A cozy, full house.

The women were in the parlor with tea when Alex pressed his face against the front window. Maggie giggled, and Melissa rose to welcome him. He gave her an absentminded kiss before rushing for his friend.

"Magdalene!" Alex spun her around and kissed her cheek. "You stayed away too long, and I've been good. Don't punish me like that."

"I had to get over my shock before feeling social." Maggie blushed under his attentions and went to smooth a loose tendril into her bun, but Alex stilled her hand.

"You look lovely." He kissed the top of her head as he held her hands. "It does me a world of good to see you."

"You're making me nervous, Alex," Melissa said. "Please sit and remove your hands."

Alex took Maggie's elbow and returned her to the sofa he'd plucked her from. "Says the woman who—"

"Don't even go there." Melissa's voice was hard.

Alex laughed, his bright eyes filled with mirth. When the doorbell chimed, he raced to it. From the entry, his laughter rang out once more.

"How convenient is it," Alex said as he returned, "that Claudio happened to come at the exact time I called on you?"

"Melissa told me of the scheduled visit last night." Claudio crossed the room to Maggie, and she stood for an embrace. "I was invited to see my dear friend."

Alex waited until Claudio kissed Melissa's cheeks before opening his mouth. "And what exactly were you doing with Melissa last night?"

Maggie gasped at the pointedness of his question.

"Comforting someone in need." Claudio stepped away from Melissa's chair and took a seat on the other side of Maggie.

Alex smirked and shook his head. "He wasn't even gone twelve hours, you scoundrel."

"He held me as I cried, nothing more." Melissa shoved a teacup at Alex. "Unless you keep to the topic you said you were coming to discuss, I suggest you stay quiet."

"Feisty, isn't she, Magdalene?" Alex raised a conspiratorial eyebrow as he set his cup on the coffee table. "Almost like a woman with something to hide."

Claudio had him by his shirt and flung him out of his seat.

"Claudio," Maggie pled, "please let him go. I'll keep him in line."

"You would claim responsibility for this man?" Claudio shook Alex teasingly.

"Yes, *Deacon* De Fiore. Return him to the sofa."

Alex crowed. "You've been demoted, Priest. Unhand me as the lady says!"

Melissa had forgotten the Seacliff Cottage friends' penchant for jesting. Without Douglas there to mediate, she was sure the three could get into plenty of mischief. Alex snuggled against Maggie, and Claudio took the seat nearest Melissa.

She turned her attention to Alex. "What did you wish to discuss?"

He straightened but kept full contact with Maggie. "I'm worried about Lucy. She speaks of dying, her moods are erratic, and she's not written anything other than letters to Frederick and a few poems in the past several months. She's given up fiction altogether."

Melissa scoffed. "I bet her letters have plenty of fictional embellishments."

"You've become bitter."

"I'm sick of the way she manages to turn everything to revolve around herself, including Douglas and Freddy leaving."

"She's hurting, and it's worse than ever. I'm scared for her, for all of us, but I'll not put her through what Opal endured."

Melissa gripped the armrests. "You're comparing her to—"

"She started beating me yesterday morning. Naomi had to pull her off me."

Maggie gave him a wry smile. "I've hit you plenty of times, Alexander."

Alex pulled his cigarette case out of his pocket and flipped it in his palm. "Not like this. Her whole fury was behind it. It didn't hurt, but it scared me when I saw how frightened Naomi was. She was there the day Opal attacked."

Melissa frowned. "If you can't control her, she needs—"

"Never! I've seen what those hospitals are like when I investigated them for Opal five years ago. They're barbaric in what they do, especially to females. Opal was used sexually from the time she was twelve. I'm no doctor, but I'm sure that contributed to her moral and mental decline."

"Surely improvements have been made over the years."

"I'll not do it!" Alex nearly crushed the metal case in his hands.

Melissa went to the window and opened it fully. "Go ahead, if you give me one."

Alex lit up for both of them, and Claudio retrieved one for himself. "What would Freddy do if he knew we were smoking in his house?"

Melissa ignored the question. "What do you plan on doing?"

"Naomi and I already agreed not to leave her alone. If she lost control with one of the children...." He exhaled a cloud of smoke. "We can't allow that to happen. I thought that with Clara Jane here, I might hire her to—"

"You can't ask a girl to shoulder that type of responsibility," Maggie said. "I'm sure Joe and Claire would be upset if you even asked."

"*Sí*, you need someone with experience, if not with Lucy, then with what ails her. Someone mature and stronger than she is."

"I fear she'll soon need medical help to calm her, but for now, I think she would be fine with a familiar face. Naomi's good as gold, but she's got a man friend now and—"

"Bless her heart," Maggie said. "It's about time."

"He's terrific for her, a widower with his own company, grown kids, and grandbabies." Alex grinned. "And I'm responsible for the kindling romance."

Maggie punched his arm. "That's just like you to take credit rather than Naomi's pleasant nature and sweet face for catching a man."

"Oh, she did that all right, but I put Paul Rollins in front of her. As I was saying, I don't want to ask Naomi to work more than she does already. Lucy would be fine with one of you with her. Would you be willing to take turns a few times a week to come over on the pretense of a playdate with one or two of the children?"

Melissa paced in front of the window, dragging deep from the cigarette. "The last time I was there proved I can no longer hold my tongue where she's concerned."

Alex took Melissa's hand. "She's sick. It's not her you hate— it's what she says and does. That's not my Lucy, but I can redirect her when she drifts away."

"I assume you're referring to how you typically handle your ups and downs. How will someone else be able to reach her if she slips while you're not there?"

"Call me, and I'll race home."

"And we're supposed to say, 'Alex is on his way to seduce you?'"

He gave her a look of contempt. "You're not trying to understand."

"I'm giving this every rational thought I can muster!" Melissa countered. "When Lucy isn't acting like herself, who are you thrusting against when you're supposedly healing her?"

Maggie gasped, but Melissa didn't remove her cold stare from Alex.

He snaked a hand around the base of her neck and the other on the small of her back. "You've never had the pleasure of being within my arms, but the thrill of my contact returns her to me." He dropped his voice. "Only after she's focused on the present do I bring my queen healing with climatic success."

Alex pressed his body against Melissa, face inches from her own. "If you doubt me, I'll give you a demonstration."

"*Calmati, amico.*"

They continued to stare, neither moving. Every burn mark and laugh line on his arrogant face fell beneath Melissa's scrutiny as her curiosity grew. *Is he so full of himself that he would think I'm tempted?* The slight tilt of her head earned a smirk from Alex in the affirmative, and then Claudio yanked them apart.

"You must stop this display of superiority, the both of you." Claudio crossed himself. "Focus, Alexander! We need to band together and pray to help Lucy, as well as Frederick and Douglas, and those left to care for their loved ones. None of you can do it alone."

Eighteen

Claudio and Magdalene took the first watch the following Monday. He met Magdalene at the Davenports' house and walked with her, Tabitha, and Simon to Government Street, where they rode the streetcar around the loop to the stop closest to the Mellings' home. Naomi answered the door, and when she brought the group to the morning room, she told Lucy she was off on errands. Asher grabbed each friend by a hand and ran with them for the stairs.

Lucy appeared gray next to Magdalene's rich coloring. After the women greeted each other, Claudio came to her.

"Lucy, will you allow me to bless you? You look as though you could use fortification."

"Alex kept me in bed all weekend."

"*Sí*, that is where he most enjoys seeing you."

Magdalene laughed, a wistful smile on her pretty face to which Lucy scowled.

"You must leave by two o'clock. Asher will need quiet time before Alex returns from work, and I'm sure Melissa will miss her house guests."

"Magdalene, you should see Asher's wonderful room. I shall keep Lucy company." When she left, Claudio settled beside Lucy and gathered her hands into his. He prayed over her, joyful to see a smile on her lips when complete. "It does not do well for you to be unhappy."

"I only feel alive when I'm in Alexander's arms." Lucy rested her head on his shoulder. "Tell me, Claudio, do you and Melissa have an understanding?"

"We are friends, as I am your friend."

"But at supper the other week, she refused to look upon you. I would never do that. She hid from your gaze as though embarrassed by a previous encounter." Lucy's arms went about his middle. "I'd rest better knowing she turns to you in her grief rather than my husband."

"We have been over this, Lucy. Alexander is devoted to you."

"But he loves much and cares for many. You could ease my fear of one of my competitors with a short phrase."

"There is no competition. Alexander married you. You have born him a son."

"But I did that for Frederick—giving him two daughters. It wasn't enough."

"It is not comparable. You were the one who left him."

"And now it is my time to be spurned. Alex loves Magdalene. You've seen them together. If Douglas doesn't return, he'll comfort her and—" She pressed her lips together.

"It is good to comfort a friend." *Deliciously good and easy to go too far.*

"He will wish," she spoke with trembling lips, "that I was not in the way."

"It is not so."

"But she told me, Claudio! Magdalene told me of their promise to each other. I never thought it would amount to anything, but with Douglas at war, it's more probable than ever."

"What promise?"

"When Asher was an infant and Maggie still nursed Simon, the men took the other children to Monroe Park, and we stayed home." Lucy took a deep breath. "She told me when they made amends in Seacliff Cottage, they kissed and promised that if they were left widowed or alone, they would give their relationship another try. Alex promised to love her and any members of her family. She told me the promise still brought her peace."

"There will be nothing more as long as either of us is married." Alexander told me as much, but how would that sound to a grieving wife?

"Don't you see, Claudio? Magdalene is the one who got away! Alexander's only unfulfilled conquest. You know how he is. To think he won't meet the opportunity to win her if Douglas leaves this earth prematurely is illogical. The desire between them is already there. They share a history that rivals the passion I have with him. The fact they never completed the ultimate means Alex will yearn to experience it all the more. I'll be a noose around his neck the moment Douglas is gone."

Claudio could not reply, for he caught glimmers of truth in Lucy's words. He hugged her tighter and kissed her blonde head.

"Magdalene will be better for him than I ever was. I'll give up my life rather than stand in the way." Her whisper stabbed the quiet like a viper's fangs, and Claudio was all too familiar with the venom.

***

Unless called upon, Alexander was supposed to stay away while others saw to Lucy, but he arrived after the group settled in the dining room for a simple lunch. Like an enraptured puppy, he bound straight to Magdalene. True, he supposedly had not seen her in months, but knowing Lucy's thoughts about Magdalene and seeing her countenance crumble at their innocent contact had Claudio ready to beat his friend to the ground.

"Poppy, did you know Tabby and Simon were in town? Kade too!" Asher hugged his father when he stopped by his chair.

"I heard. It's great to see them. Shall we host supper on Friday, Lucy?"

"If you wish." Her voice was weak, withdrawn.

"None of that half-heartedness, my queen."

Alexander pulled her to standing and kissed her until color rose to her cheeks. Rather than take one of the empty seats on the edges of the table, he planted himself in Lucy's and tugged her onto his lap, facing Claudio. There he fed Lucy and himself with plenty of caresses in between bites. Though annoyed with Alexander's actions, Claudio was glad Asher could not see his father's groping touches.

"Poppy, will you take Kade with you to the riding club this week?"

"I'd be happy to, Asher, but that's up to Miss Maggie."

Lucy sighed as Alexander's hand crept beneath her hemline, shifting the red lace higher on her legs.

"Just to watch, not ride," Magdalene replied. "I know he'd enjoy it, thank you."

"What would it take for me to be able to put him on a pony?" Alexander's hand went for Lucy's thigh beneath the fabric.

"I'd want two adults so if one of the ponies were to bolt, there would be someone to stay with the other," Magdalene replied.

"That's very motherly of you." Alexander smiled as Lucy took a sharp intake of breath.

Magdalene stared at Lucy's closing eyes and followed the deliberate motions of Alexander's arm. Biting her lip, she looked at him and raised her eyebrows. He only winked and increased his efforts. Where Melissa would have thrown sarcasm at him and Darla gone off on a tirade, Magdalene watched him with interest. Claudio could almost see the longing in her eyes and felt Lucy's pain anew.

"Alexander," he whispered, "you need to excuse yourself and Lucy."

He laughed and slowly removed his hand from under her dress. "My queen, is there something you need to see me about before I return to work?"

Lucy's green eyes opened with sparkling purpose. "In your den, my angel."

Alexander's hands trailed her hips as she stood. Then he was beside her, looking back at their guests. "Tell Kade to plan for Wednesday afternoon, Maggie."

"When you are done eating," Claudio told the children, "you may play in the yard."

Asher and Simon were up immediately, but Tabitha still had chocolate cake. "Why couldn't Beth come?" she asked after taking another bite.

"Miss Lucy isn't well enough for a big group today," Magdalene explained.

"Wouldn't she want her daughter here?"

"Maybe next time." Magdalene kissed her hair. "You'll see Beth in a few hours."

When Tabitha ran out to join the boys, Claudio offered his arm to Magdalene. "*Posseduta*, you must control your feelings. You look upon Alexander with Seacliff eyes, as Douglas would say."

She laughed. "What would you have me do when Alex—"

"It was a show. He was proving how he can redirect Lucy when she appears out of sorts."

"I never doubted him. Do you forget I've felt his touch?"

"No, but it would be well if *you* forgot. The passion is plain on your face. It is not good for Lucy to witness your longings when Alexander is being intimate with her."

"Then tell *him* not to do so in my vicinity." She laughed—a thin, guilty sound.

When they passed the den, an enraptured cry pierced the heavy door, followed by a lower moan.

"They are insufferable."

"They're blessed to share such passion, Claudio. I only envy them because Douglas is not with me."

***

Friday afternoon, Claudio walked into Melling and Associates.

Alexander's secretary greeted him with a smile. "Welcome, Father De Fiore. Mr. Melling is in his final appointment. May I get you some coffee while you wait?"

"No, thank you."

He settled in the chair closest to Alexander's door and heard a decidedly feminine laugh. Claudio strained to hear what transpired within. When the door opened, Alexander was obscured by a woman in a black hat, a watch dangling from a gold chain around her neck.

"Father De Fiore," she said with a smile, "it's good to see you."

"Ms. Stuart." Claudio bowed and looked beyond her. "Alexander."

"Make yourself comfortable, Claudio. I'll be with you as soon as I see Kate downstairs."

Claudio lit a cigarette and stared out at the park. When Alexander returned, the priest patted his cheek roughly before squeezing Alexander's face with his hand.

"You are burning with intrigue, and it does not become you." Claudio glowered and blew smoke at his face, but Alexander only laughed.

"I despise Kate Stuart, even if she dropped her ex-husband's name. She was never kind, and her magazine caused my mother to treat Lucy with contempt. Please don't mention to Lucy I had an appointment with her."

"I will refrain if you promise not to fondle your wife in front of guests. What you did Monday was despicable. With supper tonight, I want to make sure you know your behavior must be respectful. It is not fair to Lucy to be used in such a manner as to display your control over her. And Magdalene—"

"She had no objections."

"You do not need to provoke emotions in her. Lucy will not be blind to them."

"Lucy has always tolerated it, except the time I was oppressed."

"It is different now. Douglas is not here and—"

"I can control myself."

"Control is not what you displayed with Melissa last Friday or your shameless display during lunch Monday."

"You're going to drag Melissa into the conversation?" Alexander lit a cigarette and grinned. "This is going to be good."

"Forget I mentioned her and focus on Lucy. You have much to concern yourself with on that front, but you must stop flirting with Magdalene!"

Alexander adjusted himself and exhaled. "Impossible. There's something between us that begs to be toyed with."

"Then you will drive your wife to an early grave."

The grim line of Claudio's mouth must have shown Alexander how serious he was. Clamping the cigarette between his lips, he took the priest's shoulders. "Tell me!"

After sitting him down, Claudio disclosed his conversation with Lucy Monday morning. Alexander barely breathed as he listened, the cigarette in his hand forgotten.

"She has it in her head that she must die for your happiness should Douglas not make it back," he said.

"And here I thought she was concerned only for Freddy, but it's for Douglas as well. No wonder she feels ill so often." Alexander snuffed out his cigarette and grabbed a few mints off his desk. "I must go to her!"

Nineteen

Naomi carried a pot of soup to pour into the lidded tureen when Alexander rushed in the backdoor.

"Where's Lucy?"

"In the front room with her mother and Phoenix Asher." Mrs. Easton's month to stay with them wasn't until August, but she was invited to supper because she'd enjoyed herself so well the last time. "Mr. Maxwell brought her over last hour."

Alexander hurried through, and then the priest entered.

"Are you well, Miss Naomi?"

"Yes, thank you, Father De Fiore."

"Let us pray this supper party is not as explosive as the last one."

He smiled in his pleasant way, making Naomi remember the words she'd overheard between him and Alexander weeks ago. *Who could fault Melissa if something did develop between them when he glowed like that with a simple smile? But the pain it would cause Mr. Frederick—the poor man has been through enough!*

"Miss Lucy is no stranger to drama these days, Lord bless her."

"I plan to do so tonight." The priest winked.

Definitely bold, though he'll never be as audacious as Alexander.

Sharon returned from setting the dining room and helped with final food preparations. The sounds of arriving guests often eclipsed the noise in the kitchen. Minutes before suppertime, Bethany ran in.

"Miss Naomi!" She was all smiles. Seeing her family's cook, she curtsied to her as well. "Evening, Miss Sharon."

"Hello, Sugar." Naomi set the silver ladle on the tray. "What's got you excited?"

"Sissa and Momma only mend. I was wondering if you sew."

"Here and there, but not as much as I used to with helping in this big place."

"Do you, Miss Sharon? I want to learn to sew."

"Same as Naomi. My mother taught us."

"Could you both teach me, that way I can learn at either house? I want to make pretty dresses for mine and Tabby's dolls."

"Of course, Sugar."

Sharon nodded in agreement. "And our style is the same, so there won't be any crossed lessons."

Bethany hugged each of them. "Thank you. Could we start next week?"

"We'll see what we can work out." Naomi laughed as the girl ran out. "It's good to see that one excited about something. She takes after her father with her quiet ways, and I fear she is often overlooked because Phoebe is so boisterous."

"The oldest is a spitfire and getting harder to manage." Sharon transferred the rolls into the serving dish. "There won't be anything cute about her moods in a few more years, just like her mama."

"Lucy was sweet as anything until this past decade."

"Maybe they can marry her off before she's too far gone. Bless Mr. Frederick for dealing with these fair-headed she-devils."

"Those are my girls you're talking about, so you best hush up." Naomi took a tray and nodded toward the one she wanted Sharon to bring.

With the Adamses, Campbells, Davenports, Claudio, and Mrs. Easton over, the children numbered the same as the adults with Clara Jane Walker between the two groups. Eight boisterous bodies aged ten and under, though they sat mostly still for supper. But for all the children's antics, Alexander was the most exuberant. Every time Naomi was in the dining room, he stayed in animated conversation with one of their guests or had a caressing arm around Lucy.

After supper, Naomi carried in the birthday cake for Magdalene, who celebrated thirty-four years on Monday. Alexander requested a lemon cake for her and appeared pleased to see her satisfied as he led the group in singing "For She's a Jolly Good Fellow." He kissed her hand and told her "Happy Birthday" before handing her the first slice of cake.

After supper, Maxwell stopped in to greet everyone before taking his mother home, and Alexander teased him about becoming a grandfather in a few months. Then Phoebe and Kade led the others in a lightning bug catch in the camellia garden, and the women settled in the morning room while the three men stepped onto the patio for a smoke. Having sent Sharon home after the dining room was cleared, Naomi enjoyed the entertainment through the kitchen windows as she washed dishes.

The men congratulated Henry over Darla expecting their second child.

"Lucy had room to grow, but Darla's always been well-endowed. What shall you do with more of a bosom than you already have to handle?"

Henry laughed. "You're supposed to be the expert, Alex. Use your imagination."

"I'm an expert because I ask questions. But if you don't wish to share your techniques with me, I understand."

"Darla would kill me!"

"She uses fear? What do you counter with? Dominance? Subservient romance?"

The priest slapped him on the back of the head, and they all laughed like drunken fools though there were no spirits to be found in the house. Too soon, they put out their cigarettes and headed for the den.

"I want at least one more Turkey Trot with Darla before she retires her dancing shoes," Alexander said as they disappeared into the house.

***

Saturday morning, Naomi woke to knocking on her apartment door. Fearing something wrong with Lucy, she pulled her summer housecoat over her sleeveless cotton gown and rushed from her bedroom without buttoning it closed.

Expecting an anxious Alexander, she came face-to-face with smiling Paul.

"Morning, Honey. I brought breakfast, fresh from the bakery."

He held out a box, but her hands went to her nightcap. "Paul, that's awfully sweet, but I'm in no state to host you."

"It's one of your few mornings off, and I don't want to miss spending it with you. I could brew the coffee while you dress."

She laughed and brought the edges of her housecoat closed as she stepped to the side. "Come in. I'll just be a few minutes."

Before getting to her room, Paul set the food on the table and hugged her. "Not so fast, Naomi. Won't you give me a chance to enjoy waking you?"

The warmth of his touch dropped her inhibitions as his full lips pressed on with fervor. Lowered to the settee, he tugged the floral housecoat off and kissed her bare shoulders before settling at the base of her throat.

Naomi snuggled in his lap, arms about his neck as he caressed over the thin nightgown. "You make me feel beautiful."

"You are beautiful." He held her gaze a moment, and she kissed his square jaw as he pulled her against him. "Now, you better get dressed before I get us in trouble."

She changed into her lavender work dress and tied a fresh head wrap around her hair to keep the sweat out of her eyes that July day. Then Naomi joined Paul in the front room. He'd set the little table, and a minute later, he carried in the coffee and poured for them.

"You get first choice of the pastries," he said as he held the box before her.

She lifted the lid and stared at the arrangement of Danishes. On top of one lay a white corsage with a golden ring.

Paul went to his knee beside her chair and kissed her hand. "Will you allow me to wake you each morning and kiss your sweet face as the sun rises?"

Naomi could neither speak nor move.

Seeing her overwhelmed, Paul continued. "We don't have to rush the wedding. But if you need time to consider—"

"I'd be pleased to have you for my husband, Paul. I hope you'll be satisfied with me."

"You'll give me everything I need and more, Honey." He pinned the miniature rose bouquet by her collar and slipped the ring onto her finger. "I love you."

She'd heard the words for weeks, but they still felt as fresh as they had the first time. "I love you too."

By the time they finished kissing, they had to warm the coffee.

"Do you want to wait or have the ceremony soon?" he asked as they returned to the table.

"I'd like a bit of time to prepare and allow the weather to cool. October is a fine month. Is that all right?"

"Anything you want. You've already made me a happy man." He kissed her hand after he set his cup on the table. "I could bring you to my house for a few minutes after we eat so you can see what you're signing up for. I'm no great housekeeper, but my girls pitch in once a month to see that it's taken care of properly."

"I don't mind about that, Paul."

"You must be interested in the house itself then. Three bedrooms, a full bath, big kitchen, and front and back porches."

"It sounds lovely." She took a bite of pastry and fingered the ring. "Would you expect me to stop working?"

"I can support us, no trouble."

"I know you can, Paul."

His hand took one of hers, enveloping it in its warmth. "Part of the thrill of being married is coming home to a kind face at the end of the day. I won't dictate because I know how you feel about the Mellings, but I want you to know where I stand on the subject."

Naomi nodded and closed her eyes. She tried to imagine life without putting supper on the table for Lucy and her family, without Bethany wishing to learn to sew, and without Phoenix Asher getting into everything. No longer watching over Lucy for agitated moods or soothing Phoebe from a tantrum.

What would they do without me? What would I do without them?

"Three months would be ample time for them to find someone, but I'm not sure if I'd want to give them up completely."

"You'll decide what's best. Now let's eat so you can see my house before you have to work."

Paul's home was finer than anything she ever imagined living in—let alone being the woman of the manor over. He proudly showed off the improvements he'd made on the craftsman row house, including the fully enclosed back porch with a three-person swing and several rocking chairs, just like the cozy front porch. The furnishings were simple but well-kept, and the details had a decidedly feminine touch. He didn't often speak of his deceased wife, but Naomi knew Willa was a major part of his life. The day she moved in, she wanted fresh bedding to adorn their bedroom and planned to sew a new quilt.

Naomi returned to the Mellings' house before Alexander arrived from his time at the stables with the girls. Darla and Horatio were with Lucy and Asher since Henry accompanied the riders that day. She was elbow-deep in coating chicken to fry when Asher ran in.

"Hide me, Miss Naomi! Poppy's almost here, and I broke Momma's vase!"

She wiped an itchy spot on her cheek with her sleeve and gestured to the pantry. He was safely inside before his father came in the back door. Alexander and Henry greeted her and continued through the house.

A few minutes later, Alexander returned. "I'm looking for a wayward boy, Naomi. Have you seen one?"

"I don't have time for scoundrels, big or small."

He went to the pantry and pulled Asher out by his collar. "Did you break Momma's vase?"

"Yes, Poppy." Asher's blue eyes were huge.

"Did you do it on purpose?"

"No, Poppy," his voice quivered.

"Were you doing something you weren't supposed to?" Alexander's tone was forcibly hard as he removed his belt.

"Horatio and I were playing ball in the front room."

"Did you tell Momma right away?"

"Yes, Poppy."

"Did you take responsibility?" Alexander towered over his son.

"Yes, Poppy. Horatio's only three and a half. He doesn't know better."

"Did you help clean up the mess and say you were sorry?"

"I did, Poppy. And I won't play ball in the house ever again!"

Alexander went on his knees before him so they were eye-level, and with his gravest voice he probably used in the courtroom, he said, "You know what this means, Phoenix Asher Melling?"

The boy shook his head.

"It means you're a man!" Alexander dropped the belt and hugged him. "You didn't lie, and you didn't blame others. You were honest, took responsibility, and worked to repair the damages you caused. It took me decades to learn those things. I'm proud of you, my son. You'll never be in trouble with me if you tell the truth. Honesty is everything when it comes to character. Always remember trust is more powerful than fear."

Alexander kissed both his cheeks and ruffled his hair. "I love you, Ash."

"I love you too, Poppy. May I go play with Horatio now?"

"Go on."

Asher scampered out, and Naomi smiled at Alexander. "You're doing a fine job, Mr. Alex."

"I think he's already forgotten any lesson I might have possibly taught." He pulled himself up and tossed the leather belt over his shoulder.

"That boy will remember this moment for years to come."

Lucy came in and clung to her husband. "I wondered what kept you."

Naomi washed her hands and turned to the Mellings. "He had a glorious father-son time."

"Naomi, what a pretty corsage. Did you have a date with Paul this morning?" Lucy stepped forward for a closer look.

"You might say that."

Lucy snatched her left hand and clutched it to her chest. "Naomi, I'm so happy for you!"

Then tears fell from Lucy's eyes, and she ran to the hall.

Alexander came for a hug. "He'll treat you well, but when will we lose you?"

"You'll never lose me completely, but we're speaking of October. I can work and train someone until then, and after, I'd be happy to come during the weekdays to help."

"Bless you, Naomi." He hugged her. "You deserve all the happiness in the world."

Twenty

Melissa tolerated two weeks of Alex and Maggie flirting when he picked up the three children for riding. On a Wednesday afternoon at the end of July, Melissa went inside her house to see what the delay was, leaving all the children in the yard with Clara Jane.

Alex had Maggie before the parlor mirror, artfully arranging her loose hair about her shoulders.

"You've got three children in your automobile who are dying to get to the stables in this heat." Melissa folded her arms and narrowed her stare. "Get yourself out there, Mr. Tight Pants."

Alex kissed Maggie's cheek and turned to Melissa. "Are you jealous?" He swaggered to Melissa. "You haven't the length of hair to stroke, but I would dance with you. Share my rhythm with you, darling Sissa."

Melissa laughed and pushed him toward the door. "Maybe Friday night, dashing Poppy."

"He does behave himself Friday evenings," Maggie remarked as she twisted her hair to get it off her neck before stepping onto the porch.

Melissa sighed as she watched Alex drive away with Phoebe, Bethany, and Kade. "Yes, and we can thank Lucy's moods for that. Possibly the one good thing to come out of her issues."

"He's not so bad when he's here either."

"You two are shameless!"

Maggie blushed. "We have more decorum than we did at Seacliff."

"That's something to be proud of."

"It is when you're us."

They both laughed, and then Maggie's eyes followed Tabitha encouraging Louisa and Simon toward Clara Jane, who headed for the shade of the gazebo. Tabitha—a year older than Bethany—was a huge help with the younger children. Even though she wasn't quite eight, she had the patience Phoebe lacked and more awareness than Bethany. An old soul, Grandmother Stone would have called her.

"Some days, I ache for Douglas's touch," Maggie whispered. "Alex means well, but it makes it worse because I can picture Douglas urging me along to make Alex jealous."

Melissa put an arm around her shoulders and led her toward the swing. "I know the feeling. I can go days without pain and then find myself sobbing like Freddy leaving happened all over again. Strong, independent Melissa used to travel the globe alone, but now I'm a love-starved stepmother."

"We have enough love," Maggie said as she sat on the swing.

"From all the wrong people." Melissa fingered her rings. "If we could bottle Alex's carnal appetites, perverse humor, and sultry ways, we'd be millionaires. We could call it 'Essence of Alex' and guarantee the purchaser gyrating movements, naughty jokes, and at least one swooning woman an hour."

"Two if he wears a tuxedo and three if sporting riding clothes." Maggie's laugh turned into a groan. "Sometimes he's cruel. He knows I'm attracted to him, and yet he continues to flaunt himself."

"That's Alex for you."

"And when he calls me 'Magdalene,' it's even worse. One of these days, when he leans over me, I should kiss those playful lips and see what he does."

"And what would Lucy and Douglas do?"

"Douglas would blame Alex. But I'd never do it in front of Lucy or the children."

"I'm glad you have your limits."

Maggie opened the folding fan she wore on a bracelet. "Thank you for inviting me here. It's good to be away from the island, and the children enjoy the company. They get along splendidly, and Kade has the opportunity to ride. I loved horses as a child."

"The visit has been great for us as well."

"Melissa, I'm here if you ever want to talk about anything. I survived Seacliff Cottage. There isn't much that would shock me."

She shook her head. "Not now, but thank you."

The friends were still on the swing and the younger children in the yard when Alex returned. Phoebe and Kade ran hand-in-hand toward the sounds of games behind the house, and Alex brought Bethany to the porch piggyback.

"This one isn't tired of riding yet, but I need to be put out to pasture."

Bethany slid off his back, brown waves that had come undone from her ribbons falling about her shoulders. "Thank you, Poppy."

"It's my pleasure, Knight Bethany."

She kissed his cheek and then Melissa's. "I'm going to wash up and sew in the kitchen while Miss Sharon finishes supper."

Alex plopped between the women on the swing as soon as Bethany went inside.

"It's too hot." Melissa nudged him, but he ignored her. Seeing the mischievous glint in Maggie's eyes, she moved to the railing to be out of their way.

Alex shifted sideways to face Maggie. "Is it too hot for you?"

"Much too hot. If I were on the island, I'd be in the water."

"There's a sight I'd like to see." He touched her cheek, trailing his fingers to her ear. "How about we all spend the weekend at Seacliff Manor? Melissa has agreed to come with us while Freddy's gone. You can come too."

"Melissa doesn't have a shared history of the location like we do."

"Magdalene, my sweet." He went to his knees on the swing, precariously balanced as he took her hands. "Come with the children and play in the bay. Lucy will be there, Melissa too if she'd like. All of us. My big, happy family."

"Your harem?" Maggie gave him a devious smile. "Eliza's attic would have been perfect for that."

"You in nothing but a purple sheet." Alex fell back with a moan of frustration. "The images you invoke, you vixen! I'd never wanted you more than when I returned the end of that summer."

"Enough of memory lane. That was more than ten years ago."

"Then come make new memories. Allow your island children time in the water once more. If you're fearful of me, Claudio could join us."

"That would be even worse." Maggie put her arms around herself as though chilled.

Alex leaned closer. "Do you remember how I warmed you, Magdalene?"

She closed her eyes, a single tear rolling down her cheek. "Yes, and that's the problem."

Immediately his arms were around her. "I went too far. Forgive me."

"Don't ask me to go there without my husband."

"I won't." He embraced her fully. "I'm sorry, Magdalene."

With a fluid movement, Maggie lifted her face to Alex. Rather than mischief, her brown eyes showcased a level of desperation that hurt Melissa to see because she was sure that look found her own face several times in the past months.

"Don't ask it of me, Alexander. Don't ask it because I'm not strong enough on my own." Then her hands were about his neck, her lips on his.

Several seconds later, Maggie pulled away. For an awkward moment, the two stared at each other. Then she bolted inside and ran up the stairs.

Alex covered his face with his hands. "My God, what did I do?"

"Though I don't claim to be a deity," Melissa said, "I'd say you finally discovered constant flirting leads to heartache."

The dining room curtain moved without a breeze. Staring through the screen into the dimness, Melissa saw Bethany's silent form clutching a blanket.

Leaving Alex on the swing, she went inside. "Did you want to show someone your sewing, Beth?"

She took a hesitant step toward Melissa. "Yes, but Poppy looks sad. Miss Maggie did too. Is that why they kissed, to try to feel better?"

Melissa hugged her. "Yes, but showing Poppy your doll blanket will help him be happy."

"Should I kiss him too, Sissa?"

"Only if you want to."

They walked onto the porch holding hands. Alex was still slumped forward on the swing.

Bethany released Melissa's hand and approached him. "Poppy, would you like to see how good I'm doing with my blanket for Baby?"

He rubbed his eyes before looking up. "Yes, Bethany Iris, I'd love to." His voice caught, but he managed to give her a smile as he held open his arms.

Bethany snuggled in and showed him where she sewed around the edges to connect the front and back panels and her practice stitches around the flowers on the fabric to bind the pieces together as she learned to keep a steady hand.

"It's wonderful," he told her with his winning smile. "Momma's going to be proud when she sees it."

"When will I see Momma again?"

Alex covered her ears and looked to Melissa. "Could I bring the girls to—"

"Yes."

The dimpled grin that charmed him out of trouble flashed as he lowered his hands from Bethany's ears. "We're going on a family trip this weekend. You, Phoebe, Asher, Momma, and me. We'll leave Friday afternoon on the ferry for Seacliff Manor. Be sure Sissa packs everything you girls need."

"I heard you invite Miss Maggie. Is Tabby coming too?"

His smile faltered. "No, just Momma's family for now. Sissa needs to stay here with the Campbells."

Bethany kissed the discolored spot on his jaw. "Please don't be sad Miss Maggie isn't coming. I know Momma loves you. Phoebe and Asher and I do too."

She dashed into the house.

Alex looked to Melissa, blue eyes swimming with remorse.

"She was in the dining room window."

He covered his face, and Melissa laid a hand on his shoulder. "Beth doesn't blurt things out like Phoebe. Don't mention it to her, and she'll think nothing of it. She asked me if you kissed each other to feel better because you were both sad. Don't complicate it."

"I didn't mean to hurt Magdalene."

"I know you didn't, and she knows you didn't, but you need to stop tempting each other. I understand the pain and loneliness she's going through and you offering physical comfort is overwhelming."

"Tell her I'm sorry."

"I will, but go home, Alex. Telephone to tell me what time to have the girls at the dock Friday, but stay away from Maggie."

He nodded and trudged to his automobile.

***

The Mellings decided to stay across the bay more than a week, not to return until the following Sunday. Feeling guilty for the respite from her stepdaughters and two Friday suppers, Melissa planned to host the Adamses and Claudio the second Friday night. All week, she and Maggie planned the evening from food to music. She had Sharon study pasta making, even accompanying her to an Italian restaurant to get pointers on creating the best spaghetti sauce.

Thursday night, Melissa and Maggie settled in the parlor with a bottle of Scotch after the children were in bed. Melissa poured them each a snifter, and Maggie held it under her nose.

"Alex stopped sending it when the state outlawed liquor, but Douglas always made the bottle last for months." She took a sip and sighed. "It tastes like him."

"We'll have wine tomorrow, but we have to wait until the children are upstairs with Clara Jane. We can serve it with a cheese tray after dancing. What do you think?"

"I think I want a Scotch-laced kiss." Maggie drained the glass and leaned back.

"Unless you expect a miracle—"

Tapping on the window broke Melissa's words. Pulling back the drape, she laughed.

"What?" Maggie reached for the bottle.

"A miracle has arrived."

Melissa opened the door for Claudio.

He stepped into the unlit hall, a hand going for her arm. "I felt you were in need of my assistance, *Eroina.*"

After kissing both cheeks, he hesitated before her mouth. It had been weeks since they last kissed and a month since she kissed Freddy goodbye. Melissa was ravenous, and knowing Maggie needed his friendship that night, she wanted a piece of Claudio before his attentions were turned. She took his hand and stepped into the darkened dining room.

He massaged her back as they kissed, and she clutched around his waist, locking their bodies together as they deepened their connection.

"It has been so long, *Eroina.*" He kissed her neck. "I could not wait until tomorrow when the house will be full. How are you?"

"Well enough. His letters are still regular, though they'll be slower in coming now that he's in England. Alex and Lucy at Seacliff with the children this week has been a bit of a relief, but it's Maggie who needs you tonight. She's had no letters from Douglas for two weeks. Come see her."

"Anything for you, *Eroina.*"

The sincerity in his voice was eclipsed only by the passion in his kiss. Warmth spread through her body as yearnings to cleave to him drove her further against him. After a frenzied minute, he stepped back.

"That will have to hold you for now, my passionate one." With his arm linked through hers, Claudio led them to the parlor.

Maggie finished draining her glass for at least the second time. When she saw the priest, she laid the length of the sofa. "Bless me, Father, for I have sinned. I kissed Alexander last Wednesday."

"*Posseduta*, have you not remembered the lessons of the past?" Claudio knelt beside her and took her hands. "Now is not the time for you and Alexander."

Melissa returned the Scotch to the study to prevent her friend from drinking more. Claudio prayed over Maggie, his Italian words filling the room with love and peace.

Several seconds of silence followed, then Maggie touched his face. "You still have exquisite lines, Deacon De Fiore."

"And you had too much to drink, *Posseduta*," he countered.

"It's better to taste it from the tongue of another than to drink it. I might be dreaming, but I smell it on your breath."

He returned her smile. "Perhaps you are dreaming."

Maggie shifted suggestively. "Kiss me so I may know."

"I think it would be better for you to go to bed." He released her hand and straightened.

"You wish to see me in bed, Priest?" Her laughter burbled.

"And now Melissa knows your secret, that you are a fine lady except when drunk or possessed. Then you are a brazen seductress with humor as disturbing as Alexander's."

"He still wants me. He kissed me back, and his lips were the same—hot and tangy." Her hands roamed down her torso.

"You need to rest, *Posseduta*." He kissed her forehead and moved toward the door. "Sleep here—it would be safer than navigating the stairs."

"Is she drunk or possessed?" Melissa asked.

"Possessed by drunkenness." Claudio winked at Melissa and nodded to the door.

Outside, he took her hand and brought her into the shadows of the porte-cochere between the house and automobile. They clung to each other as their lips roamed.

"Will you need me on Sunday?" he whispered.

August fifth—Freddy's birthday. She rested her cheek on Claudio's shoulder. "Do you pray for his safety?"

"*Sí*, because it is your happiness I am concerned with. I wish to ease your pain, see a smile on this beautiful face." He lifted her chin and kissed her lightly on the lips.

"Maggie returns to the island next Friday, and the girls will stay with Lucy for the month after their riding lessons Saturday."

"I will come to you that night if you wish it."

"Please do," Melissa whispered.

Twenty-One

Naomi awoke with the dawn on the first Saturday of August. Feeling disoriented and hot, she opened her eyes to her front room. Paul sat with her, his breath rising rhythmically beneath her cheek. He'd come over for supper, and they spent hours talking. The last thing she remembered was cozying beside him around ten o'clock. Relief that the Mellings were across the bay and wouldn't see Paul's truck parked overnight helped her relax.

Paul's shirt was damp from their shared body heat, and his eyes half-closed. Naomi had never seen him look more handsome.

"Morning, Honey."

"I can't believe I—I'm sorry. You probably want to get home." Naomi stood.

Paul followed her upright, and his arms went around her. "In two months, we'll be waking in bed together."

The image he evoked proved overwhelming, and she wasted no time pressing her lips to his. As though sensing Naomi's plan to bring them back to the settee, Paul held her at arm's length and smiled. "I remember you said you had a lot of work to do today. May I run to the bakery to get breakfast before you get started?"

She nodded, disappointment touching at the corners of her mouth.

"You're much too pretty to spend time pouting." Paul kissed her.

Naomi responded by opening the buttons on his shirt—a task Alexander and Lucy made look easy but proved difficult to execute with unpracticed hands. It took half a minute to realize Paul was unmoving beneath her attentions as she felt her way down his broad chest. She turned her blind side to him before resting her cheek on his skin. His scent caused further stirrings.

"Are you ready for more?" His deep voice caressed as though he willed her to request the next level of intimacy.

In response, she kissed down his torso, glorying in his tightening muscles. When she reached his belly button, he hauled her upright, his penetrating gaze further heating her core.

"Why don't you take the day and think about things. I'll pick you up for supper, and then we can see if what you want right now still holds true."

"I'm not a child," she whispered.

"You're naïve—almost as naïve as Willa was when things got heated between us."

"That's not a fair comparison. You were married at sixteen. I'm twice that, Paul."

"But still a woman who's untouched by the world."

"You may be my first beau, but that doesn't mean I don't know what I want."

His smile brought hardness to her face. "You may know, but I want to make sure you understand. Willa was my first. Though we didn't wait for marriage, I was true to our relationship her whole life."

"You didn't wait?"

Paul shook his head. "Her daddy caught us in the barn, and we were married the next week. We would have married eventually, but it forced me to grow up quicker."

"And after she passed?" Naomi crossed her arms. "I caught how you phrased that. I'm not as naïve as you think."

"Perhaps you aren't, but I don't want you jumping in without thinking through everything." He cupped her cheek in his big hand before kissing her. "I made a few mistakes that first year without Willa. I'd been with her twenty-four years, gave her my youth and prime. I was bitter and angry with God for taking her from me and spent a couple of weekends in the country with a cousin who had a friend who made moonshine. They had a private gambling club with women who kept you company for a price."

Hearing the rawness in his rumbling voice moved Naomi to embrace him.

"Mattie and Jessa found out and railed on me, setting me to rights." His lips lowered to her ear. "I ain't never been back or been with anyone else since that time of pain. You're the only other woman I've loved, and I promise I'll be true to you my whole life. I'm blessed to have found true love twice and won't look further."

She allowed him to hold her a minute before pulling away. "I need to get to work, as you said. If I finish readying the house, I'll be free tomorrow."

"I'll get you some breakfast."

"Don't worry about that. I'll just have some coffee and toast." She kissed him. "What time will you get me for supper?"

"Six-thirty."

She nodded. "I'll be ready."

***

Naomi saw to the heavy cleaning in the mansion earlier in the week, so only a light sprucing was needed. As she dusted, her mind raced between Paul's stumbling after his wife died to thoughts she might not be ready for him physically. But she decided that she wanted her first time to be in her own space, where she'd be more comfortable and could see to tidying up afterward—for she knew from her years of housekeeping for the Mellings' that things could get messy.

She cleaned until noon, then planned the next week's menu and called in the Monday grocery order while she ate a sandwich in the kitchen. Alexander had told her he'd seek a new cook when they returned from across the bay. As much as she looked forward to life with Paul, she didn't look forward to sharing the Mellings. But with her marrying, there was nothing she could do to stop a stranger from joining them.

Returning to her apartment, she stripped to her underclothes in the afternoon heat, fixed a glass of sweet tea from the pitcher in her icebox, and settled at the sewing machine in her bedroom with an electric fan pointed her way. She'd made great strides on the quilt for her wedding bed with all her quiet time that week. The yellow, orange, and blue floral prints weren't too feminine, and the colors were good for their autumn nuptials. Naomi smiled to see her handiwork being used to plan for her own life. Over the last few years, she hadn't lifted a needle except to patch the children's clothes or sew ripped seams on the Mellings' things torn during their zealousness. The memory of fumbling over Paul's buttons made her think it might be easier to rip things off, and she found comfort in knowing she could fix the damage if clothing casualties were in her future.

Once the completed squares were sewn together, Naomi set her alarm clock for five and lay on her bed to nap. When she woke, she showered and arranged her hair with two silver combs Lucy gifted her last Christmas. She waited until after six to pull on a lightweight sheath—a hand-me-down from Lucy. The pale blue showcased her bronze skin, and the sleeveless cut accentuated her toned arms, compliments of her domestic work. Seeing her reflection in the mirror, she appreciated the finery but realized she hadn't proper shoes for the ensemble.

Knowing Lucy would insist on lending her something, she took the house key and her wrist bag and dashed barefoot through the yard. Naomi picked a pair of silver shoes from the master bedroom closet and hurried back. As she reached the gate, Paul parked his truck in the driveway.

He smiled as he lifted the fedora off his head and bowed. "Will such a fine lady agree to accompany me this evening?"

Naomi curtsied. "I'd be honored."

They ate under the bright moon on the patio of a restaurant on his side of town, laughing and talking in the heat of the night. Paul's hat and suit jacket were long since removed, and his white sleeves rolled above his elbows when the live ragtime music began. She pulled him to the dancefloor. Letting herself completely loose, Naomi danced like she never had before. Sensual, gyrating movements when the songs allowed them—quick footwork and flirty when that was the better match.

Half an hour later, Paul brought her back to their table with fresh drinks and sat beside her. Glistening with sweat and chest heaving from the excursion, Naomi could do nothing but smile.

"You're a great dancer, Honey. Do you want to keep at it or go somewhere else?"

She kissed him, lips hot and salty. "Let's go to my place."

When Paul parked in front of the garage, he turned to Naomi. Her heart pounded at the sight of him. In her apartment, she set her bag on the side table and slipped Lucy's shoes off while he hung his hat on the doorknob. They stood staring at each other for a silent moment, and then Naomi began moving her hips to the rhythm of the music they'd enjoyed. Paul kicked off his shoes and came at her with a dance that didn't stop when he pressed against her.

Their swaying contact heightened in fervor. The heat was intense, so when Naomi led him to the bedroom, she turned the electric fan on high. To allow herself more movement, she pulled the dress over her head, displaying her best underdrawers and camisole set. She returned to dancing without waiting for comment.

Paul indulged her for several minutes. Then his hands grasped her slim middle. When he lifted her, Naomi linked her ankles around his waist and wrapped her arms about his neck. They kept the pulse of the music with their kissing. The tingling sensations she'd first experienced two months ago returned as Paul's mouth teased across her collarbone.

"I love you, and I love the way you make me feel." Her breathy words momentarily cut through the humming of the fan.

"You haven't felt anything yet." He tugged the straps off her shoulders, kissing across the open expanse. "Are you ready for me?"

"Yes." Naomi clung to him. "Make love to me, Paul."

***

Not until the sky began to lighten did Naomi release her hold on him.

"Are you finally satisfied?"

"For now." Her fingers trailed over his bare middle.

Paul laughed. "I always knew you had a mind for what you want. I just didn't expect you'd want so much."

"Can you blame me with a lover like you?"

"Flattery is good." He shifted closer. "And you're a firecracker, Honey. Thank you for sharing yourself with this old man."

"Get some sleep, Paul." She kissed his cheek and snuggled beside him despite the heat.

Later, she awoke to his caressing but kept her eyes closed, enjoying the sensations. Only when she could no longer deny a response did she open them. Quarter past eleven.

"Morning, Honey. How do you like being woken up like this?"

"Sign me up for it daily."

Pleased that there was no self-consciousness between them, they shared more before showering. Naomi happily went about in fresh underclothes in an attempt to ward off the August heat while they cooked brunch.

"It's Frederick's thirty-fifth birthday," she remarked as they ate omelets. "I hope Melissa is holding up all right."

"I'm sure she'll cope well, especially with her family and friends around. But what of Naomi Joyner? How do you think she'll handle everything she experienced this weekend?"

"I hear Mr. Rollins knows how to treat a woman. I'm sure she'll be happy as a lark after the wedding."

He smiled over his coffee cup. "And Mr. Rollins considers himself the luckiest man alive. He looks forward to sharing a bed with Naomi once again."

The moment their eyes met, she knew that the next time she wanted to give herself to him would be their wedding night.

"What is it, Honey?"

Touched he'd read her signals, she leaned over to kiss him. "Wondering how I'll do with you is one less concern I'll have as I prepare for the wedding, but I don't want it to lose its specialness."

"You want to wait until then before we—"

"You aren't mad, are you?"

He laughed. "It might take until the wedding for my body to recuperate. You wore me out, woman."

"We can do other things, should the opportunities arise." She smiled.

They talked, touched, and laughed long after they finished eating. At three o'clock, Naomi pulled on a cotton sundress, and they went to air the Mellings' house. Starting on the top floor, they opened the windows and turned on the ceiling fans. When they were in the dining room, the telephone rang.

Naomi answered the extension on Alexander's desk. "Mellings' residence."

"Now, there's a voice that does my heart good."

"Good afternoon, Mr. Alex. I stopped in a few minutes ago to air the house."

"Thank you. We'll be on the evening ferry and have a hired automobile ready. Rosemary insists on cooking us supper today, so we'll be fed before we get home. The girls are staying the night, and then I'll bring them to Melissa on my way to work in the morning. They're staying there for the week to have the Campbells' final days in town with them."

"I'm sure a little quiet will be good for Lucy after your vacation. How is she?"

"She's been golden." The smile was audible in his voice. "She's her old self. Carefree, daydreaming, and loving. We've had some magical moments."

"I don't need the details, Mr. Alex."

He laughed. "It's been good for everyone, unless, of course, you've been heartbroken without us."

"I've managed fine."

"Remember Mrs. Easton is coming Tuesday to stay through the month."

"I already planned the week's menu with her in mind."

"What are we going to do without you, Naomi?"

Twenty-Two

Monday morning, Melissa sat on the porch swing with a cup of coffee as she read over her article in the newspaper. It discussed women banding together in friendship when their husbands were gone. Though she didn't mention Maggie by name, that's who she based the story on. She set the extra newspaper aside to later cut out her column and send it with the next letter to Freddy. Then she braced herself for her stepdaughters' return. She'd missed them, but with a house full of Campbells, the time passed quickly. Alex's automobile pulled into the driveway, and Phoebe hopped out.

"Hi, Sissa!" she hollered before throwing open the screen door. "Kade, I'm home!"

Bethany carried her doll and tiger, while Alex followed behind her with two small suitcases. Her tanned face shone, and her dark hair was lightened a bit from her time at the bay.

"Welcome home, Beth."

She ran over for a hug and kiss. "I missed you, Sissa. I missed you and Louisa. Daddy too."

"We missed you here as well, and Daddy sent you a letter. It's on your bed."

"Excuse me." She ran inside with her toys.

Alex set the suitcases down. "Did you miss me as well, darling Sissa?"

Melissa smiled, pleased to see him joyful. "I missed two Fridays of dancing with you, but you appear no worse for my neglect."

He waltzed over, set her cup on the railing, and pulled her upright.

"Lucy took excellent care of me." Alex started them on a tango. "Twice a day and more, we made sweet love. One night, we even snuck to the beach. I'm sure the cypress trees never stood guard over such passion."

"I don't know about that. Freddy and I might have retreated there several times over the years."

"Naughty Sissa." He kissed her cheek. "Lucy was much better at Seacliff."

"Because she shared you with no other women."

His smile faltered. "She refused to get out of bed before I left this morning. She can deal with you but no longer with Magdalene."

Alex spun Melissa back to the swing, kissed her forehead, and looked to the door.

"Go say hello if you wish."

He shook his head. "No, but I'd like to tell her and the children goodbye Wednesday."

"I'll let her know, dashing Poppy."

"I love you, darling Sissa. I'll see you Wednesday afternoon as well." He jumped off the porch and returned to his automobile.

While Melissa finished her coffee, Maggie joined her.

"He wishes to say goodbye when he brings the children riding Wednesday."

Maggie looked sheepish. "I listened at the parlor window. It's wonderful he and Lucy had a lovely time. But all good things come to an end."

"You still have four days, Maggie. Let's make the most of it."

"Drinks every night?"

"Not after your display last week."

"I had one glasses of wine Friday night along with everyone else."

"I'm referring to Thursday night with the Scotch and Claudio."

"I don't remember what I did, but I had a headache when I woke on the sofa. Keep me away from Scotch."

"And Claudio. Don't you remember?" Melissa's incredulousness flared. "You propositioned a priest!"

"When drunk or possessed, I wish to do more with my handsome friend." Maggie blushed. "But don't judge me too harshly. I've seen the way you two look at each other, and there's nothing holy in his gaze."

They stared at each other, Melissa feeling Maggie's dare to speak the truth. Bethany and Tabitha came out, each with a doll.

"May we play in the gazebo, Sissa?"

"Yes, but where are Louisa and Simon?"

"Playing in Louisa's room with Clara Jane."

The girls ran for the back, and Melissa stood. "I'm going to check on Phoebe. I've only had two words from her this morning."

"She and Kade were in the study a few minutes ago."

Instinct had Melissa enter the house quietly and make her way to the corner room.

"I had a fabulous time with Poppy, Momma, and my *real* sister and brother."

"I had Tabby, Simon, and Louisa, but they don't play like you."

"I do make the best games."

Melissa shuddered at the Lucy-ness of Phoebe's tone. Too often had she been on the receiving end of that attitude.

"I wish we could stay another month." Kade's earnest voice was the sweetest thing.

"And then you'd be here for my party. Poppy throws the best parties. Miss Naomi is splendid with cakes, and Momma wears the prettiest dresses. They're from Paris. I'll dress as pretty as Momma when I get older."

"That doesn't matter to me."

The sound of a pencil being batted across the table followed by giggles filled the air.

"Mama says I'm the man of the house while Papa's gone," Kade said.

"Poppy's the man of the house still. He's too old to join the war."

"But Papa's older than him."

"He loves my momma too much to leave her."

"My papa loves my mama too! I bet your poppy's too scared to go. He's not as strong as Papa or Mr. Frederick. The Germans would squish him."

"They wouldn't be able to catch him!" Phoebe screeched. "He'd ride his militia horse past all the bullets and—"

"He's been hit by bullets before."

"Not on Apollo he hasn't! He's the fastest at the riding club. Just because he doesn't punch people for fun doesn't mean he isn't strong!"

"He's a big sissy."

"You better take back what you said, or you'll never go riding with us again, Kade Campbell!"

The charged silence between the friends was as disturbing as their argument. Then a fist hit the table.

"I'll give you one more minute, Kade Gabriel Campbell!"

"Your poppy is fast on a horse…for an old man."

"Go rot on that island with freckle-face Abe Walker for all I care! I'm not speaking to you ever again!"

The rest of the day, Phoebe ignored Kade.

At the supper table, Bethany filled the others in on their adventures across the bay, including a wayward sea turtle that washed ashore. "Asher wanted to feed the turtle, but Momma made him stay away from its mouth."

"How big was it, Tiger?" Kade asked.

"It was this big," Bethany said as she spread her hands more than a foot apart.

"Poppy scooped it up by the sides of its shell," Phoebe interrupted. "He carried it safely back to the water and then returned to Momma with a fantastic story idea about a giant sea turtle. Two lovers climbed on its shell, and it swam them to a magical island where they lived happily ever after."

"That's no type of story I'd want to hear," grumbled Kade. "Maybe if the turtle brought them to an island under attack and the man led the inhabitants to victory against—"

"Maybe the *lady* was a knight, and she trained the islanders." Phoebe huffed. "After the turtle was back in the bay, Rosemary and

Priscilla came to the beach for the afternoon, and Poppy carried Momma all the way up the cliff path."

"Why'd he do that?"

Phoebe's chin went up. "Because he's strong and brave."

"And he brought her back down? Was he showing off for the turtle or something?"

"Kade Campbell, you're the most ridiculous boy I know!"

"You shut your mouth, Phoebe Davenport." Tabitha crossed her arms. "That's my brother. Only I talk to him like that!"

"I'd rather be called Phoebe *Melling*." Her pert nose went higher as she glared down the table at Tabitha. "And besides, Poppy didn't bring Momma back at all. She must have been tired because he returned an hour later without her. He probably had to get her ready for a nap. Poppy says Momma is a connoisseur of all things bedroom and takes her naptime seriously. We're not to disturb them."

Melissa covered her mouth with a napkin, Clara Jane turned redder than her hair, and Maggie excused herself—but could be heard laughing in the hall.

After supper, Maggie insisted on helping Sharon with the dishes, saying she needed to get back into the routine of domestic duties. Melissa and Clara Jane settled on the glider swing under the magnolia while the Davenport and Campbell children chased fireflies in the dusk.

"My mother warned me about the Mellings before I agreed to come with Miss Maggie. They're even more forward than the Campbells with their love," Clara Jane remarked.

The sixteen-year-old helped her mother with midwifery as Darla was raised doing, and Melissa knew she had an understanding of life. "As embarrassing as it can be, it's also beautiful."

"I remember my father and Mr. Alex sitting on this swing one visit. I'd climbed the tree earlier in the afternoon with a book to get away from the little ones, and they came for a smoke, not knowing I was there."

Melissa gave an inward groan, knowing from experience that Joe Walker was one of the few that didn't stop Alex's stories. "Did you get an earful?"

"It made me the most knowledgeable twelve-year-old on the island." She turned crimson once more.

"You're wise beyond your years. Do you plan on working with your mother when you return?"

"Yes, but also helping Miss Maggie." Her voice lowered. "Our family's worried about her. That's why I came, but I've had fun."

Melissa took her hand. "I'm glad you're here, but I hope you aren't missing your family."

"Not too bad, and everyone stays busy at home. Emmett is training with my father this summer in hopes of captaining his own ship next year to fill the void Captain Douglas left in the fleet. Mary Louella is thirteen now and as big of a help around the house as me. She gets food on the table if our mother is called away. Only Abraham needs looking after, but in another few years, he'll be on the boat, and hopefully the wildness will tame out of him."

Melissa smiled at the thought of the youngest Walker, who was the same age as Phoebe and Kade. "These ten-year-olds think they're grown up, don't they?"

Clara Jane nodded. "I feel sorry for Kade, but he doesn't seem to mind Phoebe's controlling nature. They're a funny pair. I wouldn't be surprised if they end up together."

It would be like Freddy and Lucy all over again. Phoebe would destroy his sweet nature, and he'd happily allow it just to see her smile.

Twenty-Three

Anxious over Lucy's decline since the Mellings returned from Seacliff Manor, Naomi watched the family as they finished breakfast Wednesday morning.

"Are you sure, my queen?"

Lucy nodded and folded her hands on the table.

"Shall I call?" Alexander asked.

"I'll do it." She raised from her seat and crossed the kitchen.

Alexander took Asher's hand and smiled at his son as Lucy picked up the telephone.

"Good morning, Melissa." Lucy twisted the sash on her kimono as she listened, turning paler by the second. Naomi stepped closer in case Lucy went faint. "I wanted to invite you to bring Louisa and the Campbells over after Alex picks up the girls and Kade. It would give the others a chance to play with Asher and for all of us to say farewell."

She smiled. "And Mother's here for the month. She adores speaking with you. We'll have cookies and lemonade, nothing to spoil supper." And a few seconds later, she concluded with, "We'll see you after three. Goodbye."

As soon as she replaced the receiver, Alexander had her in his arms. Naomi retreated to the sink.

"Did you ever look over those papers in my den?" Alexander's voice sounded muffled through the veil of Lucy's hair.

"Take me now, Alex."

He lifted her into his arms and carried her down the hall. Naomi's body heated with the recollection of her time with Paul Saturday night. *It'll be difficult to tolerate their passion if it stirs my own each time.*

"You've got friends coming this afternoon, Asher," Naomi told him when he finished his cold cereal. "Be sure your room's tidy and check if your grandma's up—without waking her."

"Yes, Miss Naomi." He brought his bowl to the sink and ran for the stairs.

Naomi made the rounds to open the downstairs windows when the Mellings emerged from the den. Lucy's robe was untied, exposing her lacy nightgown. Her curling smile matched the spark in her green eyes above her rosy cheeks. They stopped at the front hall, Lucy's arms going about Alexander's neck and his hands caressing her waist as they tasted deeply of each other. Her body began to move against his in a stroking rhythm, to which he responded by grasping her buttocks.

"Take me again, Alex."

Naomi hurried into the dining room, still hearing their exchange as they fondled their way back to the den. Her own body smoldering with memories, she bit her lip as she tied back the drapes.

Lucy's piercing cry of ecstasy broke the morning quiet, followed by "My angel, oh Alex!" and another exclamation of delight.

Naomi took refuge in the kitchen. When Alexander came through on his way to work, he stopped and starred.

"You've been different since we returned from Seacliff. If I didn't know better, I'd say you respond to our lovemaking as if you understood it."

Naomi turned her blind side to him and remained quiet.

"Why Miss Naomi, I never would have thought! Do I need to challenge Paul for your honor?"

He took her hand, but she pushed him away. "I've told you to leave my business alone."

"But I'm at your service. Talk to Lucy if you have any questions. Does she know?"

Naomi shook her head.

"You better tell her before she guesses, or she'll be sad you didn't confide in her."

"With all she's going through—"

"The distraction would be welcomed." Alexander placed a brotherly hand on her shoulder.

Naomi nodded, and as his hand lifted off her shoulder, she turned to him, leaving a quick kiss on his cheek. "I love you both and will be Lucy's friend forever."

"We love you too. Paul's a lucky man," Alexander said in parting.

When Mrs. Easton came down, she asked to dine on the patio. "It sounds like Lucy's in the shower, so I'll bring Asher with me. He's gathering some toys."

"I'll have you ready in about ten minutes, Mrs. Easton."

"Alex told me a bit of Lucy's troubles after supper yesterday. Is she really that poorly?"

"It comes and goes, but she's had issues this summer. We're keeping a close eye on her."

"I'm sure Alex is doing a fine job staying close. I'm surprised they only have one child, the poor dears. But maybe it's better for Lucy this way."

Asher ran through the kitchen with his fire engine while Naomi poached two eggs and toasted bread for his grandmother. Naomi added a glass of orange juice for Asher on the tray before delivering it outside.

Not long after, Lucy came into the kitchen wearing a sensible skirt and blouse—her attempt to look respectable when Melissa and Maggie arrived that afternoon.

"That looks nice on you. The green top makes your eyes sparkle."

"That's more from Alex than the clothes. He was extraordinary this morning."

"So I heard."

"Was I loud?"

Naomi laughed. "It's a good thing I'd sent Asher upstairs, or someone would have to explain to him why paperwork requires such excitement over your angel of a man."

"He's perfection." Lucy grinned. "I'm going to his office midday to surprise him."

"But he leaves early on Wednesdays for the riding club."

"I already called his secretary, and his eleven o'clock hour is open. I'll take the streetcar and be there to fill the vacancy."

Naomi knew what drove Lucy—the need to see Alexander satisfied before he and Maggie said goodbye—but she wanted to protect her.

"Could I accompany you? There's something I need to shop for and would like your opinion."

"Of course. Mother would be fine with Asher for a few hours. What do you need?"

"Lingerie," Naomi whispered. "I only have two good sets, and Paul saw them both already. He stayed over with me Saturday night, and I'll want new things before the wedding."

"Oh!" Lucy hugged her. "Are you all right? Is it what you wanted? Was he gentle?"

"Yes, yes, and yes." Naomi laughed. "He had me wait all day after I told him to make sure I was ready. I kept him up all night, and then we slept away the morning in each other's arms. Now I know why you shine afterwards. I never felt like such a woman."

***

Naomi waited under the "Melling & Associates" sign at noon. Alexander—an arm wrapped about Lucy's waist as he held the door open—smiled at her before frowning.

"You should have come inside to wait. It's a tad cooler in here."

"I'm fine, Mr. Alex."

Lucy took her arm. "What did you find?"

Naomi gave a cutting look. "You won't hear a word in front of him."

Laughing, Lucy leaned to her husband for another kiss and caress before leading Naomi across the street. Alexander wasn't the only one watching the duo. Everyone looked to glowing Lucy Melling—the great Olive Kent—and whispers raced around the square.

She dropped Naomi's arm and tilted her head conspiratorially. "So, where are you bringing me back to?"

"I found nothing because the department stores refuse to show their finest pieces at the colored counter."

"What stores?" The spark in Lucy's eyes darkened to a dangerous gleam. "Where did you go and we'll march in the front doors and demand—"

"You don't need to make a scene for me. I was hoping to be shown silk drawers, and lace gowns like you have. It's all too fine for me anyway." She sighed and waved a dismissive hand.

"Nonsense!" Lucy took her arm once more and started toward the center of the shopping district.

They stopped directly in front of Mademoiselle Bisset's. Naomi opened her mouth to protest.

"Give me one minute." Lucy disappeared inside.

Soon, Mademoiselle Bisset herself opened the door. "Come in, Miss Naomi. I'm pleased to serve you this day." She flipped her OPEN sign to CLOSED and locked the door behind them. "Miss Lucy tells me you're preparing for a special occasion, and I offer you my congratulations."

"Thank you," Naomi stammered.

"Let us take your measurements first."

Naomi heated to be disrobed in the curtained room with two white women, but the owner raved over her pleasant proportions when given the paper with Naomi's measurements.

"You'll be as fun and easy to dress as Miss Lucy herself. Come sit by my dearest customer, and I'll bring out my best for you to browse."

Lucy patted the chair next to her. "Don't worry about the prices. This will be my wedding present."

A wealth of silks and lace in a rainbow of colors and lengths followed. Underdrawers, brassieres, slips, nightgowns, garters, and everything else. Lucy insisted on three undersets and three nightgowns for Naomi and bought a naughty purple number for herself that looked like something a showgirl would wear for a late, late performance.

"Could you wrap this," Lucy asked, "and deliver it to Mr. Melling within the hour?"

"I would be delighted to," Mademoiselle Bisset said with a wink. "It's wonderful to see passion enjoyed between husband and wife. Now, who requires dresses—dresses meant to be seen by all?"

Lucy asked for some to be shown to Naomi. "Nothing too fussy, and in colors that will take her through fall with ease."

From her reticule, Lucy pulled a small notebook and composed a letter to go with the delivery while Naomi tried on a cornflower blue dress that wasn't too fancy for church, as well as an emerald green satin gown that showcased more skin than she was comfortable with. *It's one thing to dress up in Lucy's hand-me-downs, but quite another to try on things that cost more than three months' salary.*

"I see you aren't completely comfortable in that, but we'll take the blue one," Lucy declared as she pulled the page she'd written from her book. "Here, Naomi. See how to keep playfulness alive in marriage."

Naomi looked to the page with trepidation, her cheeks warming as she read the words from Lucy's flowing penmanship.

Alex,

Keep this in mind while at the stables this afternoon.

I'm positive you'll find tonight's entertainment as

stimulating as riding Apollo, though boots and crop are optional.

All my love, forever,

Lucy

"I could never put words like that to paper!"

"Paper isn't needed. A whispered word in an attentive ear does wonders." Lucy slipped the note into the box with her lingerie and addressed the delivery card herself. "This to Melling and Associates, Mademoiselle Bisset, and the rest to our home. Please send the bill with the packages, and I'll send the courier back with a check."

"Of course, my dear. It has been a pleasure serving you and Miss Naomi today. Be sure to tell that handsome husband of yours I hope he enjoys your pretties."

Twenty-Four

When she heard Alex pull into the driveway, Melissa stayed in the back with the other children and Clara Jane while Maggie followed Phoebe, Bethany, and Kade running for the front. Maggie returned a few minutes later with a crystal bud vase holding a stalk of lily of the valley.

"I'm going to bring this inside."

Melissa followed her to the guest bedroom.

Maggie set the vase on her dresser and sunk to the bed. "He makes me remember everything like it was yesterday."

Melissa sat beside her and put an arm about her shoulders. "I'm here if you want to talk."

She quieted a minute and then sighed. "On my first full day at Seacliff Cottage, Mrs. Melling sent Alex to purchase flowers to mark Eliza's mausoleum location. He brought back buckets of lilies, and his mother put me in charge of arranging them. We kissed for the first time in the dining room with the lilies. Then he danced me around and pulled my hair loose. It was the most sensual moment of my life until that point. Even if driven by demons, Alexander had plenty of magnetism of his own. He still does."

Melissa smiled. "And he knows it. Are you ready to go?"

"Could you give me a moment?"

"I'll see to the children."

Ten minutes later, Melissa and Maggie loaded their youngest into the automobile, leaving Clara Jane behind for a few hours of peace while Sharon cooked supper. Melissa parked near the Mellings' garage, and Louisa, Tabitha, and Simon dashed through the gate. Asher ran from the patio and met the three with open arms while Lucy held her position beside her mother on the wicker loveseat.

When Melissa and Maggie were a few feet away, Lucy stood. She hugged Melissa first and motioned her to her own seat, where Mrs. Easton smothered her with a hug.

"How are you, my dear? Your newspaper column makes me weep every week. You can be sure I pray for Freddy's safe return morning, noon, and night. Those girls of his need him, as do you, and dare I say Lucy as well."

Lucy turned from hugging Maggie. "Mother—"

"Now, don't deny it, Lucille. We all know you love Freddy. There's no shame in admitting you've been out of sorts since he left. We're all women here and know what it means to miss a man overseas. My James took several voyages to the orient and Europe when his business was young, and he needed to make connections. He was gone for months, often only home long enough to get me pregnant before he was off again."

"Mother!" Lucy turned crimson against her green blouse.

"There's only one way all of us became mothers, and it wasn't the same way as Blessed Mary. Don't deny our actions. Your father could be completely feral in bed. I assumed he learned a few bad habits in an exotic brothel at some time or another, but he never gave any other clues and doted on me so well I had no complaints, God rest his noble soul."

Lucy groaned and flung herself into the hammock, her arms hanging off in a way that made one think of a distressed fish in a net.

"Do you think I'm deaf in my old age, Lucille? I heard you with Alex this morning, among other times. There's no need for you to cause a scene over me mentioning anything about your father when you and your husband are more untamed than we ever were."

Lucy tried to pout, but a giggle slipped out as Naomi came through the screen door with a tray loaded with a pitcher of lemonade and glasses.

"Naomi," Mrs. Easton said as she set the tray on the nearby table. "Don't you think Lucy has a double standard when it comes to intimate subject matters? She has no qualms with trumpeting her time with Alex, but if anyone else brings it up, it's shameful."

"It's not my place to speak of, but I'll say the Mellings are the most amorous couple I've ever encountered."

"There, you see! Even Naomi knows of your moments."

"*Moments*, Mother?" Lucy's face split into a wicked grin as she stood and straightened her skirt. "Alex can go on for hours."

It was Mrs. Easton's turn to redden while the other women laughed.

Naomi delivered the cookies, and the children ran to the patio to collect them. They retreated to the camellia maze, each with a glass of lemonade and clutch of pecan cookies in their fists. The four women settled into tamer topics of discussion, but when the conversation turned to war, Melissa excused herself to check on Louisa.

"She and Freddy haven't been the same since Junior died." Mrs. Easton's voice carried across the lawn. "It's such a shame what that man has endured."

Melissa quickened her steps. In the camellia maze, she came upon Simon and Tabitha first.

Tabitha raised her finger to her lips. "Asher told us to hide from him."

Melissa smiled and nodded before continuing. Rounding the last corner to reach the center, she met the sight of Asher kissing Louisa's cheek. Her daughter wiped it off with a frown.

"I'm not gonna play if you keep changing the rules," she declared. "You can't kiss the losers *and* winners."

"I kiss whoever's pretty!" Asher laughed and ran for the other path as Melissa entered the clearing.

"Everything all right, Louisa?"

"Asher is being a pest."

"Why don't you return to the patio with me? I'm sure Grandma Easton would love to see you again."

Louisa settled beside Mrs. Easton and Melissa took a chair by Maggie. Lucy was back in the hammock, this time lying more composed as though she sought the best stance for Alex to see her in when he returned. The automobile pulled into the driveway, and Asher led the two Campbells to the gate as the others came in. Phoebe and Kade were quick to disappear into the maze, but Bethany had Alex's hand and walked with him toward the patio after he hugged his son.

"Grandma!" Bethany released her stepfather and went for Mrs. Easton.

"There's my little Davenport." She kissed Bethany. "I hear you're learning to sew."

With Mrs. Easton distracted, Alex went for Lucy. He trailed his hands down Lucy's front and back up to hold her face as he kissed her. Maggie smiled as he bent to lift his wife from the hammock and watched as he whispered something about a special delivery.

Lucy laughed as Alex set her on the ground. "Mademoiselle Bisset hopes you enjoy it."

Maggie violently shivered, causing the Mellings to turn her way.

"Could you gather the children so we can say our farewells?" Alex asked Lucy.

She straightened her clothing and went across the grass on bare feet.

Alex wasted no time taking Maggie's hands in his own and kissing both cheeks. "I forget that shop is one of nightmares for you. Maybe one day you'll have a dress from there that brings you happiness, unlike the one from the Seacliff Cottage days."

"Thank you, Alexander." She kissed his cheeks in return and then hugged him. "And thank you for teaching Kade to ride. It means so much to the both of us."

"I'm happy to bring you along whenever you wish, Magdalene."

She looked up at him through her dark eyelashes. "Lucy wouldn't stand for it, as you well know. Besides, I'm too old for play."

"You're a vibrant woman, Magdalene. Don't give up on yourself because Douglas is away. Your children and friends need you." Alex clutched her to his chest. "I'm here for you. Never forget."

The Campbell children clamored around Alex while the Davenport girls said goodbye to Grandma Easton. Lucy hugged Maggie last while Alex stared over the two women with hungry eyes.

***

After a quiet Saturday with Louisa, Melissa showered and dressed in a thin blue tea gown. She secured the sides of her hair to get it off her neck, thinking about having it cut even shorter.

The phonograph in the dimly lit parlor played one of Valentino's Mozart recordings, and Melissa stretched the length of the sofa, eyes closed as she imagined dancing with Freddy. *His hand kneading my hip as it shifts lower. Lips pressed to my temple. And when the passion swells too high, he lifts me against him, and I wrap my legs about his waist....*

Down the hall, the front door opened, followed by Claudio's soft voice calling hello.

Melissa sat up and patted the spot beside her when he came in.

"It is dark."

"The lights put out too much heat," she told him as he kissed her cheeks. "The humidity is agony today. Take off your cassock and be comfortable. I put a bottle of wine in the icebox."

His smile brightened her heart, but it didn't translate to her face.

"You are sad tonight. I must make you smile." Claudio helped her stand.

Melissa opened the buttons on his priestly covering and then went at the shirt beneath.

"*Eroina*," he said before trailing into Italian that caressed her soul as he spoke. His dark eyes bore into hers with yearning as she opened the cufflinks of his shirt, and he stepped out of his shoes.

She laid his shirt on the back of the nearest chair, leaving him in a slim-fitting cotton undershirt and his pants. Before she reached the hall, Claudio had her in his arms, hands traveling her back as he pressed her against him. Afraid her passion would carry her away, Melissa kept the kissing subdued.

As he kissed down her neck, she broke the moment. "Did you bring cigarettes?"

"*Sí.*" He slowly made his way back to her lips, a look of disappointment on his face as he went for his cassock to retrieve the smoking items from his pocket.

"Let's sit in the breakfast nook tonight. Would you ready the wine while I get my notebook?"

They sat beside each other at the glass-topped wicker table with only the light from the kitchen shining through the doorway and window. Claudio watched her as she brought the wine to her lips. She set it beside the notebook and looked to him with a questioning brow.

"I wish to taste it from you first."

Melissa felt as though she were falling into a pool as Claudio's hot mouth chased the chill of the wine from hers. He murmured in Italian as he held her, languid and delicious to her senses.

"What did you say?" she whispered when he untangled his hold.

He looked at her over the top of his glass. "I am sure you can guess."

Refusing to comment, Melissa drained her wine and held out her hand. "A cigarette, please."

Claudio set it between her lips. "What are you working on?"

She exhaled a cloud of smoke. "Topics for my column. Some weeks it's difficult to choose. I'd like a list of ideas to turn to when I'm stuck."

Claudio lit a cigarette for himself and shifted so he could stretch his feet under the table to the opposite chair. "Your words are always eloquent."

"It's more difficult to write for a newspaper than a magazine. Being a weekly contributor to a local readership welcomes everyone I meet into my life. If I go in a store, I'm remarked over for having bravely sent my husband to war. At church, the ladies cluck over me for having cried myself to sleep one night. It's suffocating at times. I need to be careful what I share."

"So I need not fear you will encourage other women to grab the nearest priest for companionship?"

Melissa laughed, feeling freed from her loneliness for the moment. "I'd never encourage people to seek outside their relationships. And with you being the most handsome priest in town, there would be a mob."

Claudio's eyes crinkled at the corners. "Then I shall stay happily yours, *Eroina*."

He poured more wine into their glasses, and she sipped while trying to calm her emotions. Being with Claudio kept the pain of Freddy's betrayal away, but it reminded her she was not being fair to her husband. Melissa focused on the page and jotted a few ideas—planning for the holidays, absentee birthdays, and relief efforts—then tossed her pen and notebook onto the table.

Claudio passed Melissa her drink. "Do you consider us lovers?"

The question startled her in its bluntness, and she coughed at swallowing wrong. His hand settled on her arm as he leaned closer. In his brown eyes were concern, love, and devotion like she only thought she'd see in her husband's gaze.

"We're friends, Claudio. I do love you and these moments with you help me feel human. I wouldn't be who I am right now after the last year without your companionship."

"But lovers?" He lifted her free hand and kissed her knuckles.

"We love and express ourselves." Trapped at speaking the words, she realized how shameful her actions with Claudio were becoming. "But I don't … I don't know if I could—"

"I would never ask that of you."

"Do you want more from our relationship?" she whispered.

His smile was bitter. "What I want and what I need is different. It is your needs I am concerned with." A hand on her cheek, he caressed her lips with his thumb and brought his mouth to her ear. "I would give you everything you ask of me. *Ti do tutto quello, Eroina*."

Melissa slipped onto his lap and kissed him until the thoughts of her unethical choices were drowned in passion.

Twenty-Five

The Monday afternoon of Phoebe's birthday, Naomi stepped onto the patio to get away from the ovens, but the August humidity did little to cool her. She lay on the hammock and used her apron to fan herself until the wind blew the hint of a thunderstorm in from the gulf. Phoebe was determined to be like her mother, going so far as to ask for Lucy's favorite cake for her tenth birthday. But while Lucy would be fine with celebrating on the nearest Friday, Phoebe demanded her party on the actual day.

Eyes closed, she heard the screen door snap shut.

"Miss Naomi?"

"Yes, Phoenix Asher."

"Momma and Grandma are sleeping, and I need to get something ready for Phoebe before she gets home."

She opened her arms, and he climbed onto her lap. "What did you have in mind?"

He grabbed her hands and kissed them. "A sign to hang in the dining room for her party."

"You'll need lots of paper, crayons, and fasteners to connect them. Maybe some ribbon or yarn to tie it to the drapes."

"Grandma's crochet basket?"

"I bet that would be fine, but let's work on the paper first and ask her about the yarn when she wakes up."

Naomi checked the carrot cake before going to the morning room with Asher. Between taking the cake out of the oven and preparing supper, Naomi helped Asher with his sign at the kitchen table. She wrote HAPPY BIRTHDAY, PHOEBE! over the space of seven sheets of paper for Asher to color. He decorated around the words with butterflies and flowers done precisely for someone his age.

Lucy came in an hour later, looking dazed in her kimono. "Asher, that's lovely."

"Miss Naomi helped me."

Lucy hugged her. "Thank you. I had to nap. Mother's still snoring on the porch, the poor thing. If this storm doesn't come any closer to cool things off, I think we'll all be on the porch tonight."

Naomi narrowed her eyes at Lucy.

She sighed. "I know. It will be torturous because there'll be no way for Alex and me to spend time with the girls and my mother here. And Asher's too old now as well. He used to sleep through anything."

Naomi laughed. "I think you two can survive a night without."

"No, I better think of something."

By the time Melissa arrived with Louisa and Bethany, Asher's sign hung in the dining room, complementing the pink roses in the Tiffany vase on the table. The two Davenport girls in their white party dresses played croquet in the yard with Asher in his short sailor suit while Lucy, Melissa, and Mrs. Easton watched from the shade of the patio. Alexander and Phoebe arrived in their sweat-stained riding clothes. Lucy urged them inside to shower, and Naomi began her thirty-minutes-to-supper countdown.

Lucy paced at the bottom of the stairs while Naomi brought platters of food into the dining room. Phoebe bound down the steps, fresh in a pink tiered dress and her hair in a ribbon-adorned ponytail.

"You're lovely, Phoebe Camellia." She kissed her daughter. "Go gather the others."

On Naomi's next pass, Alexander—outfitted in white shirt and pants—held Lucy in an impassioned pose, lips tasting her décolletage along the gold trim of her turquoise gown. Desire flushed Lucy's cheeks, and a smile graced her lips.

The children clamored to the washroom, not paying them any mind.

"Really, you two!" Mrs. Easton's voice was too light to be taken seriously. "The things you subject the children to are scandalous."

Alexander sauntered to his mother-in-law as he buttoned his shirt. He took her in his arms as if to waltz, kissing her cheek in the process. "There's no need to be jealous, Mrs. Easton. I will shower you with attention whenever you wish."

She laughed. "There was no chance for Lucy when you charmed your way into her life."

When Naomi met Melissa in the hall, she paused to hug the woman. Melissa's summer gown showcased her lean form, and her shortened hair made her sleeveless dress appear more freeing.

"We all miss him," Naomi whispered, "but I know he'd love to see you dressed up and enjoying yourself."

Melissa's broad smile was as pretty as ever, and she fingered her emerald necklace. "Thank you, Naomi."

The doorbell rang, and in the others' rush to oversee the children washing up, Naomi welcomed Father De Fiore inside.

With just herself to see to the party, Naomi kept busy going between the dining room and kitchen. After serving the cake, the group piled their presents in front of Phoebe. Naomi's small offering was a pink porcelain camellia that fit in the palm of the girl's hand.

"It's beautiful, Miss Naomi. Thank you!"

The priest gifted a leather diary, Melissa a novel, Mrs. Easton a white crocheted sweater, and Bethany a handmade pillow of pink florals. Her mother and Alex offered a pile of new dresses, and then a special box tagged as being from her father contained a letter from Frederick and a string of pearls.

Phoebe ran over and showed her mother the necklace.

"Those are a real treasure, Phoebe Camellia. Your father gave me a similar necklace on one of my birthdays too. May I fasten it for you?"

"Poppy can."

Phoebe didn't see the pain in Lucy's eyes when she turned her back, but Alexander did. He mustered a smile for his stepdaughter, but his eyes held concern. After he clasped the pearls on her, he turned Phoebe to him and kissed her forehead.

"You're a young lady now, Phoebe. Be sure you treat those around you with love and respect."

"Yes, Poppy."

"Now go on and choose which music you want, and I'll give you the first dance." Alexander looked to the priest and Asher. "I'm afraid we'll be over-worked this evening, gentlemen. Between the three of us, we must see that all the ladies have a fine time. No rest until they each have a turn. And that includes Miss Naomi."

"I can do it, Poppy!" Asher crossed the room to Melissa and offered his arm. "Would you care to accompany me to the morning room, Mrs. Davenport?"

"I'd be delighted, Master Melling."

The priest and Alexander escorted the ladies down the hall while Naomi took two loads of dishes to the kitchen. When she came back for a third trip, only Lucy was left, her lips trembling.

Alexander put his arms about her when he returned. "She didn't mean to slight you, my queen."

Lucy shook her head. "She doesn't need me. She'd do well with you and Frederick."

"Every girl needs her mother." He kissed her neck. "Allow me to bring you in so you may watch our dance. Then I'm coming for one with you after I see to the others. I want my obligations fulfilled so if I get the urge to take our dance somewhere private—"

Lucy's lips were on his, and she fingered the buttons on his shirt, opening the top two. "My angel in white."

Naomi gathered another tray of dishes while the Mellings shared more passion. When the doorbell rang, she found Maxwell Easton on the veranda, worry lines a mile deep.

"I'm sorry to cut in on Phoebe's party, Naomi, but I must speak with Mother."

"They're in the morning room, Mr. Maxwell."

"Uncle Max!" Phoebe shrilled. "You're late for my party!"

Maxwell emerged from the morning room with Mrs. Easton on his arm, followed by Lucy and Alexander. The four gathered in the front room, and Naomi stood around the corner to listen.

"I received a telephone call from the asylum last hour," Maxwell said with a catch in his voice. "Opal got a hold of a knife. By the time they found her, it was too late."

Mrs. Easton broke into sobs, and Lucy rushed from the room. The sound of her retching in the hall bathroom had Naomi hurrying to follow, but Alexander got to her first.

"My queen, she'll never hurt you again." He held Lucy's hair off her neck and turned to Naomi in the doorway, blue eyes filled with sorrow. "Could you tell Melissa what happened and ask her to take the girls home?"

In the other room, Melissa danced with Father De Fiore— the two laughing and enjoying themselves—while Asher danced with Bethany. Naomi approached the older couple, laying a hand on their shoulders to still them.

"Opal's killed herself at the asylum," she whispered. "Alexander would like for you to take the girls home with you tonight to give Mrs. Easton and Lucy a bit of peace. But don't mention the reasons to the sugars."

Melissa nodded. "I'll bring Asher too."

"Allow me to attend you all," Father De Fiore said. "We can move Phoebe's party to your house so she does not grow too melancholy."

Melissa turned to the children. "There's been some sad news for Grandma Easton. Poppy wishes a quiet evening for her, so we'll host the rest of Phoebe's party at our house. Naomi will help Asher pack a bag for a sleepover, and Uncle Claudio will ride over with us to continue the dancing and games."

"I get to go to Louisa's house!" Asher ran for the stairs.

"I want my party with Poppy and Momma!"

"You've already had your gifts and danced with Poppy. We'll have a nice time with Uncle Claudio and Doff at the other house." Melissa took Phoebe's hand and ushered her out.

Once the others were gone, Alexander escorted his mother-in-law upstairs before coming for Lucy.

Maxwell headed for the door but stopped Naomi in the hall. "Alexander told me you were going to the office with him in the morning to interview potential cooks. I'll come to sit with Mother and listen out for Lucy as well."

"Do you think we still should?"

He took her hand in his. "Don't let the Easton drama hold you back, Naomi."

***

A quarter after eight Tuesday found Naomi taking coffee in Alexander's office as they awaited the first interview. On the ride over, they'd discussed Lucy's need for a sleeping draught the night before, as well as Mrs. Easton's haggard appearance that morning, but it was time to plan for the future rather than worry about Opal's final upset.

"I chose the ones with the best experience for us to see," Alexander remarked. "What is it you think we should look for beyond cooking references?"

"A matronly, plump figure." Naomi sipped the coffee but noticed his confusion. "You don't want to bring home a woman Lucy might get the idea you fancy."

He laughed, rubbing a hand over his unshaven face. Though he shaved more often than not the past few years, Naomi noticed he allowed the stubble to cover his marks on days he felt vulnerable. Seeing her seriousness, he sobered.

"Could she really think that of me?" When Naomi continued to stare at him, he groaned. "Though I've made a few mistakes, my heart has been devoted to her since we first kissed."

"There's no telling what her mind will think in the days ahead, but it's best not to tempt her with possibilities. Any help you hire needs to be plain. And if the woman is of fair complexion, don't let her look like any of your admirers."

His eyebrows went up, and he quirked a smile. "My admirers?"

"Miss Maggie, Sister Pru—"

Alexander paled and set down his cup with a clatter. "You know about *that*?"

"Lucy doesn't have many people to confide in."

He looked to her with an impish smile. "But you admire me, don't you, Miss Naomi?"

She laughed. "I know too much about you to be enamored, but you're a fine man."

The first interview was with a lady almost as old as Mrs. Easton. Though spry, Naomi didn't trust she'd have the means to contain Lucy should her help be needed physically. The second woman, a buxom brunette, appeared to have something in her eye, such she did wink at Alexander. If the third candidate hadn't been an improvement, Naomi would have lost all hope in Alexander's skills at selecting applicants.

Charlotte Ivey was several inches taller than Alexander with dark skin and hauntingly large eyes. Though younger than Naomi, she possessed an air of maturity. She wore a respectable skirt and blouse that hung well on her thick frame, sensible shoes on her large feet, and her hair parted in the middle and secured in the back. While pleasant, all her features combined would keep her out of suspicion where Lucy was concerned.

"I've been working at the hotel the past ten years, but aim for a kitchen of my own where I don't have to share it with a dozen other cooks and bumbling wait staff. I'd run a tight ship but know my place as it'd be your home I'm in, Mr. Melling."

"We have no other help besides Naomi," he said, "but rather than a wait staff to get on your nerves, we have children. My wife and I have a son that will be five in December, but her two girls from her first marriage are with us more often than not because their father is serving in the Army. There's also his daughter from his current wife, who I claim as much as the others, plus our friends and family often come for suppers and gatherings. The children have free run of the house, including the kitchen. Right now, there are five regulars to feed—plus yourself and Miss Naomi—but there can be as many as two dozen people at a supper party."

"Coming from the hotel, I've got no problems with crowds. As for the children, so long as they aren't mine to deal with, it's all good. I'm not set for that in my life."

"No husband or beau to speak of?" he asked.

"I had me a man at seventeen, and he went and left me for my cousin he got in the family way the week before we were to be married." She shook her head. "That was a decade ago, and I'm none the worse for it now, but don't aim to try my heart again. Being played the fool once was one time too many for me."

"Mrs. Melling and her children have cravings for sweets," Naomi said to change the subject. "I keep cookies on hand at all times and bake cakes and pies several times a week."

Charlotte clasped her hands in her lap and straightened. "You don't get a figure like mine from being a poor baker."

Alexander cleared his throat. "Everything seems good so far, though there is one more matter I'd like to discuss."

Her prominent eyes held his gaze. "Yes, Mr. Melling?"

"Discretion is important in my household. My wife is a private woman, and with her career and history, gossip hounds are always looking for tidbits about her. What you see and hear at my home does not need repeating anywhere, save under police questioning if someone is in danger." He winked.

Charlotte stared at him for several seconds with a calculating gaze which Naomi immediately admired. "You seem a kind man, Mr. Melling, but I don't stand for flirtations. I demand professionalism where I work. While I'd give leniency to children, a grown man should know my limits. I don't aim to work where I'm expected to grin and bat my eyelashes because the boss is full of himself."

Naomi couldn't stop the laugh that blurted out.

Alexander blushed. "Well said, Miss Charlotte. I'll do my best to control my impulses around you."

"If you have a fancy for the help, I'll see myself out now." She stood.

Alexander was on his feet as his face turned serious. "I'm afraid you misunderstood, Miss Charlotte. I whole-heartedly assure you that you're in no danger of molestation in my home."

"Mr. Melling is a flirt," Naomi said, "but that's all. Now that he knows you don't take kindly to his mannerisms, he'll respect that."

"Yes, do excuse me. If you're still interested in the job, I'd like you to come over a few times and see how you get on in our household on trial with full pay," Alexander said. "We'll work around your current job's schedule so we don't place you in jeopardy if things don't turn out."

Charlotte sat on the edge of her chair. "I'm off work Thursday and Friday this week."

"That would be perfect," Naomi said. "A quieter day at the house and then the supper party Friday evening for Miss Darla's birthday."

"I'm up for it." Charlotte smiled fully for the first time.

Twenty-Six

Claudio hesitated on the veranda of the Mellings' house. If he did not have Darla's birthday presents from himself and Magdalene in his arms, he would have turned around rather than face the heartache of the Easton women or Alexander's admonishing over his behaviors with Melissa.

Phoebe answered the door in a lavender dress that he recognized from her pile of birthday presents.

"Uncle Claudio!"

"*Principessa.*" He kissed her cheeks without having to lean over too far because of her recent growth spurt.

Stepping into the front room, he deposited his gifts before greeting Mrs. Easton, Asher, Bethany, and Lucy—who he went to last. She put on a brave face, but sadness hid behind her green eyes.

After kissing his cheeks in return, she said what he least wanted to hear. "Alex wants to see you in the den before supper."

He nodded, placed his hands on Lucy's head, and whispered a prayer.

On his way to the den, a dark woman came out from the kitchen with a tray of provisions. Upon seeing him, she dropped into a shallow curtsey. "Good evening, Father."

He smiled and motioned her ahead, wondering how a lady with her set expression found her way into the chaotic household.

In the den, Alexander rose from his desk. "The door, Claudio."

After a brotherly hug and kissed cheeks, Alexander sat on the chaise, and Claudio followed.

Wishing to avoid the conversation, he spoke first. "There is a new face here."

"Miss Charlotte. It's her second day on trial, but I believe she'll work well for us."

"She looks serious."

Alexander laughed. "The dear scolded me at her interview, impressing Naomi to no end. Maybe it's time to have someone who will keep us in line. Many of us are drifting into dangerous waters these days."

Claudio met his cold stare with one of his own. "Speak freely, *amico*."

"Keep your hands off Melissa," he hissed. "She's glowing in your arms, and that's not good. Not to mention you going off with her and the children the other night."

"I did that for Phoebe. You know how she gets when her plans are spoiled. But would you rather Melissa be melancholy or dejected, have her go about without a will to live like your wife?"

Alexander's blue eyes narrowed dangerously as he scowled like his father. "Don't compare her situation to what ails Lucy."

"Then do not pass judgment without attempting to understand her situation. You have no idea what she has suffered."

"Her sister didn't slash herself to death." Alexander took a drag on his cigarette. "Maxwell told me Opal left a note saying she chose the birthdate of Lucy's oldest while their mother was in her house to wound Lucy the most. We've kept that from the women, of course."

"Melissa has been in agony well over a year. Do you not remember she lost her son last July?"

"Of course," Alexander waved his hand. "But she and Freddy got through that."

"They did not! Frederick emotionally abandoned her during their pain. He saw the girls to bed at night but was a silent partner for nine months. He barely touched her, nor did he speak beyond common exchanges that you might give an acquaintance. She suffered her pain alone, all while keeping the household running and seeing to the girls. Did you not notice how she wasted away last winter?"

Alexander grew pensive as though trying to remember Melissa's change. "But she's confident and self-sufficient. And Freddy, God bless him, is a saint among men."

"Melissa's clothing was hanging off her like sacks, her face like a starving street urchin! I wanted to kill Frederick when I learned he neglected her all that time. And when she told me he finally made love to her the day he registered for the Army, I lost all respect for the man. He is just as flawed as you and me, but God stayed my hand when I saw him here the night of Lucy's party. By then, he was trying to make things right, but Melissa did not know how to deal with his attention because it had been too long."

"Had it been too long, or was she already fulfilled because you'd been seeing to her in his absence?"

"Do not be a fool."

"You're the fool, Claudio! She and Freddy had sex right here in this room during that party. She doesn't love you." Alexander's blue eyes burned with contempt. "Stay away from her, or I'll cut off your invitations to Friday suppers."

"Do you not think we meet elsewhere?" They stared at each other a moment. "I will not allow Melissa to suffer loneliness because everyone else is fussing over your wife. I will not deny her caring arms and a few kisses that fortify her against utter despair."

Claudio downplayed the depth of his attachment, but what he spoke proved to be the root of his motivation—his growing love for Melissa that surpassed what he had ever felt for Eliza.

***

On Wednesday nights, Claudio spent hours with Melissa at her home. Friday evenings found him dining and dancing at the Mellings' house. Once or twice a week, he also took a meal with Melissa and Louisa, eager to ensure that the youngest in the family did not lack a father figure in her life. In between those events, he numbly carried on with his work for the archdiocese, never feeling alive unless he was within sight of Melissa.

October twelfth found the group of regulars plus a few extras at the Mellings' house for yet another Friday celebration—two to be exact because, much to Darla's horror, Horatio shared a birthday with Alexander.

Lucy, radiant in a red dress that showcased her sexy and bold, commanded the attention of the supper guests with a fork *tinging* against her glass. She stood at the table surrounded by Claudio, the Adamses, Davenports, Edmund, Oscar, Asher, and her husband.

"On behalf of Alexander and our family, I'd like to thank you all for coming to celebrate both his thirty-fifth and Horatio's fourth birthdays."

Alexander took her right hand and pressed his lips to it as he gazed up at her.

Lucy's eyes further brightened. "We love you all and are blessed to share with you our milestones and yours. Tomorrow morning, our family will be on the ferry for a weekend at Seacliff. Alexander will find his present waiting for him in Montrose."

"And what do you have planned, my queen?" He grinned like a schoolboy.

"A new automobile for Seacliff Manor. The touring motor is more than a decade old. I thought it time for a new model."

"Magdalene learned to drive behind that wheel. A ravishing sight in her goggles," Alexander said. "And Douglas lording over as if it were his own—both the vehicle and the woman."

Lucy's countenance fell, and she dropped to her seat as Naomi and Charlotte came in with jugs of apple cider. Taking command, Claudio stood and led the group in a toast.

"To Horatio," Darla added in a whisper, "may he not grow up to be like the man he shares a birthday with."

Melissa laughed and met Claudio's eyes across the table. Her bright smile warmed him more than the spiced cider. Since Alexander spoke to him at the end of August, Claudio did not hide his admiration of Melissa. They openly conversed, danced, and even flirted at gatherings. Darla often gave him cutting looks as she rubbed her growing belly, but no one said anything.

When the men gathered on the patio after supper, Edmund punched Claudio on the shoulder. The priest stumbled back before he found his footing. Taking another drag on his cigarette, Claudio stared at Lucy's brother.

Edmund's eyes were hard, adding toughness to his bearded stature. "Consider that a warning. Alex might be too much of a cad to say anything, but that's Freddy's wife you're hanging on. I don't think he'd appreciate your attentions."

"On the contrary. When Frederick was home this summer, he thanked me for watching over Melissa."

"Freddy is a trusting fool, but I know those with holy vestments aren't always saints."

Henry came forward. "Leave it alone, Eddie. Just because—"

"It's because I've run around that I can see the sin in others. I've heard of your cousin's exploits, *Father* De Fiore, and know yours as well." Edmund shoved Claudio with both hands. "But let it be known that I made Eliza a woman before she ever laid eyes on you."

Alexander flung himself at Edmund. "Don't speak of my sister!"

Edmund laughed and held him back with one arm. "You and Lucy with your double standards. You could have your way with my sister, but I better not touch yours. What did she think would happen when she sat down to drink with a bunch of Dardennes? She knew exactly what she was doing, both with me and later with Sean. Lucy was a love-blinded dupe, but Eliza was a temptress. She begged me, Alex. She begged me to show her how—"

Ducking below Edmund's reach, Alexander came up swinging. He caught Edmund on the chin with his fist as well as one of the boxers could have, but when Alexander turned away, his nose bled.

Henry was at him with a handkerchief, but blood had already dripped onto his shirt.

"It's nothing to worry over." Alexander held the cloth to his nose. "It means autumn's coming."

A chill settled on the usually amicable group. With a hand on Alexander's shoulder, Henry looked to Edmund, but he only rubbed his whiskered jaw and walked back to the house. The other three soon followed.

Edmund made his rounds through the morning room with the excuse to see his son home.

"Uncle Eddie," Phoebe whined, "it's not even nine, and Oscar's older than me."

"But Oscar's mother is Mary Margaret, and she doesn't stand for late nights at the Mellings' house."

She crossed her arms and frowned, causing her uncle to laugh.

"There's a face I saw often growing up." Edmund looked to Lucy.

She began to smile, but Alexander walked into the room with the bloody handkerchief. "Alex! What happened?"

"Just the changing of the seasons, my queen."

"Let me help you clean up." She escorted him to the hall bathroom.

Edmund said goodbye to the Adamses and kissed Bethany and Louisa. "You girls be good and keep your big sister out of trouble."

They promised, and he deliberately crossed the room to Melissa. "Freddy is like a brother to me. He's been nothing but good in his life. You better not be unfaithful to him because I'll see you regret it in more ways than one."

She stood, looking him in the eyes. "How dare you?"

"No, Miss New York, how dare *you?*" He glanced at Claudio to drive his point home and turned back to her with a smirk.

Indignant, Melissa slapped his face. Darla and the children gasped.

"Good night, *Mrs. Davenport*, lest you forget who you are." Edmund kept his hard gaze on her. "Freddy sure knows how to pick his women."

As soon as Edmund and Oscar left, Phoebe stomped to Melissa. "I'm going to write Daddy and tell him you hit Uncle Eddie!"

"She slapped him, *Principessa*." Claudio gently laid a hand on the girl's shoulder. "A lady has the right to do that when a man speaks improper things to her."

"What did he say, Sissa?"

She stared at her stepdaughter with tranquil coldness. "Nothing I'd ever repeat to a young lady. Excuse me. I need a glass of water."

Louisa took her mother's hand as she left the room.

Lucy and Alexander returned, and he was bare from the waist up. "Lucy insisted on soaking my shirt to keep it from staining. There are no complaints, are there?" He opened his arms and winked at Darla.

She huffed and rolled her eyes. "You're a perpetual scoundrel, even in your old age."

Alexander laughed and rubbed a hand down his scarred torso.

"Momma," Phoebe said, "Sissa slapped Uncle Eddie."

"Whatever for?" Lucy asked.

"Uncle Claudio says a woman has the right to strike a man if he says something rude, but she wouldn't tell us what he said. How can we be sure Sissa isn't being mean without reason?"

"I don't know." Lucy's eyes narrowed.

"I'm going to tell Daddy in my next letter," Phoebe declared once more.

"You don't need to worry your father over what will be forgotten in a few days," Alexander said. "What we need is music to lighten the mood. Henry, would you do us the honor of choosing the first song?"

As the music began, Alexander had Lucy in his arms. Her hands traveled his abdomen until they settled in position for the dance. Melissa returned as Lucy lowered her head to Alexander's bare shoulder.

Not caring what anyone thought, Claudio took Melissa's hand. "Are you all right?"

"Yes, thank you."

Her smile was not as strained as he expected, so he dropped to his knee, looking at Louisa beside her. "Will you dance with me, *Principessa?*"

Her cherubic smile melted his tension. "Yes, Uncle Claudio!"

When he stood, he rested his hand on Melissa's cheek. "Save a dance for me, *Eroina.*"

"Always."

Twenty-Seven

While the Mellings were across the bay for Alexander's birthday, Naomi spent time packing her belongings. By Sunday evening, all she had left in her apartment were a few dishes, enough clothing to see her through the week, and her honeymoon suitcase. The rest of her things had been hauled to Paul's house—including the new quilt she'd made for their bed, which Bethany declared was the prettiest thing ever.

Naomi spent her final days at the Mellings' house doing light housekeeping and sitting with Lucy. Charlotte was settled into the family's routine in her kitchen responsibilities and had survived Alexander's birthday supper, complete with him running around half-naked the final hour.

When Naomi went to the kitchen midafternoon on Wednesday to collect tea for Lucy, Charlotte proved eager to talk.

"Does Mr. Melling take supper in his pajamas every Wednesday?"

Naomi laughed. "He often does since he showers when he returns from the riding club."

"I'm cooking breakfast for dinner tonight. Might as well tell the lot of 'em to come in their nightclothes."

"The children would love that, but I don't think you'd want to see Miss Lucy's gowns." Naomi placed teacups on the tray while waiting for the water to boil.

"If she's as daring as her husband, I might need to rethink my invitation. Lord help me with these people."

"They're good folks."

"But the emotional state of the house is more fluid than fresh gelatin."

Naomi laughed at the image, but her heart weighed heavy with the truth.

Back in the morning room with Lucy, Naomi served tea for them. Lucy still wore her kimono and was curled in the corner of the sofa.

"Miss Charlotte will be serving breakfast for dinner and thought the children would have fun coming to supper in their nightclothes."

Lucy smiled, eyes brightening. "They'll love that, and I suppose that means I won't have to dress. Despite her seriousness, I think Miss Charlotte is a good addition to our home."

"She'll take good care of y'all." Naomi settled in the chair adjacent to the sofa.

"I'll miss you." Sadness swept Lucy's countenance once more.

"It's not but a few days. I'll be back here next Wednesday for a good scrubbing of the house."

"Everything's changing."

Asher, face flushed from sleep, bound into the room and straight for Naomi. "I'm hungry!"

"Go on and see Miss Charlotte for a snack. She's the food lady now."

He hugged Naomi and then went for his mother, snuggling against her silk wrap. "Did you nap, Momma?"

"No, Phoenix Asher. But I've been resting." Lucy kissed his cheek.

Before Alexander and the girls arrived, Asher was bathed and in his pajamas. He built a castle out of blocks in his room, and Naomi helped Lucy tidy her closet.

Alexander strode into the bedroom. Seeing Lucy sitting at her dressing table in her robe, he hurried to her. "Is everything all right, my queen?"

"Naomi's bringing my autumn clothes to the front of the closet. How was your ride?"

He fingered the opening of her kimono, a gleam in his eyes. "Not as good as the one I hope to enjoy with you tonight."

"Alex, Naomi is right there!" Her tone of outrage was too playful to be taken seriously—especially coupled with her reaching for his belt.

Naomi stepped out of the closet. "I'll go tell the sugars to dress for bed after they wash."

"For bed?" Alexander looked to Naomi.

"Miss Charlotte is cooking breakfast for dinner and invites everyone to come in their nightclothes."

An air of intrigue lit his face. "Then I should come as I typically sleep."

Lucy caught his hand. "You must save something for my eyes only, Angel."

"I'm all for you, my queen."

***

Friday morning, Naomi woke before the sun, nervous energy fluttering in her stomach as her wedding hour approached. She forced herself to stay in bed until seven o'clock. Then, she pulled on her robe and went to the kitchen, where she had her teapot, one cup, and a partial packet of crackers remaining.

A soft knock sounded on her door. Curious if Paul surprised her with a bakery delivery on their wedding morning, she rushed to answer it.

Lucy held a covered tray before her. "Happy Wedding Day, Naomi. I've cooked you breakfast."

"You didn't need to do that, but thank you." Naomi took the tray from her, trying to read the emotions behind her misty eyes. "Do you want to come in?"

Lucy pulled her kimono tighter and followed her to the table and chairs—the only remaining furniture in the room.

"Sit with me, if you'd like. But if you need to get back, I understand."

"Alex is cooking for the children. He told me to take my time."

Naomi removed the covering and found an omelet, toast, fruit cup, and coffee. "You'll have me spoiled with breakfast and then your house across the bay all weekend."

"The Watts family will take good care of you. I readied your room myself while we were there last weekend. And the new automobile is the most comfortable thing in the world."

"I do appreciate it." Naomi took a few bites while Lucy silently watched her. "Even though I'm your employee, you're my dearest friend. That won't change on my side."

Lucy smiled and bit her lip as it began to tremble. "I suppose we'll need to hire someone else to help with the house because you might decide taking care of your own home is plenty, especially if you have a baby."

"Paul's already raised his kids and has his grandchildren to coo over."

"But with a younger wife who keeps him up all night—"

"Don't start talking like your husband."

"It might happen. Melissa was over thirty when she had her two, and the men are willing to keep trying." She laughed and hugged herself. "Have you really waited since that weekend?"

Naomi nodded and kept eating.

"Do you want any help with dressing?" Lucy asked as she gathered the tray.

"No, thank you. Sharon will be here before long."

"Then I'll see you at the ceremony."

By the time Naomi traveled across town, the little chapel held numerous extended family members. Escorted into a small room to wait, Sharon fussed over Naomi's blue dress—the one Lucy bought for her at Mademoiselle Bisset's shop. *If she only knew what I wore underneath, she'd cluck even more!* Aunts and female cousins peeked into the room to give their blessings and gush over her.

When she walked down the aisle on the arm of an uncle, the crowded chapel threatened to overwhelm her with tears of gratitude. The Melling and Davenport families were easy to spot in the crowd, and Naomi took a moment to smile at them. Then she focused on Paul Rollins before the pulpit wearing a crisp gray suit and a huge smile. Her breath caught at his handsome figure and the fact that he only had eyes for her.

With pounding heart, she made it through the ceremony with what felt like the ocean in her ears. Naomi said, "I do" at some point, but it was all a blur until Paul's lips were on hers.

"You're prettier than ever, Honey." His deep voice rumbled her ear. "Let's go see the guests."

While Sharon orchestrated the setting of the food tables in the side yard, Naomi and Paul stood on the porch of the church and greeted their wedding guests as they exited the chapel.

When the Mellings got to the front of the line, Lucy took her in a wordless hug that threatened to suffocate Naomi.

"Easy there, my queen." Alexander took Lucy by the waist.

"I hope you two are wonderfully happy," she said in her breathy voice.

"Thank you, Miss Lucy." Paul shook her hand and then Alexander's. "And thank you for your generosity in allowing us the use of your house across the bay for our honeymoon."

"It's our pleasure." Alexander kept an arm about Lucy's middle as he smiled at Naomi. "Being Mrs. Paul Rollins looks great on you."

Naomi dipped her head. "I'll see you Wednesday. And you, Phoenix Asher, better have a clean room when I arrive."

Phoebe and Bethany hugged her, and then Louisa and Melissa, who wished Naomi and Paul well. After that, the two families went to their automobiles, but most of the other guests stayed for dinner. So busy speaking to people in the following hours, Naomi didn't eat more than a few bites of the food her cousins and aunts had prepared. Then Paul hurried her to his truck so they could make the ferry.

She didn't mind the stares from the well-to-do crowd at the dock, and they spent the ferry ride leaning against each other on a bench behind the engine room.

At the top of the hill from the Montrose pier, a dark man around the same age as Paul waited beside a shining black automobile. "Mr. and Mrs. Paul Rollins?"

"Yes," Paul replied. "You must be Mr. Watts."

"Leroy is fine, Mr. Rollins. Allow me to take your suitcases."

"Then call me Paul," he said as he handed over their luggage. "This is my bride, Naomi."

"Pleased to meet you both. The Mellings are excited for you to stay at Seacliff Manor, and we were given instructions to make sure you both have everything you need."

As soon as they turned off the main road a few miles south, Naomi eagerly looked through the wooded lot, anticipating the first glimpse of the house. She had heard stories, seen photographs, and even looked over the blueprints while it was being built but had never accompanied the family on their trips. A shingled Craftsmen bungalow, charming though massive, sat long on the lot so it wouldn't loom over arrivals with its two and a half stories. Its wooden sides and green roof blended well with the forest.

"They sure have fine taste," Paul remarked as he helped Naomi out of the backseat.

Before they reached the porch, a woman opened the door with a beaming smile. "Welcome, Mr. and Mrs. Rollins."

"They're wishing to be Paul and Naomi," Leroy said as he carried the suitcases. "This here is Rosemary."

She was quick to embrace Naomi once she stepped inside. "I've heard so much about you from Miss Lucy. I always begged her to bring you, but she insisted you needed the time away from them to keep your head on straight."

"They have nothing but kind things to say about you and your family, Rosemary."

"Go on up with Leroy and see your room. You're in the front suite, where Mr. and Mrs. Davenport stay. The Campbells, too, though they don't come as often, which is sad because I love them like family. Bless their hearts with all they went through at the old house. And now Mr. Freddy and Douglas are overseas, the brave men." Rosemary took a deep breath. "Don't mind me. I'd talk a spoon into stirring a pot for me if I could manage it. I'd run on forever if Leroy didn't stop me."

The crisp white and blue bedroom was sparsely furnished with the white canopy bed the focal point. Simple dressers with fresh gardenias, bedside tables, and two wingback chairs before a fireplace were the only other furniture in the room. The door to the bathroom stood open—equally gleaming white with a claw foot tub perched on the blue tiles.

Leroy placed the suitcases on top of two luggage racks beside the closet. "Would you care to see the rest of the upstairs before you settle in?"

"Yes, please." Naomi took Paul's hand.

They were shown two other smaller bedrooms and a bath most often used for children as they housed several single beds, though one had a double as well.

"This is the Mellings' side," Leroy told them.

There were two more snug rooms, another bath, and the master suite. Though no bigger than the front bedroom, it was decorated with sumptuous lavender and silver, the details of the carved furniture adding richness to the space with the undulating thickness of the posters around the massive bed and scrolling details on the dressers and chairs. It faced the cliff, and peeks of the bay could be seen glimmering through the trees in the final light of the setting sun.

Naomi looked into the bathroom, which was silver and red. "It's like walking into Lucy's wardrobe."

"Take your time," Leroy told them. "I'll be downstairs."

Not wanting to keep the Wattses waiting, Naomi and Paul washed for supper. On their way to the dining room, they were shown the parlor, library, another bath, and game room—a relaxed living area intended for the children to play and gather in. The yellow dining room was trimmed and furnished in sturdy oak, the table as large as the one on Government Street though not nearly as pretentious. The head of the table and the seat immediately to its left were set with the Mellings' formal china and silverware.

Seeing her eye the familiar pattern only used for special occasions at the main house, Rosemary smiled. "The dishes in this house are functional pieces. Miss Lucy brought these last weekend so you'd have something fine on your wedding night. She also said to set the table like this, but if you'd rather—"

"No, it's perfect. Thank you." Naomi sat in the chair Paul pulled out for her. "She went to so much trouble for us."

"She cares for you, Honey."

Feeling almost ashamed, she whispered, "I didn't realize how much."

After supper, Paul lifted Naomi into his arms and carried her to their bedroom. A blue silk robe hung over one of the chairs, and the aroma of rosewater filled the space. A hot bath had been drawn with the scented additions. Naomi would have shown more gratitude over breakfast if she'd known how Lucy planned everything.

"It's all lovely. Would you mind if I bathe first?"

"Not if you allow me to undress you."

Paul's hands trailed her neck, going to the little buttons at the nape of it as he kissed her collarbones. He helped her into the tub and retreated to the bedroom.

She settled into the heat, a sigh of contentment escaping as she lounged—her silent husband almost forgotten. While she washed in preparation to lay with him, Naomi couldn't help but remember the feel of his hard body against her. With quickening movements, she finished and reached for the plug.

Paul offered a giant white towel. "There's a perfect view of the tub from that chair."

"You watched me?"

"Every blessed minute."

His absolute manliness when he placed her on the silk sheets left her expectant. Before he could straighten, she unbuttoned his shirt, kissing down his chest.

"Are you ready to make love, my wife?"

"I've been ready since that August night."

Paul was as warm and attentive as their other shared time, but Naomi found everything more fulfilling. It wasn't something forbidden she snuck time to explore. It was beautiful because it was *them*—husband and wife—becoming one for the rest of their lives. His body belonged to her, and she wanted to know everything about it, from pleasure to pain. Naomi unleashed her longings with each exhale, no matter the volume of her passion, as she maneuvered complimentary to him. She found as much pleasure in giving him attention as she did when he aroused her or they mutually benefitted from being joined. Safe in the arms of love, Naomi slept completely at ease in the strange location.

***

The sounds of the forest, from skittering squirrels to tweeting birds, brought the world to wonderful life along with the rising sun.

"Good morning, Husband." Naomi snuggled closer.

"How about a walk to the bay this morning, my hot little honey?"

They dressed and went to the only room they didn't see the day before. The kitchen was glorious, from the oak cabinets to the marble counters. On the massive prep table, a note waited.

Orange juice in the refrigerator, coffee fixings on the side counter.

Help yourself to anything. I'll be over around nine o'clock to prepare brunch.

-Rosemary

They each took a glass of orange juice to save time, bringing it onto the back porch. Naomi sat in Paul's lap, and they watched the critters in the underbrush.

"Do you mind if we go to the mausoleum first?" Naomi asked.

"The what?"

"Eliza Melling's tomb. It should be down that path there." She pointed to the neatly raked section of forest beyond the old barn. They went for the path holding hands. Naomi lowered her voice as the forest surrounded them. "Eliza was Alexander's younger sister. She died after a fall from her horse when she was nineteen."

The gleaming white walls of the mausoleum were seen through the trees before they arrived in the clearing. Lying on the steps to the door was a bouquet of roses, faded and crumbling. Naomi reached for the note tucked between the stems. Written in Lucy's flowing hand were the words:

Rest well, Eliza.

I'll join you soon.

Naomi went to her knees, choking on despair.

Paul pulled her into his arms. "What is it?"

She sucked air around the lump in her throat. "Lucy's planning her death."

Paul took her to the lone bench under an ancient oak. There he cradled her in his arms until her breathing settled.

"I'm sorry," her voice rasped several minutes later. "It was a shock to see it in words though she's been hinting at death for months now."

"I'll make coffee, and we can take our walk this afternoon."

The Watts family found Paul and Naomi sitting at the corner table in the kitchen when they arrived.

Rosemary introduced a beautiful young lady with a heart-shaped face as their daughter, Priscilla. Then she pressed for the reason behind Naomi's upset. After hearing of the note, she gasped. "Miss Lucy's been as good as gold when she's here. I'm sorry to hear there's been trouble with her."

"The outlook isn't good," Naomi informed the Wattses. "Her younger sister committed suicide in August. As a precaution, someone is always with Lucy now. Alexander knows he'll need to hire more help at some point, though it's difficult to do so without alarming her."

"She's a shy lady if there ever was one. I remember the day she came when they were engaged the year before the fire. Like a pale mouse, she was on Master Melling's arm. I don't think I heard her speak more than a few sentences."

"Please, think of me," Priscilla said. "I've finished my schooling and turn sixteen in February. I adore Miss Lucy and would be happy to help however I could. Housekeeping, sitting with her, watching the children, anything."

"I'll inform Mr. Alex," Naomi answered. "He's determined to keep her at home, but it will take everyone we can gather to keep her there."

Twenty-Eight

Melissa meticulously dressed for Bethany's seventh birthday party held the Friday evening before her special day. The last month had been more difficult than ever, and in an attempt to cheer herself, she used several weeks' worth of the newspaper money to purchase a new evening ensemble. Seeing her body draped in the chiffon sleeves of the pale pink and black gown with her ankles and much of her calves exposed wasn't as exciting as she expected. Not without the admiration of a man.

Freddy—now Major Davenport—was firmly installed on the western front in France while autumn turned to winter. His letters came monthly though she continued to mail his notes weekly. His previous one mentioned something she'd written about in June, so she knew the post was slow to find him and return to her, but she took heart in his loving words and humor. He always shared something amusing though she knew horror met him each day.

"Mommy," Louisa said as she came into the bedroom, "I need help with my bow."

Louisa turned her back, and Melissa tied the blue sash on the new dress. Her daughter had grown leggy over the summer and required more clothing for the cooler season. "Be sure to pick a wrap, Sweetie. It might be chilly on our way home."

"You too, Mommy." Louisa fingered the sheer sleeves when she turned around. "Those won't keep your arms warm."

Melissa embraced her. "Hugs are my favorite wraps. Daddy gives the best hugs, warm and strong. I miss him, and I know he's thinking of us extra this weekend with it being Bethany's birthday."

"Uncle Claudio will hug you tonight."

She nodded and tried to ignore the excitement that rushed through her body at the thought of Claudio's touch.

They gathered the gift boxes for Bethany and drove to the Mellings' house, where the birthday girl in an orange dress that matched her stuffed tiger welcomed them. Melissa kissed her forehead, unable to hug her with arms full of gifts.

"Happy Birthday, Beth."

"That's a pretty shawl and beautiful gown, Sissa."

Alex came to the doorway of the living room. "So it is. And daring to show so much of your shapely legs. All those walks do them a world of good."

She ignored his wink and went for the dining room to place the gifts on the side table. He began to follow, but Lucy called out. "Alex, please take Louisa's cape."

She heard Alex's remarks about my legs. Serves him right!

When she returned, Claudio came in the front door with his hand clasped around Bethany's. He paused, his gaze traveling Melissa's body as she removed the black shawl from her shoulders.

"Doesn't Sissa look beautiful?" Bethany asked.

"*Sí*, she always does, *Principessa*."

The three entered the front room. Lucy was curled in Alex's lap, his arm about her and a hand caressing her hip through the purple silk dress.

Melissa caught Phoebe's eye, who sat on the other side of her stepfather. "Did you have a good week at school?"

"Yes, Sissa. And Uncle Claudio stopped in yesterday and ate lunch with us." She giggled. "He brought us tiny cakes. The sisters hate when he does that because it makes the other children jealous."

Claudio frowned. "Why have you not told me, *Principessa?*"

"Because I enjoy the cakes, and it's fun to see pinched faces on the nuns."

Alex laughed, and Lucy looked at him as if to say, "she's yours."

"But the newest sister is quite pretty. She—"

"And what of you, Bethany?" Claudio asked. "Do you enjoy the cakes, or is it too much trouble for me to continue bringing them?"

All eyes on her, Bethany lowered her gaze to her dress, trailing a finger over the organza ruffle. "I like to see you more than receiving the cakes."

Phoebe rolled her eyes as the doorbell rang. Bethany escaped the conflict to welcome the Adams family. Horatio fell in with Louisa and Asher on the floor with a handful of tin soldiers. Melissa hugged Henry, who she hadn't seen in weeks, though she often spoke to him over the telephone.

"You look well," she told Darla.

"I'm keeping my energy up so far, which is a good thing since I'm still working four days a week with Dr. Hughes."

Melissa took her friend's hand. "As I reminded you at Hattie's science meeting, if you ever need someone to watch Horatio, bring him over."

"Thank you. It's handy to have Mrs. Warner next door, but she only has two months left of her pregnancy."

When the group moved to the dining room, Alex escorted the birthday girl on one arm and his wife on the other, placing both of them on either side of him. Phoebe reluctantly chose to sit between her half-brother and Claudio, Melissa across the table between Louisa and Darla.

Halfway through the main course, Lucy turned her attention to Melissa. "Did you decide about the Thanksgiving invitation? Maxwell asked me when he rang today if I'd heard because you've yet to respond to his invitation."

Maxwell would host Edmund's and Lucy's families the following Thursday, and invited Melissa and Louisa to join them. Melissa could think of a hundred other things she'd rather do than have dinner with Edmund—who she'd managed to avoid since his scathing remarks at Alex's birthday supper—but none were good enough excuses to keep her daughter from her half-siblings and extended family on a holiday.

"I have learned we are a few volunteers short for the community Thanksgiving dinner," Claudio said. "I was going to ask if you would care to help us."

Lucy's eyes narrowed, and she looked to Claudio.

"It does a soul good to be of service to others," he said in answer to her glare.

"I often helped at soup kitchens on holidays in New York, but I'm afraid it wouldn't be fair to Louisa."

"Louisa could come with us," Alex offered.

Melissa looked to Alex, knowing he had his hands full with three children and Lucy. "It wouldn't be too much for you?"

"Not at all." Alex leaned forward to catch Louisa's eye. "Would you like to be with your poppy on Thanksgiving, Littlest Princess?"

Hearing Freddy's name for her daughter dropped Melissa's heart into her stomach.

"Yes, please!" Louisa glowed.

"Then Melissa may fulfill her charity service, and Claudio needn't look further for helping hands."

"But she isn't even Catholic!" Phoebe blurted.

"God does not care where our faith lies," Claudio said as he clasped his hands. "He only wishes his children to show their love for him by helping others."

The conversation dropped.

After chocolate cake, it was present time. Phoebe insisted on being the first giver. She gifted Bethany a set of princess paper dolls, to which Asher offered a complimentary one of a prince. After a pile of dresses was presented from Lucy and Alex, Claudio gave Bethany a white leather illuminated Holy Bible and the Adamses a sketch pad and pencils for drawing ideas to sew. Bethany adored the assorted yards of fabric Melissa picked out and the coordinating ribbons and threads from Louisa.

The last offered gift was from Freddy. As with Phoebe's birthday present, he saw to it himself when home the few weeks between training and deployment. Melissa only knew it was jewelry from Mr. Hofstedder's shop.

Eyes shining, Bethany read the personal note. Still clutching the paper, she retrieved a golden locket on a long chain from the white box. When Bethany slipped it over her head, it hung below her heart—the perfect length to grow into. She opened the oval locket and smiled at what lay inside before going to her mother.

Lucy looked at the locket, and a hand went to her mouth as if to cover a sob. Bethany turned to her stepfather, who gave a bittersweet smile.

"It's lovely, Bethany." He kissed her cheek and then Lucy's. "Come, my queen. Let's ready the music for dancing."

The children surround her to see the necklace.

"Handsome Daddy and beautiful Momma!" Phoebe declared.

Melissa turned cold. Henry and Darla stopped to look and followed the children into the morning room, leaving Claudio and Melissa behind.

Bethany came to her stepmother, holding the letter out. "Don't be sad, Sissa. Read this."

Dearest Bethany,

Happy seventh birthday to my beautiful Little Princess. I am sorry I cannot be there with you, but I am sure Momma and Poppy have a wonderful celebration planned in my absence. It has been many months since I last kissed you goodbye, and you are bigger and smarter than ever. Here is a special gift you can keep close to your heart for many years to come. Just as all my children are special to me, all your parents have a special place in your heart. When you open the locket, you will see your momma and me, as we will always be your parents. But you are blessed with Poppy and Sissa, who love you as well. I thought it best to include them. When opened, look for a tiny latch inside the locket. Momma's picture will swing on a hinge. Flip it, and you have the opportunity to see me and Sissa together and then Momma and Poppy on the other side. This can be your secret from me, or you may wish to show it. Know your family loves you, Bethany Iris, this year and always.

I Love and Miss You,

Daddy

Melissa, shedding silent tears, took hold of the locket around Bethany's neck. The front held an engraved iris, and the back read "To Beth, Love Daddy." Inside were two miniature paintings styled from photographs of Freddy and Lucy. When she sprung the latch and flipped the painting, she gazed at noble Frederick Davenport and herself. Lucy's portrait then faced Alex's—both fair and sensual.

She brought Bethany into her arms. "Your daddy loves you, Beth."

"He loves you too, Sissa." She kissed her and then straightened. "Poppy will want to give me the first dance. You'll come in, won't you?"

Melissa wiped her cheeks and nodded.

"I'm going to show Momma and Poppy the secret, but I wanted to show you first."

When Bethany left the room, Melissa gave up trying to be strong and pressed her face into her hands. Claudio moved to stand behind her, a warm touch on the back of her thin gown until she gathered her emotions.

Later, when she danced in Claudio's arms, Melissa whispered to him. "Thank you for inviting me to help on Thanksgiving. I do miss helping in the community."

"I am pleased to hear that because I feared my motivation was entirely selfish, *Eroina*."

A wave of heat flowed over her. Melissa was about to tell him to come to her that night when a hand went to Claudio's shoulder.

"I'm cutting in, whether you like it or not."

Alex took Claudio's place. "You need to check your emotions at the door when it comes to him. You two grow more obvious each week."

"Obvious of what? We're close friends."

"Too close. It will turn into a scandal, and he will be sent away or lose his position or both. Then Freddy will kill him, so it won't matter anyway. He's already beaten Claudio twice. What do you think he'll do when he learns the priest bedded his wife after all his other infractions?"

Melissa tried to free herself from his hold, but Alex didn't release her. "You speak as though we've lain together, but we haven't."

"How much longer do you think it will be before control is lost?"

"We're stronger than that."

"You're both human, and mistakes will be made."

"Is love a mistake?" she countered.

Looking annoyed, Alex released her. Melissa went to Henry, who waltzed Phoebe around the room, requesting to Turkey Trot with him for the next dance. Melissa took a seat opposite Lucy and watched as Bethany showed her mother the secret to the locket.

Twenty-Nine

Claudio waited outside the Baptist fellowship hall on the north side of town as Melissa parked on the side street. A fine sight behind the wheel of Frederick's massive automobile in a sensible skirt, white blouse, and her short hair pulled back on the sides with gold combs.

"Thank you for coming," he said as he took her hands. He kissed both cheeks, and she did the same to him.

"I'm happy to help." She leaned to his ear. "Same as I told you last night."

Her smile and the spark in her brown eyes brought the remembrance of the taste of her kisses to the forefront of his mind.

Claudio gripped her arm with one hand and his crucifix with the other, steering them to the door. "*Eroina*, you bring both joy and pain."

Claudio escorted her to the elderly nun who ran things inside the fellowship hall. "Here is our extra set of hands, Sister Mary. This is Melissa Davenport."

She looked up at Melissa towering above her. "Leave it to Father De Fiore to bring the prettiest volunteer. I hope you can work hard. We have one hundred and fifty souls to feed today."

"That should be no problem as I've served meals for over five hundred people on several occasions when I lived in New York City."

"New York! You'll be another foreigner like Father De Fiore." Sister Mary stared at Melissa until her smile gave her away. "Bless you, dear. I'm not as senile as that. I was born after New York was granted statehood."

Melissa laughed. "Of course, Sister. How may I help today?"

"At the dessert station with Sister Prudence. That's the best place for friendly smiles."

"I think Melissa might be more comfortable working at the front of the food line," Claudio said in a rush.

"So you can keep an eye on your friend?"

He straightened under the woman's gaze. "So I may answer any questions she might have."

The nun patted his arm. "Then work the potatoes, Father De Fiore. I know how you Italians love potatoes."

"That is Iri—" Claudio stopped and laughed. "God bless you and your humor, Sister Mary."

The nun took Melissa to her work location and introduced her to Sister Prudence—the very person Claudio wanted to keep her away from. He settled with a deacon rolling silverware into linen napkins at a nearby table to observe the two.

"Do you mean to tell me," Sister Prudence said, "that you're part of *the* Davenport family?"

"Frederick Davenport is my husband."

"Then you write those newspaper articles and have those darling girls. I recently started work at St. Mary's School and have already taken a liking to Phoebe Davenport. She's so fair and bright like—" She looked to Melissa, biting her lip.

"Do you know her mother?" Melissa sliced into a pumpkin pie.

"Only by name." Sister Prudence cut into another pie. "I suppose it's silly to say, but she reminds me of her stepfather."

"Alex!" Melissa looked up in surprise. "You've seen him bringing the girls into school?"

"I haven't been fortunate enough for that." She looked sideways at Claudio, but he averted his gaze. "I've known him for years."

"He does love the cathedral." Melissa kept slicing.

"He's the most magnificent man I've ever met." Sister Prudence's cheeks colored.

"And you came to that conclusion from seeing him at Mass over the years?" There was no denying the piqued interest in Melissa's voice, but Sister Prudence didn't know her inflections.

"I was blessed to know Alexander in a less formal setting before he married, and I took my vows."

Melissa's eyebrow rose at the words, but she wasted no time defending her friends. "I didn't know him before he married Lucy, but he was a scoundrel from what I've heard. He's completely devoted to her, and everyone that sees them together remarks on their love. Their son is darling, and Alex dotes on our stepdaughters like nothing I've ever seen."

To Claudio's relief, Sister Prudence took Melissa's declaration of Alexander's devotion to heart, sobering the unrighteous yearning on her countenance as she settled back to work.

**

The following Monday, Claudio stopped by St. Mary's School to see Bethany and Phoebe before having lunch at the Davenport house. He found Sister Prudence leaning over Lucy's oldest in the cafeteria. Claudio silently came up behind them.

"And how does your poppy ride his horse?" The nun put a hand on Phoebe's shoulder.

"Like a commandeering militiaman! He's the fastest rider at the stables."

"I'm sure he is, Miss Phoebe. I caught a peek of him this morning when he dropped you off."

"I could introduce you, Sister Prudence."

Claudio expected her to lie and seek an invitation to speak to Alexander.

"You're sweet to offer, but we knew each other when we were younger, and five years ago, he helped a friend of mine. He's a fine man, though I doubt he'd be pleased to speak with me again."

"You are exactly right, Sister Prudence. Mr. Melling would not be interested in rekindling a connection with you."

"Uncle Claudio!" Phoebe hugged him, eyeing the brown paper bag he held as she did so. "Did you bring me a treat today?"

"*Sí, Principessa.*" He kissed her forehead. "I brought something to keep you out of trouble."

He retrieved a shiny red apple, and Phoebe turned her nose up, though accepted it. "Thank you, Uncle Claudio. But I think you were rude to Sister Prudence."

Claudio smiled at the nun. "But you do not think I was harsh, do you, Sister?"

She shook her head and looked away. "Not at all, Father De Fiore. I'll see you later, Miss Phoebe."

Claudio excused himself to visit Bethany.

She happily accepted her gift. "Thank you, Uncle Claudio. I love apples."

"Does Sister Prudence speak to you much?"

"No, but I see her often with Phoebe. Everyone likes to talk to her more than me, but that's okay." Bethany's soft voice lowered more, and she looked to Claudio. "I don't like Sister Prudence. She makes me feel itchy. Does that make me bad?"

"No, *Principessa*, it means you are in tune with the spirit." He did the sign of the cross over her. "I will see that she leaves you both alone."

She hugged him. "Will you be at Friday supper?"

"I wouldn't miss it."

After saying goodbye, he found Sister Prudence coming out of a classroom around the corner and stopped her in the middle of the hall.

"You must stay away from the Davenport girls. Nothing good will come of it."

He was used to her being meek, but she boldly met his eyes. "Maybe nothing good in the long run, but there's plenty to satisfy me temporarily."

At the Davenports' house, Louisa looked out the screen door with her intense eyes.

"Uncle Claudio!"

"Open the door for him," Melissa called from the kitchen.

He lifted the girl into his arms. "*Ciao, Principessa.*"

She kissed his cheeks and leaned to his ear. "I missed you, *Father* Claudio."

He pulled her away from him a few inches and frowned. "What did I tell you months ago, Louisa?"

Clinging to him, she buried her head beneath his chin. "I miss Daddy, and I love you."

"*Principessa...*" He stepped further inside, and she wrapped her legs about his middle as though afraid he would put her down. The moisture from her tears soaked through his cassock and shirt. Rubbing her back, he sang an Italian lullaby before speaking. "I love you as well and will be here as a friend, but I cannot be your father."

"Don't you want to, Uncle Claudio?"

"I would love to, *Principessa*, but it cannot be." Opening his eyes, his gaze fell to Melissa, heartache etched on her face. He continued to speak softly to Louisa. "You will have to be satisfied with me sharing meals and coming to play."

Louisa raised her head a few inches. "And making Mommy smile? Be sure you hug her, Uncle Claudio. She cried last night after she tucked me in bed."

Melissa's hand went to her cheek and she abruptly turned back to the kitchen.

"Come, *Principessa*. Dinner smells too good to stand out here with sad faces. What did you prepare today?"

"Soup and sandwiches."

They washed in the hall bathroom before joining Melissa in the kitchen. Claudio did not take it personally when Melissa barely kissed his cheeks.

Worry over Sister Prudence's schemes and Melissa's melancholy weighed Claudio, but he managed to smile for the precious girl. Unlike Phoebe and Bethany who favored one parent over the other, mother and father could never deny Louisa.

Would it be easier to attempt to step into Frederick's place if he was not looking at me through his daughter's eyes? Would I have already taken his wife and claimed his child without that reminder? God help me; I am as bad as Sister Prudence in coveting that which is not mine!

After eating, Louisa climbed into Claudio's lap and snuggled against his shirt. He had opened his cassock to help the tear spots dry, and the sides of his black covering served as a blanket.

"Would you like me to bring you to bed for your nap, *Principessa?*"

"May I stay with you, Da—Uncle Claudio?"

He looked to Melissa. She pressed her lips together and gave a shallow nod.

"Yes, Louisa." He left a kiss on her forehead. "But let us go to the sofa."

With Louisa snug on his shoulder for the relocation, Claudio used his free arm to capture Melissa's hand. She joined them without protest but took the armchair by the window rather than beside them. Melissa observed her daughter's descent into slumber before speaking.

"A letter came Saturday that I can't get out of my head." Her voice dropped lower. "Freddy sounded different, discouraged. With all the censoring of the mail, he can tell me nothing of where he is, other than the weather turned cold much quicker than it does in Mobile because it was only September, and he needed wool socks and a coat. I don't know how I'll survive this winter knowing he's suffering and depressed with a group of young men he's responsible for. Claudio, if he loses any, it will shatter him. How can I enjoy the comforts of life while he suffers?"

"You do it because you must. He went willingly. You being left was no choice of your own. You accept the help and support you need so you can be strong enough to care for his precious daughters. Not to mention Alexander and Lucy. And with the newspaper, you reach even more to cry with them and lift them. You need to be comforted and cared for so you might care for all those who rely on you, and it is many, *Eroina.*"

Melissa settled beside Claudio, rested her head on the opposite shoulder from her daughter, and whispered her thanks.

Thirty

Paul dropped Naomi at the end of the Mellings' driveway Tuesday, December fourth, at the same time Melissa drove up with Louisa. Naomi let them in the kitchen door with her key. Alexander sang "I'm Always Chasing Rainbows," one of the new songs he collected as soon as the sheet music was printed, hoping the children would want to learn piano so they wouldn't have to rely on the phonograph for all their music.

"It does my heart good to hear that," Naomi said to Melissa as she set her purse on a hook near the pantry. "Lucy's been in good spirits the past few weeks, and if that man's singing a peppy tune, it's more good news."

"But does he know I'm taking Lucy to a lawyer this morning?" Melissa whispered.

"I expect he does." Naomi pushed through the swinging door when his song faded.

While the children greeted each other, Naomi followed Melissa's lead to the morning room and found Lucy dressed in a plain skirt and blouse.

"Morning, Miss Lucy. Don't you look business-like today?"

"That's the point, Naomi." She smoothed the hairs around her chignon.

While her hands were still fussing about her hairstyle, Alexander came up behind her, arms going about her waist as he kissed her neck. "Shall we reschedule our morning appointments and return to bed, my queen?"

Lucy turned to him with equally roaming hands and their typical kissing—much too familiar for polite society. Melissa caught Naomi's eye and shrugged, taking a seat on the far side of the room.

"Alex." Lucy giggled as his lips migrated to her throat. "Remember to meet us at Mr. Spunner's office at ten."

He frowned. "I still don't understand why you insist on using Sean for legal matters."

"I want to make sure it doesn't look like someone in your practice influenced me, and Sean has always been kind." She kissed Alexander on the cheek and stepped out of his arms.

"My queen, what are you up to?"

"Updating my will, which should have been done years ago." The three others in the room stared at her and then exchanged nervous glances. Her hands went to her hips. "Have I not been steady these past weeks? Would each of you say this day I'm of sound mind?"

Cold seeped into Naomi's bones, and she laid a hand on her stomach. *How difficult has it been for her to keep her moods steady, to balance her emotions, knowing she needed to be "of sound mind" to do what she wants to be done?*

"Yes, my queen, but there isn't much to change. Surely someone at my office could handle adding Asher and dividing your royalties and savings by three instead of two."

"Come at ten, and Mr. Spunner will read through it with all of us in attendance so there will be no questions of what my wishes are when I'm no longer here."

Phoebe ran into the room. "Come on, Poppy! I want time to see my special friend before school."

Melissa stood. "Good morning, Phoebe."

"Hello, Sissa." She paused as if thinking that was enough before she crossed the room to her stepmother for a hug and kiss. "How's Doff?"

"Doff is good and will be as pleased to see you as I am after school." Melissa kissed her forehead and then sat down heavily when Phoebe turned away.

Once Alexander was gone with the oldest girls, Lucy hurried Melissa out the door. Naomi constantly checked the nearest clock as Asher and Louisa frolicked in the yard the first hour. Once the children were settled in the morning room with a jigsaw puzzle, she slipped into the kitchen to make a telephone call.

"Good morning," the cheerful voice answered.

"Hello, Miss Darla."

"Naomi! Charlotte is nice enough, but Friday suppers aren't the same without you."

Naomi laughed. "I miss y'all as well. I'm watching Asher and Louisa at the Mellings' right now if you and Horatio want to stop in."

"That would be great, thank you. I wasn't feeling good yesterday, so we stayed home all day. Dr. Hughes made me promise not to work, but I feel fine. We'll be over in half an hour."

Once their friends arrived, the three children took Asher's ball into the yard to throw around. Naomi brought coffee to the patio for her and Darla, telling her how Lucy had been the last few weeks and the morning appointment.

"She's stubborn, and I can see her willing herself to keep her moods in check to accomplish what she wants." Darla stirred cream into her cup. "But what of you, Miss Naomi? You've got a healthy glow about you despite your worries."

"I think…I mean, I wondered if you would possibly take on a colored patient."

"Oh, Naomi!" Darla was out of her seat for a hug. "There's no question, and you know it! Are you certain?"

She smiled and smoothed her skirt. "About as certain as I can be. I haven't had a monthly since before my wedding, and I've felt queasy this past week."

Darla squeezed her hand. "Have you told Paul?"

"I will over supper tonight. I used to be scared, afraid he was done with children since his girls were raised, but the last few weeks, he's been reminiscing about when they were babies, how he loved their sweet sounds and their tiny fists gripping his finger. I think he'll be pleased."

"Of course he will!" Darla's grinned. "What man doesn't want the opportunity to feel virile and he with a second chance at youth with a younger wife? You're blessed to have his maturity to draw on. He won't be like Alex without a clue in the world."

"And how was Mr. Henry when it was your time with Horatio?" Naomi asked.

Darla grinned. "He'd assisted with horses when he was growing up, so he knew enough. But I warned him if he patted my rump and told me I was a good mare, I'd sock him."

They laughed so much the children ran over to see what the matter was.

"Can Horatio stay for dinner, Miss Naomi?" Asher asked.

"He and his mother are welcome to."

Louisa took Darla's hand. "Please do!"

"All right, Louisa."

"What will we eat?" Asher asked.

"Soup and sandwiches." Naomi stood. "I'll get them going."

"That's what we had with Uncle Claudio yesterday," Louisa said before running back into the yard with the boys.

Naomi and Darla looked at each other.

"He lunches with them twice a week," Darla said. "It's better than him going over at night."

Naomi made a motion of buttoning her lips.

Darla sighed. "I can only be a friend and pray for them—and Frederick."

***

Their guests were still over when Lucy and Melissa returned. Lucy immediately seized Darla and brought her into the den, leaving Melissa with Naomi in the morning room.

"What is it?"

"She updated her will and spelled out every detail of what she does and does not want after her death." Melissa flopped onto the sofa, a hand on her head. "Poor Alex was in tears and begged for Sean to stop, but Lucy insisted it be read in full. She even had Alex sign a statement declaring he would honor all her wishes."

"What all was it? Surely the children splitting her assets wouldn't be difficult to hear."

Melissa looked to the doorway and waved Naomi closer. "She's putting me in control of all literary decisions, including rights to her books and any possible printing of her other writings."

"You're the best choice for that."

"She's splitting her money between Alex and her three children, with ten percent being pulled first to upkeep the Seacliff estate. If one dies, fresh income is divided between the remaining people unless there are new dependents for the one who passed. That allows for the girls to mature and have families of their own, protecting their legacy, but also spelled out that it goes for Alex as well, should he remarry. That set him off, and then it got worse."

Naomi groaned.

"She insists on being buried with Eliza in the mausoleum with Claudio offici—"

Lucy and Darla returned.

"Thank you for inviting me and Horatio, Naomi. We enjoyed our time, but I need to get home so I can rest before supper."

They said goodbye, and after Darla and Horatio were gone, Melissa spoke. "I should find Louisa and be on my way as well."

"Do you need a bite to eat?" Naomi asked, hoping to get time to speak with her more.

Lucy was quick to reply. "We stopped at a restaurant on the way back, though she didn't eat much."

"I have the leftovers in the automobile." Melissa went for the hall.

"I suppose you'll be angry with me for a while," Lucy said. "I didn't think you'd mind handling my literary affairs, especially as you know the publisher."

Melissa met her gaze with coolness. "It's not that, and you know it."

Lucy gave her innocent stare, widening her eyes with a slight sulk to her lips.

"There was no reason for you to make Alex hear things like that with an audience and then force him to sign a note swearing he'll see to your wishes as if he's a stranger you can't trust."

"It's nothing to you how I handle my husband."

"It is when you drag me in as witness! You were cruel, Lucy. An absolute bitch, especially when he begged for it to stop!"

"He's stronger than he gives himself credit for. I can't trust that he'd keep to my wishes if he felt them wrong when he's in an emotional state."

"Alex never denies you anything!"

Lucy's chin was high. "And this will see that he never will, even after I'm gone."

"It'll do nothing but drive a wedge between you and urge him to old indulgences."

"I'm sure compassionate Melissa will be there to comfort him."

"Maybe I would." Melissa sneered at Lucy. "You're too full of yourself to recognize you've pushed Alex to the edge. You know he needs validation, but you ran him dry today—and in front of one of his oldest friends."

Fear flicked across her countenance. "He'll go riding and return home fine as anything."

Melissa shook her head. "You keep telling yourself that, and maybe it will make it true."

***

Wednesday afternoon, the Mellings' front door banged open before three o'clock when Alexander typically didn't return until after five from the stables. Naomi looked to Lucy, who stood from her desk in the morning room.

"I don't understand why we can't go riding!"

"Go to your room, Phoebe," Alexander's voice was harsh.

"But Poppy, you like surprises!" Her shrill voice carried down the hall.

"Go!" Footsteps raced for the stairs then the door to Alexander's den slammed shut.

Bethany wandered into the room, eyes wet. Lucy opened her arms and Bethany rushed to her mother for a hug.

"Can you go play in your room, Asher?" Lucy asked over Bethany's shoulder.

"Yes, Momma."

Lucy pulled her daughter into her arms. "What's the matter, Bethany Iris?"

"Phoebe says I shouldn't tell."

"What does Poppy say?"

"He was too mad to say anything. I'm scared, Momma. I never liked Sister Prudence, and she tricked Phoebe into surprising Poppy."

Lucy paled.

Naomi came to their side. "You did fine, Miss Bethany. None of this is your fault. Go on to Asher's room and play with him, Sugar."

"Melissa was right," Lucy said when Bethany left. "I drove him to old indulgences."

"I'll hear none of that. Sit a moment, and I'll make tea."

Lucy ran to the den, throwing the door open. "Alex!"

"I can't see you right now."

"Don't leave me! Please don't—"

"Get out!" His red-ringed eyes burned as a cloud of cigarette smoke curled around him.

Naomi took Lucy's arm, urging her toward the door. "You can discuss this when everyone is calmer," she whispered.

"I was too cruel this week! He'll go back to the arms that find no fault in him. The one who offers herself because she adores him more than her covenants with God!"

"Shut up!" Alexander roared.

"My angel, I need you," Lucy whispered, reaching for him.

With a cold stare, he looked to Naomi. "Get her away from me."

"Don't hate me!" Lucy screeched as Naomi pulled her out of the den, the door locking behind them.

Lucy pounded on it a few times, and then Naomi forced her to the morning room while she went for the telephone on the desk.

"Davenports'."

"I need you to come get the girls, Melissa," Naomi said in a rush. "Do you think you could handle Asher too?"

"Of course, Naomi. What's—"

"Could the children spend the night?"

"Yes, I'll—"

"Come quick!" Naomi hung up the telephone while Lucy hugged herself, ridged body rocking as tears coursed her face.

Thirty-One

Melissa rushed to Sharon in the kitchen. "I need you to watch Louisa. There's an emergency at the Mellings,' and I'll be bringing the children home. If there isn't enough to feed everyone, I'll do without supper."

Once at the mansion, Melissa hurried through the yard.

"Quite a day," was all Charlotte said as Melissa burst through the backdoor.

Naomi stood guard at the juncture of the downstairs hallways.

"What can I do?" Melissa asked.

"I need to stay with Lucy, but we need to find out what all happened." She recounted what Bethany said and then explained to Melissa the history of Sister Prudence and Alex.

"I should speak with him."

"You need to get the children out of here. I'll keep with Lucy until Alex is on speaking terms with her."

Charlotte came from the kitchen. "I can go upstairs and watch the children."

"Thank you, Charlotte. That will be a great help," Melissa was quick to say. "I'll check Lucy with you and then see to Alex."

Lucy still sobbed, but Melissa and Naomi got her to the sofa and made her lie on her side.

"It's as you said. I drove him to seek old comforts, and now you'll finish him off with your sophisticated airs. I'll never have him again once he has you. Don't go to him!"

It took all her self-control to walk away rather than slap Lucy. Melissa went to the kitchen and out to the patio to try the French doors. Unlocked.

Alex sat in his desk chair facing the entry as he nursed a cigarette.

"May I beg a smoke, dashing Poppy?"

"Anything for you, darling Sissa." A smile tugged at the corner of his mouth as he pulled his gold case free. "I suppose Lucy sent for you."

"On the contrary. She begged me not to come." Melissa remembered Lucy's words from the time of Hazel Kline's pretrial— that it was good for Alex to fill his reservoir by flirting with their female friends rather than *other sources*. Sources she now knew were like Sister Prudence. Pulling from that information and the desperation on his face, Melissa leaned over him, a hand on his knee. "She thinks my sophisticated ways will spoil you."

"I could use a good spoiling." His blue eyes brightened, and he caressed her lower lip as he placed the cigarette in her mouth.

Melissa straightened, taking the unlit smoke with her. She locked the patio door and pulled the drapes shut with a fluid motion. When she turned back to him, Alex shone like brilliant fire in the lamplight.

"Lucy treated you dreadfully at Sean's office."

"She was cruel, but she tried to make it up to me last night."

"Did it work?" Melissa stepped closer.

He took her wrist, a fingertip swirling along the inside of it. "I may have asked her to try again this morning."

She laughed at his honesty as she brought a hand to his shoulder. "And have you been good since then?"

He snuffed out his cigarette though he still hadn't lit hers, and leaned back in his chair. "I'm always a gentleman, even when women throw themselves at me."

"Alex the Angel."

"I might not reach sainthood, but it would be heaven to kiss you." He stood, clutching her hips in a way that caused her to gasp in pleasure. His enchanting smile filled his face, dimples on full display above the discoloration of his old burns. "I bet you didn't think I could stroke that sound from you. There is much I could do for you, Melissa."

She leaned against him, her cheek resting on his temple. "What could I do for you?"

Alex's lips brushed her throat. "Put me out of my misery from wondering over the taste of you all these years."

"Why, so you can throw it at Lucy when she's being cruel or boast to Freddy?"

"You, Melissa Stone Davenport, are the one secret I'd be willing to take to my grave."

He grasped her hips once more and then pressed in just the right spot with his thumbs that made her reflexively thrust against him. Mouth gaping in surprise, Alex brought a finger to her chin to close it and then trailed his touch across her jaw.

"Darling Sissa, we share the girls as stepparents. We can share a kiss." Beneath the thin layer of bravado was the sensitive soul of the true Alex—vulnerable as he waited for acceptance.

She set the unused cigarette on his desk. "First, I need to know why you shut Lucy out."

He raked a hand through his hair. "Because I didn't trust myself to speak rationally. I was raving mad at Phoebe for playing into Prudie's schemes, but more so at that woman for involving a child in her attempt to snare me. I couldn't look at Lucy because it was like looking at Phoebe. I needed to clear my head."

"You aren't mad at Lucy?"

"I've gotten over the sensational demands in her will, though the day I'm forced to deal with them will be a different story. I'll need you beside me, Melissa." His hands cupped her face, a thumb teasing the corner of her mouth.

Feeding his needs—and paying back Lucy for every unrighteous thing she'd attempted with Freddy after their divorce—she lowered herself to the chaise so he towered over her.

"Show me your prowess, Alex."

He pulled her back upright, a hand going to the small of her back. "The chaise is for my wife. As a dear friend, I'll have to offer you a chair."

Seeing he was in control enough to stay true to Lucy's furniture helped Melissa relax. When Alex brought an armless chair into the middle of the room and sat upon it, she willing hiked her skirt past her bare knees and straddled his lap. His arms went about her waist, and she placed hers around his neck. They gazed at each other for several seconds, Alex grinning like a boy who'd caught the biggest lightning bug.

"It's nice, isn't it?" he asked.

"Nice?" She tilted her head. "I thought you were trying to make me swoon."

"You're going to be like that, are you?" He tried to keep his gaze sultry, but his smirk got in the way.

"I am. And I'm catching a chill. Unless you wish to warm me, I suggest you release me so I can set my skirt properly."

He laughed and leaned his forehead against hers.

"I almost hate to break our fun to show you a proper kiss." Both hands kneaded her hips. When she instinctively arched back, his lips went to her neck, trailing toward her mouth as his hands migrated over her ribs. "To taste you is divine."

Her face lowered to look at him, crisp eyes sharp as ever. Fingers played over her throat like misty rain as he brought his lips to hers. An expert at switching pressure, he read her responses to each movement while his heady scent of sandalwood and cigarettes enveloped her. Hands on her back, he pressed her toward him, nibbling and licking, but didn't force his way into her mouth. Melissa willingly opened to him as he wore down the boundaries. Inhaling her very soul, he made a believer out of her in the power that was Alexander Randolph Melling.

Such was his perfection in pacing the kisses that Melissa wasn't breathless when they finally separated. Smiling, she hugged him. "You're exceptional, dashing Poppy."

"And you're delicious, darling Sissa." He helped her stand. "But not a word of this to Lucy."

"And you never ask for another kiss."

"Fair enough." He caressed her hand before stepping away. "I'll just give and take without asking."

She slapped his rear, causing him to laugh.

"Naughty Sissa."

Melissa slung an arm around his shoulders and kissed his cheek. "Lucy is blessed to have you."

"And Freddy better get back before someone else claims you."

She caught her breath, willing the lump in her throat to drop. "I miss him more each week, and with Junior's birthday approaching—"

"You aren't alone." Alex hugged her fully. "I thought it would be nice for us to spend Christmas at Seacliff Manor, all seven of us. It would be a good change of scenery for the holiday week. What do you think?"

"I'd love that, Alex. Thank you." Melissa took his hand. "Naomi telephoned and thought I needed to bring the children home with me. Would you like me to?"

"That might be best, but let me see to them first."

They separated in the hall, and Melissa went to the morning room. Lucy immediately sat up, studying her.

"Alex is saying goodbye to the children. I'm taking them all home with me for the night. I'll bring the girls to school in the morning and Asher back later in the day. Telephone when you're ready for him."

"And Alex? Is he leaving me too?"

Melissa couldn't help smiling. "He wants the evening with you because he knows you've had a shock. He'll tell you about it after I'm gone." Turning to Naomi, she continued. "Thank you for calling. I'll see you both sometime tomorrow."

Asher ran in, jumping at Lucy. "Goodbye, Momma! I'm going to Louisa's house!"

Then Bethany kissed her. "See you tomorrow, Momma. I love you."

Phoebe—arms crossed and frowning—trudged across the room. "I don't like being sent away. I only did as Sister Prudence asked me."

"You aren't being sent away, Phoebe Camellia," Alex said. "That's your house too. I'm sure Doff will be pleased to see you again."

"But I don't understand why we can't go riding when I only—"

"Later, we'll talk about how you can distinguish if someone is trying to make you do things that aren't proper. Sister Prudence is not to be trusted, and Uncle Claudio will let her know that she's never to speak to you girls again. You, in turn, are not allowed to speak to her either. Do you both understand?"

Bethany smiled. "Yes, Poppy. Thank you."

"Phoebe?"

She sighed dramatically. "I'll stay away, even though she's the prettiest nun at the school."

Lucy gasped.

"Come on, girls." Melissa put a hand on each of their shoulders. "Let's find your brother and go home."

***

After supper, Bethany, Louisa, and Asher worked at the library table in the study, creating maps of Kingdom Davenport and Melling Empire while Phoebe curled under a side table lamp in the parlor with a novel and her cat.

When the telephone rang, Melissa picked up the extension in the kitchen. "Davenports'."

"*Eroina.*" The name rolled over her like a caress.

"I'm glad you called. There—"

"Alexander telephoned. You have your hands full tonight. Would my coming to play a game with them be helpful?"

"I appreciate it, but I think a quiet evening for us would be best."

"Know I am here if you need me."

"Thank you, Claudio." Her voice dropped. "I'll miss you."

"Until Friday supper, *Eroina.* Save a dance for me."

At bedtime, Asher insisted on sleeping in the extra bed in Louisa's room that was left there since the summer visitors. Half an hour after lights out, Melissa had to tell Louisa and Asher to quiet their chatter. When the giggles started back a minute after she climbed in bed, Melissa hugged Freddy's pillow and tried to feel happy that her daughter had a brother-figure in Asher though it brought out her pain and loneliness all the more.

In the morning, Melissa managed to make coffee, a pot of grits, and a pan of bacon before the children woke. Bethany came into the kitchen first, fully dressed but still sleepy and holding her tiger.

"Good morning, Sissa. Here's a hug from Daddy." She greeted her that way every morning she was home.

Melissa smiled and smoothed the girl's hair. "Thank you, Beth. I hope you slept well with those noisy ones across the hall."

"Asher's silly, but they didn't bother me."

After dishing bowls of grits for the two youngest and placing the bacon platter and milk bottle within reach, Melissa settled at the table with Bethany. Asher and Louisa soon arrived, dressed but hair rumpled.

"Good morning."

"Mommy!" Louisa kissed her in greeting, then took Asher's hand to bring him to the chair next to hers.

"Morning, Sissa." Asher grinned like his father.

Phoebe came last, Doff on her heels. She saw to the cat's food and water before sitting.

After breakfast, the children pulled on coats. Melissa stayed uncovered in her wool suit, happy to feel the first real nip in the air. The telephone began ringing as soon as she closed the front door, but she ignored it. Bethany and Phoebe led the way across Catherine Street to St. Mary's, Louisa and Asher holding hands next while Melissa watched over them from behind.

When they reached the school, Bethany held the door for everyone.

Screaming met their ears as they crossed the threshold.

Looking panicked, Phoebe ran toward the commotion around the corner. "Momma!"

"Bethany," Melissa said as she took her arm, "stay here with Louisa and Asher."

Melissa hurried down the hall. Phoebe clung to a red-cloaked Lucy as she tried to get around an ancient priest who shielded a cowering nun.

"She's harassing my children and tried to molest my husband! My daughters will never step foot in this den of filth again!" Lucy yelled as her fists pounded the elderly man. When he finally stumbled against the wall, she lunged at the nun. "He was never yours!"

"Momma!" Phoebe clung to Lucy's cloak. "Stop, Momma! She's my friend!"

Melissa snatched Phoebe, pulling her several feet away from the altercation.

"You can never have him, you whore!" Lucy screamed as she struck. "He married me!"

More administrators arrived on the scene, but none of the frocked and habited people knew what to do. Then Alex rushed in, taking Lucy from behind.

Lucy kept yelling even as her arms were pinned to her sides. "I give him everything he needs!"

"Momma!" Phoebe fought to free herself from Melissa as Alex brought Lucy past them.

A helpless look of devastation on Alex's face met Melissa's gaze. "Please take them all home." And to the priest, he called out, "I'm sorry, Father Ines!"

Tucking Phoebe to her side, Melissa followed the path Alex cleared through the spectators. Standing at the front door with her arms around the two others, Bethany silently cried. Louisa ran to Melissa, and she picked up her daughter.

"Poppy!" Asher reached for his parents as they neared.

"Go back home with Sissa, Phoenix Asher. I'll come for you as soon as I can."

With Louisa on her hip and Phoebe clutched in her other hand, Melissa led the children home.

Thirty-Two

An eerie silence met Naomi as she let herself in the unlocked kitchen door. Alexander's automobile was gone, but there might have been an emergency at the office.

"Lucy," she called as she made her way to the morning room.

It looked as it had when she left yesterday, minus Alexander and Lucy necking on the sofa. All the downstairs rooms were uninhabited. A sense of unease spread quicker than the life growing within her womb. The bedrooms were all empty. Laundry and a damp towel were in the middle of the carpet in the master suite. Naomi hung the towel on the rack and noticed the disorder in the bathroom.

Someone left in a hurry.

Naomi returned to the kitchen and put water on for tea. Out the back window, Alexander carried Lucy across the yard. Once they were on the patio, she saw the dried tears on Lucy's face as well as panic in her green eyes. Naomi opened her mouth to speak, but Alexander shook his head to quiet her.

"I'm taking her to bed. Please bring tea and toast." He kissed Lucy's forehead and continued. "We're home, my queen. We're safe."

While mulling over the odd situation of Lucy dressed for a day out in her grandmother's old cloak and Alexander without a tie or jacket, Naomi urged the water to boil and the toast to brown. She went to the bedroom with the tray but halted in the doorway. Alexander lay curled against Lucy, who was stripped to her silk underwear, pillows propped behind her head. His lips were at her throat. One hand tangled in her loose hair and the other below her waist, unseen beneath the sheet. Without another glance toward the bed, she stepped over the newly discarded clothing to set the tray on the table between the armchairs in front of the unlit hearth. She pulled the door shut on the way out.

Naomi checked the children's rooms for things to tidy. When Lucy moaned in passion, she retreated to the guest rooms in the other wing. After finishing her work, Naomi parked herself on the hall bench near the top of the stairs.

Alexander soon joined her, his usual swagger replaced with defeat as he dropped beside Naomi. "I'm letting her rest."

"What happened?"

He shifted forward, resting his elbows on his knees, and exhaled. "I thought she was stable after we talked and made love last night, but she ran off while I was in the shower this morning. I received no answer at Melissa's, and fearing retribution, I drove to the school. Lucy had beaten Father Ines and attacked Prudie. Melissa held Phoebe back to keep her safe, and Bethany had the other two huddled inside the front door, but they still heard every blasted horror."

"The poor sugars."

Alexander took Naomi's hand and pressed it to his lips before rubbing her knuckles over his forehead. "I've never been so scared. Not even having a gun pointed at me felt like this. I fear I won't be able to refocus her much longer."

"You've got a good support system. None of us are going to abandon you or Miss Lucy."

"Alex!"

They both rushed to the bedroom. Lucy sat upright, clutching the blanket to her chest, frenzied exhaustion burning in her eyes.

"Alex, I'm sorry! May God punish me for doing it!" The tears came in torrents as he cradled her.

Naomi went to the bathroom and readied a washcloth with cold water to apply to the back of her neck. She delivered it to the bed, and Alexander smiled as he smoothed Lucy's hair out of the way.

"I love you, my queen."

Lucy looked upon him, complete anguish in her eyes. "I'm broken, Alex. I feel my thoughts shattering and control slipping. I'll not be a fit mother or a respectable wife much longer, if I ever was to begin with."

"You've been perfect for me, and you'll continue to be perfect the remainder of our days. I need everything you bring to my life—all we share together. If I were willing to settle for what society thought best for me, I would have gone through with that marriage to Beatrice Kirkpatrick. But I didn't want a society doll that would spend more time basking in the attention she received from the press than what passion we shared in private."

"Did you love her?" Lucy fingered the wet patch on his shirt.

"I loved the way she looked on my arm and the thought of seeing what lay beneath her fashionable gowns, but I barely tolerated her companionship." He nuzzled into Lucy's neck. "But with you, I can never get enough. I miss you as soon as one of us parts. I'm half a man without you by my side. I need you, my queen. I need you like rain needs sunlight to create a rainbow."

Naomi couldn't blame Lucy for straddling her husband's lap and kissing him after his passionate declaration. As they lowered to the mattress, Naomi pulled the door closed on her way out. She called Melissa from the kitchen telephone to check on the children and hear the rest of the story. Melissa whispered about Lucy's cruel words and beating fists, as well as Phoebe's desperate pleas to save the nun.

"I've asked Darla to come. I thought Horatio being over would at least distract the younger two from what happened," Melissa said. "She might want to check on Lucy."

"That'll be fine. Thank you, Melissa."

Alexander had Lucy eat the toast and drink a cup of tepid tea before he administered a sleeping draught leftover from one of her other anxious times. By noon, Lucy slept peacefully. He collapsed at the top of the stairs, afraid to go too far in case she called out. One hand rubbed the scars on his bare chest, and the other rested in a tense fist.

"I've got to go to the office for an hour or two at least."

Naomi leaned against the banister. "I'll have a coffee and sandwich ready for you in five minutes. Charlotte will be here by three, and I can stay until four. Darla will probably be by before long to check on Lucy as well."

"With Darla in her condition, I don't want her alone with Lucy. And in another month or two, it'll be best you aren't either. We must protect your growing dear ones."

Naomi's heart dropped. She hadn't considered the thought of violence but knew Alexander was right.

***

Lucy still slept, Charlotte worked in the kitchen, and Darla was gone when Alexander returned at four in his riding clothes. Naomi assisted him in packing a bag for Asher as the children were staying the weekend with Melissa. When the telephone rang, Naomi answered the extension in the upstairs hall while Alexander finished packing for his son.

"Mellings' residence."

"Is Alexander there?" His voice was pained, but his accent flowed languidly.

"Yes, Father De Fiore. Just a moment."

She told Alexander of the call and then continued on to peek at Lucy.

"It would kill her!" Alexander shouted. "I don't care if some part of her would be pleased—the tender part of her will feel nothing but guilt!"

Naomi hurried back to the telephone.

"I'd rather the girls not know either, but I'm sure word will reach them eventually. I already promised Lucy they aren't going back."

He ran a hand through his hair as he listened.

"I'll be there in a few minutes. You can take Melissa for a walk and let her know everything. I'll sit with the children."

He gave a dry laugh. "Yes, I'm sending you off with her alone. I know she needs a bit of a break, even if the news she gets is heavy. I'll trust you not to make an ass of yourself in public."

Alexander hung the receiver and collapsed against Naomi for a hug. "Prudie went back to the convent and hung herself. Lucy mustn't know. God knows I wish I hadn't been told."

"What can be done?"

"Shelter Lucy from the truth." A moment later, he straightened. "I'm sorry, Naomi. I've put you through too much. I might not be home until after five. I need to see to the children and allow—"

"Paul can wait today."

"Have Charlotte give him my supper if needed. I don't think I'll be able to eat tonight."

"You need to take care of yourself as much as you care for her." She undid his collar. "But for now, you need to change. You don't want Phoebe seeing you dressed for riding when you didn't bring her along."

He sighed. "It's less than two weeks until Asher's fifth birthday, and then he'll be clamoring to ride as well. Maybe we should settle at Seacliff even earlier than I planned, so I needn't worry about taking the children to the stables the rest of the month."

"You'll figure it out, Mr. Alex. You've done well with your family and will continue to do so."

Thirty-Three

Friday night the following week, Melissa grabbed the hollow book labeled *Paradise Lost* and stalked to the breakfast nook, barefoot and wearing only a cotton house dress. The cold night air in the screened room helped her feel each muscle beneath her goose-pimpled skin that had spent too much time indoors with demanding children. The words from Freddy's letter raced through her mind as her body chilled to life.

> *Thanksgiving approaches, and I pray you'll spend it with those you cherish. Please tell the girls I think of them all the more on holidays and birthdays. My sweet Bethany will be seven, but I'm sure all the girls have grown much these past four months. What I wouldn't give to hug them and feel your arms around me during the long, cold nights. I hope they like what I have hidden in my dresser for Christmas. Don't forget to slip those boxes into everyone's stockings.*

She'd forgotten the gifts he lovingly tucked away in June. It was a blessing his letter arrived the day before she left for Seacliff Manor because they weren't planning to return until after Christmas.

Retrieving a cigarette and match from the metal case in her pocket, Melissa lit up and leaned back as best she could in the wicker chair. Upstairs, Louisa slept in bed with Bethany in her older sisters' room, a cozy fire in their hearth to keep all three warm during the winter night. Their suitcases were in the hallway, ready to catch the morning ferry across the bay. Melissa wanted to escape the pressure of keeping Phoebe and Bethany away from people who might mention the strange case of a nun hanging herself a few hours after being accosted by their mother. She could stop burning the newspaper delivery each morning before the girls could pick it up and get away from the house to somewhere other than the mile drive to visit Lucy.

She opened the bottle of brandy and drank straight from it, allowing it to coat her throat and warm her empty belly. After a second swig, she finished off her cigarette, laid her head on the table, and cried. Missing her husband and deceased son, despising the Lucy-inflicted banishment, and the ever-oppressive guilt over missing Claudio because she didn't want him coming at night when Phoebe and Bethany were there drowned her heart.

"*Eroina*." His voice came from the dark, bringing hope to her desolation. He slipped in the unlatched screen and pulled her into his arms as he kissed her cheeks. "I cannot stay away when you need me. You are cold and drinking alone. You will be sick before Christmas."

Claudio repacked the bottle into the hollow book and steered her inside. In the study, he used the ambient light from the hallway to place the spirit in its spot on the shelf. Melissa closed the door, locking them in the darkness. She felt the heat coming off Claudio's body as he moved closer. Pausing, he removed his cassock, placing it on the back of her desk chair. She pressed against him until he was wedged between her and the bookshelf, her hungry mouth seeking his. Claudio smelled of fresh incense and tasted of wine. Remembering the peace she felt when he blessed her during her first visit to Mobile, Melissa sought temporary relief with his lips. It had been almost half a year since she shared space with Freddy. Claudio was now the familiar figure in her life. He was home, love, and comfort.

And she needed more.

Her hands slid under Claudio's shirt, traveling up his hot torso. When her fingers met the soft hairs on his chest, she wrapped a leg around him. "Touch me, and please don't make me beg because I would, shamelessly."

Loving hands worked in tandem as they migrated over her green dress. "I give all you ask for, *Eroina*. I will not allow you to suffer."

Claudio's shirt was off, and the top of Melissa's dress was half unbuttoned as he kissed across her collarbones. Then footsteps roamed the upper hall. Melissa's heart caught in her throat, body alternating between panic and disappointment.

"Stay here," she whispered as she fastened a few of her buttons before opening the door.

"Sissa," Bethany said from the steps.

Melissa met her at the foot of the stairs. "What is it, Beth?"

"Louisa had a bad dream. I didn't know if I should wake her, so I held her until she slept peacefully again."

"That was just the thing to do, Sweetie. Thank you." Melissa hugged her and her tiger, hoping the girl wouldn't remark on her rumpled clothing or hair.

Instead, Bethany breathed deeply as they embraced. "You smell like Uncle Claudio after Mass. It's nice."

She held her stepdaughter tighter in response.

"I'll miss him when we're at Seacliff," Bethany continued in her quiet voice. "He told me he would make sure Sister Prudence left me and Phoebe alone."

Melissa forced her voice to action. "You don't need to worry about any of that now."

"I miss school and my friends. May we go back in January?"

"You'll start at a new school next month. I'm discussing with Poppy where it will be."

"Daddy would know. I like being home with you, but it makes me sad because he isn't here. It's easier to stay with Poppy because I don't think of missing Daddy as much. Is that why we're going to Seacliff for Christmas?"

"That's Poppy's reasoning. He loves you as much as your father does."

She nodded and rubbed her eyes.

"Do you need me to walk you back to bed?"

"No, Sissa. Good night." Bethany hugged her once more.

Melissa listened from the bottom of the stairs until Bethany shut her bedroom door. Claudio stood by the desk in the same state of undress. He was nowhere near as strong as Freddy, but every bit as pleasing to look upon. She wanted to continue where they'd left off—going so far as to press her lips to the hollow of his throat and kiss a path to his mouth. But there she paused, gazing into his brown eyes in the shadowed room.

"I will leave if you wish," he whispered as he trailed his hands around her back.

"Beth," she breathed out. "She could smell you on me."

He smiled, the hint of mischievousness brightening his face as he fingered the highest closed button on her dress. "It was beautiful to bring you pleasure, *Eroina*."

"Do you enjoy it, Claudio?"

His smile turned bittersweet. "*Sí*, much more than I should."

Melissa kissed his shoulder and rested her cheek in the curve of his neck. "And then Freddy's daughter interrupts, reminding us of our situation."

For several minutes, they stayed nestled together. Melissa's hand rested over Claudio's heart, feeling the strong beat as a silent message of love. Her hand slowly lowered until she tucked two fingers into his waistband. Her other hand cupped his cheek as she kissed him, slow and deep.

"Merry Christmas, Claudio. I'll miss you the next few weeks. We all will."

***

The following Monday, the Davenports and Mellings were settled at Seacliff Manor. Alex took Lucy and Asher out to a midday dinner for the boy's fifth birthday and returned with fresh evergreen swags and other items to spruce the house for Christmas. Alex led them in decking the halls, Christmas Carols playing repeatedly on the gramophone with him and Phoebe singing the loudest. Lucy was all smiles, and Bethany spent much of her time close to her mother.

The Watts family helped tremendously during those days on the Eastern Shore. Even when Alex took the morning ferry across the bay to work on Tuesday and Thursday, Melissa was free to go for long walks after lunch because Priscilla watched over Lucy and any of the children who stayed behind. The mornings Alex was home, he sent Melissa on solo walks or drives.

When she returned from a solitary motor outing to Fairhope Friday morning, there was a message for her to call the newspaper. Fearing her latest article was lost in transportation across the bay, she hastily shut herself in the library to make the call.

"Mrs. Davenport," Benjamin Paterson's voice crackled over the line, "I trust all is well with you despite the scandal associated with your stepfamily."

"We're having a lovely time away, and none of us care to discuss the unfortunate circumstances."

He laughed. "Very well. I'm calling to extend an invitation on behalf of Order of Mayhem. They would like for you to give a short speech at their New Year's Eve ball, paying tribute to our men in the military and what we can do to support them going into 1918. This will be one of the only official Mardi Gras society festivities this season, and the organizers would like the speech to be given a few minutes before midnight, a solemn reminder before the changing of the year. We can print your speech as your article the following week to save you extra work. What do you say?"

"Could I think about it for a while?"

"Call me by three o'clock, Mrs. Davenport. I'll be able to secure four invitations for you if you agree to it."

"Thank you. I'll telephone as soon as possible."

Melissa hurried to Alex, who lounged on the sofa in the parlor.

"Any trouble?" he inquired.

"I've been given an opportunity I'm not sure I'm up to."

Alex swung his legs down and was up in a second, reaching for her hands. "Whatever it is, darling Sissa, you'll be more than equal to the task."

"Giving the New Year's speech at Order of Mayhem's ball?"

"You'd do the community a great service in accepting. I suppose they want it about noble Frederick and the other thousands of Mobilians serving in the armed forces."

"Exactly, and they'll print my speech for my column the following week."

He looked to the doorway where Lucy stood and crossed the room, hands roaming Lucy's hips over the red dress.

"That was mine and Lucy's first ball together. She stunned the crowd in a gorgeous black gown." A primal growl spread from deep within, and he clutched Lucy's backside, tugging her against his manhood. "It hugged your curves in ways that sent mine and every other man's blood racing. Do you have any idea how I restrained myself on that carriage ride? I wanted to unleash my passion but knew I needed to wait."

"What we did share that night was magic, my angel." Her arms were about his neck, the flush of pleasure on her typically pale cheeks. "You awoke more of my sexuality, as you had with every kiss and touch the two weeks previous."

"Thirteen years of being in love with you." Alex kissed her as his sinuous moves continued to stroke their bodies together. "You've been my everything."

Melissa knew where they were heading and moved her conversation to a close. "I have until this afternoon to decide, but thank you for your vote of confidence, Alex. He said I'd be given four tickets. Do you think it would be appropriate if I attended alone, or would I need an escort?"

"You need an escort, darling Sissa. I'd be happy to be of assistance."

Lucy took Melissa's hand. "I'd love to go to the ball this year."

Melissa looked to Alex, seeing the hope in his eyes. "But what about the children, and who would I ask for my escort?"

"Henry!" Alex offered exuberantly. "He's your husband's business partner. So it would be completely respectable, and Darla could watch the children."

"I know his parents are coming down for Christmas since Darla can't travel, but have you heard from them lately?" Melissa felt a flutter of unease, realizing it had been over a week since either had called. Henry usually checked on her every few days.

"No, but I'll telephone the office and ask about securing them for New Year's," Alex said.

"Is it fair to ask Darla to look after four children in her condition? Not to mention taking away her husband for the evening."

"I'll see if Priscilla would help in Mobile for a few days. She could stay with us and watch Asher and Lucy's girls at least." Alex dashed from the room.

Lucy watched him go, a spark in her green eyes. "I'd like to give him one last pleasurable society outing. I wish we could have shared more over the years because I know he enjoys them."

"Are you up for it, Lucy?"

"I am today and will do my best to remain so. Alexander holds me together with his love, but I'm still crumbling. The more broken I am, the less sway he'll possess over me. I'll do what brings him happiness as long as I'm able."

Lucy settled on the sofa, and Melissa paced the room until Alex returned.

"Henry would like to speak with you, Melissa." His eyes betrayed his concern.

Melissa hurried to the library telephone.

"Henry, how are you?"

"As well as can be expected. I must apologize for not checking in. Davenport would have my hide, but I think you'll understand when I explain." His voice sounded aged, heavy with worry. "I received my order of induction to the Army and leave for training in January. I've been trying to get things in order at the office and console Darla this past week. I knew you were safe with Alex, but I should have called."

"You have your family and the office to see to. Don't worry about—"

"I did write Freddy. I'm sure he'll officially send word to Alex, asking him to pick up when I have to leave, seeing after your well-being and any help you might need. Mr. Peabody will take over managing the office, which includes seeing your deposits are made at the bank. Of course, if you need more, he'll be able to assist you in all things financial. The same will go for Darla. My mother and youngest sister will be staying with her until the baby is born. And I hope you'll be there for her as well, Melissa."

"You know I will." Tears swelled in her eyes. "I'm sorry you have to miss such a momentous occasion. It makes me ill to think of it."

"I don't worry over Darla in the birthing room, but I'm concerned about our child not knowing me. At least your girls are old enough to remember their father when he returns. This baby might shriek at me when a stranger comes home."

"Hold them all close and try to enjoy Christmas, Henry."

"And New Year's Eve with you."

"I couldn't."

"We already discussed it, and Darla insists I bring you. Consider it my final requirement for the Davenports before I turn command of your care over to Mr. Peabody and Alex. I'll be able to tell your husband I Turkey Trotted you into the New Year."

She managed a laugh. "All right, and Merry Christmas if we don't talk before then. Be sure to tell Darla I appreciate her sharing you."

After hanging up the telephone, Melissa covered her face and sobbed.

Thirty-Four

Claudio arrived at the rectory Friday afternoon to a message confirming his appointment with the bishop the following Thursday, as well as an urgent one to call Alexander at Seacliff Manor. He made sure the housekeeper was out of earshot before picking up the telephone in the study.

"Good afternoon."

"And a blessed day to you, Miss Rosemary."

"Father Claudio, it's good to hear your voice!"

"As it is to hear yours. It has been too long."

"We aim to remedy that, Father."

"How so?"

"Mr. Alex gave the message to me should you call while he's *otherwise engaged*. It's Miss Lucy's naptime, as he tells the children."

Claudio laughed. "The Mellings' infamous naptime. What is the message?"

"They had some upsetting news. He wants to know if you can take the ferry over and spend tomorrow with the family. He's most worried over Melissa."

His stomach tightened, fearing the worst. "And did he share the problem?"

"Their friend, Henry Adams, has been drafted and leaves next month. Should I tell Mr. Alex to expect you on the morning ferry?"

"I will be there."

The relief over it not being devastating news about Frederick was short-lived. Claudio grabbed his overcoat and headed to Henry's house. He reflected on Magdalene as he rode the streetcar, wondering if Darla had told her and what the latest news was on Douglas. Then his thoughts drifted to the invitation to the New Year's Eve ball he was given the day before—his fifth masquerade invitation since he moved to Mobile, but he always turned them down.

Claudio soon found himself staring at a vaguely familiar young woman with blonde hair who opened the door at the modest two-story home.

She looked up at him with a smile. "Father De Fiore?"

"*Sí*, I am here to see Darla and Henry."

"Henry isn't home, but Darla is in the sitting room. I'm Bonnie, Henry's youngest sister. I haven't seen you since the wedding."

"You have grown much since then."

He followed her to the parlor, where Darla sat with her legs on the sofa, the red square of a knitting project on her round middle. Henry's parents were in adjacent chairs, but knowing Darla was in the greatest need, Claudio knelt at her side and kissed both cheeks.

"Why must I hear such important news over the telephone all the way from Seacliff rather than from your own lips?"

She shrugged, her blue eyes wet with the threat of tears. "It's still difficult to talk about."

"And have you told Magdalene?"

"I wrote Maggie at the end of last week and already had a reply. She's willing to come to me after Mother and Bonnie leave. They're staying until after the baby is born, and I'm settled, but Father needs to return after Christmas."

Claudio stood and bowed to the others. "Please excuse me for failing to address everyone. It is good to see you again, Mr. and Mrs. Adams."

Horatio ran in on a hobby horse and went for a hug. "Father Claudio!"

Several minutes of polite conversation followed while Horatio bounced on Claudio's knee. "I visit your friends across the bay tomorrow. Shall I give Louisa or Asher a message from you?"

"Tell Louisa my father is going to be a soldier like hers."

"You don't often go there," Darla remarked. "How long are you staying?"

"Only the day as I have work to see to on the Sabbath."

"I was going to wait until they returned, but would you be able to bring their Christmas gifts from us?"

"I would be honored to."

"Help me up so I can collect them now. I'm liable to forget otherwise."

Claudio helped her stand and marveled over how much she had changed from the young woman who grew flustered over Valentino's attentions when he first met her seven years before.

Darla set several packages into a box and turned to him. "You'll have to come see us on Christmas for yours. Do you have somewhere to eat Christmas dinner?"

"No official invitation, but I am sure one will turn up."

"We'd be happy to have you."

"It would be my pleasure. Thank you, Darla."

Henry arrived. After a few minutes of family conversation, he brought the priest into the small study.

"I assume you talked to Alex." After he nodded, Henry continued. "I'm sorry I didn't think to tell you. I've had too much on my mind, but when Alex called to ask me to escort Melissa to the New Year's Eve ball, I knew I had to explain the situation."

"Melissa is attending the New Year's masquerade?"

"She's to give the speech before midnight."

The image of himself in a tuxedo dancing Melissa around the grand ballroom washed Claudio's mind of all else. "I am happy you can bring her to such an important event. I must go now, but I will see you at Christmas dinner. Darla invited me."

"I'm glad to hear it, Father De Fiore. Have a good weekend."

Claudio planned to do just that.

***

Staring absentmindedly across the choppy gray water, Claudio kept one hand on the box beside him on the ferry bench. He had added his own stash to Darla's gifts, but a special present for Melissa was in his coat pocket. He did not know if he would be brave enough to give it to her, but he felt better for being prepared.

Alexander waited for him on the Montrose dock, his soul shining with joy. They greeted each other, and he took the crate of presents from Claudio before walking up the hill to the automobile.

"Your countenance does not match the pleading note in your message for me to relieve anxiety."

"I'm glorious because Lucy is. She's doing well this week."

Claudio looked at him out of the corner of his eye. "Meaning you just finished bedding her before driving over?"

"That too." Alexander laughed. "But I don't have to touch her to level her moods. She's seducing *me*! You should see the suitcase she brought packed with boudoir outfits. She's free and loose this week, my first and last love affair."

"Do you not think she tries too hard? That this might be a ruse to get you thinking she is well?"

"You can't fake what she's doing. She *is* well, at least for the moment, and we're enjoying it." Alexander climbed behind the wheel and let out a groan of yearning. "I'm relishing every encounter, and I'm ready for more!"

"Do not allow it to affect your driving. It will do no one good if we fail to make it back." Claudio paused until they were on their way. "I saw Darla and Henry yesterday. His parents and younger sister are there for Christmas, the women staying until the baby is born."

"I'm glad to hear it. Darla's been good to everyone. We need to care for her."

When they wound their way up the driveway, Claudio held his breath until the house came into view. "It is always a shock not to see Seacliff Cottage when I come here."

"Good riddance to that hell house. The manor has far better memories than the cottage."

"Because you have bedded Lucy more times here?"

Alexander nearly wrecked the automobile laughing as he drove into the old barn. "I never thought of it that way, but you could be right."

"I'd like to pay my respects to Eliza before going inside."

"See your old love before greeting your new flame?"

Alexander's eyes were teasing, but Claudio did not smile.

Fingering the gift in his pocket, the priest turned toward the forest, leaving the box for Alexander to carry. In the peace of the woods, Claudio's soul darkened with regret. He fell to his knees on the steps of the sepulcher and rested his head on the weathered copper door.

In Italian, he cried out, "Must I be cursed to love those I cannot have? I love thee, Lord, but is not love between a man and woman good as well? Should I not have joined the priesthood? But if I had not, I never would have met these women. Is my path to walk the earth in the shadow of love? You took Eliza from me so I would stay the course, but please do not take Melissa. If Frederick returns, I will leave, but should he not make it back, I will care for her and Louisa. I leave it to thee, but have mercy on this sinner."

He crossed himself and laid a hand on the door. "Eliza, *la mia rose*, you showed me much, but my needs are different now. I think you understand, unlike your brother. Rest well."

He stayed on his knees a few minutes more and then went to Eliza's rock on the cliff. Like a message from above, he found Melissa perched there. Her hair fluttered around her face, but her long coat was snug about her as she gazed across the water.

"*Eroina.*"

Her face held a mix of relief and love—completely beautiful. They each moved for the other, embracing in a hug that left no room to kiss her cheeks.

"Claudio." Her breath was hot on his neck. "What are we to do for Darla?"

"Frederick is liable to have won the war before Henry can cross the ocean, but we will be family to her."

Melissa leaned back enough to look at him, eyes glistening with moisture. Her hands were in his hair, tugging him closer until their lips met. He tasted the bitter tea she enjoyed and savored the experience as heat pooled in his loins. Claudio allowed the passion to consume him until she shifted away.

She touched his cheek and met his stare. "Don't take this the wrong way, but what are you doing here?"

Laughing with her felt as good as kissing.

"Alexander called me yesterday. He wanted me to come for the day and try to cheer you, but I did not expect to find you out here. I came to pay my respects to Eliza." He motioned to the boulder. "She often sat there, sketching ships on the bay."

"Do you miss her?"

He cradled her face in his hands. "I have been over missing her for years, but my time with her helped me understand the power of the human body. She was a beautiful, tortured soul. Her upbringing ruined her as much as it did Alexander. Eliza was raised to be as lovely and alluring as possible, and Alexander to take all the pretty things he wanted without thought of the repercussions. But they both escaped, and I rejoice in that."

Thirty-Five

At the house, Melissa followed Claudio into the game room after he greeted Rosemary. Priscilla, who had watched over the group, silently excused herself to give the family privacy. Four jumping children immediately surrounded the priest. Sitting in the middle of the floor, he pulled Louisa onto his lap. Melissa smiled to see him give her daughter special consideration despite Phoebe and Asher being more vocal.

Melissa went to Alex and Lucy. "I'm going to go work on a few ideas for my speech. Send someone to get me for dinner."

Ignoring Alex's protests, Melissa closed herself in the library and settled on the leather armchair and ottoman with her notebook. She jotted a page of thoughts before she leaned her head back and allowed the sleepless night to catch up with her while the sounds of happy children shrilled in the distance.

Over an hour later, a sweet voice woke her. "Mommy, Priscilla says it's time to wash up."

"Thank you, Louisa." Melissa went to her room to freshen— grateful she did as the mirror revealed her tousled hair from her time on the cliff. Melissa took a minute to brush and pin it back from her face. Letting it grow a bit for the winter, the tips almost reached the shoulders of her green dress. She leaned closer to her reflection, seeing the lines ever-deepening around her eyes and mouth that showcased her thirty-five years of life.

After the midday meal, everyone tromped to the shore, bundled in coats to brave the chill wind. The children each had a metal pail to collect things they found. Claudio and Melissa took the lead while Alex and Lucy followed behind the children as they walked north. Absorbed in a conversation about Italian Christmas traditions with Claudio, Melissa failed to notice the others stopped a hundred yards back until he took her arm and pointed behind them.

"I do not think those with shorter legs wish to continue, for they will only have to walk that much further home."

Smiling, she looked to Claudio. "I could go on walking with you for hours."

His fingers tightened pleasantly around her arm. "And I with you. Just as you devote much to your writing through research and details, you bring vibrancy to a conversation."

She felt her cheeks warm despite the nippy air. She'd received praise for her last article about Christmas traditions the soldiers might encounter abroad, but none meant as much as Claudio's kind words. Taking his hand into hers, she turned south but didn't move toward the others who had already begun their return journey to Seacliff.

"If I had but one reader for the articles I write, I'd wish it was you."

"But you have thousands of readers, and your most important one waits eagerly for your clippings to arrive."

Looking to the sand, she sighed. "He had several instances of having to use his gas mask this fall. Some of his men took ill from toxins, and several were killed by grenades."

He hugged her to him, kissing her forehead. "Have faith in his safe return."

"It isn't easy."

"Nothing good ever is."

Melissa leaned into Claudio's side, and he placed his arm around her to continue walking.

"Do you remember the boxing tournament my first autumn here, how I grew faint from the heat, and you stood behind me so I could watch Freddy?"

"*Sí*, it was an honor to assist you."

"Why?"

"I have respected you since we first met and have grown to love you. Have I not made myself clear in that regard?"

"Claudio," Melissa breathed out his name with longing.

He stopped and faced her. "I have something for you. A Christmas present, though I do not wish to give it to you in front of everyone. Would you receive it now?"

"If I can." She turned to see if they were watched, but he stopped her with a gentle hand.

"It is just us for the moment, *Eroina*." From his pocket, he pulled out a brightly colored box that fit in his hand.

Thinking it jewelry—of which she could never accept—her heart fell to her stomach. Inside she found a silver cylinder that she easily palmed. It felt good in her hand, heavy and calming. She ran her fingers over the carved peacocks and scrolling ivy that decorated it.

"Allow me." He stood closer to shield the wind and flipped open the metal case, exposing a striking gear. With the flick of his thumb, a flame lit. "Now, I will always be able to offer you a light, even when I am not here."

"It's wonderful, Claudio. Thank you." She quickly kissed his cheek. Placing the box into her coat pocket, she continued to hold the lighter in her other hand as she claimed Claudio's warm grip.

They were quiet a minute as they strolled.

"I cannot walk here without thinking of Magdalene and Douglas. We spent many hours on the shore that summer. She has always been a good correspondent, but her letters are sporadic since Douglas left. I hope she stays for a long time when she visits Darla next year."

"She is welcome to stay with me again as well. I'll be sure to let her know."

"But her being in Mobile will not be good for Lucy."

"It's unfair to ask others to change their lives in an attempt to pacify Lucy."

"*Sí*, but Alexander thinks the world revolves around them. He will take everything we do contrary to his wishes as an attack against his queen."

"Then I declare Kingdom Davenport for the win!" Melissa raised their linked hands with her shout.

They laughed and kept their conversation light from then on. When they neared the cypress grove, Claudio joined the children in corralling a crab. Alex left Lucy in an Adirondack chair to partake of the fun. Melissa took a seat nearby as she fingered the lighter in her pocket.

"You're glowing," Lucy remarked.

"Claudio is fine company."

Lucy looked as though she wanted to say more. *Alex probably told her not to bother me today, but it's clear she's biting her tongue over something sharp about me dishonoring Freddy.*

"Thank you for hosting Louisa and me all this time. We're enjoying ourselves."

"You're family," Lucy replied gracefully.

The crab was caught, observed, and set free. Then Claudio began a game of European football with the men as captains. He took Louisa and Bethany on his side, and Phoebe and Asher stood with Alex to make their plans. Fair against dark.

"Claudio loves them all," Lucy said, "but he does lavish attention on Louisa."

So much for holding her tongue. "The others have a claim on Alex."

"Alex allows her to call him Poppy and loves her too."

"But she knows it's not the same because Phoebe constantly reminds her it isn't."

"So you let a priest fill the void to help your daughter feel loved?"

"It's not that simple. Louisa—"

"Who named her?" Lucy held her chin high.

"Louisa Constance?" Melissa faltered. "Constance was Grandmother Stone's name."

"But Louisa?"

"I admire Louisa May Alcott's work."

"I bet it was Frederick." Lucy smiled challengingly. "It's the perfect blending of our names."

She might as well say, "He loved me first and longest. He loves me still. When you break his heart, he'll know you're no better than me and what I did to him."

"I wrote him about that last week," Lucy continued. "I want him to know that I understand he still cares for me. Give him a reason to return."

Melissa wanted to yell at Lucy to keep her fantasies to herself but held her temper. Before marriage, Freddy let Melissa know Lucy had only penned him a goodbye letter throughout their whole relationship. Surely in all her babbling letters, he could tell Lucy wasn't right in the head. No matter how flowery she penned things, she wouldn't be able to fool him. But the most anxiety was worrying over what Lucy might say about *her* in the letters.

When the game ended, Alex put Asher on his shoulders. "Hot chocolate time!" The children cheered, and he looked to Claudio. "Would you walk with Lucy while I get things started?"

"Of course." Claudio collected his cassock he'd removed during the game and helped Lucy out of the low chair.

Phoebe bound ahead with Alex and Asher, and Bethany took Louisa's hand. Melissa turned toward the shore, allowing the gentle lapping of the bay to calm her nerves.

"Er—Melissa," Claudio called as his cassock billowed around his legs, "I am happy to escort you as well."

"Thank you, but I'll be a minute."

She didn't need to look at Lucy to know she had a smile of triumph. Still gazing at the water, Melissa sat on the cold sand, smoothing the knolls the children's feet made while running. Gathering a handful, she felt the grains shift between her fingers.

Just like life, I can't cling to it. Junior slipped away, and with him Freddy. When I thought I'd caught hold of him once more, the wind blew him across the globe.

Standing, she kicked a mound of sand and watched the granules scatter. Tears threatening to erupt, she hastily went for the path. Hoping the family was in the dining room, Melissa let herself in the front door and ran upstairs. She managed to close her bedroom before the first rivulet streaked her face and caught hold of one of the bedposts to steady herself from the wave of despair. Collapsing on the bed, she curled on her side and let the tears fall.

The door opened several minutes later, but she didn't care who saw her in misery. She'd played all her strong cards.

"Darling Sissa." Alex's scarred hands enclosed one of hers as he kissed her cheek.

Then he was gone. She could have dreamt it were it not for the fact that she had his monogrammed handkerchief in her cold hand. Melissa wiped her nose with it and tried to breathe as the tears slowed. When her door lock clicked, followed by the weight of someone on the bed behind her, she tensed.

"Alex!" she gasped as the body settled snugly behind her. But the arm that surrounded her was Claudio's.

Alex's laugh came from near the fireplace. "Do you think I'd climb in your bed with Lucy under the same roof?"

"I don't know anymore." Melissa relaxed beneath the comfort of Claudio's warm embrace.

"Freddy may kill me, but I know you need support. I'll chaperone a few minutes." Alex built up the dying fire. "Get the tears out of your system before we return to the family."

"*Eroina, amore mio.*" Claudio's whispers tumbled into more Italian as he continued to hold her.

Calm radiated from her heart outwards as she pressed against Claudio's healing form. She lifted his hand to her lips. When she released him, he touched her shoulder and trailed his fingers the length of her arm.

"Just keep those hands where I can see them," Alex goaded.

"You are crass, *amico*. Especially for one who brought me to a woman's bed."

Alex exhaled with flustered annoyance. "When you say it like that—"

Melissa laughed, the sound strangling the tears in her throat. "You two are wonderful."

"Wonderful?" Alex stuck his face in front of hers. "I risk a beheading by Major Davenport, and you call me *wonderful?*"

"I do."

"I have half a mind to crawl in the bed with the two of you and—" Claudio reached for him, but Alex laughed and kissed Melissa's forehead before jumping away. "I may be a cad, but I'm not stupid. Come on, let's get downstairs before someone comes looking for us."

In the game room, they all played charades until the early supper hour approached. Bethany went to her mother with her tiger tucked under her arm.

"Momma," she said as she rested a hand on Lucy's knee, "you missed your naptime. Did Poppy forget to bring you to bed?"

"Poppy didn't forget, Bethany Iris. We're having such fun today that I didn't want to miss anything." Lucy gave a sharp look at Claudio and Melissa.

"I'll be sure she goes to bed early tonight," Alex said with a wink.

After supper, Alex sent the children to say goodbye to Claudio and instructed Phoebe to start the baths.

"The rest of you gather your pajamas. Momma and I will be up soon." The children scattered, and Alex waved Melissa away. "Get him to the ferry."

"Alex—" Lucy began, but he stopped her with a quick kiss.

"No protests. Remember you missed your naptime and need to get to bed early." He kissed her deeper. "I insist on getting you in bed as soon as possible, Lucille Melling."

Her enchanted laugh filled the room. "Then allow me a head start so I may prepare myself." Lucy turned to Claudio and hugged him. "It was good to see you. Have a Merry Christmas."

As Claudio helped Melissa into her coat, Alex paused at the foot of the stairs.

"I know exactly how long it takes to get to the Montrose pier and back, darling Sissa. I'll give you five minutes leeway. Nothing more."

Lucy stopped on the stairs. "Five minutes is plenty of time to get in trouble."

"Not for a priest who's out of practice." Alex narrowed his gaze at his friend. "And you better be *way* out of practice, Claudio."

Thirty-Six

Claudio stumbled through the next week—Midnight Mass, Christmas dinner with the Adams family, and his interview with the bishop—all while dreaming of Melissa. When she drove him to the ferry the previous weekend, she stopped halfway down the secluded driveway and climbed in his lap. They lavished attention on each other for several minutes, needing the drive to Montrose for her to lose the flush of passion. If Melissa insisted on bringing them to the edge with moments like that, he knew he was capable of falling.

During his appointment with the bishop, Claudio confessed he battled feelings for a married woman. The bishop advised him to throw himself into service and decide what his larger goals were in regards to the priesthood. He would meet back with the bishop in January to discuss his progress. After the meeting, he dedicated himself to planning for the New Year's Eve Ball and the opportunity to hear Melissa's speech—her evening to shine though she did so because Frederick abandoned her.

The other priests and deacons in the house left for quiet New Year's festivities. When alone, Claudio shaved and dressed in his rented black tuxedo, leaving the tails off until he coated his face with a fine powder to disguise his olive skin. Then his hair was combed through with a graying solution that aged him a decade. With a top hat, mask, and gloves, he would not easily be recognized.

Claudio arrived at the Battle House by hired cab at ten. Immediately, his eyes fell upon the Mellings wearing silver masks in the middle of the dancefloor. Alexander shone in a white tuxedo while Lucy mesmerized the room in a pale pink gown that trailed from her voluptuous hips to the floor while most of the other women wore fashionably shorter gowns that showcased a bit of leg. The couple only had eyes for each other as they spun and dipped under Alexander's erotic lead.

As much as he enjoyed seeing his friends enraptured at the moment, he scanned the crowd seeking the glow of copper hair under the chandeliers. Not until a man led her onto the dancefloor from the far side of the room did he see her. Melissa wore a gold mask and tiara. Her dress, gauzy black and layered, had a square neckline showcasing the emerald necklace Freddy had given her for her birthday. The lines of the gown tapered at her narrow waist and stopped well above her ankles. On her wrist that rested by her partner's shoulder was a gold and emerald bracelet that matched the jewels around her throat.

Frederick should know she will not forgive him based on expenditures.

Going boldly across the floor, Claudio almost lost the courage to cut in when he recognized the arrogant bearing of Melissa's partner.

Before he could lose his nerve, Claudio tapped Eliza's old fiancé on the shoulder, purposely keeping his head lowered as he said in his best mimic of Douglas's Scottish brogue. "Pardon me, sir."

Claudio took hold of Melissa and danced her away from Sean Spunner. Melissa studied his lips and her hand on his shoulder quested, causing him to grin.

"Claudio!" She laughed. "What did you do to your skin and hair?"

"It is the price I pay to hear your speech without being hassled for my profession."

With the pause between songs, she stepped back to study him. "I wish I could see you dressed like that without the alterations. You'd look even more handsome."

He suppressed a shiver as her black glove trailed his sleeve. The next tune began—a modern song with a Latin flair. Claudio pulled her snug against him, hand low on her back as he led her in a tango. He allowed his passion to drip from the movements as he held Melissa.

Toward the end of the song, a strong hand clamped his shoulder. "A word with the lady, please."

Henry Adams.

The three moved to the edge of the dancefloor. Claudio kept his head down as the young man leaned to Melissa's ear. He could not hear Henry's words, but she answered firmly.

"Thank you for your concern, but I'm enjoying myself."

His cheeks reddened, and he turned back to Claudio. "She's a married woman, sir, and a guest of honor. See that you act with decorum."

Claudio nodded and had her back in his arms as soon as they stepped away. He placed his right hand in a more respectable location, and their bodies were not as close as they were before. Wanting nothing more than to plant his lips on the ones beneath her sparkling mask, he imagined the passionate way she liked to kiss— tasting, nipping, and touching—and raced through ideas on how to abscond with her to a private location.

"*Eroina*, after this song, wait a minute and then go out the back door on the right. Down that hall is the orchestra's storage room. Meet me there."

The song died away, and he purposely left her on the opposite side of the room, kissing her hand in farewell before weaving his way through the crowd. Halfway to his destination, he saw Alexander watching him. The curve of surprise on Alexander's mouth could not be mistaken. A grimace immediately followed it. Rather than going for him, Alexander looked the way Claudio had come as though seeking Melissa.

Claudio took the moment to slip through the nearest door. He reached the storage room and tried to slow his pounding heart with deep breaths. The door swung inward, and the hall light created a halo of warmth around Melissa's figure. She stepped in, and the door shut, leaving them in safe darkness. They held each other, Melissa curling onto his shoulder. She rested there a moment and then unbuttoned his tuxedo jacket.

"You felt so good the last time." She ran her hands down his shirt. "Was it too scandalous that we kissed like that in an automobile?"

"Do you think a storage room is any better?"

He felt her smile as their lips met. Claudio caressed her bare arms as they surged together. The world was naught while he held her like that. Heaven and Hell ceased to exist because he dwelt in Paradise. His mouth was at her décolletage, his hands feeling every inch of her backside through her thin gown when the door swung open, and the light switched on.

Alexander ripped Claudio from Melissa and slapped him across the face before shoving him into a pile of cello cases.

"Melissa." With one word, Alexander showcased his disappointment.

She didn't waver as she held his glare. "Did you need something, Alex?"

"You're less than an hour from giving a speech on the noble service of our city's men, yet you dishonor your husband with your actions. I expected better from you." He turned abruptly and stalked down the hall.

Melissa helped Claudio stand and handed him his fallen hat. "I need to collect my papers and review the speech, but I'm delighted you're here, Claudio."

Left alone, he fell to his knees and reached for the crucifix that was not there.

***

When Claudio returned to the ballroom, he found Alexander and Henry huddled around Lucy on a corner settee.

"May I be of service?"

Henry looked at him, startled as he recognized his voice. "That was *you* dancing with Melissa? Claudio—"

"And you finally call me by my name!"

"I always told you I would when you weren't dressed as a priest." Henry took his arm, and they stepped away. "When Alex stepped out, Kate Stuart approached Lucy. I didn't catch the opening words, but she asked Lucy how she felt being responsible for killing a nun."

"She didn't understand, did she?"

"Kate said enough to make it clear before I could whisk Lucy away."

Claudio moved to go toward the Mellings, but Henry grabbed his arm.

"Why are you dressed like that?"

"So I may hear Melissa's speech without being judged for my vocation."

"Not wearing your collar doesn't give you leave to dance like that with another man's wife."

"You completed your chaperone duties. I changed to more respectable ways after your words."

"I shouldn't have to tell you, Claudio."

"Melissa is magnificent. We enjoy each other's company."

"A little too well," Henry grumbled.

Claudio knelt beside Lucy, shocked no tears stained her face. "Do you require a blessing?"

Alexander grabbed his shoulder and hauled him up. "You'll not lay your hands on my wife until you've gone through confession! You must think me daft to allow it after what I saw you doing, De Fiore."

"I will pray—"

"Pray for yourself!" Alexander pushed him. "And you're uninvited to Friday suppers."

Claudio took a seat nearby and watched Alex settle with Lucy. She shifted into his side, allowing him to hold her completely. A single tear fell, but she quickly wiped it away. He knew they would have left if not for Melissa's speech and was happy they made an effort.

Henry, with Melissa on his arm, returned through the main door. They stayed near the dais as her time approached. When the Order of Mayhem's spokesperson came forward, Alexander led Lucy to a corner near an exit. He kept an arm around his wife as Melissa stepped to the center of the platform.

"I stand before you on the threshold of the New Year because my husband chose to safeguard his country against the rising evil in a foreign land." Her papers were in her hand, but she spoke without looking at them. "A man content to run his office, travel regionally with his family, and knock out a few opponents in the boxing ring from time to time"—the audience laughed—"answered the call to serve when Uncle Sam sought brave men."

The love in her voice caused Claudio's heart to crack, but he couldn't look away from her radiant figure. Clear and strong, she continued on another minute about Frederick Davenport, which warmed the crowd because they all knew him.

"Though I am a spokeswoman for the military wife, I am by no means alone in my hardships. Tens of thousands of wives, sweethearts, children, mothers, fathers, sisters, brothers, nieces, nephews, cousins, and more are praying for the safe return of their loved ones. All of those left behind struggle with something—from loneliness to financial hardships to despair. Beyond writing letters and sending goods to our men overseas, let us not forget those soldiering on within our city."

The crowd shifted together as the conviction poured from her with each word.

"Reach out to your neighbors and extended family to help meet the needs of those who are close enough to receive a hug or handshake. Enjoy the young men still here because we don't know when their time to serve will come. One of the supports in my own circle was called this month. Henry Adams, my husband's business partner, and previous middleweight boxing champion will report for training next week, leaving his four-year-old son and a lovely wife who's soon to birth their second child.

"Rather than ask God 'why,' I shall step forward and give Darla Adams all the help I can, from childcare to a shoulder to cry on. That is our fight—the ones left behind—to see to the care of those around us. Let us not slip into idleness and depression. We are the Homefront Army and must not allow our allies to fall by the wayside in want of nourishment. Let us make 1918 a year to show our strength, resolve, and generosity. Please join me in pledging to do your part, no matter your circumstance. There is something we all can do. Thank you."

Melissa bowed her head while applause rang through the ballroom. Alexander whistled while leading Lucy out the door. Then Henry was beside Melissa, decorously kissing her cheek.

As the seconds ticked closer to midnight, Claudio worked his way toward the stage. While the crowd sang *"Auld Lang Syne,"* he stopped before Melissa long enough to kiss her lips before tipping his hat and heading into the cold.

Thirty-Seven

The telephone ringing was an unwelcome sound even after ten in the morning. Naomi shifted away from Paul's warm body, her bare arms feeling the chill of winter.

"Stay, Honey."

"It might be one of the girls needing something."

Naomi tied her robe around her growing middle and hurried to the telephone. In the last few months, she'd become close to her stepdaughters, especially Mattie. She was the youngest and expecting her third child within a month of Naomi's baby.

Hoping nothing was wrong, she answered the telephone with a cheerful "Happy New Year."

"And God help us."

"Mr. Alex, how did everything go last night?"

"Priscilla was wonderful with the children. All three were sleeping peacefully when we returned, even with Lucy sobbing."

"Was the evening difficult for her?" Naomi rubbed her feet together in an attempt to stay warm on the bare hardwood.

"She did well, and we had a lovely time dancing. Then Claudio stole away with Melissa, and I had to find them. While I was gone, Kate Stuart went to Lucy and let her know her actions against Sister Prudence caused her death."

"And you've gone weeks without her finding out!"

"It was quite the blow, and right before Melissa's speech, but my queen held steady for it."

"And Melissa?" Naomi cautiously asked.

"She'd be able to start a revolution with her stirring words."

"Do you need anything from me today?"

"Your listening ear was enough. Can you still come tomorrow?"

"I'll be there at seven-thirty."

"Thank you, Naomi. And I'm sorry to bother you."

"You're no bother, Alex. Telephone any time."

Naomi put the kettle on in the kitchen and dove back under the covers.

"You best get that robe off if you're with me, Honey."

"I'm chilled from being up."

"I'll warm you in no time."

Paul's mouth was on her neck as his hands opened her robe. Her husband pulled her attention to the moment, leaving behind all thoughts of the Mellings. Strong hands, hot kisses, and rhythmic touching were all she knew.

***

Paul dropped off Naomi on his way to work each weekday. She stayed until three o'clock, except on Wednesdays, when she left at noon after Melissa and Louisa arrived to have lunch with Lucy and Asher. On Wednesdays, the Davenports kept Lucy company until Alexander returned from the stables with Lucy's children. Phoebe and Bethany were enrolled at a tiny private school at the home of two spinster sisters from an affluent family who were members of the parish. Phoebe was underwhelmed with the small setting, but Bethany flourished. Besides the school change, the girls' new schedule was staying with Melissa Sunday nights through Wednesday mornings, which took the pressure off Lucy and Alexander.

On the last Tuesday in January, Naomi sat at the kitchen table for lunch with Lucy and Asher. Usually well-behaved, the little imp slurped his soup. When Lucy or Naomi gave him the eye, he stopped. As soon as they looked away, he started back.

"Phoenix Asher Melling, I need you to stop." Lucy's tone was even, but her leg jiggled with nerves.

"Yes, Momma." He dunked his toast into the broth and settled down to eat without noise.

But Lucy's leg kept wiggling.

When Asher brought his near-empty bowl to his lips to drink the final bit his spoon couldn't reach, he sucked in the liquid with more racket than ever.

Lucy covered her ears. "Get him out, Naomi!" she shouted as she rocked back and forth. "Get out!"

Asher jumped from his chair, his bowl shattering on the floor. "Momma, I'm—"

"Go away!" She squeezed her eyes shut and bit her lip.

"It's okay, Phoenix Asher, but go to your room." Naomi nudged him out the door and stopped at the telephone to ring Alexander's office. "Tell Mr. Melling to come home at once," she said to the secretary.

Naomi pulled Lucy's chair away from the table to get beside her. Alexander had told her not to handle Lucy if she was belligerent, but she didn't know how long it would take him to arrive, and there were too many potential dangers in the kitchen. Slowly, she reached to remove a hand from her ear.

"Let's get you somewhere more comfortable, Lucy."

"Is he away?" Her lips trembled with the words.

"I sent Asher to his room."

"He needs to be safe."

"Safe from what?" Naomi helped Lucy stand.

"From me!" The tears came, and she clutched Naomi's arms, fingernails digging through the sleeves of her blouse. "Don't leave him with me! Don't leave any of them with me! Promise me, Naomi. Promise!"

"I won't leave you alone with the sugars." Tears came to her own eyes—both from the pain from Lucy's grip and the despair seeping from her like heat off a furnace.

By the time Naomi walked Lucy to the foot of the stairs, Alexander had run in.

Lucy collapsed against him, tears wetting the shoulder of his gray suit. "I didn't mean to scare him. Please don't be mad!"

"I'm not angry, my queen, but let's get you in bed so you can rest."

"You must keep the children safe! Don't leave me alone with them. I already made Naomi promise."

"We won't, Lucy. We're watching out for you. I'll get us more help so you needn't worry." He kissed her as he scooped her into his arms.

Naomi followed them upstairs.

"Go to him, Alex," Lucy pled. "Leave me and tell Asher I love him. Tell him Momma would never—"

"Hush now, my queen." He stood her by the bed. "I'll see to you and then Asher."

"Help him know I'm sorry. Take him riding or somewhere to spoil him because I've broken that dear heart of his."

"I will." Alexander tenderly removed Lucy's dress and tucked her into bed. As he collected her medication, Naomi went to Asher's room.

Sniffling came from beneath the desk Paul built. She tried not to think of the way she'd come undone for the first time while perched on the surface, but once the thought slipped in, it was difficult to remove.

Naomi sat in the armchair near the fireplace. "Phoenix Asher, you can come out now."

He pulled the desk chair closer, pinning himself in. "But Poppy's home. I'll be in trouble for making Momma holler."

"You didn't make her holler, Asher. The only thing you did was eat your soup too noisily, and that ain't nothing in the scheme of things. You just need to make sure you follow directions and stop when you're told next time."

"I'm bad, Miss Naomi. Poppy's gonna know how bad because Momma got upset."

"You remember when you broke that vase last summer?"

He nodded.

"Did you get in trouble for that, young man?"

He shook his head.

"Then tell the truth, and you needn't fear Poppy."

Alexander walked in with the last words and nodded at Naomi. He'd removed his shoes, jacket, and tie. Settling himself in the middle of the plush carpet, he faced the desk.

"Phoenix Asher Melling?"

"Yes, Poppy," his voice squeaked.

"I need to speak to you, man to man. Come out when you feel brave enough. That shouldn't take long because you have a courageous heart."

The chair moved out two inches. "Do you think I'm as brave as you?"

"I hope so, but without being so reckless. My courage caused me a lot of wounds, as you can see on my skin. But I've also damaged my soul with some of my choices. Even though you can't see those scars, I feel them inside me."

"Are you better now?" Asher asked as the chair moved out a little more.

"I try to be but still make mistakes." Alexander unbuttoned his shirt and draped it over the end of the bed. He pointed to the bullet wound on his arm, the burned flesh on his forearms, and then placed a discolored hand on the puckered marks on his chest. "You see all these scars?"

Asher was out from under the desk, nodding.

"You've felt them before?"

"Yes, Poppy."

Alexander opened his arms, and his son crawled into his lap. He hugged Asher to him before setting him back so he could look him in the eyes.

"I need you to understand something about Momma. She has scars too, but you can't see them. She has damage up here." He fingered Asher's forehead. "Her scars in her head are getting bigger, but it doesn't affect what's in here." He brought Asher's hand to his heart.

"She still loves me?"

Alexander cradled him. "She loves you so much that she yelled for you to get away because she didn't want to hurt you. The scars in her head make her sound mean, even to people she loves. And though her head scars are trying to take over, I love her as much as ever. Because I love her, I want to keep her at home rather than send her away when the scars cause trouble. But we'll need to be brave when the scars are louder than her heart. We need to remember when she seems angry or sad that it's the scars, not her or you or anyone else. Can you do that, Phoenix Asher?"

"Yes, Poppy. And I'll try to be good."

He kissed his little face. "You *are* good, Ash. Never doubt that. Now dress for riding, and we'll tell Momma goodbye for a few hours, okay?"

As Asher ran for his closet, Alexander collected his shirt and went to Naomi. He handed her a handkerchief for her tears. "We'll be back by four. See if you can keep her awake while we change, please."

Still sniffling, Naomi settled in a bedside chair in the master room, holding Lucy's hand.

"Is Asher okay?" Lucy asked.

"He's doing good. That husband of yours is a fine man."

"He'll raise our son well."

Asher came to the doorway, and Naomi waved him in.

"I'm sorry, Momma. I love you."

Lucy turned to her side and reached an arm for him. "I love you, Phoenix Asher. You listen to Miss Naomi and Poppy. They'll help you when I am unable to, all right?"

"Yes, Momma."

Alexander joined them. "Your men are going riding, my queen. Take a lovely nap, and we'll be home before long."

Lucy nodded and tilted her head up for a kiss. As father and son walked away, she sighed raggedly. "You'll stay with me, Naomi?"

"I'll never leave you."

Thirty-Eight

When Melissa returned home from bringing Phoebe and Bethany to school on January thirtieth, the telephone rang.

"Davenports'."

"Happy Wednesday, darling Sissa."

She smiled at hearing his voice, proving how lonely life could be with three children to care for and no man in sight. "Happy Wednesday to you, dashing Poppy. The girls are more than eager to see you this afternoon."

"I'm glad to hear it. Do you have a moment to talk?"

"Of course." She listened as Alex told of Lucy's breakdown the day before and how he'd already spoken to the doctor and Darla—that they were going to help him find a qualified nurse to sit with his wife while he was gone during the day.

"But what can Darla do in her condition?" Melissa asked.

"She insists on being involved but will do no more than inquire about the applicants—make a few telephone calls at most."

"And what about on your side of things? Will you interview them with Naomi like you did with Charlotte?"

"Yes, but we'll need someone to sit with Lucy during it. Hopefully, one day next week."

"You know I'll help, Alex. Just give me a day's notice. The only person I've been seeing is Hattie, and I can stop by the Spunners' practically anytime."

"Thank you, darling Sissa."

As soon as she hung the telephone, a heaviness settled in her heart. She had hoped it was Claudio on the telephone. She hadn't seen him since he kissed her goodbye on New Year's Eve. Last Friday, she'd mailed him a letter stating she'd missed their friendship and invited him to come over Wednesday for either supper or a drink afterward. He'd yet to reply, and it was now the fateful day.

Not wanting to sit around worrying, she called for Louisa. "How would you like to go to the library before we go to the Mellings' house?"

"Yes, please!"

They spent the morning browsing the little library, paid the fees for their borrowed books, and then took lunch with Naomi, Lucy, and Asher. The children were in the morning room with a pile of books for quiet time when Alex arrived. Lucy dozed on the sofa, so Melissa slipped across the hall to the den, hugging him.

"Thank you," he whispered. She shifted against him, relishing the contact. Alex nestled into her neck a moment before stepping around to place the desk between them. "God help me, you smell good. I suppose I can't continue placing the full blame on Claudio. Would you like him to come back to Friday suppers?"

Melissa nodded. "He hasn't contacted me since the ball. I wrote him last week, but I still haven't heard anything."

"I hope I scared some sense into both of you."

She clutched her heart. "Your words struck me hard, but I had to put on a brave face for my speech. Henry saw me crumbling on the way home and insisted they keep Louisa the rest of the night so I could go home and grieve. I know it isn't fair to Freddy, but I've been lonely since Junior died. I'll admit Claudio and I were getting too familiar with each other, though we tried to keep things respectable."

"It hurt me to see you two tangled together. I don't want any of you in pain because you're disrespecting your vows." Alex looked to the door and leaned closer. "But once to test a kiss is different."

"Because nothing you ever do is wrong according to your standards." Melissa kissed his cheek.

"I only want what's best for you, darling Sissa. And Frederick officially put me in charge now that Henry's gone."

"As though I need a man in charge of me. I spent over a decade on my own in New York City and around the world."

"And there's that spark you need to combat your unholy yearnings."

Melissa shoved him toward the hall. "Go change so you can get out of here."

***

After saying goodbye to the Mellings and her stepdaughters, Melissa stopped at Klosky's restaurant and purchased a loaf of crusty bread, garlic vegetables, and a carton of ravioli. At home, she started a fire in the parlor hearth and spread a tablecloth on the floor in front of it. She turned on the gramophone and settled on the floor with the picnic Louisa set with their best china.

"A party for two, Mommy!"

"I love having your sisters here, but it's nice with only you."

"It's nicest when Daddy's with us."

"Yes, it is." Melissa dished up their food, hungry for the first time since the trip to Seacliff Manor at Christmas—which was good because her clothes were too loose once more.

Every few bites, Louisa danced like a ballerina to the strains of Vivaldi's "Four Seasons." Melissa found herself laughing and smiling more than she'd done in weeks and decided it was due in part to her conversation with Alex that afternoon.

After Louisa did another pirouette, her eyes looked to the open window, and she dashed to the front door. "Uncle Claudio!"

Before Melissa could stand, Claudio carried Louisa into the room, her arms and legs wrapped about him. "We've missed you, Uncle Claudio! Why did you stay gone so long?"

"I had much work to do, *Principessa*, but I thought of you and your mother every day. Will you forgive me for not coming?"

"Only if you promise to come every day from now on!"

Claudio's dimpled smile brightened the space more than the firelight. "Even if I would like to, I cannot come daily, Louisa. But I will do my best to come for lunch once a week like I used to, and I will be back at the Mellings' house for Friday suppers."

Louisa squealed and hugged him. "Will you eat with us now? Mommy bought plenty."

Melissa's and Claudio's eyes met for the first time. "You're welcome to join us. I shopped with you in mind."

"I would love to. Thank you." Setting Louisa down, he kissed her cheek. "Allow me to wash before I sit at your lovely spread, *Principessa*."

Louisa danced around the room while they waited for him. As soon as Claudio returned, she brought him to Melissa's side. "Sit by Mommy. I'll get your plate."

"Slow and careful, Louisa," Melissa reminded her. Turning to Claudio as Louisa left, she smiled. "It's great to see you again. I've missed you."

She kissed his lips first, in case Louisa returned quickly, and then went for his cheeks while he did the same. Their foreheads rested together a moment as they breathed in each other.

"I missed you as well, *Eroina*."

Louisa laid the gleaming plate on the red tablecloth before collecting the silverware.

"Happy belated birthday," Melissa whispered. "Lucy remarked over your absence for the typical birthday supper the other week. You're as handsome as ever at thirty-seven."

Claudio laughed. "Do you prefer an older man? I hear that husband of yours is younger than you."

"Three months, but he loves to tease me about being his older woman between my birthday and his."

While he dished up his food, she collected a bottle of *Brunello di Montalcino* and three glasses—one of which she filled with juice for Louisa.

Melissa took another helping of everything. By the time she and Claudio were on their second glasses of wine, her face was sore from smiling. Louisa finally danced herself to exhaustion when the gramophone completed all four seasons. Claudio chose a quiet piano movement and tucked the girl on the sofa to rest. He carried a load of dishes to the kitchen while Melissa placed the remaining ravioli into the icebox.

They resettled on the tablecloth before the fire, Melissa's shoulder brushing his arm. Taking her hand in his, he angled closer.

"How have you been this month?"

"Lonely and depressed for the most part, but I have the girls Sunday through Wednesday mornings and sit with Lucy Wednesday afternoons. I finalize my column Thursdays and deliver it Fridays. Otherwise, I stay busy in the garden or walking. I stop in to see Hattie Spunner once or twice a week, often for her Monday afternoon science club meetings, so Louisa can play with Brandon."

He knelt before her, his hands going about her waist, feeling her ribs. "So you care for everyone except yourself. You must do better for yourself, *Eroina.*"

Melissa pulled him back to her side, resting her head on his shoulder. "I've ached for Freddy and you this month. Working in the yard has been my solace."

"I should go now."

"We haven't even shared a cigarette."

Claudio stood, pulling her to her feet as well. "You always have my light." He hugged her and then laid a hand on sleeping Louisa's hair. "Sweet dreams, *Principessa.* You are loved."

In the hall, Melissa clung to him for another embrace.

"I should not come again at night, *Eroina.*" He fingered through her hair. "What day is best for lunch?"

"Tuesdays or Thursdays, but I'll leave it up to you as your schedule might change. Telephone me the night before if you wish, or let me know at Friday suppers."

"I will." He smiled down at her, causing a pull in her core that craved more.

Melissa wrapped her arms about his neck and tugged his lips to hers for a firm kiss. "Thank you for caring for me, Claudio."

Thirty-Nine

On St. Valentine's Day, the telephone roused Claudio from his morning coffee. Being the closest, he picked it up but was not given time to speak.

"I need Father De Fiore, please." Melisa sounded unsure of herself, and Claudio hoped she hadn't called to make a declaration of love because three other men of the cloth stared at him over their coffee.

"Melissa?"

"Claudio, it's time! Can you come to Darla?"

"*Sí*, I will be there as soon as possible."

He hung up the telephone and gathered his dishes.

"You are forever running off to damsels in distress, De Fiore. That or your Melling friend," a priest commented.

"Sometimes one's flock does not consist of the parish where you are assigned. Those who need assistance will find their way to you through God's hand." He placed his dishes in the sink and returned to the table. "Would you please let Bishop Allen know I have been asked to be on hand at Darla Adams's house as she is having her baby?"

The priest nodded, knowing better than to say anything negative about service to a woman whose husband was at war.

Claudio grabbed his bag filled with blessed items. Darla had looked well when he visited her Sunday afternoon, but he knew four days were a lot at that stage of pregnancy. Rather than waiting for the streetcar, he ran along the sidewalk until he saw one going his way and caught it at the nearest stop.

At the Adams's front door, he paused to catch his breath. Bonnie let him in, and he settled with her, Horatio, and Louisa while they awaited news.

Louisa climbed into his lap. "You won't be able to come over for lunch today."

"I was just there Tuesday, *Principessa*," he whispered.

Her little arms went about his neck. "But it's Valentine's Day, and we need love, Uncle Claudio."

"You and your mother have plenty of love." He hugged her, hoping Henry's sister did not listen. He purposely chose Tuesday that week to avoid seeing Melissa on St. Valentine's Day.

God apparently had other plans.

Louisa kept her hold on Claudio and settled against his chest. She refused to join Horatio when he tried to entice her with his new building set. Dr. Hughes emerged from upstairs and said everything progressed well, and then Louisa fell asleep in Claudio's arms. He continued to hold her as Bonnie, and the cook brought buckets of boiled water upstairs though he knew he should be helping with the physical work. Louisa felt helpless with her pouf of auburn curls framing her cherubic face as she slept. He could not put her down.

A little while later, Melissa smiled over them. "Darla would like a blessing before she begins the final stage," she whispered. "Lay Louisa on the sofa. She'll be fine. I had to wake her at five this morning. This nap will catch her up with sleep."

When they were in the stairwell, Claudio entwined their fingers. "Happy St. Valentine's Day, *Eroina*."

"And you, Claudio," she whispered in reply. "I do love you."

His heart soared with thoughts of this being the turning point for them. Maybe the heavens were preparing him for taking Frederick's place as they supported their friend in bringing a baby into the world. He would be with Melissa on this day for lovers as she received word about her husband failing to return. All this and more swam around his head as he laid his hands on Darla. He prayed in his native tongue, lest his thoughts over-power the prayer, and he began babbling about his devotion to the woman who gazed at him across the bedroom with her alluring smile.

"Thank you, Claudio," Darla said. "Are you able to stay?"

"*Sí*, I will be with the children. Send for me whenever you wish."

Her smile turned to a gasp as her hands went to her large belly. "I believe it's time."

A fraction of an hour later, the lusty sound of a baby's cry rang through the house.

Bonnie ran for the stairs and shouted down. "It's a girl! She and Darla are well!"

Claudio paced the room as the bustle of cleaning happened around him. Often he carried Louisa across the space. She loved to hang off his arms and swing up-side-down by her ankles. The girl missed physical play with her father, and Claudio was pleased to be there.

A short while later, Bonnie collected Horatio so he could meet his sister. After Dr. Hughes left, Melissa brought down a load of laundry and joined Claudio in the parlor.

Seeing her exhaustion, he opened his arms to enfold her in an embrace.

"I held Darla through the birth in the modified position she had Alex use with Lucy. It brought it all back." She sighed, sounding as though she tried to breathe around the threat of tears. "Freddy's strong arms supporting me as I labored to bring our children into the world. Then I thought of how Henry must have been for her when Horatio was born. I'm no substitute for that strength and love."

"You were wonderful, *Eroina*. Darla is blessed to have you as a friend."

From the top of the stairs, Bonnie called down. "Father Claudio and Louisa, come meet Virginia Henrietta Adams!"

***

On Friday, March first, Claudio arrived at the Mellings' house at four o'clock. Alexander was at the club riding with the children but had requested his friend to see to Lucy the hour before they returned.

"Good afternoon, Father De Fiore," Charlotte said briskly. "I've got to get back to the kitchen, but I expect you know how to find Miss Lucy in the morning room."

"*Sí*, thank you."

Lucy, Mrs. Easton, and a nurse sat in the bright space. Claudio greeted Mrs. Easton first and then the nurse, Bertha. As he kissed Lucy's pale cheeks, her mother spoke behind him.

"It was good to have you here today, Bertha, but I think we have things covered now. I'll be pleased to see you on Monday."

"Thank you, Mrs. Easton." The nurse nodded to the older woman and then turned her solid form to the lady of the house. "You enjoy your supper party, Miss Lucy."

"Thank you."

Mrs. Easton rose to see the nurse out, leaving Claudio beside Lucy on the sofa. He took her hand, resting it between them.

"You look tired today, Lucy. Are you sleeping well?"

She shook her head. "I'm dreaming about Sister Prudence this week. The horror on her face as I yelled at her haunts me. I imagine what she looked like dangling from the rafter, heartbroken for Alex because he married a woman capable of beating an elderly priest and berating a nun in front of her children."

"That was not you. The Lord does not judge you for what is out of your control. Have you told Alexander or your nurse about the sleep disturbances?"

She curled beside him. "Alex is aware of what goes on when I wake up screaming several times a night. He's good enough to help get me back to sleep each time, but I think it finally broke his stamina. The doctor gave me a new sleeping draught today. Maybe it's wicked of me, but if it does work, I'll miss the middle of the night interludes with Alex."

Claudio smiled and kissed her forehead. "I am sure he will miss those as well."

Mrs. Easton came in and eyed Claudio's arms about her daughter. "Father De Fiore, while I appreciate your concern over Lucy, I worry what Alex would say if he saw you like that."

"Alex is the one who sent him to me, Mother. Does it make you feel better to know I was discussing how Alexander's midnight attentions are the best medicine of all?"

"Really, Lucille! I didn't raise you to speak like that, especially in front of a priest!"

"If you want scandal, wait until you see Claudio and Melissa tango after supper. Much has changed since your last visit."

Claudio felt his ears go red. "I am sure there are other things more important to discuss than my dancing habits."

"But you're a fine dancer. Dance with me now." Lucy swept across the room to the gramophone and put on a Tchaikovsky recording. "Dance with me, Claudio."

Her voice dripped with giddiness, and her cheeks flushed mauve, matching her lacy dress. Unsure what denying her would accomplish, Claudio spun her around the room.

Lucy pressed against him provocatively. "I feel like I'm on fire. Pretend I'm Melissa so I may know why she shirks Frederick for her moments with you."

"Lucy—" he tried to pull away, but she clutched him tighter.

"Frederick is an ardent lover. That means you must be equally tantalizing."

"Lucille Amelia!" Mrs. Easton snapped.

Lucy giggled and then dashed from the room. "I need to dress for supper!"

"I should have kept the nurse until Alex returned." Mrs. Easton stood. "Walk me to her room, and I'll do my best to contain her. Is she naughty like this often?"

"Her moods come and go," Claudio admitted as they climbed the stairs.

Mrs. Easton tried the knob on the locked master suite. "Lucille, open this door!"

"I'm naked, Mother! Surely you don't want the priest to get a glimpse when you didn't even want me sitting next to him!"

Mrs. Easton clutched her head.

"Go rest for a while," Claudio suggested. "I will call for you if needed, but I am sure Alexander will be home soon."

Mrs. Easton made her way down the hall, Claudio watching until she was safely in her room.

From below, voices and laughter drifted skyward. Asher and Phoebe clamored for hugs at the top of the stairs.

"Wash and dress for supper," Claudio said as Bethany joined them. "Your mother and grandmother are resting a minute. Make sure you bathe well."

"That means you stink, Beth!" Asher laughed.

"If she does, you all do." Claudio ruffled Asher's blond hair.

They were in their rooms when Alexander came up. "What's going on?"

Claudio informed him of Mrs. Easton sending the nurse home when he arrived and Lucy's subsequent behavior. "Did she tell you of her dreams?"

Alexander shook his head. "I only helped soothe her back to sleep."

"She is dreaming of Sister Prudence."

"Thank God the new medicine was delivered this afternoon."

"Lucy is happy for the moment, but it reminds me of Magdalene when she was possessed. She is all laughter and sensuality. Tread carefully, *amico*. There is a full house tonight."

Just as they reached the bedroom, the door opened. Lucy, in a navy gown with a butterfly emblem on the low décolletage she spilled out of, grinned like she had a mouthful of sweets.

"Welcome home, Angel. Do you like what you see?"

"You know I do, my ravishing wife." He grabbed her hips and pulled her to him. After kissing her on the lips, he dipped his head to her chest.

Afraid one false move with Alexander's mouth would set free what little remained covered, Claudio looked away.

"But you cannot wear this to supper, my queen. This was your dress when you were an untouched young lady, and now you're a woman. Your amazing breasts grew as they mothered the spawn of your sexuality."

Claudio nearly choked at Alexander's words as his hands went to her waist, kneading upward, and she arched into her husband's touch.

"These beauties are mine, and I don't wish them on display at the supper table. May I help you change?"

"Take it all." Lucy wore an expression of complete surrender as Alexander stepped into their bedroom, pressing against her as he went.

Claudio had to close the door for them because Alexander had already lowered her to the bed—his riding clothes a striking sight above the delicate gown. Standing guard because it was not locked, Claudio heard each noise that escaped the door. It stirred his yearnings, wanting to share that with Melissa more than ever.

Bethany returned first. Her steady gaze—so much like her father's—cooled Claudio's passion.

"Would you see to your grandmother, *Principessa*? She had to lie down because of a headache."

"Yes, Uncle Claudio." Bethany tucked her tiger under her arm.

When she turned to go, Lucy yelled, "Faster, Alex!"

Bethany's steady, brown eyes went back to the priest. "Momma sounds happy. Is she having a good day?"

Claudio nodded and bit his tongue. Fortunately, the next vocal display happened after Bethany was down the hall and the other children had not yet emerged. When they were all washed, he sent the children to the stairs before him and escorted Mrs. Easton down the steps. Once the others were settled in the living room, he stationed himself at the top of the stairs, where he could only hear the loudest of Lucy's cries.

The Mellings had still not shown themselves when the doorbell rang. Going to the middle landing, Claudio watched Phoebe open the front.

"Good evening, Sissa!" She hugged her stepmother and then kissed her half-sister. "Did Doff eat well today?"

"Yes," Louisa said before dashing into the front room.

"Good heavens, Louisa!" Mrs. Easton cried. "You must have grown five inches since I last saw you. Come here, dear."

Thinking herself unobserved, Melissa peeked around the corner into the front room. Her hand went to the emerald necklace when she smiled. *The smile she only gives when overcome with love. She loves her husband—the child she created with him. What I give her will never be enough.*

Her eyes lifted as she removed her wrap. Catching Claudio's gaze, her broad smile returned.

Maybe I could be enough.

They met at the foot of the stairs, kissing cheeks and holding the other's hand. A final keening from Lucy pierced the air.

"It is going to be a long night, *Eroina.*"

Melissa laughed. "Or a very short one for the guests."

Forty

Naomi rode to the Mellings' on a Wednesday morning mid-March, grateful for a short day. Her pregnancy was halfway through, and tiredness had plagued her the last week.

"Are you sure you're up for it, Honey?" Paul asked when he pulled his truck into the Mellings' driveway. "Alex can hire another girl so you don't need to come so often. From what you've said about her this month, it sounds like Lucy will need more care anyway."

She kissed him and leaned against his arm. "I'll talk to Alex about dropping my hours again. Maybe he can find a housekeeper at the end of the month when Mrs. Easton moves on to Cora's for April."

"You take it easy. I don't want you risking yours or our baby's health for that woman."

"Lucy's my best friend."

He kissed her forehead. "I know, but take it easy."

The fuchsia azalea bushes lining the yard were in full bloom, and the back doors were open to the cool morning. Alexander's singing about trains rang out, followed by Asher's laughter. The man of the house two-stepped around the tiles, arms moving like they were shunting along train tracks.

"All aboard, Naomi!" Alexander danced her to the hook, where she hung her purse and coat. Under his breath, he whispered, "She had a restless night. Bertha will be here by nine. If she doesn't improve, telephone Melissa and ask if she'd bring Asher to her house instead of coming here."

Naomi nodded and went to Lucy, who stared at a cup of coffee at the table. "Did you eat breakfast?"

She shook her head, tousled locks shifting over her silk robe.

"Would you like to lie down?"

"Yes, please."

"Allow me." Alexander stepped between them and lifted his wife into his arms. "Give us a few minutes, Naomi."

Asher shoveled sugared oatmeal into his mouth while Naomi cleared the rest of the breakfast table and rinsed the dishes. "I'll be in your momma's room until your grandma wakes. You want to play in your room a while, Asher?"

"Yes, Miss Naomi." He ran ahead of her.

In the master suite, Alexander was curled beside Lucy on their bed, a hand under her robe as he nibbled her neck.

"You needn't try to pull me out of the darkness this morning. I feel nothing today, but don't let that stop you later. Even if I'm despondent tonight, be sure you get your release."

"I want to pleasure you, my queen." His hand shifted lower.

"Some days, I'll be beyond pleasure, but it helps knowing you can take what you need from me."

"I don't wish to take—I wish to share." He leaned over her as though searching to connect to her soul through her empty eyes.

"That might be the only way I can share. No matter my response, I'm telling you now to take all you need when you want it. My body is yours, and I want you to use me while you can. Last summer, you had me promise to fight to keep what we have alive, to love you to the end, and allow you to love me. This is how I can fulfill that promise. Don't take it from me."

Alexander pressed his face into her curtain of hair, hugging her to him. Naomi folded her arms across her belly, looking away from the intimate scene.

"I love you, my queen. I'll see you this afternoon."

"I love and appreciate all you do. No one understands how good you are." Lucy watched him put on his tie and jacket—a slight hint of longing in her faraway gaze.

He slipped on his shoes and came for a kiss. "Try to rest, my queen."

Seeing Lucy stay idle, Naomi began cleaning. She heard Alexander tell Asher goodbye, and then the boy came in with a picture book.

"Why don't you look at it in the chair while I clean the bathroom?"

By the time Bertha arrived, Naomi was done with the master suite. The nurse settled in the armchair with her knitting—her medical bag at the ready beside her. Naomi took Asher into his room to point out what needed tidying. He helped her in the children's bathroom as well, and then Mrs. Easton needed breakfast.

When she finished eating, Mrs. Easton stopped Naomi. "I telephoned the office and invited Max and Eddie to take lunch with me. I figured with Lucy in bed, Melissa wouldn't be coming."

"Melissa's getting Asher at eleven-thirty. I'd be able to fix y'all something as soon as he's gone."

"Thank you, Naomi. And nothing difficult, mind you. Those boys are used to eating at luncheon counters. Anything will do."

After final plans were made, Naomi called Alexander at his office.

"Everything okay?" he asked.

"She's been sleeping all morning. Melissa's getting Asher before lunch, so you need to pick him up there."

"I'm grateful I don't need to see Lucy until I'm home for the day. I know that sounds awful, but her words nearly killed me this morning."

"I understand. Mrs. Easton invited her sons for lunch. I'll see to that before leaving."

"Our home is hers when she's with us, but I hope that doesn't put you out any."

"Not at all. I enjoy the Easton family, but there's something I need to speak with you about when you have the time."

"Go ahead."

"I'm running tired lately. I'd like to reduce my hours next month."

"I planned on phasing you out of housekeeping, but I didn't want to run you away. We're blessed to have you whenever you come."

"Thank you, Alex. I'm glad to help as much as I can, but that's changing each week."

"I understand, and I'm happy for you and Paul. I'll see you in the morning."

***

When the Easton men arrived at noon, Edmund's sour mood shadowed the gathering.

"Why is Alex hiding Lucy? Ever since their flamboyant display at the New Year's ball, she's been an enigma."

"She's unwell, Eddie." Mrs. Easton said from the head of the massive table.

"But we're family." Edmund crossed his arms, pouting like he did as a child.

Maxwell's gray hair and gentle mannerisms made him look exactly like his father. "Since when are you overly concerned with Lucy and Alex? You barely spoke to them for years."

"I was close with them once, and we're family, even when we have our differences."

Mrs. Easton poured tea. "She didn't sleep well last night, and she's been resting today. Maybe you'll be able to see her next time."

"Is that cad keeping her up all hours to satisfy his needs?"

"Edmund Albert Easton, I don't know where you and Lucy learned to speak as you do! It's completely inappropriate for people raised as you were in a respectable home."

"Then why all the secrecy with Lucy? It's like we're being lied to. What's she sick with? Why is she not taking visitors?"

"She's not well. I'll leave it at that. Talk to Alex if you must."

"I'm not going to wait for Alex to return my calls. I'm going straight to Lucy."

Naomi blocked the door. "Please leave her be, Mr. Edmund. Today's not a good day."

"Even the help knows! It's not right!" He nudged Naomi out of his way.

"Stop him, Maxwell!" Mrs. Easton cried.

He ran past Naomi, and she followed the men upstairs.

Bertha stood unwavering in the bedroom doorway. "Mr. Alex said she's not to be disturbed."

Maxwell pulled on his brother's arm. "Leave it be, Eddie."

"I want to see my sister!"

"Bertha, it's all right." Lucy sat up, the bedspread falling to her waist and exposing her slinky red nightgown. "I can speak to my brothers."

The nurse clicked her tongue but moved to the wingchair in front of the fireplace. Edmund filled the void, leaning over to kiss Lucy's cheek. "You look well, maybe a little pale, but otherwise good."

She smiled and held an arm out to Maxwell for a hug as Naomi settled by Bertha. "I've missed you both. I hope you and your families are well."

"Why is Alex hiding you away?" Edmund demanded. "There doesn't appear to be anything wrong."

"It's my choice to be here, though I'd rather be on his arm for the world to see in our final months together."

"Final months? So he's leaving?"

"No, Edmund. Never. It's I who's to leave this world."

He took her hand. "Are you diseased? Did he infect you—"

"It's not from Alex! He's nothing but good to me!" Fire burned in her eyes as she stood.

Maxwell took Edmund by the arm and stepped back.

Naomi went to stand, but Bertha stopped her as she opened her bag, a hand maneuvering for items within. "If she goes off, those brothers have it coming to them. But I'll not have you mixed in the middle of it in your condition."

Lucy continued her tirade. "Alex is a devoted husband and a wonderful father! He's every bit as good as Frederick was to me. It makes you look shallow when you blame him for everything that goes wrong."

"Then what the hell is it?" Edmund yelled. "What's wrong, Lucy?"

"Insanity," she whispered. "Rather than go the way of Opal, I'm willing myself to die."

Edmund laughed. "You and your dramatics! I know you had that spell at St. Mary's before Christmas, but there's been nothing else. Why hasn't Alex locked you in an asylum?"

"Alex knows what those places are like and won't have me treated as such. I pray daily to go quickly so I don't prolong his misery as I lose myself to darkness."

"What darkness? Screaming at a nun because Alex used to bed her when she was a prostitute?"

Maxwell moved back. "Eddie, we should—"

"Prudie saw the madness in my eyes as I beat Father Ines! She looked at me with fear because she knew Alex was strapped to a woman who had no grasp on reality! It broke her heart all the more for him, so much she took her life because of me!" Lucy struck Edmund's shoulder before Maxwell could step between them, but she pushed against her eldest brother to yell around him. "And I'm sorry you lost one of your old whores when she took her life, especially after you lost Hazel Kline when your filthy friend had his way with her. But you have no right calling Alex a cad when he's been faithful to me the whole time we've been together! You ran around for years while Mary Margaret cried at home, left to rock the babies you insisted on filling her with while your gluttony left you a fat, miserable excuse for an Easton!"

Maxwell went to take her arm, but she yanked away.

"I'm not done!" She clawed at her brother. "At least Alex is man enough that he outgrew the Dardenne ways. In your pathetic mind, you're still that Mystics of Dardenne member protected by your mask and costume. But I see you as you are, Edmund, and it makes me ill!"

"This isn't madness," Edmund sneered as he got in Lucy's face. "You're nothing but a spoiled wife looking for attention, trying to capitalize on your little sister's legacy."

"You know nothing!" Lucy threw herself at him. Despite her slight frame against his thick mass, she clung to his neck with one arm and wailed on him with her other as she screeched curses.

Bertha commanded Maxwell to hold Lucy from the back, locking her arms behind her. Then the nurse covered Lucy's mouth and nose with a chloroform-soaked cloth for several seconds. She took up Lucy's feet as Maxwell held her upright. Once Lucy was laid in bed and covered, Bertha looked to the men.

"I assume you'll be on your way now, gentlemen. Please direct any further questions to Mr. Alex."

Ready to flee the unfortunate scene, Maxwell stepped into the hall.

"Mother, what is it?" He caught Mrs. Easton as she collapsed. "Call the doctor, Naomi!"

Forty-One

On the last Friday in March, Melissa and Louisa eagerly awaited the arrival of the *Mary Louella*. When Captain Walker brought the boat in, the Campbell family waved excitedly from the railing. Joe and his oldest son, Emmett, turned down the noon dinner invitation because they had cargo to secure before steaming back to the island. Still, they personally loaded the Campbells' luggage into the Davenports' automobile. After wishing the Walkers a blessed Easter, Melissa drove the group across town.

Kade took charge of the children as they played in the yard. Sharon prepared a hot dinner while Melissa and Maggie sat on the front porch exchanging the latest news.

"Lucy's worse than ever," Melissa explained how the woman wished to die to save Alex further heartache, especially after she attacked her brothers. "Mrs. Easton overheard everything Lucy said to Edmund and collapsed. She's been in the hospital two weeks now, but Lucy hasn't been told about her mother."

"Bless her heart. What's the latest on Freddy?"

Melissa exhaled. "He had a week of relief time according to the last letter, but he's back on the front somewhere in France."

Alex parked in the driveway. Fresh from Holy Friday Mass, Lucy's girls rushed from the automobile in new pink and white dresses. Asher wasn't far behind in his gleaming suit as they ran for the back. Alex removed his dove gray suit jacket and smoothed the sky blue suspenders that matched his bowtie.

With a smile that let the women know he was aware of their attention, he stopped a few feet from the swing, arms open. "Magdalene."

She hesitated a moment before flinging herself against him. His arms were about her in a tight embrace, and he kissed her forehead.

"Magdalene, you feel wonderful."

"So do you, Alexander." She nestled against his neck.

Melissa couldn't be sure, but Maggie might have kissed beneath his shaved jaw. Whatever Maggie did, Alex responded by pressing fully against her and whispering. Having no right to judge, Melissa kept quiet.

Alex escorted Maggie to the swing and settled between the two women, a hand on each of their knees. Turning to Melissa, he offered a smile. "Thank you for having us over for dinner and accepting my invitation to return the favor on Sunday. Hopefully, Lucy will join us at the table for Easter Dinner. Some days she refuses to eat—says she can't swallow around the sadness choking her. She's sedated today because she wouldn't sleep last night."

Claudio came up the driveway, and Maggie ran to him. He lifted her off her feet in a hug, kissing both her cheeks.

"Should I be jealous she didn't run to my arms like that?" Alex teased.

"Her greeting to you was heart-felt."

He grinned. "Are you and Claudio behaving yourselves, naughty Sissa?"

"He only visits during the day while Louisa is in attendance." She wanted to add "unfortunately" because the ache for a deep kiss overwhelmed her.

A quarter of an hour later, the seven children and four adults settled around the dining room table. They were reverent for Claudio's prayer, but the children returned to the energetic level typical for the Davenport-Melling-Campbell gatherings.

Toward the end of the meal, the doorbell rang. Melissa excused herself to answer it, her heart falling to her stomach the moment she saw the uniformed men on the porch.

One spoke through the screen. "All isn't lost, Mrs. Davenport, but we wanted to send word in person rather than a telegram."

Alex was behind her in a flash, taking her by the elbow. "Come in, gentlemen."

He closed the doors to the parlor, staying beside Melissa as she perched on the edge of the sofa.

The army officer held his hat. "There is a campaign happening near the Somme River. General Pershing is doing his best with our men to help, but it's a long, nasty fight. Major Davenport's unit took things heavy right off, and you know his bravery."

Alex's arm went around Melissa.

"Some of his boys got in trouble, and he rushed in to save them. He took two bullets to his leg and another in the shoulder but still managed to carry Lieutenant Brady to safety though it was too late for the man."

"Chuck," she choked on the name. "Rachel will—"

"We just came from seeing Mrs. Brady."

"And what of Major Davenport?" Alex asked.

"He's still in France. The goal is to get him stabilized and moved to England. From there, transportation to the East Coast when he's well enough. I'll keep you posted myself, Mrs. Davenport. Try to have a Happy Easter."

As soon as they were gone, Melissa sobbed on Alex's shoulder for longer than she thought possible.

"Thank you for being here, Alex." She wiped her face with his handkerchief. "Will you tell the girls for me?"

"Of course." He kissed her cheek. "Thank God he's alive."

"All sorts of complications could arise. Infection, amputa—"

"He's alive!" Alex gripped her arms. "Hold to that, and we'll all continue to pray for his safe return."

He slipped from the room, and then Claudio and Maggie were on either side of her.

"I'm sorry he's wounded," Maggie said. "But the fact he's alive is great news."

"*Sí, Eroina.* Be brave a little longer, and you will see all will be well."

Melissa leaned against him, tucking her head to his shoulder. "Hold me, Claudio, and keep telling me Freddy will be fine."

***

Sunday morning, Melissa took all three girls to Trinity Episcopal as she did bi-monthly. News of the Somme Defensive reached the newspaper that weekend, along with the updated list of local men wounded or lost thus far. The church members rallied around the Davenports, promising to pray for Freddy and offering help. By the time the service ended, Melissa was ready to crawl into bed and hide for a week. But Phoebe had to make her social rounds. Louisa tagged along, eager to learn from her oldest sister. Bethany held Melissa's hand and her locket with her other while they waited to the front steps, smiling when greeted but otherwise straight-faced.

"Will Daddy be home soon?" she whispered.

"He has to be well enough to travel, and securing transportation across the Atlantic is difficult during war. The best I can say is that it would be a month at the very least, but probably more. We need to be patient, Little Princess."

Bethany smiled at her father's nickname for her. "I can be patient, but Daddy is strong. I know he'll get better."

Once they were home, Melissa fed the girls finger sandwiches to hold them over until dinner and allowed them to work on a jigsaw puzzle while she lay on the sofa. Closing her eyes, she imagined the times Freddy stretched himself on the sofa after a weekend meal, often napping or reading the newspaper. *Will he ever lie here again? He's been gone so long his scent isn't in the house, and I can't remember his face without looking upon a photograph.*

Misty-eyed, she crossed the hall to the study. Sitting at her desk, she lifted the frame that sat on the corner opposite her lamp—the silly edition of Freddy and the girls on the porch swing the morning he left for training. The one of just the two of them was on her bedside table.

"Please make it home," she whispered.

When the Davenports arrived at the Mellings' house, Melissa parked by the Adams's automobile.

Alex was quick to greet them in the driveway, handing a basket to each girl. "Find three eggs each, Darlings."

"Thank you, Poppy!" Louisa kissed his hand.

Bethany stopped for a one-armed hug as she clutched her stuffed tiger in the other, but Phoebe snatched a basket and tore through the gate, yelling for Kade as the Campbells were staying with Darla.

"You look lovely in blue." Alex kissed Melissa's cheeks like Claudio always did and smiled. "Lucy would like to see you. Would you be willing to go to her room and help her downstairs?"

Melissa nodded, greeted Darla and Maggie, and then climbed the grand staircase while thoughts of the impassioned moment Freddy threw her over his shoulder and carried her to one of the guest rooms replayed in her mind. She was lost in the memory of being wrapped around her husband when she entered the master suite.

Lucy lay on top of the covers in a lacy pink gown, and Claudio sat beside her in one of the armchairs pulled close.

Claudio stood. "You look flushed."

"I felt dazed a moment." They clasped hands and kissed cheeks. Then Melissa took in the full sight of Lucy. Hollow-cheeks and dark circles around her eyes cast a shadow of unrest over her pretty countenance.

"Claudio, would you leave us? Melissa can see me down."

He looked to Melissa, and she nodded. "We'll be fine."

Lucy motioned to the seat Claudio vacated. "Is everyone here?"

"Darla and Maggie with their children, but I'm not sure if any of the Eastons—"

"No Eastons today. How does Magdalene look?"

Knowing Lucy would see soon enough, Melissa didn't lie. "Pretty, as always. She grows lovelier each year while I see more lines on my face every time I look in the mirror."

"You're beautiful in a different way, Melissa. Magdalene is soft and alluring. You're strong and modern." Lucy folded her hands in her lap. "Alex told me about Freddy. I'd like to see him one more time. I've decided to hang on a little longer."

"Lucy, you—"

"I stopped writing him last month. I help the girls when they're here, but I've not penned a letter of my own. I worry I was saying the wrong things, that he must think me ... he must know I'm not the same." She sighed, long and loud. "You need him here. The girls need him. And Alex will need him."

Melissa took her hand.

"As much as Alex claims Claudio as his best friend, it's Frederick who's been there for him. He helps us through our mistakes and knocks sense into Alex when he needs it." Lucy's eyes took on a fierceness Melissa hadn't seen in a while. "I'll not debate that Claudio loves you, but I'll stand firm in saying that he's not what you need when you have Frederick Lionel Davenport. You're perfect for each other. Promise me you'll love my best friend as long as you live, that you'll be a devoted lover because everyone needs one in their life."

"I promise, Lucy. Claudio and I never did what everyone thought we were doing. And since New Year's, we've done nothing that we haven't done in front of everyone else. I still love Freddy and Claudio knows it. I'll tell Freddy when the time is right. He'll hear from my own lips how I weakened though my love didn't waver."

Lucy smiled, casting her emaciated face in further shadows. "Help me downstairs so I can see that no mischief happens between the Seacliff friends. I'll be forgiving today because Alex will wish to ease Magdalene's pain on her husband's birthday. I'm not yet so heartless as to deny Alex his pleasure in comforting a friend in need."

Melissa had to hold in an exclamation of shock at feeling how light Lucy had grown. She thought she'd be able to carry her if needed, but Lucy got to her feet steady enough. At the foot of the stairs, Lucy released her hold on Melissa's arm and made her way to the patio alone.

Alex stood with an arm around Maggie. She seemed to swallow her surprise at Lucy's appearance but came forward to embrace her.

"That's a lovely gown, Lucy. I'm glad you're able to join us."

"Yes, my queen." Alex wrapped her in a hug. "I'll stay by your side forevermore."

Forty-Two

Claudio saw the change in Lucy the moment she joined the others on the patio. Always a gracious hostess, but every smile taxed her. After the other guests left, Claudio offered to stay and watch Asher so Alexander could see Lucy to bed. Alexander emerged from the bedroom over an hour later and immediately hid himself in his den. Claudio left Asher in the morning room and joined him, lighting his own cigarette.

"She was brave today, *amico*."

"And I was weak. As much as I love her, I'm finding it difficult to meet her demands. She's unresponsive most of the time, and it strips my passion. If I don't complete the task, she'll think I'm going elsewhere, especially when Magdalene's in town."

"It cannot—"

"She's ruthless, Claudio! Even though she appears to gain no pleasure, she wants to see me climax. But she's no longer my soft, sensual Lucy. She's cold, stiff, and wasting away. It's painful to see her beneath me, but if I close my eyes and drive on, it feels like what I did to her in the duplex." He wiped a tear with the sleeve of his shirt. "If I hadn't been a sex-crazed fool all these years, she might not be this insistent. I ruined us both."

Over the next several weeks, Claudio went to the Mellings' house often. They hosted no supper parties, but they always had visitors in the form of Lucy's watchful helpers. Priscilla Watts was brought from across the bay as a housekeeper and an extra set of eyes on Asher. When Naomi came in the mornings Mondays, Wednesdays, and Fridays, Priscilla did her heaviest cleaning, and Naomi kept Asher and Lucy entertained—even though Nurse Bertha hovered in the background.

By the end of April, the Campbells returned to Dauphin Island, bringing Darla and her children with them for a visit. Alexander—at Melissa's insistence—took riding time alone with Apollo a couple afternoons a week. During his Saturday afternoon rides, Melissa saw to Lucy and all the children and Claudio joined her, either watching the children play in the yard or sitting with Lucy while Melissa took charge of the other duty. He did not get much time to see Melissa, but being near and helping together gave him a sense of peace. And what peace he could experience was a blessing because Freddy convalesced in an English army hospital and was expected home within the month.

On the first Friday night in May, Claudio climbed the porch steps to the Davenports' house at nine o'clock. The parlor drapes were closed, but he tapped lightly on the window. A minute later, Melissa held the door open.

Once it closed behind him, he took her hands. "Happy birthday, *Eroina.*"

He went to kiss her cheeks, but her lips caught his in a delicious surrender. It had been months, but Claudio remembered the feel of her attentions. His frock was soon on the floor and they stumbled to the dim parlor, Claudio's hands roaming her blouse.

His own shirt open, she kissed his chest as though famished as she urged him to the sofa beneath her. The length of her beautiful figure on top of him brought Claudio to the edge. Grasping her hips, he pressed her against him as he trailed kisses down her neck.

Melissa's breath grew ragged. "I can't." She buried her face in his shoulder. "I feel your need and I thought I could give you this to thank you for all you've done for me, but I can't."

He kissed her until the hardness of disappointment softened to a tender longing.

"I have been here this past year for your needs, not mine. I am happy Frederick is returning. Do not worry about me. I have been planning for my future."

She shifted as though she wished to stand, but he held her. "Stay, *Eroina*. Allow me to hold you a little while longer."

Claudio trailed his fingers across Melissa's back. He felt her body meld against his as she released her tension. The heat of her cheek on his skin and the rhythm of her heartbeat were as wonderful as he hoped they would be. Memorizing the scent of her hair and the way her body fit with his own caused a smile to find his disillusioned face.

It is enough to hold her like this. A man in my position has no right to expect more. If she broke her vows to her husband I could not love her as much. But she sleeps in my arms, our bodies as close as they will ever be. I will be selfish enough not to wake her until morning because I wish to spend one night with her.

"*Buon compleanno, amore mio*," he whispered before closing his eyes.

***

Claudio woke when Melissa's touch roamed his torso. Her hand made its way to the morning stubble on his face.

"I'm sorry, Claudio. I didn't mean to fall asleep." She shifted, but he wrapped his arms around her.

"Do not be sorry, *Eroina*. It was a blessing to share a night with you." A finger brushed her lips. "Remember after Darla's wedding, when you and Frederick took the girls to his house? I came in and found you two sleeping on the sofa. It was not the only time I was jealous when it came to you, but I am happy to have had a taste of it."

"Claudio." She kissed him fully.

His hand ran through her hair. "It is enough, Melissa. It has been too much in the eyes of the world, but I am satisfied to have shared these moments with you."

"Your loving care has kept me from hysterics and been a blessing to Louisa." She sat up and smiled down at him. "But Alex doesn't need to know you spent the night here."

They laughed and straightened their clothing.

"Would you like some coffee or to stay for breakfast? It's Pancake Time today."

Claudio kissed her cheek. "It is good you keep Frederick's traditions. I would be happy to share your morning."

When Melissa went upstairs to freshen, Claudio retrieved his discarded vestment and buttoned it over his clothes. Then he saw to his morning prayers before putting water on to boil. The two sat in the breakfast nook drinking coffee and chatting until Louisa woke.

"Uncle Claudio!" She jumped into his lap, snuggling against him as Doff rubbed his legs. "Did you hear Daddy's coming home in a few weeks?"

"I did, *Principessa*, and am most happy for you and your family. Today I am here to inspect how well you do Pancake Time to be sure your father will be pleased when he returns."

"It's better when Phoebe and Bethany are here, but I do my best."

After the boisterous breakfast, the three settled on the front porch swing. Claudio was about to say goodbye when a courier pedaled over.

"Mrs. Davenport?"

"Yes." She met him at the top of the stairs.

"Urgent message, fresh off one of the boats from the island."

She stepped inside to take a quarter from the credenza and handed it to him. Recognizing Darla's handwriting, she returned to the swing. "I hope everything's all right."

Claudio watched as her face turned ashen and the page trembled in her hand as she read.

"Mommy!" Louisa touched her arm as Melissa shook with tears.

"Give her a few minutes, *Principessa*. Could you sit in the rocking chair?"

Louisa nodded and moved across the porch. Claudio hugged Melissa, carefully prying the note from her hand.

Melissa,

Excuse the brief letter, but I wanted to send word as soon as possible. Last evening, Maggie received word that Douglas's cargo ship was torpedoed by a German U-boat in the Mediterranean. Though most of the crew was rescued, Douglas didn't survive. They promise Lieutenant-Commander Campbell died a hero as he tried to save others and went down with the ship, but that does little to console Maggie at this time. I plan on staying until she is through the worst. I'll send Joe to collect more things from my house next week and would appreciate your help in securing the proper items. Please tell Claudio and Alex the news. They need to hear the words in person.

Love to all,

Darla

"Douglas," Claudio spoke the name with an ache in his chest.

Melissa straightened. "I'm sorry, Claudio. I was supposed to tell you."

"Darla's words were as kind as possible, but it is something best heard from a Seacliff friend." He linked their fingers and kissed her wet cheek. "I will tell Alex myself and secure passage to the island. I must go to Magdalene."

"She could ask for nothing better at a time like this." Melissa opened her arms toward her daughter. "Here, Louisa. I've sad news to share."

She crawled into her lap, taking one of her mother's and one of Claudio's hands into her own.

"Mr. Douglas's ship was sunk by the enemy. He won't be coming home like Daddy."

"Tabby, Simon, and Kade won't have their papa home?" Her brown eyes filled with concern.

"Not everyone's father makes it home from war. But your friends still have Captain Joe, Uncle Claudio, and Poppy to help them. We can help them, too."

"May I make them a feel better picture?"

"I think that would be nice, Louisa."

"Yes, *Principessa*. And I will go see them as soon as I can." Claudio stood. "I will hug them all for you."

"Alex will be at the stables," Melissa told him.

"I'll see to transportation and packing first."

Melissa drove him to the docks and he secured passage on the boat that brought the letter for a two o'clock departure that afternoon. Being from Joe Walker's fleet, Captain Kevin O'Farrell insisted he couldn't accept payment when he learned Claudio was going to comfort Maggie.

Melissa then dropped Claudio at the rectory.

"Please tell Alex I'm here for him," Melissa said in parting. "I'll take the girls and Asher tonight if needed."

Claudio nodded and hurried inside to pack. Once ready, he left word of his departure—not permission—with his superior. He took the trolley around Government Street to the Mellings' house. Phoebe, still dressed in her riding clothes, let him in the front door.

"I need to speak with Poppy, *Principessa*. It is most urgent."

"He's showering, Uncle Claudio."

"And where is your mother?"

"In the morning room with her nurse. I'll bring you."

"Claudio! What a nice surprise."

She held her hands out to him, and he kissed her cheeks, forcing a smile. Claudio's soul ached at seeing Lucy happy because her wounds would open anew.

"Doesn't Momma look pretty in her new dress?" Phoebe asked.

"*Sí, Principessa*. Lucy is always lovely in purple."

"Alex brought it to me yesterday from Mademoiselle Bisset. Phoebe, be sure you get your shower. Bethany should be done by now." Lucy motioned to the woman in black sitting across from her. "Nurse Stephanie, this is Father De Fiore. Claudio, this is Stephanie. She helps on weekends and fills in during the week as needed."

The nurse—though small—had a strong handshake.

"It is good to meet you and see that Lucy has more wonderful helpers." He turned back to Lucy. "I need to speak with Alexander when he is presentable."

"You should know by now I'm never presentable." Alexander waltz in, beltless pants riding low and his blue shirt unbuttoned. He hugged Claudio's shoulders with one arm and kissed his cheeks before going to Lucy. "Can you do without me a few minutes, my queen?"

"I'll try to contain my disappointment, Angel." She fingered his scars as they kissed.

Claudio saw the long-lost spark in her eyes when Alexander straightened, and dread pooled in his chest as he followed his friend to the den.

"She's glowing today," Alexander sang out with a swivel to his partially covered hips. "She rode me this morning like a wild Gulf wind."

"That makes what I am about to tell you even more difficult, *amico*."

He gripped his shoulders. "What is it, Claudio? Did you and Melissa—"

"No!" He realized his denial was too intense and spoke all the faster for it. "It is not about me. It is Douglas. His cargo ship was torpedoed. He did not make it onto the rescue boats because he helped the injured. He went down with the ship."

"Not Magdalene's Scot—he's invincible!" Torment raked his face.

"She was given word last night while Darla was with her. This morning, Darla sent a letter to Melissa, asking her to tell us. I have passage on the boat returning to the island to go to Magdalene. I have little time, but I would tell the children or Lucy for you, *amico*."

"It will break my Lucy." He ran his discolored hand through his hair. "But Magdalene is already broken. Promise you'll send my condolences, Claudio. Tell her I would be there if I could, but I cannot leave Lucy at this time. I'll send help however I can."

"I think she will be relieved you cannot come."

He hung his head, tears dripping from his eyes as he rubbed the scars on his chest. "I always meant to do right with her."

"Cling to Lucy. Melissa said she would take the children tonight."

Alexander nodded. "Take care of Magdalene for me. I'll see to my family here."

Forty-Three

When Naomi arrived at the Mellings' on May fifteenth, she found Alex frowning at a pot of oatmeal.

"What did those oats ever do to you, Mr. Alex?"

"They taunt me. Yet another food my wife refuses to eat." The sorrow in his blue eyes was a punch to Naomi's protruding stomach. "She refused food and drink yesterday, and her night was just as miserable."

"And how are you holding up?"

"I'm smoking too much and wishing for a bottle of brandy at least five times a day. But Ash is holding on, the brave soul. Even when Lucy started raving, he came to kiss her goodnight." Alex sighed and dished up a bowl for his son. "I'm glad he'll get to play with Louisa today. Priscilla is great with him when you aren't here, but he needs to be around his peers now the girls are with Melissa more, and Horatio's still gone with Darla."

"He's resilient." Naomi kissed Alexander's cheek. "Do you wish to take breakfast with Lucy? If so, send Asher down, and I'll watch him so Priscilla can get started on her work."

Alexander nodded and readied a tray for two with honeyed oatmeal, fruit, and coffee while Naomi poured milk for the boy.

Asher clomped downstairs, and Priscilla followed, gathering dusting items from the closet.

"Everything working out for you here?" Naomi asked.

"It's lovely, except worrying over L-U-C-Y. She doesn't look right today. Mr. Alex hoped to bring the family to S-E-A-C-L-I-F-F this month, but I don't think that will happen."

Naomi nodded and settled at the table with Asher. When he finished eating, she sent him ahead to the bathroom to wash his face.

"Naomi, can you come up?" Alexander called from the stairs. He met her in the hall outside his room. "Will you look at her and tell me what you think?"

"I'm no doctor, Alex."

"I know, but I want to see if you think the same thing."

Naomi followed him into the master suite.

"My queen, you have a visitor."

Lucy's normally pale skin was yellow tinged against the white pillow. Naomi gave a prayer of gratitude Frederick would be home the following week because she didn't know how much longer Lucy would survive. "Did you eat breakfast, Miss Lucy?"

She shook her head.

"You need to drink to keep yourself hydrated. Mr. Frederick will be here in nine days."

"Nine days?" Her voice scratched out the words.

"That's right." Naomi took her limp hand. "Melissa will be able to tell you more when she comes today."

Lucy pushed herself to sitting, exposing her jutting collarbones and sagging breasts beneath her low-cut nightgown that was now too big for her. "I'll try some coffee."

Alexander smiled with relief as he scooped her sugar into the cup. "You need to eat *and* drink, my queen. Freddy will appreciate you welcoming him home."

"And you can use me a few more days, my angel."

She took the cup from him, and Alexander turned away, gritting his teeth.

Asher skipped into the room. "I couldn't find you, Miss Naomi."

"She came to tell me good morning." Lucy smiled. "Would you tell me the same, Phoenix?"

"Yes, Momma!" He climbed across the red bedspread to leave a sloppy kiss on her hollow cheek. "Good morning, my beautiful mother. May I brush your hair?"

She laughed, but the sound lacked its former chime. "After I finish drinking. Thank you, Phoenix Asher."

Alexander and Naomi watched Asher brush Lucy's waist-length hair. It brought back some of the shine but lacked the full luster it previously held. Alexander paced the room, flipping the light switch in the bathroom off and on as he came and went as though trying to decide if he would shave or not.

Naomi caught his elbow when he came near the door. "She looks jaundiced."

"I was afraid of that."

"If you want to leave—"

"I want to personally speak to Bertha." He shifted toward the hall and dropped his voice. "But thank you for getting her to drink. I don't wish to hang Frederick's homecoming over her but—"

"Don't leave!" Lucy cried out as she clutched Asher's hand. "Don't leave *us*. You promised!"

He hurried to her side, bringing their clasped hands to his lips. "I'm here, my queen."

Nurse Bertha managed to get Lucy to drink a cup of water an hour. At noon, she bundled Lucy in Alexander's velvet robe and moved her to the morning room to get sunlight through the large windows. Naomi stayed to take tea with Melissa and Lucy while Priscilla served Asher and Louisa lunch in the kitchen.

"Happy Anniversary, Melissa," Naomi told her as she poured tea.

"Thank you. It's only been six years, but much has changed in that time."

"When is Frederick to come home?" Lucy asked.

"He's supposed to be on the train next Friday," Melissa replied. "I'll know for sure next week. A telegram is supposed to be sent when he boards the train in Washington D.C."

"You'll keep the girls home from school to go with you?"

"Yes, and Alex wants to be there to help with them like he did last year when Freddy came back from training. It's nice to have another set of hands to help with the girls. I'm thinking about having an open house for him sometime. I'll decide when I see him and judge how he'd take to it all. I've read reports about wounded soldiers returning drastically changed, not tolerating noise or crowds. I wouldn't want to overwhelm him."

"Not my Frederick. He'll never change." Lucy's eyes brightened for the first time in weeks. "He's stalwart to the end."

Naomi caught Melissa's gaze, but there was no arguing with Lucy in her current state.

"He'll want to take you dancing," Lucy continued her fancy. "You two will be glorious on the dancefloor."

After taking two bullets to his leg? Alex hobbled around for weeks after he was grazed by one. Bless Melissa for having to sit through Lucy's fantasies, but I can't take it anymore.

Naomi stood. "I need to get home so I can nap before fixing supper."

"Thank you, Naomi." Lucy took her hand. "You'll be here on Friday?"

"Of course." She turned to Melissa. "Take care of yourself this week. Be sure to ask Sharon for more help if you need it around your house."

Naomi stopped to say goodbye to the children and Priscilla and then waited for the colored streetcar, transferring lines twice to make it across town with the least walking. At home, she checked each room for things to tidy on her way to bed. With a sigh, she curled on her side, snuggling Paul's pillow as she inhaled his scent from the linens. She didn't understand how Melissa coped all those months alone, how Magdalene would survive without her husband, or how Darla carried on each day, not knowing if Henry would ever see their baby.

"God spared me by having me fall in love with a man too old for war but still healthy and strong," she murmured into the pillow.

Naomi slept until almost four and woke disoriented. In her rush to prepare supper, she stumbled over her recipe for greens, cube steak, and potatoes, which she had prepared perfectly for two decades.

Paul found her crying at the stove when he returned from work. "Honey, what is it?" He hugged her, and she leaned against his broad chest.

"She's dying, truly dying. I didn't believe it until today, but her skin is yellowed, and she's nothing but a pile of bones."

Paul turned off the burners, steered her to the living room, and held her as she cried.

"I fear I'm losing my mind too. I can't cook a meal without messing something."

"That's not your mind, Honey. That's the baby. Baby Bumbles, Willa called it when she grew forgetful when pregnant. Don't let that worry you."

"I over-salted the greens and burned the potatoes."

He kissed her, soulful eyes keeping her blurry gaze focused on him. "None of that matters. We're together at the end of the day, and that's all I care about."

"I'm afraid to go back, Paul. I don't want to see her worse than she was today. She spoke nonsense about Frederick. It was all I could do to hold back from reminding her he's wounded, that he won't be the same man he was when he left. And dear Asher, still caring for her like she's a princess while Alex can barely keep the tears off his face."

Paul held her tighter. "You're home tomorrow, Honey. Rest and care for yourself. Wear one of those new dresses, and I'll bring you out to supper when I get home. We haven't done that for a while."

After a few more minutes, she dried her tears, and Paul helped her back to the kitchen. Over their meal, he spoke about his project redoing the trim of a mansion in Spring Hill. His deep voice soothed her nerves, and by the time the kitchen was cleaned, she relaxed in the bath he'd drawn for her.

When she returned to Lucy Friday morning, she carried the extra love from Paul as a talisman against the sorrow that oozed from the blonde like molasses. Thanks to her will to see Frederick, Lucy was no worse. She drank to stay strong and nibbled enough food to keep alive though Alexander looked worse than ever with his unshaven face and dark-ringed eyes.

Saturday, Naomi sat on her back porch with Paul as he sanded the cradle for their baby. He skillfully rounded each curve of the oak boards he'd crafted. To the soothing sound of Paul's motions, Naomi hand-stitched yellow and green quilt squares together while the electric fan whirled overhead. She did her best not to think of the Mellings, but their shadow darkened the corner of her mind.

Forty-Four

Up before the sun the following Friday morning, Melissa dressed in a sensible green walking suit. Forgoing all jewelry except her rings, she used gold combs to hold back her hair, plucking the gray strands that sprouted along her forehead the past month.

She took the framed picture off her bedside table, fingering her husband's face. Much had changed, but still, her love for him burned. *Will he feel the same for me? When he telephoned from New York, his voice sounded changed, but that could have been the connection or the fact I haven't spoken to him in almost a year.*

When the girls clamored to the kitchen, Melissa was reminded how she'd prefer to greet Freddy alone. She couldn't explain her reasoning to those excited faces, though she prayed Alex would understand and keep them back a minute. Phoebe wore her pearls and pink Easter dress. Bethany was dressed in her white one with a pink sash—locket bright against her torso. Louisa had already outgrown her spring clothes and wore a new white dress bought earlier that week.

"When are we leaving, Sissa?" Phoebe asked after the dishes were done. She preened her hair as it tumbled over her shoulders.

"Ten o'clock. Poppy is supposed to meet us at the station."

Bethany frowned. "I think he'd better stay with Momma instead of coming with us."

"He'd be at work anyway." Melissa had reminded the girls how sick their mother was throughout recent days, but only Bethany seemed concerned. "She has Miss Naomi this morning."

"Daddy will want to go see Momma." Phoebe flipped her hair with an air of superiority.

"Phoebe, please arrange your hair properly before we leave."

"It's how Momma wears hers."

"Your mother is an adult and may wear her hair any way she chooses. You are yet a girl and need to arrange your hair appropriately for your age."

"I could help you," Bethany offered.

"I don't require assistance!" Phoebe snapped as she stalked out of the room.

By the time they drove downtown, Phoebe's hair was braided and tied with white ribbons. She sat in the front passenger seat, waving at everyone who caught her eye.

The train station teemed with The Salvation Army Band and a crowd of people. Melissa had to circle two blocks to find a parking place. Her annoyance soon turned to understanding as they were greeted warmly by everyone they passed. Because of her newspaper column, her family members were public figures and Freddy— whether he wanted to be or not—a local hero, both from her words and his valiant actions. Phoebe glowed with the attention, and her poise served her well as she answered questions from several reporters about how she felt having her father return. Bethany clung to her older sister's hand and remained silent. Melissa continued through the multitude with Louisa.

"Melissa!" Alex waved from a small stage in the corner of the waiting area. Seeing the girls surrounded, he dashed for them. He lifted a stepdaughter in each arm to carry them to the platform. When they were all together, he leaned to Melissa's ear.

"I secured permission for you to board the train so you and Freddy can have a few minutes before being in the limelight."

Melissa hugged Alex. "I could kiss you right now!"

"Save that for later." He winked. "There are a few dozen other men returning home, but Davenport will be the lead interest. Don't detain him too long, naughty Sissa."

She laughed as a conductor came for her.

"Stay with Poppy," she told the girls. "I'll be back soon with Daddy."

After the train pulled in, Melissa was escorted to one of the cars before anyone disembarked. Her hand quaked as it gripped the railing. There were dozens of khaki-clad soldiers between them, but Melissa only had eyes for the one standing in the back. The music of the band and cheers faded. Rushing up the aisle, she felt her face would break from her huge smile.

Freddy had more gray at his temples but was as handsome as ever. Noticing he had a hand on the seat beside him and his other arm rested in a sling, she embraced him gently so as not to knock him off balance.

"Beloved." His free arm tightened around her. "Do you forgive me now that I've returned?"

"You know I do." She kissed his lined cheek and stared into his brown eyes. They were shadowed with loss but still open and warm. "I never stopped loving you, Freddy."

Their lips met, and everything that had dimmed in his absence returned. Arms resting about his neck, she deepened the kiss to renew the remembrance of his taste. His good hand went to the small of her back and pressed her to him as he worked his sensuous tongue about hers.

"Major and Mrs. Davenport?" the conductor said from the door.

Freddy pulled away first, looking at her with an awed smile.

"I love you." He took her into his one-armed hug and spoke over her shoulder. "Yes?"

"I don't like to interrupt, but it's time. I'll see to your luggage."

Melissa startled at the empty car, unsure how long they'd been in each other's arms. Freddy kissed her once more as his right hand went for a cane balanced against the seat. He winced when he took his first step but motioned her in front of him in the narrow aisle.

At the door, she stepped to the side so Freddy could take the lead. The fanfare began anew and hundreds of little American flags waved as cheers filled the air. Melissa tucked her left hand under his upper right arm and smiled as she waved at those gathered.

"The girls are to the left," she said directly into his ear to be heard over the din. "I'm sure a path will clear for you."

The crowd did part, several people thanking him and many more smiling and waving. Then Rachel Brady pitched herself at Freddy. Melissa did her best to steady him discreetly.

"Thank you, Frederick." Rachel cried on his shoulder and he on hers.

They stood together a minute, then he straightened. "I'm sorry I couldn't save him. I—"

"You did everything humanly possible. He couldn't have asked for a better friend. I'm glad you're home. Your family needs you." She kissed his cheek. "I stayed in town until you returned, but I'm heading north to spend the summer with my grandparents. Promise me you won't fret over what happened."

"I've worried two months now," he admitted.

"Then stop, for all our sakes." She hugged him again, then Melissa. "Take wonderful care of him."

Rachel was swallowed by the crowd before they could tell her goodbye. They made their way to the platform where Phoebe posed like a queen, Bethany peeked from around Alex, and Louisa waved a flag atop his shoulders. Alex motioned the girls back from the steps, but rather than climbing the two stairs, Freddy sat on the edge of the platform, his cane clattering to the ground as Phoebe and Bethany went to their knees beside him. His massive arm brought them both to his heart for a hug as he kissed each one.

"Daddy! I missed you so much!" Phoebe smiled as she snuggled him, turning her face toward the nearest photographer while Bethany hid in the crook of his arm.

"I missed all my princesses. Have you kept the Kingdom safe?"

"Yes, Daddy, though I worked more with Melling Militia. You should see how I can jump on a horse!" Phoebe reluctantly stepped to the side when Alex approached with Louisa.

He lifted her off his shoulders and set her beside Freddy.

"You must have grown a foot, Littlest Princess."

Melissa choked on the lump in her throat as Freddy hugged Louisa and kissed Bethany's head. Then Alex received a handshake, and the men exchanged words.

Alex stepped back, relief on his face. "I'll prepare her for your visit."

Freddy took a few minutes with the reporters, answering questions about being awarded a Distinguished Service Cross when he stopped in Washington D.C. Then the family posed for photographs, and Melissa drove them to the Mellings' house.

In the grand hall, Naomi hugged him in welcome.

"It's wonderful to see you with child, Naomi. I wish I could have been here for the wedding."

"Don't worry over it, Mr. Frederick."

"It's my afternoon to go home on the ferry," Priscilla told him. "I'm glad to see you so I can tell my parents you're well."

"Please send Leroy and Rosemary my greetings," he replied.

Melissa had to hold Asher back from climbing up Freddy's side like he used to, but he bent to hug the boy.

Priscilla and Naomi kept the children downstairs as Melissa ascended the stairs with Freddy. When they paused to rest on the middle landing, she looked to him.

"Lucy doesn't have much longer. What improvements she made at the end of last week were waning when I was here Wednesday."

"Alex warned me she's no longer the glowing muse she once was."

"Guard your heart. She's liable to say and do anything."

He nodded and started on the next half-flight of stairs. At the top, he sat on the hall bench and stretched his left leg.

Melissa joined him. "Where did the bullets go through?"

He pointed to the back of his calf and then just above his kneecap. "An inch lower, and I would have lost my leg. I think that lucky kiss you gave me prevented it."

"I'd like to think that's true, Handsome." She smiled.

"I missed you, Beloved." His finger trailed her laugh lines, caressing down her neck. "Imagining you beside me kept me strong until everything shattered along the Somme. I was broken, not myself for many weeks. I—"

"I was afraid I'd have to carry you up here." Alex came to them. "Melissa, did you warn him about Bertha?"

"No," Melissa said, wishing they hadn't been interrupted.

"Bertha's our weekday nurse. Lucy talks about anything and everything around her, so don't be embarrassed if personal things come up. Bertha's the one who had to put Lucy out when she attacked her brothers."

Freddy tried to jump to his feet but stumbled as he righted his cane. "Lucy what? When?"

"Don't worry about that," Alex assured him. "She only struck Max because he blocked her from Eddie. She's too weak to be a danger at the moment."

Freddy stood his ground, glaring at his ex-wife's husband. "What's happened to her?"

Alex sighed and clasped his hands behind his back. "She had a violent few months over the winter. Since then, she's been willing herself to die so she doesn't end up like Opal. None of us wanted to worry you with the details."

"I knew from the tone of her letters that she wasn't the same, but she stopped writing me several months back."

"It's taken a group of us, but we've managed. Naomi only comes a few days a week to sit with Asher and Lucy, but we now have Priscilla in the garage apartment. She's cleaning the house and keeping track of Ash. Bertha and Stephanie are the nurses, and Charlotte is the new cook. Not to mention Melissa. And Darla, when she could help before Ginny was born, and now she's on the island with Magdalene."

"I heard about Douglas. War is terrible."

Silence hung in the hallway like a Victorian mourning veil. The three exchanged apprehensive glances.

"Come to her, Frederick," Alex whispered. "She's stayed alive to see you. I placed a chair beside the bed."

Freddy's pace quickened as soon as he stepped into the room. He bypassed the armchair and perched on the bed, leaning over Lucy's face as his cane slid to the floor. Her skin was sallow, and she looked to have two black eyes.

"Goosy, my maiden." He kissed her, and she smiled in her broken way.

"I knew you'd come, Frederick." Her skeletal arms slowly encircled his waist. "I want to see you with our girls. I know Melissa and Alex will care for them, but I wanted to be sure you were here before I let go."

He smoothed her hair along her gaunt face. "Don't talk like that."

Her arms fell to her sides. "Clinging to my sanity has been like chasing a butterfly's shadow. I can't be a noose around Alexander's neck. I've already been one around someone else's. I know you'll help Alex through it. You've always been there for us. Be happy I'm escaping the madness."

"You don't know what you're saying, Goosy." Freddy's lips went to her forehead.

"This time, I do. Protect them, my knight." Her head turned toward Melissa and Alex. "Will you get my daughters, please?"

Knowing Alex was too emotional, Melissa hurried from the room. On the back patio, she called for Phoebe and Bethany, bringing them inside to wash. Taking each by a hand, they climbed the stairs.

"Your mother is very sick, but she wants to see you. Don't be alarmed if she looks different, it's just how it is for her right now."

Upon entering the master suite, Phoebe forced her way between her parents. "Momma, what's the matter?"

Bethany quietly went to the opposite side of the bed and settled beside Lucy.

"I won't be with you much longer, girls, but I want you to know I'll always love you, as will Daddy, Sissa, and Poppy." She took each daughter by a hand. "Be good sisters to each other and to Asher and Louisa too. We're all family, no matter what."

"But Momma—"

"Phoebe Camellia, you'll do well to listen to your parents—all of them." She kissed her hand and turned to her middle child. "Bethany Iris, I know you'll do well with whatever you set your mind to. Keep us close to your heart."

Lucy fingered the locket and then kissed her hand as well.

"I love you, Momma. I'm sorry you've been sick, but I'm glad you got to see Daddy."

"Me too, Bethany. I'm sure he's eager to get home. You let him rest tonight, but then have the best Pancake Time ever tomorrow morning." She took Freddy's hand. "You know I'll always love you. Kiss me once more, Frederick."

Forty-Five

The mile drive home was quiet, with the oldest girls in the backseat and Louisa between Melissa and Freddy in the front. They stopped in the yard so Freddy could see the vegetable garden before bringing his haversack into the house. Sharon had a simple lunch spread waiting for them, but no one ate much. They spent the afternoon in the living room, the girls piled around their father as he propped his leg on the coffee table. Melissa looked on from the armchair by the window as she wrote her next article in longhand while Freddy told about some of the interesting things he'd seen on his travels. After an hour, she slipped into the study to type her column about Freddy's homecoming and called for a courier to bring it to Mr. Paterson's office.

When the girls were settled in bed after supper, Melissa found herself truly alone with Freddy for the first time in over ten months. He looked at her the same shy way he did while they were courting—the perfect arch of his eyebrows framing his brown eyes with distinction.

"Would a bath be easier than a shower for you?" she asked.

"Yes, though I might need help stepping over the tub."

"I'm happy to assist you." She went to him, unbuttoning his shirt with a teasing smile. "I'll be your personal nurse as long as needed, Major Davenport."

He tensed and took her hands.

"No, Melissa. Please be my wife. I've waited forever to be with you." Freddy released her hands and held her against him with his good arm.

"I didn't mean to frighten you." Her voice trembled. "We don't need to rush anything physical. I understand some soldiers suffer from reoccurring nightmares. That—"

He pressed his lips to hers. After a breathless minute, he tottered to the edge of the bed and patted the spot beside him.

"I started to tell you earlier, but Alex interrupted us." Freddy took Melissa's hand again. "I want to confess so we can start back with no secrets, just as we were when we met."

Melissa's heart filled with dread as rampant images of true-hearted Freddy behaving as shamelessly as she had with Claudio played through her mind. A line of French women grateful for his help and ready to show him.

Not wishing to hear his declaration, she blurted her own. "I never stopped loving you, but I weakened. I'd suffered from losing Junior and you the year before and I sought loving arms to fill the void while you were gone."

He took her chin in his hand, his gaze softening. "Claudio?"

She nodded, eyes wide with surprise.

"I saw how he looked at you when I was home after training. Lucy even alluded to it, but I didn't want to hear it at the time. My guilt was still fresh. It wounds me to this day. I should never have left you to deal with your grief or joined the army without discussing it. My selfish actions only made the pain of losing our son worse because we lost each other as well."

Freddy's lips were gentle at first, but then his fervor increased. Breath hot on her neck, he kissed her ear. "I don't blame you for what you did, Melissa. It's my fault for leaving you, but if you'll have me back—"

"I never let you go. Claudio knows I always loved you, that I was seeking relief, not a replacement. He was kind and loving and never pushed for more. He'd come to me after Louisa was in bed and hold me. We talked, drank, smoked, and kissed. A few times a week, he'd join us for lunch. He was another father figure to Louisa but never a replacement. No one can take your place, Freddy. We might have been lovers of a sort, but you're the only one I've given my body to. I'll be pleased to go to my grave with that truth."

He leaned his forehead against hers. "Don't speak of graves. I've seen enough death to last me a hundred lifetimes, yet soon I'll see my second wife laid to rest."

"Allow me to love you through it this time. Don't withdraw—"

"Never again, Beloved."

Kissing led to touching. She gently removed the arm sling and then his shirt, fingering around the raw scar just below his shoulder.

"The sling is to remind me to rest the arm as much as possible so I don't stress the healing muscles, but I can use it."

She smiled and lifted his left hand to her blouse. Kissing her collarbones once her shirt was opened, he settled his head against her heart.

"There was a British nurse at the field hospital in France. Her face and my pain are all I remember from those days. I must have said or done something while out of my head that made her stick closer to me than the other patients. When my fever broke in the middle of the night, Sandra was holding my hand."

Melissa ran her fingers through his hair, knowing he needn't have said anything to gain the attentions of a nurse. Any woman could look upon him and crave a touch—see the kindness in his brown eyes and fall under his spell.

"I was there several more days and learned to enjoy her smile and the spark in her green eyes, much like Lucy's. I'm ashamed to say I may have encouraged her affections. Her tender administrations felt heavenly after life in the trenches. I lost most of my belongings at the Somme, including your letters and my pocket photograph of us. Sandra filled the void I should have filled with thoughts of you. I was moved twice before arriving in England, and I thought of her youthful face because no mail found me during those transfers. She was a close memory, and you a distant one. When I finally arrived at the convalescent hospital near London, she was waiting for me."

Melissa couldn't help the tears that smarted at the corner of her eyes.

"It might have been the garden she helped me walk in after the sparse vulgarity of the battlefields that softened me further. One morning, she removed her headpiece. When the sunlight glinted off her copper strands, I buried myself in them, and we kissed. We spent several days sneaking moments together. One afternoon, she came to me with plans to get permission to walk me on the streets in hopes of going to a nearby hotel. Being with her made me forget Junior, the pain I caused you, failing Chuck, and all the others I saw die. Temporary relief is what she offered, and I was willing to go along with it."

Melissa didn't think she'd feel pain at hearing he had erred in their time apart, but the ache was fathomless.

"But you saved me. Saved *us*." He cupped her cheek. "Not long after she left for the day, the post arrived with over two months' worth of mail. In one of the notes you'd written of the yard, how the azaleas were as lovely as ever, you'd reaped the harvest of the last of the winter vegetables, and were readying the ground for tomatoes. The newspaper clipping was about Easter and how traditions keep life normal amid the turmoil of war. You included a photograph of the girls in their new dresses. Seeing their faces and reading your words brought my heart back to what matters most."

Melissa shifted closer, resting her head on his good shoulder.

"I didn't sleep that night. Instead, I repeatedly poured through the letters and reestablished my loyalties. When Sandra arrived the next morning, I saw her as I always should have—a nurse, barely more than a stranger. Rather than go out the front door, I led her to a bench in the garden. I told her I appreciated all she'd done for me and apologized for taking too much of her time when she could have been helping others."

Tears of relief coursed her cheeks.

"I explained how grief had overtaken me when I failed my friend and that I'd found solace in her kind ways when I had lost track of myself. Then I shared how remembrance returned with the long-delayed letters and showed her the picture of our daughters, regretting my photograph of you was lost during my last battle."

Melissa tucked further against him, the familiar rhythm of his heart balm to her soul.

"Sandra admitted she was there when I was carried in and helped the doctors remove my uniform. She found the photograph and letters I kept in my breast pocket. She cleaned the blood off the picture, but the papers were ruined. When my fever set in after surgery, I apparently called for you. 'Melissa, my beloved,' she said I cried every time I was alert enough to speak. She wanted to be the one I looked to, so she didn't return the photograph when I improved. On seeing she'd lost me, she removed it from her pocket and gave it back, saying you were the luckiest woman alive."

"I am, Freddy." Her smile was sticky with fresh tears.

"I promise never to leave town without you again." He kissed the moisture from her cheeks as he laid her back on the bed. "May we re-consummate our relationship tonight, or do you wish to wait while you decide if what I did is beyond forgivable?"

"I can't fault you when I've done the same. It's been painful to be separated, both emotionally and physically these years, but the rediscovering is exhilarating."

Melissa marveled over Freddy as they removed their final layers. His body was the size it was after Louisa's birth—when he spent no more than three afternoons a week at the gym—strong and knightly, the scars adding to his noble presence. His callused hands were a new sensation, and his passion knew no bounds, though some of his movements were stilted because of his wounds.

After releasing an exclamation of delight, Melissa restrained her sounds.

"Let go, Beloved. The girls are sleeping, but if not, they'll know we love each other as much as Alex and Lucy do."

Laughing, she hugged him. "I missed you, Handsome."

"Words can't describe how much I yearned for you."

Afterward, when they lay in each other's arms, an open glow forged the connection to her husband stronger than ever. Fingers playing over his chest, Melissa propped herself on her elbow. "I need to tell you more about what happened when you were gone."

He tucked her hair behind her ear and playfully brushed his fingertip over her nose. "Will you tell me how the Italian reminded you of your time in Tuscany you wrote about in your first book? That he drank all my wine and kept you warm this winter?"

"We didn't drink it all, but there were several intense moments. The most recent was a few weeks ago. He hadn't come at night for months, but he came to me on my birthday, not wanting me to be alone. I thought I would show Claudio how much I appreciated him by giving myself to him, but I couldn't. He held me on the sofa all night instead."

Freddy's eyes darkened. "I've missed so much with you, but I did purchase something for your birthday when I came through New York. I'm afraid it isn't much compared to last year's emeralds, but soldiers aren't known for having much money."

"I've never needed jewelry, Freddy. I just need you."

"So I don't need to dig through my bag to find your present?"

"No." She dropped upon him. "You're not to leave my bed all night."

He laughed. "Tell me something I don't want to hear."

She told how Claudio came to the New Year's Eve ball in disguise, and Alex found them in the storage room, striking the priest and banning him from Friday suppers.

"I'll have to thank Alexander the next time I see him."

"There's something that happened with Alex as well. He's been under heavy stress with Lucy's condition, especially after the episode with Sister Prudence."

Upon hearing the situation with the nun at St. Mary's School and Lucy's unleashing of her fury, Freddy's countenance fell. "It makes sense now that I know the details why the girls switched schools. I thought it odd you transferred them when it was convenient to have them within walking distance. But to know Lucy did all that with the girls there—"

"She's not been herself for months. It's pained us to see the decline. Alex has been beyond loving. He's grown much this year, but when I saw him eaten away by Lucy's cruel treatment at Sean's office over her will, I sought to refill his reservoir."

Melissa explained how Lucy told her about Alex's needs years ago, that she preferred him to flirt with friends rather than outsiders. Then she shared how she allowed Alex to kiss her, all for the sake of helping him out of his despair.

Freddy grasped her hips, urging her on top of him. "And is Alexander the Great everything other women say he is?"

"He's good, but he has nothing on you, Freddy." Relishing the feel of his skin against hers, she kissed his neck. "Only you make me feel complete. I love you."

"And Claudio?"

She swallowed her pain at him bringing up her indiscretions at such an intimate moment. "He's loving, kind, and attractive. I esteem him as a man and friend, but it's but a tiny spark compared to the love that burns for you in my soul." She pressed her lips to his in an attempt to muffle the heartache.

"We'll come through these trials stronger than ever, Beloved. Please allow me to see the splendor in your eyes as we join once more."

Forty-Six

The sun shone in the window as Claudio shifted his knees on the hardwood floor. Impressions from the rosary beads ringed his hands after he loosened his grip, switching from his outpouring of prayers in his native tongue to rote ones in Latin. As he verbally recited the memorized words of Psalm fifty-one, his mind cleared.

Create in me a clean heart, O God; and renew a right spirit within me. Cast me not away from thy presence; and take not thy holy spirit from me. Restore unto me the joy of thy salvation; and uphold me with thy free spirit.

Ever since he declared to the bishop his interest in returning to Italy to undergo Exorcist training after the New Year's Eve debacle, he started his day with heartfelt prayer and meditation in an attempt to gain control over his feelings for Melissa. When word that Frederick was wounded and returning home came two months ago, he had confirmed his desires. The bishop agreed Claudio's ties in Mobile were stronger to his friends than the church and wished him to be separated. Plans would be made for returning to his homeland as soon as travel overseas became safe. Claudio meant to tell Melissa about it when he went to her on her birthday, but the right moment never came. With Frederick in town—a sight Claudio witnessed from the back of the crowded train station—he was not sure he would ever be able to explain.

Knocking on his door jarred him from his self-imposed trance.

"Father De Fiore, there's a telephone call for you."

He stood, shaking the feeling back to his legs before he took a step. "Who is it?"

"A Melling, of course," the other priest called through the door.

Claudio slowly made his way to the study as his legs woke from their prolonged disuse. He lifted the receiver to his ear.

"Good morning, *amico*."

"Uncle Claudio!"

"Asher?"

"Poppy told me to call. He's holding Momma and doesn't want to leave her. Come help!"

"I will be there as quick as I can."

"Poppy said I'm to wait in the kitchen for you."

"I will come to the back door."

Already dressed, Claudio grabbed his bag. He ran the sidewalks toward Government Street. At the Mellings' backdoor, he hurriedly knocked.

Asher opened it, and Claudio lifted the boy.

"Are they in their bedroom?"

He nodded, arms flung about the priest's neck.

"We will go up together, Phoenix Asher."

Alexander sat against the headboard with Lucy wrapped in a blanket like a sleeping baby in his arms. The pain and horror Claudio had not seen in Alexander's eyes since the hurricane at Seacliff had resurfaced. Knowing the Lord was with him as he saw to yet another

Mrs. Melling dying in the mansion, he dropped his bag in the armchair, depositing Asher there as well.

Claudio approached the couple. Laying a hand on his friend's bare shoulder, he dropped his other to Lucy's pale face. "There is life in this vessel."

Her eyes opened—bright green like new moss though her voice was aged. "Will you give me the Last Rites, Claudio?"

"*Sí*, Lucy. I am here to ease your burdens." He turned to Asher. "Will you dress as though for Mass?"

"Yes, Uncle Claudio."

"Do not rush, we will wait for you."

As soon as Asher left, Claudio readied Lucy for Penance so she could confess without her son in attendance.

"Father, forgive me. It has been years since my last confession. I've willed myself to die as a sacrifice for my family." The wild look in her eyes burned frantic. "I beat a priest and my brothers, drove a nun to suicide, and made life miserable for all those around me."

"No, my queen," Alexander said, rocking her in his arms. "You've been my greatest blessing."

Claudio did the sign of the cross over Lucy, assured her all was forgiven, and then led her through "Hail, Mary."

Asher returned in a navy suit and tie, a sharp contrast to his shirtless father. Claudio motioned for him to sit at the foot of the bed and placed his black bag beside him. He asked for each item he needed to give the boy something to think about other than his dying mother. Nodding and smiling at him, Claudio sought to reassure Asher of his importance in the final Sacraments for his mother.

"Phoenix Asher"—Alexander's voice cracked as he spoke— "will you please go to Momma's dressing table and bring the cross from the middle drawer?"

Off the bed in an instant, Asher brought back the heirloom gold cross inlaid with garnets hanging from a black ribbon.

"Will you wear it, my queen?"

"Yes," she whispered, "but who will wear it after me?"

"May I pass it to Phoebe Camellia?"

Lucy's brilliant smile shone for a second. "Even though she has Freddy's name, she's yours, Angel. I know he won't keep the girls from you. Bethany's locket proves how he feels."

With the cross about Lucy's neck, Claudio began the Anointing, followed by Viaticum. Alexander's face was wet with tears, but Lucy remained calm.

"Thank you, Claudio. You've done so much for all of us. I wish you happiness and peace."

"And I you." He clasped her hand and kissed her cheeks. "Allow me to see to Asher."

Before they could leave, Lucy reached for her son's hand. "Will you hug me?"

He crawled beside his parents, gently snuggling against her blanketed body. "I love you, Momma. You look happy now."

"Everything is set to rights, Phoenix Asher. Thank you for helping." She kissed him. "Promise me you'll listen to Poppy and be a great brother to your sisters."

"I will, Momma. Ladies always deserve respect."

"The world will never be the same when you come of age. Tread carefully on the hearts laid before you." She gave a heaving sigh. "And save your heart for the one that matters."

"Who matters?"

"You'll know when you meet her." Lucy's eyes closed.

Alexander cradled her closer. "Claudio will help you get breakfast, Ash."

The boy was halfway through a bowl of corn flakes when the doorbell rang. Claudio welcomed Dr. Moore and the weekend nurse before returning to the kitchen. A few minutes later, Nurse Stephanie reappeared.

"Mr. Melling asked if I'd sit with Asher so you could return to him."

In the foyer, he waited as the doctor descended the stairs. "May I offer coffee or refreshment?"

"No, thank you, Father De Fiore. There is nothing further for me to do for her. Mr. Melling has instructions to telephone when the body is ready to be taken, and Mr. Spunner has already contacted me with posthumous instructions to be passed to the undertakers."

Claudio could only nod and let Dr. Moore out the door.

Lucy was tucked under the covers, and Alexander curled beside her on top of the blanket. Repositioning the armchair closer, Claudio settled and silently took Lucy's hand into his own, her grip faint.

"I gave him my blessing, Claudio. Hold him to it."

Alexander looked down at her. "You're my first and last love affair, Lucille Melling."

"You cannot live without love." She halted between each word. "You were glorious to me and deserve happiness. My season closes, but your world prepares for the next. Cherish our memories and my children. That's all I ask."

Alexander was on his knees, yanking the covers in an attempt to get to her. Her withered body appeared rigid beneath the red nightgown.

"You needn't ask me that, and you know it! You've possessed my lust from the day I saw you dancing in the fountain. You took control of my soul when we first kissed, then my heart when we spoke in the camellia garden. I gave you my everything—it just wasn't enough."

"But it was." Her voice strengthened and she sat of her own accord. "I always told you it was."

The brightness in her eyes turned to yearning, such as Claudio had never witnessed on a deathbed. Her hands roamed Alexander's scars before encircling his neck and drawing his mouth to hers. Alexander was upon her and they evoked pleasurable moans from each other as the kissing deepened and hands explored. Gradually, Lucy's movements stilled until her head fell back, displaying her neck in swanlike grace. Alexander kissed her throat, collarbone, and heart one last time before clutching her to his chest and sobbing.

***

An hour later, Claudio watched Alexander place Lucy on the bed, gently cover her, and kiss her lifeless lips.

"Will you call the Davenports and Naomi?" His raw voice showcased his despair. "Allow them the opportunity to come before she's taken away."

"*Sí, amico*. And the Eastons?"

"Just Maxwell. He'll let the others know, but discourage any from visiting. Send Asher to me and dismiss Nurse Stephanie. Take five dollars from my billfold on the dresser. That will be more than enough to settle things with her for today."

Claudio nodded and collected the money. He found Asher in the morning room with the nurse, he drawing at his mother's desk and she on the sofa with a book.

"Your father would like to see you, Asher."

When he dashed from the room, Claudio turned to the woman he had only met a handful of times. "She passed on. Alexander asked me to give you this for your time today and thank you for your service these last weeks. I am afraid he is not up to seeing anyone. Otherwise he would have spoken to you himself."

Stephanie nodded and collected her bag. "Please give my condolences to the family."

Claudio assured her he would and saw her to the front door before settling at Alexander's desk. He knew family should come first, but he telephoned Naomi to ease himself into the more difficult calls.

"I was afraid of that when I said goodbye yesterday," she responded to the news with grace. "May I come? I could sit with Asher or help in some other way."

"*Sí*, Naomi, thank you. I am not sure how much I will need to do for Alexander."

Looking at the clock and knowing Pancake Time might still be going, he told the news to Maxwell next. The eldest Easton sibling promised to tell the others and his mother, who was convalescing at his house.

"Mother won't last long after the news," Maxwell stated, "but maybe she'll be able to attend the funeral."

"Lucy wishes are for no funeral but a memorial service when she is laid to rest in the Seacliff mausoleum."

"And Alex is allowing this?"

"She had him sign a document that he would fulfill all her demands."

"He had his hands full with her, but he's proven himself this year. Shall I come help?"

"No, but thank you. I will tell him you offered, Maxwell."

Claudio then contacted a courier service to have a letter awaiting one of Captain Walker's boats at the docks with word of the death so Magdalene and Darla would be informed that day. Only when all that was done could he force himself to connect with the Davenports' house.

A joyful clamor filled the line before "Davenports'" was said. Just one word, but Melissa sounded pleased.

"*Eroina.*"

The background noise faded as though she had turned away from her family. "Claudio."

"Lucy is no longer with us. Alexander held her this past hour but has finally laid her to rest until he decides to call the doctor."

"What can we do for him?"

"He wishes you to come to say goodbye."

"Should we bring Asher here for the day?" she asked.

"That might be good."

"Freddy and I are here to help in any way."

"Is all well?"

"I believe so," she whispered. "But there's still pain."

"I was at the station yesterday. You all looked blessedly happy. I pray the girls do not suffer too much with sadness."

"Your prayers and kindness are always appreciated."

"*Arrivederci, Eroina.*"

After pausing to collect his thoughts, Claudio went to the kitchen to make coffee. He found Naomi and Paul already at work.

"You have read my mind, Miss Naomi." He opened his arms, and she accepted his hug.

"You have a tough job ahead with comforting Alex," she stated.

"I need to return to him and Asher. I just finished the telephone calls."

Naomi nodded. "Paul and I are here as long as necessary."

"Melissa offered to take Asher overnight. I will talk to Alexander about that when the time is right."

Upstairs, Asher snuggled against his mother's body, face glistening with tears. Alexander stared blankly at the scene from the armchair.

"Naomi and Paul are making coffee."

Alexander nodded and closed his eyes.

"Maxwell offered his services, and a letter is going to the island this afternoon. Melissa invited Asher to come home with her if you think that best. She will help however you allow."

Lips pressed together, Alexander nodded again and rubbed the stubble on his chin. "Ash, do you want to stay with me or go to your sisters' house?"

Asher sat up, a hand still on his mother's body. "Beth and Phoebe will be sad too. Shall I comfort them, Poppy?"

The corner of his mouth quirked as he opened his arms. "It might be best, Phoenix Asher."

The boy climbed off the deathbed and into his father's lap. Alexander kissed his head and held him. "We waited a long time for you to join our family, and she loved you much, my son."

Naomi came to the door, Paul behind her with a coffee tray. Claudio motioned them in, but Paul stayed in the hall. Naomi knelt beside the bed, kissed Lucy's cold hand, and silently cried.

Slipping from his father's lap, Asher hugged her. "Don't be sad, Miss Naomi. She was happy after Uncle Claudio gave her the Rites."

"I know she's at peace. I cry more for myself because I'll miss her."

Claudio took the tray from Paul. "Do you wish to come in?"

He shook his head. "I'm not family."

Alexander went to the doorway. "Naomi's husband is most certainly family."

"I'm sorry for your loss, Alex."

"Thank you for you bringing her." Alexander turned to Naomi. "If you can help ready Asher for the Davenports, I'd appreciate it."

Claudio prepared a cup of coffee for Alexander after Naomi and Paul took Asher out. As he turned to bring it to him, Frederick limped into the room and lowered to the edge of the bed. Dropping his cane, he caressed Lucy's pale cheek and smoothed her hair against the pillow.

Alexander went to him. "Where are the girls?"

"Home."

"Did they not wish to come?" Alexander waited half a minute for a reply, but none came. "Did they take the news too badly? Is Melissa all right with them?"

Frederick looked up, his face more lined than Claudio remembered. "I don't know. Melissa told me Lucy was gone, and I went to the automobile as quick as I could."

Alexander yanked Frederick's good arm, hauling him from the bedside. The larger man stumbled across the room to keep pace with Alexander's lead. He shoved Frederick into the armchair, blue eyes blazing.

"Did you not think Lucy's girls have the right to see their mother before she's taken away? That your wife and daughters would appreciate your embrace when they share the news? Have you learned nothing these years? Stuff your own despair and see to those around you for once!"

Alexander stomped across the room, retrieved the cane, and marched back to Frederick with it raised above his head. Images of the fury he'd released on Rupert Lyons flashed through Claudio's mind. He set the cup down and jumped to his friend's side.

"*Calmati, amico.*"

Knowing Alexander's arm and aim were strong from his time on the polo field, Claudio gripped his friend's forearm and attempted to lower it. The cane trembled under their grips.

As though realizing he threatened a man his wife loved in the presence of her body, he took control of his rage and stepped to the side as he tossed the cane at Frederick. "You deserve no respect from your gallantry on the battlefield when you can't be noble to those who matter most!" Disgust darkened Alexander's countenance. "I used to think I did Lucy a disservice by luring her away from you, but now I know I saved her. I pity Melissa for having to put up with your selfishness. I'll be sure to offer my services should she seek a way out."

Frederick remained silent, but the knowledge that Alexander's words struck him deep was noticeable in the tightening of his jaw and pain-filled eyes as the war hero limped out of the room.

Forty-Seven

Melissa thought the walk to the Mellings' would calm her, but it only aggravated the heartache of Freddy's abandonment. Not wanting to wait for a hired automobile or subject the girls to unwelcomed conversations on the streetcar, walking was the only option to see Lucy one last time. But forcing a crying Phoebe and stoic Bethany to stroll down Government Street to their mother's deathbed was a hardship no child should bear.

Naomi welcomed them at the front door, hugging each girl to her round belly. When she embraced Melissa, she whispered, "There was shouting, but things are calm now."

Asher ran down the stairs. "Sisters!"

He jumped at Phoebe, kissing her cheek, and then hugged Bethany, stroking her brunette hair as he held her tight. "It's okay, Beth. Momma was happy to go to heaven after Uncle Claudio saw her. She's sleeping peacefully now."

He hugged anxious Louisa, and then Melissa lifted her daughter to her hip and followed Lucy's children up the stairs. Asher brought Phoebe into the master suite, but Bethany froze in the hall.

"It's all right, Beth," Melissa whispered. "I'll hold your hand."

Her brave façade crumbled as she erupted into tears. "I want Daddy!"

Claudio took Louisa from Melissa so she could see to Bethany. Hugging her stepdaughter, she scanned the master bedroom. Freddy wasn't there. Looking to Claudio for answers, he only shook his head.

"Daddy!" Bethany's lanky form stiffened in Melissa's arms. "Daddy's gone!"

Not wishing to upset the others, Melissa carried her across the hall and sat on Bethany's bed. "Daddy's not gone, Beth. He came home yesterday."

"But he left us, and now Momma's gone too!"

"He's here." Alex walked into the room. "Your father needed a minute to himself, but he's in this house. You'll see him soon, Bethany Iris. In the meantime, would you allow me to bring you to say goodbye to Momma?"

She nodded and Alex handed her a handkerchief so she could wipe her nose. Melissa stood, and he wrapped her in his arms.

"Phoebe said you walked here."

Melissa relaxed against him. "There was no other choice."

"He's a selfish bastard. I'll be your lawyer whenever you've had enough."

"Take Beth for now."

When she believed herself alone, she sank to the bed and cried.

A halting figure stepped out of the shadows from the adjoining bathroom. Leaning warily on his cane, Freddy limped to Melissa.

Pain churned to anger once more, and she stood to meet him head-on. "How could you stand by while your grieving daughter cried out for you?"

"I couldn't face you in front of Beth." He kept his gaze steady though filled with anguish.

"How could you run out after what you promised me last night? Are we nothing to you?"

"You're everything to me, Melissa. You and my girls are my whole world."

"Then act like we are!" She collapsed against his solid chest, fisting his shirt until it strained against his shoulders. "I refuse to be treated as a disposable part of your life! If your behavior since Junior died is the new you, don't string me along with promises when you wish to bed me only to toss me aside when I'm not wanted."

"It's not like that." He brought his hand toward her cheek, but she slapped it.

"It's exactly like that! Ever since the day you enlisted, you've led me on with hollow promises, teasing with a taste of our old passion only to abandon me when you seek refuge elsewhere."

"I go to no one el—"

"You can no longer tell me that." Her voice was deadly, eyes brimming with pain.

He hung his head. "I'm sorry I failed you when you've done nothing but save me."

She turned her back to him.

Claudio stood in the doorway. "*Eroina*, do you require assistance?"

Hearing the concern in his voice nudged some of the anger from her. "I don't know anymore."

Freddy shuffled toward her. "Beloved—"

"Don't call me that unless your actions match the word."

Melissa took Claudio's offered arm and walked across the hall. The room was empty save Lucy's body. Her face was peaceful but otherwise looked much the same as the day before. Releasing Claudio, she smoothed the blanket. "I'll help Alex see to your wishes and do all I can for your children."

Then Alex was there, hugging her. "I'll need you, darling Sissa."

"We'll all need each other, dashing Poppy. Where are the children?"

"Naomi and Paul have them downstairs. I had Asher ready to go but—"

"I'll bring him."

"I don't want to add trouble."

She smiled and kissed his cheek. "Our children are never trouble. They're perfect."

He laughed and held her again. "Could you get the dress Lucy wanted to be buried in before you go? I don't want to send the wrong one when they come for her."

"Of course."

When she came out of the closet with the red dress Lucy wore to Ruth Melling's funeral, Alex, Claudio, and Freddy all stared.

She laid it over the armchair. "The note in her own hand is attached to the hanger if you don't believe me."

"I remember her request from Sean's office," Alex said. "It was to be her Saint Valentine's Day wedding dress, and it was her mother's before that, a Christmas dress from decades past."

"Goosy was always sentimental."

Claudio and Alex turned to Freddy. Melissa deliberately looked away, going for the door.

"Your fondness for the dead should not overshadow your love for the living." Claudio's rich voice filled the room.

Freddy cleared his throat. "I went through many losses alone and learned to cope through physical release, not talking it over. I'm doing my best to open my pain to others, but it isn't easy."

Alex sneered. "Lucy would have beaten you if she knew you allowed Bethany to cry out for you, not to mention leaving your girls to walk here in their sorrow."

"And I'd wholly deserve it." Freddy looked to Claudio. "I'd like a word with you before I leave."

"No!" Melissa shouted before she could control her emotions. "I won't allow it!"

"I need to speak to the man who saw to my family in my absence."

"*Sí*, I will hear you."

Alex looked to the bed and then the men. "Take your conversation to my den, please. Do I need to referee?"

"No, *amico*, it will be fine."

"Because I'm going with them." Melissa stepped between Claudio and Freddy.

Not knowing who to walk with, she followed a few steps behind Freddy. Claudio's hand briefly touched the small of her back as though letting her know he was there for her. On the stairs, Freddy stumbled but caught himself on the banister. Melissa went to his other side and took his elbow. When they came in view of the front room, the girls ran for their father.

He kissed and hugged each one. "It will be a few minutes more, and then we're going home."

Claudio waited for them in the den, standing before the desk's guest chair. Melissa moved Alex's chair out from behind the desk and motioned for Freddy to sit.

"It's I who should offer you a seat. Please take it, Melissa."

She did, and he brought the armless chair she had sat upon with Alex months ago to the little grouping.

When everyone was settled, Freddy looked to Claudio with humility. "Thank you for seeing to Melissa while I was gone. I don't blame either of you for how your relationship progressed, nor will I hold it against Melissa as I strive to mend the rifts in our marriage. It was by my actions that she was starved for love. My choices drove her to seek affection and support from you. I'll do all I can to make things right."

Claudio crossed his arms and angled slightly toward Melissa. "It might be too late."

"I know, especially after my behavior this morning." Freddy looked to Melissa, her anger falling away at the tenderness in his eyes. "If you'll allow me one more chance before you take Alex's divorce offer, I'll be forever in your debt."

"I don't want us to be beholden to one another. I want to be equal partners once more." She closed her eyes a moment. "Complete love, acceptance, and trust. I'll not sit by while you're off at the gym for hours while I'm left to everything at home."

He nodded. "It was wrong of me. Please forgive me for failing my family's emotional needs."

Down the hall, a man's voice yelled obscenities.

"The girls!" Freddy heaved himself from the chair, and Melissa took his arm to steady him as Claudio ran ahead.

"Where's my sister?" Edmund shouted, Paul blocking his path to the stairs as he attempted to shove his way through. Naomi stood in the doorway to the front room, shielding the children. "Why was her family not allowed to come in her final days?"

Freddy quickened his pace. "Her family was here."

Edmund's face relaxed a smidgen at seeing his old friend. "Why didn't you telephone me yesterday?"

"You haven't been close for a while."

"Because of Alex! He's done nothing but drive a wedge between Lucy and me since that blasted Christmas party in this cursed house!"

"It was one of the happiest days in my life," Alex said from the top of the stairs. "But don't blame me for keeping you away. Lucy was in no state these past weeks to be subjected to your arrogance. I couldn't invite Maxwell and not you, so no Eastons came. There's a little time before she's taken away. You're welcome to see her now, and you're all invited to the memorial service."

"To see her buried in that unconsecrated mausoleum with Eliza? I don't think so, though it's fitting to shelve all the Melling whores there."

Alex flew down the stairs and leaped upon his brother-in-law, fists striking before Paul and Claudio could pull them apart. Freddy went for the living room to console hysterical Phoebe while Melissa and Naomi gathered the others and herded them out the front door.

Melissa saw the youngest three into the automobile. "Stay with them, Naomi. I'm going back for Freddy and Phoebe."

In the hall, Phoebe frantically squirmed in her father's grasp while screeching at her uncle. Her wild bucking was too much for Freddy. Melissa grabbed Phoebe as she broke free.

Claudio supported a breathless Alex, and Paul held Edmund by an arm—all staring at the blonde wildcat who Melissa had pinned to her chest.

Edmund jerked free and wiped his bloodied nose with his sleeve. "Congratulations, Davenport. It seems you have yourself another mad as a hatter Easton. Maybe Miss New York can teach her how to host a proper tea party, if she isn't too busy copulating with the priest."

Freddy's movements were as fluid as his championship days as he advanced and clocked him clean on the jaw. Edmund went down so fast Paul barely had time to catch him before his head struck the marble floor.

Freddy grabbed the banister for balance after his follow-through. "Sorry, Alex."

"He deserved it. I only wish I could have knocked him out rather than bloody his nose."

Turning to Melissa, Freddy embraced her and Phoebe. "Don't listen to Uncle Eddie, Princess. He's a bitter man."

She took a few breaths before she was calm enough to speak. "He called Poppy and Momma bad names and tried to storm the castle!"

"He'll not do it again. Poppy and I taught him a lesson. Now we're going home."

Paul and Claudio carried Edmund to the sofa in the front room, and Alex assured them he would hold things together until the undertaker arrived for Lucy.

Melissa embraced Alex. "Cancel Charlotte for today and come eat supper with us, both of you. Asher could return with you or stay the night, depending on how you're feeling."

"I don't think I'll be able to eat today."

"Still come, Alex." Her fingers splayed across his back as she hugged him tighter. "We all need you, dashing Poppy. You could even stay in the guest room so you don't have to come home tonight. I know how lonely a big house is with only a child to keep you company."

***

The Mellings stayed with the Davenports Saturday night. If Alex hadn't been there, Melissa would have sent Freddy to the guest room, but they settled in bed together with nothing more than a vocalized "goodnight." At daybreak, Melissa woke in his arms. She breathed in his scent and then hurried from bed before emotions could overwhelm.

Claudio arrived after breakfast to see Alex and Asher to the cathedral for Mass while the Davenports attended Trinity Episcopal. It was as awkward for Melissa as it had been when she brought the girls alone. When the congregation greeted the war hero, she tried to stay to the side, but he held her hand to keep her close.

"I wouldn't be here without you," he whispered.

To the girls' delight, the Mellings returned midday with fresh supplies for another night's stay. Asher kept Louisa entertained while Phoebe moped in her room and Bethany snuggled against Freddy in the parlor. Melissa and Alex sat across from each other on the platform swing he'd bought for Lucy when they'd lived there. He retrieved a cigarette from his case and offered one to Melissa.

She shook her head. "But share with me when the children aren't nearby."

"It would be easier if you sat beside me." He winked.

She joined him and took a few puffs.

"Is Freddy getting the cold shoulder?"

"Tepid."

"I can't believe all he's put you through. I would never have expected it after how noble he was with Lucy, but maybe she wounded him completely when she left. He buried himself at the gym then too. And after his father and first wife died before that." Alex passed the cigarette to her and blew a smoke ring. "Maybe we held him to a higher standard compared to a cad like me, but he's had it rough through no fault of his own until now."

"If you'd heard the things he promised me Friday night and the confessions we shared, you'd find it difficult to forgive him running yesterday morning as well."

"I don't need to hear because leaving you and the girls alone was selfish enough, but if you wish to share the intimate details, I'd be more than happy to listen." He squeezed her knee and took a heavy drag. "I'll tell you of my Friday night. After Asher was in bed,

Lucy and I lay facing each other. She touched me all over and had me within an inch of release before begging me to join with her."

Melissa listened to his confession, trying to keep nausea from overpowering her as she thought of corpse-like Lucy. Surely his attentions were an act of mercy.

"I used the think there would be no better way to die, but now I know it would be hell for the lover. I didn't expect her to survive the night, but she did." He passed the cigarette back. "She revived after Claudio gave her the Rites. It was like old times for a minute, touching and tasting. But she faded in my arms as though I sucked the life out of her with my kiss."

Eyes blurry with tears, Melissa clasped his hand and rested her head on his shoulder. "You gave her life, Alex. Never doubt that."

Freddy limped to the swing with something clutched behind his back.

"I don't mean to intrude." He leaned his cane against the crossbar of the frame and heaved himself onto the swaying platform. "Bethany helped me unpack, and I retrieved your belated birthday present."

Freddy sat across from them and held out a crudely wrapped item.

"I don't think it's emeralds this time," Alex joked.

Melissa opened the brown paper, revealing a six-inch replica of the Statue of Liberty monument.

"We never made it to New York together, but when the ship came into the harbor and I saw Lady Liberty, all I could think of was you—brave and independent. An inspiring sight, that's what you are to me." He held her gaze, the depth of his emotions crashing into her soul. "I plead for your forgiveness as I make amends. I'll be able to face anything in life, but only if I regain your trust. Please give me another chance."

Melissa passed the figurine to Alex and climbed upon Freddy for a searching kiss.

"That's a fine sight," Alex remarked when they slowed for air. "Life isn't balanced when the Davenports are arguing."

Forty-Eight

On Monday morning, Melissa and Alex took Phoebe and Bethany to school and then met with Sean Spunner to be sure all Lucy's wishes were being fulfilled. When they returned at noon, Miss Sharon had a hot lunch ready, and they ate with Freddy, Louisa, and Asher in the dining room.

"If you're both finished with errands for the day," Freddy spoke as they stood at the end of the meal, "I'd like to go to the office and say hello. I could pick up the girls from school on the way back. I'd only be gone a few hours."

"Why don't you go with him, Melissa? You're already dressed for a day out, and you could use the time together. I've got these two ragamuffins." Alex scooped Louisa into his arms before she could rush out of the room with Asher.

"We get to stay with Poppy!" Louisa squealed.

Freddy looked to Melissa with hope. "I'd enjoy your companionship."

Melissa nodded.

"Would you mind if I brought Louisa to the stables while I check Apollo?" Alex asked.

Melissa looked to Freddy, but he inclined his head to allow her the choice. "That's fine, Alex. She'd enjoy it, but she's too young to—"

"She'll be five in a few weeks, and it would be a good chance to show her around without the girls there. Maybe put her in my lap for a leisurely trot around the corral."

"Nothing fast or jarring."

"I swear to be responsible, darling Sissa."

"I'll hold you to it, dashing Poppy." She kissed his cheek and turned to Freddy. "We can leave as soon as I brush my hair."

He reached out, fingers trailing her bobbed locks. "I like how you're wearing it now. It frames your beautiful face."

She kissed his palm. "Keep it up, Handsome."

Alex made a purring sound. "Bring the girls home and then go out to supper, if not tonight, then sometime soon. Nurture her love before you lose it, Frederick. There are too many vultures waiting if you let her go. I might be one of them."

Freddy punched him lightly on the arm. "For propriety's sake, at least wait a week."

He laughed, then sobered. "These will be the longest days of my life."

Alex and Asher stayed on with the Davenports that week. Freddy eased back into office life at Davenport and Adams Allied Accountants, and Alex went to work a few hours a day to keep on track with his firm.

On Friday morning, the two families and Claudio took one of Joe Walker's ships to Seacliff. Priscilla—who had stayed across the bay with her parents upon hearing about Lucy's passing—entertained the children while Alex and Claudio watched over the coffin in the library.

The walk up the cliff when they arrived had been tiresome for Freddy, but when he offered to accompany Melissa to the beach after lunch, she didn't want to turn him down. Restlessly shifting her bare feet through the warm sand where they sat, she gazed at the sparkling bay.

"I'll be ready for longer walks in the weeks ahead, but if you wish to stroll, I'm happy to watch you."

The yearning in his brown eyes seemed intensified in the sunlight. Melissa felt her cheeks blush and pulled the brim of her hat lower to shade her smile.

"Don't you like that your husband appreciates your figure?"

It had been a week since she'd allowed him to do more than briefly kiss her, but she felt it was time to reopen the door between them. He'd been attentive to her and the girls since last Saturday, even while working and taking strength training sessions every other day at the gym.

"I crave your touch, Freddy. I always have." Voice rich with need, she relished his contact when he pulled her to him.

His breath was hot on her cheek. "Do you remember those nights in the cypress grove?"

"Every time I come here." Melissa pressed her lips to his as she pulled him to the sand.

His hand went up her leg beneath her skirt. "Shall we go there now?"

"Tonight, in our bed, Handsome."

He pressed in for a deeper kiss as he kneaded her thigh. "Sweet torture, Beloved."

By the time their necking slowed, a boat horn sounded in the distance.

Freddy shielded his eyes from the lowering sun. "Is that Joe?"

They watched the boat grow closer.

"It is! And it looks like people are waving from the top deck. Do you think Claire and the children are coming?" Melissa asked.

Freddy righted his cane and helped Melissa stand. "It looks like more than the Walkers."

"Maggie and Darla!"

They met the bay steamer at the end of the pier. Emmett Walker was helpless against the mass of children, but a stern word from the captain settled all the Campbells, Adamses, and the smallest Walker at once.

"Proceed with caution, young ones!" Joe barked.

The children walked off the boat in their Sunday best. Horatio came to them first for hugs.

"Mr. Freddy! Did you see my dad?"

"Sorry, Horatio. His unit must have passed me when I was sent back to England. Are you being a good helper to your mother?"

"Yes, sir! Come see Ginny, my sister."

Freddy hugged Darla and cooed over Virginia, swaddled to her mother's chest.

When the Campbell children mobbed him, Melissa feared they'd take him off the side of the pier with their exuberance. She was quick to his side, throwing what she hoped looked like a loving arm about his waist though it felt more like a lifeline. Simon, Tabitha, and Kade all clamored for hugs before running the length of the planks and launching up the path toward the house.

"I've got them." Clara Jane lifted the hem of her dress and dashed after her youngest sibling, Abraham, and the rest of the children.

Maggie, pale and pretty in a black dress, stepped forward. Freddy shuffled his weakening legs, switched his cane to his poor arm, and embraced her with his good one. "I'm sorry, Maggie. He was a terrific man."

"Thank you. I'm glad you came back," Maggie whispered. "I pray Henry returns as well."

Freddy kissed her cheek and then the back of her hand.

Claire hugged Melissa and then Freddy. "Why don't you walk up with me and Joe, Freddy? I'm sure he has a few questions about your service."

Leave it to a medical woman to see Freddy's need for help. Melissa smiled at Claire and more so at Freddy when he fell in step with the captain. She hooked her arms through Darla's and Maggie's and started toward the looming red cliff.

"I'm glad you were all able to come. It will mean the world to Alex to have a full house."

"We sent a letter to Rosemary," Maggie explained, "but we wanted it to be a surprise because we didn't know if everyone would make it. More specifically, if I would make it. If I hadn't come, Darla would have stayed with me, and I knew she was needed here."

Melissa squeezed her arm. "Is it your first time off the island since—"

"Yes, but I'm not sure if I'm ready…ready to—"

"Handle Alex?" Melissa interjected.

Maggie nodded and looked to silent Darla. "She thinks I'm being overly emotional about Alexander, but I know my weakness. I wanted to master it before seeing him."

"He's the disease, not you." Darla hurried ahead and joined Claire.

Melissa leaned closer to Maggie. "He's matured a lot this year. Don't underestimate his self-control. He loves and respects you."

"I know."

Darla stopped briefly to greet Alex on the porch. His eyes turned to the yard, focusing on the widow in black. He bound to Maggie in his boyish way and paused before her.

"Your magnificent Scot was taken from you too soon, Magdalene."

"And your lovely queen, Alexander."

Alex's blue eyes managed to be tender and intense.

Maggie blushed under his scrutiny and clasped her hands before her as she lifted her head to meet his stare. "I wouldn't trade anything, even knowing how it would end."

"Me either," he whispered.

Whether they spoke of their shared past or their dead spouses, Melissa didn't know. Without further word, Alex offered Maggie his arm, and the two entered Seacliff Manor.

***

After Maxwell Easton arrived from the hotel in Point Clear in a hired automobile, the group assembled in the downstairs hall. Everyone looked to Claudio to take the lead, but Alex stepped forward.

"Maxwell, Joe, Claudio, and Leroy will help me carry Lucy to her eternal resting place. Asher will follow directly behind us. Frederick, I know you would help if you were able, but could you lead the procession with Lucy's girls and allow Melissa to stand in for you?"

"Melissa a pallbearer?" Freddy's chivalrous soul sounded offended by the suggestion.

"I'd be happy to, Alex," she replied.

Alex quickly defended his reasoning. "The coffin isn't too heavy, Frederick. Four of us carried it up the path. We'll tuck Melissa in the middle, and there will be no strain on her."

Freddy's jaw tightened, but he nodded. Rosemary and Priscilla handed candles to those wishing to carry one, and the group migrated outside. Claire and her girls kept the children in line, and Emmet collected the mortar supplies left in buckets on the back porch.

Freddy waited with Phoebe and Bethany, each with a lantern in her hand. Alex, Joe, Leroy, and Claudio brought the coffin down from the house, Maxwell and Melissa joining in the middle of either side once they were in the yard.

Freddy's pace was slow, but it worked well for the solemn occasion. Stepping into the twilight of the forest, Melissa looked to those around her for strength. Alex walked in front of her and Joe behind. Claudio had the lead on the other side, his jaw set with concentration. When they approached the open mausoleum, everyone but Alex and Joe stepped to the side, and the two carried the coffin inside single file, sliding it onto the open shelf directly across from Eliza's.

When Alex emerged, he went to Asher and held his hand, motioning Maxwell to join them. Claudio presided, reciting prayers and scriptures in English, Italian, and Latin with his lyrical voice. They closed the service by singing "Nearer, My God, to Thee," led by Alex. His and Maggie's voices were the loudest, their faces both damp with tears. When it was over, Emmett delivered the mortar supplies and an extra lamp. Joe and Leroy helped Alex spread mortar, lift the engraved slab into the space on the wall, and set the bracing beams. While the others returned to the house, Alex and Asher knelt in the sepulcher mixing the finishing grout so they could seal Lucy into the tomb.

Melissa sat on the steps to offer her silent support. Across the clearing, Maggie left a clutch of flowers on the ground near an oak— one of the invisible markers from the Seacliff Cottage days. Her candle flickered, casting her face in fractured shadows as her head bowed.

At their completion, Asher hurried for the house. Alex paused to wipe the edges of the slab with a damp cloth, cleaning the wayward lumps Asher left behind. He closed the door, passed the lantern to Melissa, and joined Maggie.

"Lydia, wherever she is, wouldn't appreciate your remembrance of Georgiana."

"I never liked her anyway," Maggie said with defiance.

"Nor I, but I appreciate you honoring my half-sister." Alex offered Maggie his arm. "Will you accompany me to the house?"

"I'm returning to the island tonight with the Walkers."

"But not until after supper." He blew out her candle and set it and his rag on the bench.

She nodded and slipped her arm through his. Melissa followed. As they came into the yard, Maggie stopped.

"I'm not ready, Alexander."

He left a gentle kiss on her cheek. "I'll wait for you."

Freddy watched Alex and Maggie pass through the hallway, then took Melissa's hand. "Have they come to an understanding?"

"He's waiting until she's ready."

"Can anyone ever be ready for Alexander Melling?"

She laughed. "I've missed you."

"You'll never need to miss me again. I'm yours completely. From travel assistant to parenting, we'll share it all once more."

Epilogue

On Monday, July fifteenth—seventy-four days after Douglas left the world—Magdalene entered Melling and Associates. She smoothed her blue walking dress as Alexander's secretary knocked on his partially ajar door.

"Mr. Melling, your ten o'clock is here."

"And his name?" he called distractedly.

"*Mrs.* Campbell."

Alexander's chair rolled back, and papers dropped as he hurried from his desk. "Magdalene, what a surprise! You know you don't need to make an appointment to see me."

She accepted his arm and followed his lead into his office. It wasn't the luxurious space his father kept a dozen years before, but Alexander had turned out nothing like George Melling. The modest office was yet another example of his level-headedness—at least when it came to business.

"I felt it best this first time," she said as she took the chair he offered. He perched on the edge of his desk, and she lowered her head. "Please, Alex. We're in your workplace."

He slunk to his chair, frowning at the desk between them. A second later, he sat full-height, smiling once more. "How may I assist you, Mrs. Campbell?"

"I had hoped, that is, I came to see if—"

"If what I spoke to you after our kiss at Seacliff Cottage all those years ago still holds true?" His blue eyes shone—not as sapphire as Douglas's, but in the crisp way that was completely Alexander—and she felt the pull once more. "It does, Magdalene. I swear to love and protect you and your children all the days of my life."

"I'm sorry I stayed away after Lucy's burial, but it hasn't been long enough."

"Tell me you wish to wait a year or two or five, and I will. But if it's the opinion of the world you're worried about, don't let that stop you. People might say we didn't love our spouses enough to wait a respectful time, but they don't know our hearts. The more we loved, the harder it is to put aside what burns within."

"Passion or possession?"

"Both." He brought her to her feet. "You've possessed a segment of my heart since you arrived at Seacliff with that homely shawl and your country ways. Your portion will blaze brighter in our season together, but Lucy and Douglas needn't haunt us. They both reside fondly in our memories. I only wish the opportunity to build a life with you from this moment on."

He nipped a kiss and pressed his body closer. "Say you'll have me, Magdalene."

Seeking to check the need for his touch coursing through her, she angled away. "I can't go into this blindly."

"I love your children, as does Asher."

"Kade turned eleven last month. He needs a man—"

"I'm not a perfect example, but I'm a better man than I ever thought possible. And speaking of birthdays, allow me to buy you a ring for your thirty-fifth tomorrow."

"Douglas gave me a ring for my twenty-third."

"And helped you become the wondrous woman you are today." He hugged her. "Private schools, horses, tutoring. Tell me, and I'll provide what you seek for Kade, Tabitha, and Simon. And if I'm not enough, they'd have Claudio, Frederick, and Henry to look to."

"Tabby always wanted to learn the piano," Magdalene whispered.

"Then she'll begin lessons straight away! The grand piano has sat untouched for years. We'll fill my house with music and love."

"Do you keep the girls much?"

"I take all three riding twice a week, but Phoebe and Bethany stay over every other weekend. Louisa sometimes comes to give Freddy and Melissa a bit of privacy." His grin was playful. "Can you imagine the antics with yours and mine always together? They'll have as much fun as us."

She ran her hand down his lapel. "What you had with Lucy was glowing, but it wouldn't be right for me. I'll never be comfortable being paraded to intimate encounters or making love while entertaining guests."

"Once you have a taste of it, you might change your mind." His puckish grin fell when she didn't return it. "Maggie—"

"You know I don't shy from contact, but I have my limits, and privacy is one. Just last summer, you were pleasuring Lucy at the dining table with Claudio looking on." She took a breath, trying to keep her voice steady. "I'll have no part of that in my relationship."

"Our relationship." He pursed his lips. "I *can* act with decorum."

"Lucy was raised in this social class and felt comfortable shirking the regulations, but I'm an outsider. I'll need my best manners to get along with your group. As a lawyer from a respected family, I know you have eyes upon you—even if you ignore them. I'm willing to play the part of society wife if you'll help guide me."

"Lucy was never a society bride. She didn't play those games, only wrote about them."

Magdalene took his hand and kissed his discolored knuckles. "I want you to gain as much from this union as I do. If I can be a respectful hostess or anything else to help you succeed, I'm more than happy to play the part so long as I keep my dignity."

"Magdalene, I'd gain all I need by having you in my arms. I dare not ask for more than your affection and to show love to my son and stepdaughters."

"I'll give it freely."

His warm hand cradled her cheek, thumb brushing her lower lip. "May I kiss you?"

Magdalene tilted her head in response, leaning toward him.

"I want to hear you say it, Magdalene."

"Kiss me, Alexander. I haven't been kissed since I stole that one from you on Melissa's porch last year. I'm feverish for your touch."

He captured her mouth, allowing the pressure and movement to build as he caressed her neck. As she responded to him, Alexander's lips became firmer, both hands at her waist, kneading to her hips. Magdalene trailed his back—so much slimmer than Douglas. Remembering the sight of her husband in Alexander's clothes during the hurricane brought warmth to her cheeks faster than his attentions.

Arching back so she could breathe, Alexander took the opportunity to kiss down her throat. Tingling with sensations and yearnings, she clung to him.

"You still feel and taste delectable, Magdalene."

"And you're still a master seducer, even without demonic help."

They laughed and hugged, exchanging a few more kisses in the process.

"How long are you in town? Are the children with you?"

"They stayed behind with Claire. I need to meet Joe at the docks tomorrow afternoon."

He kissed her brow. "Will you marry me today, or do you need a room at one of the hotels?"

"Neither of those options, Alex. Darla's hosting me tonight. She's expecting me for supper and—"

"I'll telephone her and cancel your itinerary."

"I can't do that."

"Then I'll squeeze in everything around your supper plans." He rushed to the door and flung it open. "Ms. Bledsoe, please cancel my appointments the rest of the day and tomorrow!"

He shut the door and turned back to Magdalene. "We'll go to the jewelry store first, and then the dress shop. We can—you'll have me, won't you?"

She couldn't help laughing at his exuberance. "Yes, Alexander."

"I want you to return to the island with something to remember me by. Keep wearing your rings from Douglas if you'd like, but I want you to have one from me as well."

She held out her hand. "The band was my mother's, but the engagement ring was from Douglas."

Alex kissed each one. "Fine memories for you to treasure, but we'll carve new ones. And dresses. New dresses for my society bride, as you wish to be." He nuzzled into her neck. "If you have me wait long, I'll insist on regular visits. I'll put you up in a hotel if you don't wish to intrude on anyone too often. My home is always open, but it wouldn't look right for you to stay before we're married. I won't have gossips speaking ill of my future wife."

"You've matured, Alexander Melling."

"I've tried to shed the stain of my name."

"You've done it well."

***

In the time between her visit to Alexander's office and their wedding on November second, Magdalene visited Mobile every other weekend, in conjuncture with Alexander keeping Lucy's girls. Besides dresses and gowns—most of which she kept at Alexander's house as they were no use to her on the island—he bought Magdalene riding clothes and a horse for an early wedding present. She stayed with Darla but spent most of the daytime hours with Alexander, including Saturday morning rides with the Campbell, Melling, and Davenport children. The boisterous group of nine became the focus of much attention. Freddy and Melissa often watched the spectacle, and Melissa photographed the riders.

True to his word, Alexander arranged for Saturday afternoon piano lessons for Tabitha. The nine-year-old spent much of her weekend in the mansion's front room, determined to play at least three carols well enough to accompany the group for singing during the Christmas party Magdalene planned. Magdalene prepared for Christmas because it was easier to think about than the wedding. The thought of becoming Mrs. Melling loomed in her mind from the horrors associated with the name during her time as a companion to Ruth in Seacliff Cottage.

Claudio, hoping to travel to Italy as soon as the war ended, transferred in early September to a parish in New York while he waited to return to his homeland for Exorcist training. His absence put a strain on the wedding, but the families kept it simple with plans for a small backyard ceremony amid the growing Spanish influenza epidemic.

The morning of the wedding, Melissa, Darla, and Claire helped Magdalene dress in a guest room that would become Tabitha's space. They fluffed the sheer sleeves on her sky blue gown and helped twist her hair in a sophisticated style.

"It's not too late to back out," Darla reminded Magdalene as she tucked a sprig of mums into her hair.

"When are you going to stop picking on Alex?" Melissa asked.

"When he stops mocking me."

"He's practically all but stopped," Magdalene remarked.

Claire laughed. "I know from my years with Joe that the change in Alex you see now is all you can hope for."

A knock on the door broke their conversation.

Taking charge, Melissa approached it. "Who's there?"

"Naomi."

Melissa let her in, removing the four-month-old from her arms and snuggling into the baby's curly hair. "He looks more like Paul every time I see him. Is everything well for your family?"

"Yes, thank you. I wish we could see each other more often, but it's taking all I have to keep up with things at the house with Samuel here. I miss y'all and appreciate the invitation." She looked to Magdalene and smiled. "I want you to know how happy I am for you. I remember the day you and Douglas came to the Davenports' for tea and thinking that everything was going to change for Lucy. And it did, but in ways none of us expected with Alex's return."

Magdalene didn't speak but took Naomi's hand.

"I witnessed Lucy's change from child to woman. I saw her love for Alex when it was fresh and when he tried to make things right after their falling out, and then as it haunted her for years. I saw the difference in Alex when he returned. He's been through much these past years, both alone and with Lucy, but I've never seen him as composed as he is now. You're a blessing to him, Miss Maggie."

"It means the world to me to hear that." Magdalene hugged her. "I know how much you loved her."

Magdalene soon gathered in the foyer with her children. Each son put an arm through hers, and Tabitha walked in front with a bouquet of lilies of the valley. They escorted her to the gazebo Paul Rollins built for the occasion. There Alexander and Asher waited with Father Quinn to join their families. The ceremony was quick, followed by best wishes from their usual group of friends and a luncheon provided by Miss Charlotte.

When they were halfway across the bay, Magdalene turned to Alexander on the bench beside her. "I feel guilty leaving them all in Mobile while we go to Seacliff."

He tightened his hand about hers. "We'll have plenty of time with the children. The next three days are about us."

"I'm surprised you didn't insist on staying at home and kicking everyone out instead."

"Why's that?"

"Because this trip is excruciatingly long."

He kissed her cheek. "Expectation can be almost as thrilling as the act itself."

Magdalene relaxed against his side, inhaling his sandalwood scent. She'd expected him to take advantage of their privacy during the trip, but Alexander behaved perfectly—as he had since the day he proposed.

At Seacliff Manor, Joe sent a deckhand ahead with their luggage and escorted the couple to the dock. "I saw Maggie here the first time and told her she could let me know if she ever needed anything. That still holds true. Treat her well, Melling."

"I plan to, Captain."

Magdalene hugged Joe goodbye and took Alexander's hand for the walk up the cliff. When they reached the yard, he scooped her into his arms and carried her into the house. Setting her down in the hall, Alexander stepped out to retrieve the suitcases from the porch, following her up the front stairs with them.

Gone were Lucy's lavender walls and the bold red of the bath. In its place were deep blues, the ornate furniture bringing distinction to the space. Alexander set the luggage on the cedar chest against the wall and opened his arms to her.

"We join at the location where we first met, but it's a fresh room for our new beginning."

"It's beautiful, Alexander."

"Anticipating you upon this bed kept me alive these past months." He began a slow, rhythmic motion with his hips. "May I have permission to stop being a gentleman?"

"I thought you'd never ask." She wrapped her arms about his neck, swaying with him.

Alexander's fingertips flexed into her curves as he pressed their bodies together. Magdalene gasped at the erotic dance and tasted him as he led them to the massive bed.

That night, they lay in each other's arms, the soft glow of the fireplace the only light in the room.

"Waiting a dozen years to experience this with you, I imagined all sorts of scenarios," Alexander whispered, "but I'm pleased to say you surpass them all in the most magnificent ways."

Smiling, she responded in kind. "You're everything I could wish for, Alexander."

He trailed kisses down her side. "No regrets?"

"My first weekend at Seacliff Cottage was a hollow example of all that you are, as a lover and a man."

"I aim to continuously surprise you in both regards, Magdalene."

She ran a hand over his scarred chest. "I'm ready for the challenge."

THE END

Bonus

"Mystic Misperception"

The Possession Chronicles #6.5

By Carrie Dalby

Sadie Marley hurried past the maid into the Beauchamp house and up the stairs to her best friend's room.

"Alice, you'll never guess what happened!" Sadie threw her handbag and blue coat onto the second bed.

Gazing up at Sadie over the romance novel she was reading, Alice Beauchamp raised her eyebrows, closed her book, and sat up from where she'd been lounging on her frilly bed.

"Then tell me."

Sadie perched at the foot of the bed and smoothed her slim skirt about her hips as she crossed her ankles. "I was in Hammel's, near the men's shoe department, when I overheard a few young men discussing the need to buy plain black boots for their costumes."

"What's so extraordinary about that?"

"Costumes! And they were whispering."

Alice continued to stare, unimpressed. "Discussing costumes during Mardi Gras season isn't special."

"They were mystic men—and not just any society." Sadie leaned closer and dropped her voice. "They were Mystics of Dardenne members!"

"What? They never spill a word." Alice lifted her book and opened it back up to where her finger had held her place. Ever since she was nearly ruined by an Italian violinist, Alice had been difficult to impress where men were concerned.

Sadie understood her friend's reluctance, and held her own annoyance under a layer of patience. "They didn't say the name out loud, but I received an invitation from them."

The book lowered once more. "Since when do Mystics of Dardenne members hand out masquerade invitations in department stores?"

"They didn't actually hand it to me." Sadie fingered her blonde chignon. "One of them dropped it on their way out."

"And you didn't return it?"

"They would probably get in trouble if it was found out they weren't discrete. I bet they were greenies. They didn't sound like they knew exactly what to expect."

"Who was it?"

"No one you'd know—some upstarts from St. Matthew's. Unless, of course, you're so desperate for a husband you'd look outside the cathedral parish."

Alice tossed her book onto the side table.

Sadie smiled. "Then you'll attend with me?"

"Not to a masquerade with those barbarians."

"Come on, Alice. All men are wild during Mardi Gras, even my brother-in-law, and he's a respected surgeon. It's time we see what other societies do besides the Order of Mayhem and the Mystic Order of Sirens. Or have you decided on the convent after all?"

"Not on your life, and you know it. I'd rather join a symphony in a northern city that takes women than lead a cloistered life. Besides, you only have one invitation."

"Grace Anne has told me the Dardennes never turn away a pretty figure from their masquerades, with or without an invitation."

"Maybe back when she was single a decade ago. It's 1915 now. I'm sure things are different."

"Don't you want to know if you pass inspection to make it inside their masquerade?"

"I don't care if my figure is desirable to a bunch of upstarts."

"Really, Alice, one would think you'd be pleased with the prospect of unchaperoned time with men. Don't tell me you're still mooning over that Italian. You were just a girl of sixteen back then. It's been more than four years."

"You fawned over Valentino De Fiore as well, so don't tease me."

"Everyone did when he was in town, but unless you're going to chase him around the world and try to make beautiful music together, with or without your violins, I suggest you take better note of the eligible bachelors right here in Mobile. There are plenty, but with talk of the country joining the war, they might not be around much longer."

"I have no desire to marry a man associated with the notorious Mystics of Dardenne society."

"Then come and find out who is a part of it so you can avoid them. I plan to be wed this summer and want to fully enjoy my final Mardi Gras season before marriage."

Alice narrowed her eyes. "And do *you* want to go to learn which men to ignore? It would be safer to find out who hasn't pledged to one of the respectable societies."

"Maybe, but Grace Anne says the best husbands have a naughty side."

"You'll get a reputation if you go to the Mystics of Dardenne ball."

"If I find a beau within the next month, it won't matter."

"You think it's that easy?" Alice sounded offended. "You crook your finger and a man will be at your side."

Sadie shrugged. "Something like that. I've been asked out often enough. Not to mention Grace Anne is always willing to play matchmaker at her supper parties. John has a wide array of friends ready to settle down. I'm sure I'd have an offer from at least one man before the end of Lent if I show the slightest interest."

"You scheming hussy!"

"Don't be jealous, Alice. You could as well, but you have to do more than perform your violin concertos and attend Mass to give a man the chance to talk to you. Shall I inform Grace Anne you're—"

"I'll not be pandered to by your elder sister!"

Deciding not to take offense, Sadie nodded slyly. "You *do* have a plethora of men within easy reach with all your brothers about. Their friends are always ripe for the picking, especially Richard's, but stay away from Clarence's musician friends," she said, speaking of Alice's twin. "The last thing you need is to marry a husband as obsessed with music as yourself."

Alice huffed and crossed her arms. "I'll not look to my brothers any more than to your sister as a means of procuring my heart's true love."

"Sometimes Cupid needs a little help. Begin right now by going with me to Mademoiselle Bisset's shop to look for a gown."

"I don't want to attend that masquerade."

"You don't have to, but will you help your dearest friend find the perfect dress?"

***

Richard Beauchamp, the eldest sibling, returned home at the exact moment his sister and Sadie Marley descended the front stairs. The two women were opposites in looks and temperament, but the difference in their disposition was recent. Alice had grown serious though Sadie remained as joyful as ever.

"Good Saturday afternoon, Alice and Sadie." He lifted his hat and smiled. "Going somewhere?"

"Hello, Richie." Sadie's voice managed to set the twenty-three-year-old's heart on fire, as it had for at least five years. "We are headed to Mademoiselle Bisset's for a bit of shopping."

Richard took her coat from where it hung on her arm and helped the blonde into it. "The wind is terrible. Allow me to drive you, so y'all arrive looking as fresh as you do now."

"That's sweet of you." Sadie gracefully slipped her arms into her coat. "I thought you were still in Montgomery."

"I took the train back yesterday afternoon. I plan to be here every weekend through Mardi Gras. Our state representatives can do without me that much."

"Don't they need your help to stop that prohibition bill they're threatening us with?"

Richard smiled at Sadie as he helped Alice into her coat. "I don't have that much sway yet, Sadie, but someday."

"You're certainly a well-spoken gentleman now, Richie. University and political life have agreed with you. Don't you think so, Alice?"

Alice's brown eyes looked deadly. "Don't get any ideas, Sadie Marley."

Sadie's head went back with a laugh, displaying her elegant neck beneath the unbuttoned coat. "Your sister is darling, isn't she, Richie? Are your friends from the capitol coming down for the festivities? Anyone you think would be especially interested in a pretty violinist?"

Alice stomped out the door.

Turning to Richard, Sadie placed a gloved hand on his for a few seconds. "I'm worried she's turning into a spinster. She needs to be thoroughly kissed this year."

"And you?"

Sadie's full lips quirked up at the corners in that maddening curl that sent Richard's heart racing. "Should I be worried about finding a willing participant for myself?"

He grinned. "Just say the word, Miss Sadie, and I'd be yours to command."

"Alice would never tolerate that." She tucked her arm through his. "But I appreciate the compliment."

Pride inflated to near bursting, Richard walked her to his automobile, and she slid into the backseat where his sister was waiting. They were silent while he backed out of the driveway. As he picked up speed on State Street, Sadie started talking.

"Here's the invitation, Alice. Look it over. You must come with me."

"That's not even two weeks to prepare."

Richard strained to hear more details.

"It's plenty of time." Sadie lowered her voice. "And the venue is only a few blocks from your house. Right there, I can see the roof of the third story. We can arrange that I'm staying with you. It'll be simple."

"Have you forgotten my mother?"

"Then we can ask Richard to escort us. Surely she'd let us out with your older brother as chaperone."

As he pulled to a stop along the curb outside the Parisian dress shop, Sadie leaned forward and set her hand on his shoulder. "Richie, would you be willing to escort your sister and I to—"

"No!" Alice jerked her arm. "That would be as mortifying as the event itself. I'm too old to be escorted anywhere socially important by a relative."

Sadie laughed, her breath warm on Richard's ear as she leaned over his shoulder. "Thanks anyway. We appreciate the ride."

"Shall I wait for you?"

"Mademoiselle has a delivery boy, and I'll take the streetcar home from here." She squeezed his shoulder. "I hope to see you at Mass tomorrow morning."

"I'll be there, Sadie."

Before he pulled into traffic, Richard heard Sadie say something to Alice about the Spanish Inquisition. Fearing they were in possession of an invitation to his society's masquerade, a hot lump of dread twisted through his middle at the thought of his sister stumbling into the debauched scene the Mystics of Dardenne masquerades always presented. Sadie could handle it—at least he thought she might—but never Alice.

***

After settling her luggage in Alice's bedroom, Sadie knocked on a door down the hall on the afternoon of February twelfth.

"Clarence," she called. "Are you there?"

"Of course he is," Alice bitterly whispered. "And I don't approve of you dragging my twin brother into this scheme of yours."

The door opened and Clarence Beauchamp blinked at his visitor.

"Hello, Sadie." He flickered a smile at her. "I heard you were here for the night."

"Yes, supper and then staying over in Alice's room, but listen." She leaned close, causing heat to rise to the twenty-year-old's face. "Alice and I have a late gathering to get to. I was wondering if you'd be able to drop us off to save us the trouble of arriving disheveled."

"I'd be happy to. I'll ask my father to use—"

"No, Clarence." She quickly touched his lips with a fingertip. "I don't want to worry your family. We'll slip out after your parents are settled for the night."

His brown eyes darted from Sadie to his twin behind her. "Do you need an escort?"

"No," Alice was quick to reply as she crossed her arms. "We'll be fine, Clarence."

He nodded and focused back on the blonde. "Our parents don't stay up past ten most nights, but I'll play a few lullabies immediately after supper to help them relax."

"You're a sweet one." She smiled at the plainest of the Beauchamp brothers. He didn't have his younger brother's daring or eldest Richard's square jaw and good looks, but Clarence's piano skills would earn him a woman at some point in his life. "I hate to have to miss your recital, but I'll need to dress for our outing after supper."

Clarence shoved his hands into the pockets of his trousers like an awkward schoolboy. "I practice before supper, if you'd like to join me in the parlor in about half an hour."

"That would be lovely."

"Would you like to do a duet, Alice?"

"I'm not in the mood." She grabbed Sadie's arm and led her back down the hall. Once they were safely in Alice's bedroom, she let loose. "Don't you dare string him along! Clarence is a sensitive soul. The last thing he needs is you flirting with him."

"He's a darling, but not one to flirt with. Y'all look too much alike. But I'll always be kind to him. Have you decided on your gown?"

"I don't want to be recognized in one of my previous dresses."

"That's why I tried to get you to buy a new one at the shop last week."

"I'm not willing to throw money away on something I'll have to toss out after one use. Nothing worn to this scandalous masquerade can ever been seen again."

"So are you going naked? From what I've heard, those men would like that."

Alice shot her a look of incredulousness that made Sadie giggle.

"I got out one of my mother's old dresses. It has to be from at least 1890 because the waistline is from before children. It's red like yours, though not nearly as flattering. I don't want to attract extra attention anyway. I think I'd faint if one of the Dardennes asked me to dance."

"Grace Anne told me the absolute rule of their balls is that you cannot deny one of the members if he asks you to dance. I think she's jealous we're going. She never made it to one, but a few of her friends did and told her all about them. I'll spare you the shocking details." Sadie laughed again, then wished she'd hadn't when Alice paled. "You'll be fine, Alice. Now where's the dress? I want to make sure the mantilla I brought doesn't clash with it."

She took the ensemble out of her closet, laying it on her bed. It was a splendid Victorian two-piece ball gown complete with small bustle and matching red gloves. "I embellished an old mask, mimicking the ruffled edges of the gown around the edges. It gives my face more coverage."

"Very clever, Alice. With your hair under a mantilla and lips painted to match the gown, no one will recognize you. The bustle will even keep your buttocks safe from wandering hands." Alice's face went as crimson as the silk gown, and Sadie hurried to the box holding her masquerade items. "Would you prefer the black or red lace mantilla?"

"Black," Alice said. "It will hide my hair better."

With that settled, Sadie hurried to the parlor to give Clarence her attention while Alice hid the party attire once more.

Clarence played a Beethoven piece, and then Sadie joined him on the bench to pound out a bit of Joplin with him. The youngest Marley sister was the true pianist in the family, but all the sisters had learned to play as soon as they were able to reach the keys. In truth, Sadie didn't think her mediocre music abilities, brains, or manners would help land her a husband. She knew she would be chosen for her looks, and she was fine with that. Blonde hair was fashionable, and though her chest was a tad more than the magazines displayed, she knew some men preferred a little extra on top. And Mademoiselle Bisset specifically chose to highlight that feature with the new gown.

Even without Richard in attendance, supper was lively. Seventeen-year-old Felix was more than eager to show off for the guest, explaining his latest tricks inspired by Houdini's magic. Clarence smiled and offered his thoughts, but Alice was too absorbed in her own anxiety to contribute to the conversations.

Though not as old as Sadie's parents, Mr. and Mrs. Beauchamp appeared to be tuckered out from a busy week of work and club meetings. According to Felix's reports (who happily played spy between the parlor and Alice's room while the ladies dressed), they went like lambs to the slaughter with Clarence's renditions of "Moonlight Sonata" and other dreamy pieces. The Beauchamps closeted themselves in their suite at nine o'clock.

"Come on, Alice," Sadie urged. "We have the opportunity to arrive on time. Your hair doesn't need to be perfect when you're going to have the mantilla over it."

They hurried their final preparations, donned their masks, and pinned on the mantillas. Sadie led the way down the servant's stairs and was met with a low whistle from Felix and the bulging dark eyes of Clarence in the back hallway.

"You're the prettiest girl I ever saw," Felix said.

Clarence elbowed him. "Sadie is a *woman*."

"That she is," Felix replied as he ogled her, "and in all the right places."

"Don't be crude, Felix," Alice said as she came to a stop behind her friend. "Are you ready, Clarence?"

Her twin nodded. "You'll have to tell me where to drop you off."

Felix's intelligent eyes flashed between his sister's tight lips and Sadie's smiling ones beneath their masks. "I can tell you where to bring them." He offered Sadie his arm. "This way, Miss Marley."

"You can't come with us, Felix!" Alice grabbed her brother's other arm. "You have no idea where—"

"Don't I?" He smirked. "I may be the youngest, but I've got ears."

"Shh!" Alice shushed him. "I don't appreciate my brothers being privy to my shame."

"There's no shame," Sadie said. "We're young and adventurous, enjoying what will hopefully be our final carnival season before marriage. Take Clarence's arm and let him escort you to the automobile."

Sadie winked at Felix and allowed him to caress her arm as they followed the twins to the driveway.

"I always said you were the bravest girl," Felix whispered to Sadie. "Ever since you stood up to Richard and the others when they were teasing that dog all those years ago, I knew you would never let anyone hold you back from what you wanted."

Felix helped her into the backseat beside his sister and kissed Sadie's gloved hand.

"Stop fawning over her!" Alice fussed at her little brother.

He leaned over Sadie and kissed Alice's cheek below her ruffled mask. "You look beautiful too, Alice, though I can't imagine you at a Mystics of Dardenne masquerade."

"Oh, go away!"

She shoved him. Felix laughed and jumped into the front seat of the automobile.

"You can't come along! Clarence," Alice said as her twin took the driver's seat, "make him get out."

"I'm not getting out until you and Sadie do. I want to make sure you arrive at Temperance Hall in style."

"No, and besides, we aren't being dropped off in front of the building. Tell them, Sadie."

"That's right, gentlemen. We want to be dropped a block away and arrive on foot so no one will see who brought us. We don't wish to be recognized."

"Men will recognize your luscious lips, Sadie."

"Stop with the flattery, Felix!" Alice snapped.

"How will you get home?" Clarence asked.

"We won't have trouble in that regard." Sadie patted his shoulder over the seat. "Let's get going, though. I don't want to miss their tableau. I hear it's always thrilling."

When Clarence pulled to the curb a block northwest of the hall, Alice clutched the door handle but didn't move.

"Come on, Alice." Sadie nudged her. "I don't want to be late."

"I can't." She shook her head. "I can't do it. I'd die of fright if any of those monsters wished to dance with me."

In the front seat, Felix snorted and Clarence poked him in the ribs.

"I'm not brave like you. Go on without me."

"Alice, don't be a ninny. You're dressed and ready to attend," Sadie said.

"Don't send her in there alone, Alice," Clarence said with indignation.

"I can't. Walk home if you'd like, brothers. I'll wait here for her."

Sadie huffed and exited the door into the street before hurrying around to the sidewalk. She leaned back toward Felix's open automobile window. "Take care of her."

Felix grinned. "Say hello to… never mind. Enjoy the masquerade, Sadie. We'll be here."

***

Richard adjusted the coarse black face netting and then secured the monk's cowl over his head, shadowing himself from all possible recognition when he appeared with the other Mystics of Dardenne members. To help with the air of anticipation in the ballroom, the society men waited five minutes beyond their planned arrival before they solemnly entered in two straight lines of over two dozen each. On the raw wooden tables, the refreshment spread only offered bread and wine.

Their procession of habited monks draped with huge beaded crosses was in direct opposition to the Mystics of Dardenne's reputation and elicited several laughs that turned to nervous titters as they marched the length of the party. Behind the line of the black-clad figures came one in red, arms raised for silence as he swept into the center of the dance floor.

"What heretics are you," he bellowed, "to show your faces within our hallowed walls? Our society demands purity!"

The group's president stalked between the rows of monks as he raved.

"We must sift out the unclean to allow us to focus on our indulgences! You and you," he said as he pointed to one monk and then a second, "bring another brother with you each and ferret out the heretics so our masquerade may commence!"

The two pairs went to opposite sides of the room, circling the guests on their quest. They often paused to grope females, and the men in attendance whistled to egg them on.

"Silence!" The red-robed man went to the dais beside the musicians who stood at attention. He pointed to the wall behind him and a spotlight shone on it. "Bring the heretics to the racks!"

The monks returned, each pair dragging a seemingly uncooperative female. The crowd gasped and angled closer to watch as the chosen offerings were brought toward the torture equipment.

Behind his mesh mask, Richard smirked, knowing that this display was better's than any in recent memory. The women cowered before the man in red, earning every bit of their night's wages for their performance. The leader rent the shimmery gold gown off the first woman, then the blue one off the brunette. As the women were shuffled toward the racks in their corsets and underwear, several shrieks came from the guests.

"They shall be punished until they confess their sins!" The masked president pointed to the crowd. "If you do not dance and make merry, you shall join them!"

He wielded a leather cat-o-nine tails, striking the fleshy thighs of the first woman who was restrained. When the band started a festive ragtime tune, the monks dispersed, seeking their partners for the first dance that only they were allowed to participate in. Several paused long enough to nip from the hollow crosses about their necks that doubled as flasks, drinking the liquor straight through the mesh face shield.

Richard sauntered the edge of the dance floor, seeking a pretty figure though he knew none would be as fine as Sadie's. He caught sight of a voluptuous body in a red gown reminiscent of a Spanish dancer. Gaze traveling her form, he noted the breasts were as fine as Sadie's, and her lips—they were *her* lips!

Painted red like her ruffled dress, Sadie's mouth was open in surprise as one of the monks led her onto the dance floor. When her partner's fondling hands worked from her cleavage to her succulent hips, she looked about the room for a means of escape.

Richard snatched his unknown society brother by the shoulder and shoved him away. He immediately pulled Sadie into a modified Bunny Hug and danced as quickly as possible to discourage interruption.

"Thank you," she said with a trembling smile. "I'm afraid I didn't know what I was getting myself into when I came."

Richard nodded and Sadie looked to the torture scene.

"Everything I've ever heard about your society is true. It's frightful, except for you. There's another monk following us. I think he means to cut in."

"Do you trust me?" Richard asked, forcing a deeper tone to his voice to disguise it.

"Yes," she breathed.

Richard immediately claimed her buttocks with his hands, pressing against her in a suggestive dance as his mesh-covered face went to hers. He had dreamt of kissing her for years, but not through a covering or with an audience. He leaned to her ear, smelling her perfume before he spoke.

"It needs to look like you're mine, that I'm taking advantage of you, so no one else will. Do you understand?"

Sadie nodded, and his chin lowered as his eyes fell to her heaving chest. He licked his lips, glad the net and cowl hid his face from view.

"Good, my sweet. Forgive me." His pelvis continued to move to the beat of the song as he led her in the erotic dance. He bit the inside of his cheek to keep himself from falling completely under the spell of the moment.

"You dance well." Sadie offered a true smile. "I suppose not all the members are monsters."

"A woman like you should never have come here alone."

"There are people waiting for me outside, but my friend was too timid to come in."

"It's better she didn't."

"I didn't say—"

"My turn!" a monk said as he snatched Sadie's wrist.

"I just heard a confession from the heretic. She has agreed to go to the confessional with me for penance." Richard pulled Sadie behind him. "She is *my* captive. I'll take this to the cardinal if needed."

The other man bowed and stepped back. "Enjoy, brother."

With an arm slung low and tight around Sadie's hip, Richard steered her across the room to the false front of a cathedral. The partitioned room within the miniature church was lined with alcoves made to look like confessionals. They were not divided as a padded bench ran the length of the space and only a thin lace curtain offered a semblance of decorum if used. But the three other couples already filling half the confessionals didn't bother to close the drapes as they necked and groped.

"You'll be safe here for a little while," Richard said as he saw her to the furthest bench and pulled the black lace closed.

Sadie tilted her head, lips tight as she peered through the curtain at the other couples. "Do we need to do something similar to make this appear legitimate?"

"Well…"

"After all you've done for me, I don't want you to get into trouble." She stood, encouraged him to take the bench, and then sat on his lap. She reached for the bottom of his face net, and he raised his hand to stop her. "I won't pull it up all the way. Trust me, as I trusted you."

Her full lips were everything he had imagined as they met his exposed mouth. The netting hung over the arch of his nose as they kissed each other, tentatively at first. As their mutual passion flared, Richard held her closer, feeling the skin on her arms between the long gloves and the ruffled shoulder of the gown. Sadie opened her mouth first, but he rushed to taste her as his hands roamed.

"Oh, Richie," Sadie whispered as his kisses trailed to her décolletage.

He straightened with an intake of breath, the covering falling back over his face.

"I thought it was you, but I knew for sure the instant you rebuked the last monk. Do you think I would have been so forward with a stranger?"

"I'd hope not. You don't think poorly of me after seeing how the society is?"

"It is rather shocking, but after you rescued me like that, I can't fault you." She leaned against his shoulder a moment. "Besides, Mystics of Dardenne membership is temporary—a phase many young men pass through. You'll join the society your father is in when you marry."

"That's right, Sadie." He touched her ear with a fingertip, trailing it down her cheek.

She lifted his netting once more and kissed him until she giggled.

"What is it?"

"Alice is going to have a conniption."

"I'm glad she wasn't brave enough to come. I would have had to rescue her rather than you, but don't tell me she's sitting alone somewhere in the dark."

Sadie's soft lips curled at the edges. "Clarence and Felix are with her."

"Could I escort you there or do you wish to stay?"

"I've seen more than enough of this masquerade, Richie, but I'd like to see more of you."

"Would you attend the Blithe Buckaroos parade with me on Mardi Gras Day?"

"I'd like that, and Alice never attends that one. She claims their humor is too irreverent."

Richard laughed. "It is, but it's nothing compared to this debauchery."

"It allowed me to finally find out how it feels to be in your arms, so I'll always be thankful to Mystics of Dardenne for this time with you."

"Did I pass inspection?"

"I'm going to the parade with you, aren't I?" She smoothed her gown as she stood. "I wish you could leave with me now. I hate to think of who you might grab after I leave."

"My heart goes with you, Sadie." Richard took her hand and went for the door. "I'll not speak once we're outside."

"Your secret is safe with me, Richie."

***

As soon as Sadie and Richard were a half a block from the Beauchamps' automobile, Felix jumped out.

"You didn't last long."

"It was too much for me. Alice was smart not to attend. There was one gentleman out of the lot who was kind enough to see I was not molested." She motioned to the monk beside her. "Thank you, kind sir. Or should I say Father or Brother?"

Richard gave her a silent bow and turned back towards Temperance Hall.

Felix smirked after the retreating form as though he suspected something, but soon refocused on Sadie, seeing her into the backseat.

Alice leaned close to inspect her as Clarence drove toward the house. "You appear rumpled."

"I was touched," Sadie admitted.

"Now you're sullied. I told you not to go!"

Sadie laughed. "It wasn't much. And, like I said, the one who escorted me out was kind."

"What was the masquerade like?" Felix asked.

"She already said it was horrible," Alice snapped.

"Oh, the Dardennes gave a good show, if blasphemous debauchery is considered praiseworthy. You saw the monk. There were dozens like him and a leader in red. They were the Spanish inquisition seeking heretics." Sadie paused when Clarence parked the automobile at the house and then lowered her voice. "They took two women from the crowd, stripped their clothes off, bound them, and then whipped them before the whole ballroom."

Alice shrieked, and Felix laughed.

"But you said he saved you from molestation," Alice said.

"The first monk to try to dance with me did have roaming hands, but—"

"I'll hear no more of it. You shouldn't have gone!" Alice exited the automobile.

With Alice upset, there was nothing to do but follow her inside.

"Sadie," Felix whispered when they were in the hallway. "I'm glad you went."

Understanding that he knew it was his eldest brother who had escorted her out, she smiled. "So am I, but don't tell Alice."

He grinned and hurried up the stairs.

Turning to Clarence, who responsibly locked the back door, Sadie touched his sleeve. "Thank you for the ride."

"I was glad to be of service, though I hope this is the last time you attempt to attend a masquerade like that."

She smiled kindly at his sincerity, so like his twin—and the opposite of Richard and Felix. "It was. Good night, Clarence. I'll see you at breakfast."

Sadie could feel his eyes on her the whole way up the stairs and moved as primly as possible so as not to inflame the young man. He'd get doused as it was when he found out she was stepping out with Richard.

Alice was already preparing for bed. Her gown was draped over one of the chairs and she wore a floral print robe.

"Please shower before bed," Alice told her. "I can't stand the thought of you crawling into the clean sheets after being in that filthy gathering."

Sadie rolled her eyes, collected her toiletries and nightgown, and gratefully escaped to the solitude of the bath before going to the guest bed in Alice's room for the night.

Tucked into her single bed, the remembrance of Richard's firm touch and delectable kisses kept Sadie from falling asleep. When she finally did slumber, the dreams she had kept her warm.

Her disappointment over Richard's empty chair at the breakfast table was difficult to conceal. Fortunately, Mrs. Beauchamp had gone to a fundraiser breakfast for a ladies' aid group. That left Sadie with the two youngest Beauchamp brothers, an un-talkative Alice, and their father, who read the Saturday morning newspaper.

Halfway through the meal, a door opened down the hall and heavy footsteps tread the stairs. No one remarked on it, so Sadie kept eating her omelet. A few minutes later, someone pattered down the stairs and then Richard was in the doorway to the dining room, fresh suit on though his brown eyes were slightly red and his jawline shadowed with the beginnings of a beard.

"Good morning, everyone." His eyes lingered on Sadie the longest, and she hid her smile behind a coffee cup.

Lowering his newspaper, Mr. Beauchamp looked to his oldest. "Just getting in, Richard? You look a bit rough. Did that poker game go all night?"

"Something like that," he said as he took his seat.

"So long as you aren't completely broke, I suppose you'll survive."

"My financial standing is good, Dad."

"Of course it is. I didn't raise any fools, did I?"

"At least not with the first three children." Richard grinned as he helped himself to a cup of coffee and toast from the center of the table.

Felix, in the chair beside him, elbowed him in the ribs. The cook brought in an omelet for the newcomer, placing it before him without a word.

Sadie tried to make her last bit of breakfast stretch by eating slower so she could stay at the table, but Alice must have thought her full.

"Are you finished?" she asked. "You can be excused to finish packing."

"Not quite, but thank you."

"Well, I'm going up. Excuse me, everyone."

Her brothers all rose respectfully, but Mr. Beauchamp's eyes never left the newsprint.

"Let me know when you're ready to go home, Sadie," Clarence said. "I'd be happy to bring you across town."

"Don't bother," Richard said. "I know how you like to practice the piano Saturday mornings. I could bring her so you don't interrupt your routine."

"Thank you, Richie." Sadie dropped her eyes. "I'll be ready in half an hour."

"Allow me to be the porter." Felix knocked his brother's arm. "I'll carry her luggage."

Mr. Beauchamp lowered his paper, a frown beneath his mustache. "She can't have much from a one-night stay, Felix, and you need to study. Your grades have been slipping since the holidays. Classes will only get tougher when you start college in the fall."

"Then I suppose Alice will ride along," the youngest said with a grin meant to show their plans would be spoiled with or without him.

But Alice claimed a headache from the stress of the night before and sent Sadie off with Richard.

Sadie was silent, hands clasped primly in her lap for the first several blocks.

"How was the rest of the masquerade?" Sadie asked when they passed the cathedral.

"Miserable." Richard paused. "I couldn't get you out of my head, so I drank too much. After two dances, I hid in our confessional for an hour."

Sadie smiled. "And after that, or are my feminine sensibilities too sensitive to know?"

Richard tried not to smile and a slight blush colored his cheeks. "Another time, perhaps."

"I dreamt of you," she whispered, half hoping he wouldn't hear, though she needed to confess.

"I'm sure visions of you would have flooded my mind had I slept."

As Richard drove down Government Street, his right hand went to Sadie's knee. A flutter in her middle heightened her craving for his touch. She teased the back of his hand with the tips of her fingers. He gripped her knee, fingers strong around the blue of her skirt.

"Last night was a fantasy come true. I've wanted to touch you for so long, Sadie."

"For how long?" She linked their fingers and brought their hands to the bench between them.

"Since I was sixteen." He glanced at her before returning his attention to the road. "Were you invited to the masquerade?"

Sadie laughed and told of her acquisition of the invitation.

"Those dunces, though I should to thank them for their carelessness."

Richard pulled to a stop in front of the Marleys' home. Sadie looked to the white house on the little rise, wondering if anyone was looking out form the rows of windows on either floor.

"Thank you, again, for rescuing me."

"I'm sure you would have gotten yourself out of his clutches before long. You're resourceful, Sadie. Capturing that invitation proves it."

She smiled when he came around to help her out. "If you bring my luggage to the porch, the maid will collect it."

Swaying her hips a little extra as he followed her up the walkway, Sadie felt his stare and reveled in it. Richard set the two cases on the porch to the side of the front door and leaned in, quickly brushing his lips to her cheek. The stubble on his jawline roughed her skin. His hand slipped into the interior pocket of his suit jacket and retrieved a square envelope.

"Happy early Valentine's Day, Sadie Marley."

Caressing the white paper, she gazed up at him. "Will I see you at Mass tomorrow?"

Richard nodded. "I take the evening train back to Montgomery after supper."

The door opened and a uniformed maid curtsied and went for the luggage. "Welcome home, Miss Sadie."

"Thank you." She refocused on Richard's handsome face. "Tell Alice I hope she feels better. I'll look for your family at the cathedral."

***

"You're really going to the parades with Richard Beauchamp?" Marie asked.

Sadie huffed at her little sister and continued brushing her hair.

"He's not at all like John."

"Good! I don't want a man like Grace Anne's husband." Sadie twisted her hair and secured it.

"But John is splendid." Fourteen-year-old Marie was closer to her brother-in-law than her own sister though there were two decades of life between them. "Is Alice upset about you stepping out with Richard?"

"I expect she will be for a time, but she doesn't know yet." Sadie buttoned on her purple wool cape. "I'll deal with Alice when she finds out."

"Will it be worth the trouble?"

"Richard is worth any amount of trouble." Sadie kissed his most recent letter before pulling on her decorative fur hat. "Don't try to spy on me if you see us."

Marie and their mother would be sitting in the grandstand in front of the Aethelwulf Club with Grace Anne for all the parades that day, something Sadie typically did as well. The excitement of mingling with the crowds on the sidewalks thrilled her, not to mention being with Richard.

After a cordial greeting to her mother and sister, Richard whisked Sadie downtown in his automobile. His out of the way parking space provided an interlude of isolation.

"Sadie," he said as he turned to her, "I hope you enjoy our time together."

"I'm sure I will."

"I have your father's permission to escort you through all the parades, but if you tire of me or aren't enjoying yourself, don't hesitate to tell me. I'm under instruction to bring you to your family outside the Aethelwulf Club."

"I've spent more than enough time on those bleachers. I look forward to being on the streets this time, having an adventure with you."

"But you aren't opposed to the Aethelwulf?"

"Heavens no. My father and brother-in-law are members."

"I'm next on the waiting list for a membership opening." Richard took her gloved hand. "Sadie, I hope this is the first of many outings together. Your father gave me his blessing to court you and I plan on seeing you as often as I'm in town and for as long as you'll accept me. Perhaps next Mardi Gras you'll be sitting in a chair reserved for 'Mrs. Richard Beauchamp' outside the club."

"I might enjoy that."

"Might?" Richard leaned back.

"Ask me in a month or two."

He grinned and angled for her mouth. Sadie eagerly accepted his lips, giving him a taste of what they enjoyed at his masquerade.

"You're an amazing kisser," she whispered.

"I think the same thing of you. I want to shout from the top of the Van Antwerp building that I'm in love with you."

They went at it again until a horn blared on the street behind them as a ragtag brass band stumbled down the road. Laughing, they untangled themselves and Richard helped her from the automobile. He offered his arm, but she boldly linked hands with him.

After the three block walk to the nearest parade route, they angled together to make it through the crowds. They settled in an area where no one knew them, far from Bienville Square. They laughed and joked at the political satire floats of the Blithe Buckaroos, even the one created at the expense of Richard's boss.

Twice, Richard hugged Sadie and kissed her square on the mouth, earning cheers from the good-natured crowd on the day of indulgence. By the time the second parade began, Richard's arms were linked around Sadie's waist from behind, and she leaned against his chest.

The society had more throws than the Buckaroos. Richard caught a string of purple glass beads, laying them gently around Sadie's neck with a kiss to her cheek.

"Let's go to the club now," she practically shouted to be heard over the marching band.

"Are you tired of me?" he hollered as they squeezed through the throng on the sidewalk.

"I want to show you off to our families, Richie." She kissed his lips. "Despite my misgivings about your society, I caught the best prize at the masquerade that night. Alice needs to accept me as a sister if all goes well. The sooner she begins to deal with her feelings about it, the better."

The jaunty tune carried them joyfully as they wove through the multitude. The magic of Mardi Gras could be a blessing or curse on new unions, but Sadie had faith it would be an exultation to her and Richard—that February and always.

THE END

Author's Note

With a series, it seems like the acknowledgments flow from one book to the next. Please be sure to note who has been thanked before, as it is often an ongoing help, such as the Local History and Genealogy branch of Mobile Public Library. Once again, I spent many hours researching there, this time the tumultuous years of World War I.

As always, my family has been a great support, as well as my main critique partner Candice Marley Conner. Sandra Buford offered a listening ear as I cried my frustrations and heartache along with the characters. Joyce Scarbrough and Lee Ann Ward are always available for my "Dial-a-Nerd" questions and literary support. Thank you all!

Special shout outs to beta reader Jennifer Lamont (Team Douglas), who I hope has finally forgiven me.

Last, but not least, thank you to all the readers. It's a joy to share these characters with you—even the ones that aren't so loveable. There's one more novel in The Possession Chronicles to go and then more projects in the future. For example, check out The Malevolent Trilogy if you haven't already.

About the Author

While experiencing the typical adventures of growing up, Carrie Dalby called several places in California home, but she's lived on the Alabama Gulf Coast since 1996. Serving two terms as president of Mobile Writers' Guild and five years as the Mobile area Local Liaison for the Society of Children's Book Writers and Illustrators are two of the writing-related volunteer positions she's held. When Carrie isn't reading, writing, browsing bookstores/libraries, or homeschooling her children, she can often be found knitting or attending concerts.

Carrie writes for both teens and adults. *Fortitude* is listed as a Best History Book for Kids by Grateful American Foundation. She has also published *Corroded*, a contemporary teen novel about friendship and autism, several short stories that can be found in different anthologies, as well as a multitude of Southern Gothic novels for adults.

For more information, visit Carrie Dalby's website:

carriedalby.com

Lightning Source UK Ltd.
Milton Keynes UK
UKHW011847181022
410670UK00004B/183